Back Bay Murders

Back Bay Murders

Andrew Bonar

DEDICATION

To Mama and Papa, your continued support and love is, has, and will always be everything to me.

ACKNOWLEDGMENTS

Without my amazing wife, always in my corner, I would never have had the confidence to start this story, I love you Tricia thank you for all the wonderful years.

I would also like to posthumously acknowledge my grandmother Nora. Nora was a creative soul, always urging me to explore my emotions, visions, and dreams. She showed me how to channel my experiences into retrievable memories for use in art and writings

Bag Her – 2014

It was a dry, cool night. The air felt crisp and clean as it entered my lungs. *A typical October night in New England*, I thought.

"Fall is the best time to live in New England, right?" I said to the man sitting in the shadows behind me, with no response. I hated when he did this, ignoring me, sitting there in silence. *What a sketchy dude.* "Why are you playing a mute, Jack?" I yelled at him.

"Just stay focused," the man replied. His hoarse, scratchy voice reminded me of a smoker; he was always clearing his throat. He never smelled like cigarettes though; he always smelled like chemicals—the kind you use to clean bathrooms.

"So, what do you do for your day job? You a janitor?" I asked him. I should've known more about this guy. We were in this thing together, yet any time I asked him questions, I got the same response.

"Stay focused," he replied.

We had met online in a forum website, I couldn't remember which, one of those sites with poor oversight, where controversy means dollar signs to the people who run them. It was our shared interests that had brought us together. We both liked girls. Watching them, fantasizing about them, and commenting on photos of them. Mostly, we liked photos of girls that met a specific style—over eighteen, tight, and a tease. My favorites were selfies, when girls took pictures of themselves, maybe covering their nude, perky breasts with their free hand, like an "oops, I didn't realize you were there" look. That stare of innocent seduction into the camera just made me crazy.

Commenting on a photo like that had gotten Jack and me talking to each other. One year later, after chatting over photos and private chats online, he was sitting behind me, staring out of the tinted back window of this car—barely speaking. Maybe he was chickening out on me. Part of me wished that he was.

"Hey, are you thinking about backing out, man?" I asked.

"No, stay focused," he replied firmly.

"What happened to your online chatty personality? Don't say 'stay focused.'" I added a snarl of sarcasm onto the last part.

"There she is. Stay focused," he said as he pointed out of the window.

My heart started pounding, my hands started to clam up, and my breaths were getting shorter, each breath louder and more annoying than the one before it. Was I getting nervous? I had practiced this so many times. I had watched girls before. I had practiced this before with and without my "stay focused" friend in the back seat. I fantasized about taking them.

It was different this time. We weren't just fantasizing—we were going to take this girl. I started getting nauseous at the thought. Could I do it? Could I live with this? We didn't exactly plan everything out.

"Shouldn't we wear masks or something? We don't want her to be able to identify us, right?" I asked Jack.

"That won't be a problem," he said calmly.

Oh my God, what does he mean by that? I was so excited about having someone that shared my fantasies I didn't even stop to think about what would happen when we were done with her. Surely, he wasn't going to hurt her, because I'm not into that.

"So, what are you thinking about doing with her after we're done?" I asked him, trying to hide the nerves, but they were spilling out uncontrollably in my shaking voice.

"Don't worry about that." After a moment of pause, as if he was urging me to move on from the question, Jack said, "Just be ready soon."

"We are going to let her go after . . . right?" I pressed. I needed to know. How could Jack be so cool? *I can do this. I can do this,* I repeated to myself. *I want this—I want her.*

"Just get that bag over her fast, and she'll be fine," he said calmly and smoothly from the back seat.

Time seemed to be slowing down as our plan edged closer toward execution. We had planned this for weeks, although the girl and location had constantly changed. Jack had said it was best practice to keep rotating targets. "If we don't know who we're taking, how will anyone else?"

I had probed this particular spot, finding the perfect girl to target last weekend. I had taped white cloth over my tattoo to make sure I couldn't be identified through them. I went to a popular bar in downtown Boston, starting a tab to create an alibi should I ever be suspected. After a few beers mixed with a shot of vodka to cool the nerves, I had snuck out of the back of the bar, leaving the tab open with my credit card. Jack had been waiting outside for me. He had gotten out of the driver seat and made for the back door.

"You drive," he had spat.

We had driven out of Boston and gone north into New Hampshire. The entire ride I couldn't stop talking I was so nervous. All the while, Jack had been silent. I don't think he said a word over the course of the forty-five minute drive. We had pulled into the strip mall where the girl worked as a bartender or bar help in one of the establishments. The mall was made up of a grocery store, generic take-out Chinese restaurant, electronics store, pharmacy, car rental agency, and adult film store.

"I don't know how they stay open . . . the porn shop, with all the free porn on the internet at your fingertips," I commented.

We parked a few spots from the employee parking section, positioned so that she would pass us to get to her car. We reversed into the spot so that our driver's side would be facing her car, waiting for her to finish her shift. The previous night that I had watched her, she had gotten out before closing, which had been just late enough that the rest of the stores in the mall had already been closed for the night, so traffic had been minimal. The car rental agency was directly next door to the bar, which made being in the parking lot on a slow evening not look out of the ordinary. We had checked the mall and the nearby roads for cameras as well to make sure we couldn't be seen on tape.

The moment she stepped out of the bar, we double-checked our surroundings to make sure the grab would be clear. With my heart beating out of my chest, I held my breath. My hands were tight and clammy, holding onto a bag that was not that far off from a pillowcase, albeit made with a rougher material that was ribbed horizontally with wire. It had a lip sewn into the opening with a drawstring passed through it, custom built by Jack so that once tightened, it required a screwdriver to get loose again. The ribbing made it difficult to move around inside. We both had our doors ever so slightly propped open, so when the moment was right, we could silently exit the car.

The girl was wearing tight jeans with gold trim that outlined her pockets. She wore a gray slim-fit sweater, and an elaborate scarf was wrapped around her neck. Light brown leather boots rose up tightly against her calves. She was pretty and innocent-looking with dirty blond hair that accented her slim figure—she must only have weighed 115 pounds. You could tell she had Irish in her bloodline, with a slim jaw, high cheekbones, and cheeks spotted with light brown freckles. As she walked toward her car, her head was down focusing on the messages she had missed on her cell phone, oblivious to what was happening in the world around her.

"Go," Jack said, but I hesitated. "Go," Jack quipped sharply again, and again. *"Go!"*

The waitress passed our car, and I felt nothing. I froze in a state of shock. I felt a quick pain at my side. Jack had reached around the car seat and pinched me.

"Go!" he hissed, snapping me out of my dazed, frozen state.

I quickly slid out of the car, moving on her from behind. I jammed the bag over her head and pulled it down to her waist, yanking on the drawstring. She didn't scream. She sucked in a giant gasp of air and froze. Not dissimilar to the state I had just been in, like a deer in headlights. The unexpected silence was broken by the clinging and clacking sound of her keys, then phone crashing to the ground. Jack picked them up and put them in his pocket. I grabbed her by her torso— she was a squirming, awkward lump to grapple with—as Jack looped ties below her knees, forcing her legs together. He picked her up by her feet, wakening her to the fact that she should make a sound, any sound. She started to squeak, trying to get a scream out, but all she could muster was a hoarse moan. We carried her without much effort, wiggling like a worm trying to avoid the hook. The trunk was already slightly propped open in preparation. Inside the trunk was what looked like cut-up yoga mats covered with clear plastic, taped down to the floor and up under the trunk door. *To keep her from hurting herself,* I thought.

Who was this guy? He seemed so experienced; had he done this before? A sick feeling of regret snuck up inside me. It was too late now. We shut the trunk, got back in the car and drove off.

Jack spent a few minutes playing with her phone, then threw it out of the window. He led me in what seemed like circles through back roads, highways, and back roads again. Our destination was a "safe house," as he had called it. It felt like it took forever to get to. We could hear her screaming and thumping around in the trunk the entire ride, kicking about no doubt.

"Here it is. Take your next left," Jack said.

It was a dirt driveway that was about a quarter of a mile long. We pulled up to a large house with an attached three-car garage. The farthest garage to the right opened as we got closer.

"Pull into the garage," Jack ordered, pointing. The garage was clean, almost like it was never used. I shut off the engine and grabbed the backpack I had brought with me from the bar. It contained everything I needed for tonight, for my fantasies. I had packed a twenty-one-megapixel camera, backup batteries, and a telescoping tripod to improve picture quality. I could feel energy starting to boil up through my body. I was getting excited. I couldn't wait to take pictures of her. After all, that was what this was all about. We liked photos, and we wanted to get real shots that you couldn't get anywhere else. The idea of her fear-filled, unwilling participation made the prospect of the photos all the more exciting and rarer. The fact that I could look back at the photos, knowing that I was there, on the other side of the camera, was tantalizing.

The waitress stopped screaming when we turned off the car. Maybe she had gone back into shock with the realization we had likely reached our destination.

"You have a nice house; this place is big," I told Jack.

"It's not my house. Pop the trunk," he commanded as he moved toward the back of the car. I did as I was told.

"Help me carry her," he spat.

I moved around toward the trunk and saw her still trapped in her restraints. I felt bad for her, for the fear she must've been experiencing. She didn't know it would all be all right.

"You'll be fine; we just want photos." I squeezed her leg, assuring her. Jack gave me a glare of disapproval.

This time I picked her up by her feet, which were lighter to carry but more difficult to hold onto as she squirmed.

"Please—pleeeaase. Let me go-oh-oh-oo. I'll do anything—please," she moaned out, half-crying. "People will be looking for me. Please let me go."

She continued to plead through the bag constricted over her head and torso. We entered the house through a door on the opposite side of the garage. The house had an open concept, with the kitchen counter lining the far wall, making an "L" shape, with the long end against the wall. The short end of the "L" came out from the wall on our left, housing the sink and extra cabinets. On our right was a refrigerator and a hallway leading away from the kitchen. On the other side of the short end of the "L" stood a large living room with floor to ceiling windows. The room was circular in shape. *No furniture. That's weird.*

"Jack, is this house a foreclosure or something?" I asked as he led us to the hallway next to the refrigerator. Jack ignored me. Typical. "Have you been squatting?"

As we rounded the corner of the hallway, I could see there was a door already open that led down a set of stairs to the basement.

"Dammit, we have to carry her down a set of stairs?"

I considered myself to be in shape even though I didn't frequent the gym since I walked a lot and kept a good diet. At twenty-five, my father's beer belly had just started to grow on me, but I did my best to keep it off. I went down the stairs first, using the walls to balance my weight against her kicking.

"You know you're more likely going to hurt yourself kicking like that than anything else!" I said to her as I struggled to keep my grip on her legs.

The basement was very large, fully finished with soft beige-colored carpeting and walls painted an off-white with a touch of blue. The opposite side of the basement was floor to ceiling windows again with French doors in the middle. The windows were all taped over with duct tape and cardboard. There was a long metal lockbox on the right wall with holes drilled into it.

"Put her in the box," Jack told me.

We set her down into the box, Jack quickly shutting it just as she flattened out against the bottom. She was crying something fierce now. I didn't blame her. On the other wall, there was a door that led to what appeared to be a full bathroom.

"I have to use the head," Jack said as he walked toward the door. "Start setting up. In that box, you'll find ties and equipment. Pull them out."

I examined the room for this box with equipment, spotting it lying next to the girl's lockbox, on the end facing the blocked windows. I moved to the box and gave it a few tugs, but the lid wouldn't budge.

"Hey, Jack, this lid seems jammed?" I made it more of a question than a statement.

"Keep trying. There's a latch on the side to open it," I heard him respond.

I tried again, but it seemed like I needed a crowbar to get it opened. I started to feel around for a latch. Suddenly, blackness surrounded me, and I felt something tighten around my neck. It smelled terrible, like ammonia or a cat litter box that was a week past its cleaning date. I reached up to my face.

"Jack, what the fuck is this?"

I felt the same ribbing that had been on the sack used to bag the girl. This was a little different. The material was more plastic or rubbery rather than cloth. The bag was smaller and seemed to have been made to cover just the head of a person.

"Jack, seriously, get this thing off me." I felt the drawstring and immediately knew that it would require a screwdriver to loosen. The bag seemed to be getting heavier on my head while I scrambled to remove it. My breathing started to get heavy and more desperate. I was running out of oxygen.

"Jack! Get this bag off me, man!"

I was on the floor now, on my hands and knees, feeling around for anything I could find, a screwdriver or pliers, even scissors would do. I stopped crawling, desperately trying to pull apart the hood like it was a bag of Doritos.

"Dammit, Jack!"

The material stretched a little but didn't break. Terror seized my thoughts. Darkness started to seep in around the edges of my eyes. Although my chest was pounding and beginning to ache, I could feel myself getting weaker. Then the darkness took me.

Jessica – 1986

"Hey, Kristin, you going to the party tonight?" a happy Jessica said as she was pulling outfits out of her closet.

"Apparently you are! Having trouble figuring out what to wear?" Kristin responded with a grin, then continued through the rhetorical question.

"I don't know . . . you know that guy, Ben? Well, he asked me the same question at the gym like thirty minutes ago. I don't think he's getting the message."

Kristin and Jessica had been assigned together as roommates freshman year by Northeastern University in Boston. As they entered into their sophomore year, they had moved into off-campus housing that put their tiny dorm to shame. Their new apartment was in a busy area, just north of campus on Westland Avenue. Kristin's father was a top defense lawyer in New York City and was easily convinced by his only daughter that a two-bedroom, eighth-floor apartment was necessary for her to achieve "academic success," as Kristin had put it.

"You should come—pleeeease," Jessica pleaded. "Just tell that loser you want nothing to do with him. You have to tell him straight. Why did you kiss him anyways? So gross."

"I was drunk!" Kristin paused a moment, then sighed. "Okay . . . Fine. I'll go, but you have to promise me that if I want to leave that you will leave with me." Kristin pointed at Jessica with a serious face. Repeating herself to underline her sincerity, she said, "Promise me!"

"Yes! Yesss. I promise. Now go jump in the shower—you smell like a jock."

Jessica had finally settled on her outfit for the night—for the fourth time. She was wearing patterned leggings that accentuated her slim legs, wide hips, and apple-shaped bottom. For a top, she was wearing a long green shirt that extended to her mid-thigh, tapering up slightly from her right side to her left hip. Over that she had a low-hanging black belt, which was there more for appearances than purpose. To keep warm, she had a thin, short, black leather bomber-style jacket with large cargo pockets on the breasts. Lastly, she wore black, high-heeled wedge boots that helped add a couple more inches to her petite stature—she was typically shorter than most girls in a room.

"Wow, babe, are you looking to get laid tonight or what?" Kristin said after stepping out of the bathroom with a towel still wrapped around her wet hair. "You look f--ing amazing."

Jessica blushed at the comment; she was a conservative girl naturally, yet, at the same time, she had a way to show her curves. Her skin was rarely visible; this outfit was as racy as she got. Kristin, on the other hand was wearing plain black jeans with a gray V-neck shirt. Showing cleavage was page one in Kristin's fashion book. Over that, she had a greenish, puffy jacket and an intricate scarf of blues, browns, and greens wrapped around her neck. At five-foot-ten, height was less of an issue than for Jessica, so, as usual, Kristin wore black flats.

"You look great too," Jessica said politely.

"Oh, go fuck yourself. You can be honest, ya know," Kristin said with her normal vulgarity. "Let's get to this party before I change my mind."

On arriving, they could see a line of ten people or so waiting outside to get into the house party, complete with a bouncer like at a club or bar.

"What. The. Fuck," Kristin said as they got out of the taxi.

"I am not waiting out here. It's freezing. Let's just see if we can get in—it looks like a lot of guys waiting," Jessica said, already walking toward the bouncer.

"Go ahead, ladies." The bouncer opened the door and moved aside as soon as they were close.

"Shit. That's awesome. We didn't even have to say anything," Kristin said, feeling more confident about herself than when she left her apartment, a huge smile stretched on her face.

Jessica was busy smiling at a dark-haired guy standing third in line, who was tall and lanky with a goofy, but handsome, look.

"Hey, stalker, let's get inside." Kristin was poking fun at Jessica's long stare at the boy in line. "Let's go, for fuck's sake! And wipe that smile off your face. He's probably not going to get in."

Jessica felt a hand squeeze her by the shoulder as Kristin dragged her from the entryway. "Now, where can we can we get a drink, like now?"

The house was a large two-story brownstone with an open-floor concept where the kitchen, dining room, and living room were all completely accessible without any walls in between. There was nothing separating the rooms except support beams. The kitchen appeared to come straight out of a home-cooking magazine with polished stainless-steel countertops and matching appliances. The walls in the entire home matched the brownstone on the outside, giving the feeling that you were in a restaurant or club located in a rustic mill building. The rest of the floor was made up of an area that had a large dining table, where a group was gathered for beer pong. Adjacent to that a large living room spread out with what must have been the biggest white leather couch Jessica and Kristin had ever seen. There was a DJ spinning music from the entertainment system near the couch.

"Hey, ladies, welcome! Can I get you something to drink?" A cute, muscular jock-type came out from the kitchen area holding onto two Bud Lights.

"Sure," Kristin responded quickly and snatched the drinks, giving one to Jessica.

"My name is John. This is my best friend's place. He's somewhere around here." John glanced over a mostly full apartment, his head extending from side to side. "He looks like a complete dork, but he's cool, and his parties rock. If you girls need any more drinks tonight, you can come to me; we have some mixed cocktails and fruit punch that will be coming out in a while."

As he moved away from the girls, he yelled out, "Hey Jay-cob!" to another friend he saw.

"He's cute," Kristin said, winking at Jessica.

"If he's so cute why don't you take him?" Jessica replied sharply.

"Oh, no. He is way too f-ing short for me. We're like the same height. I'm pretty sure that's against the law. No, I can only date guys that are, like, six-two or taller."

As the night went on, more people packed into the apartment. The music seemed to get louder with each body that came through the door. The large white couch had been pushed to the side of the living room to open up a large area for the dance floor. Jessica loved to dance. After a couple more Bud Lights, she was grabbing Kristin and dragging her into the middle of the floor. They danced for so long that both of them had long removed their jackets and fought off multiple advances. Sweat was starting to boil up through their skin.

"Uh oh. I think your friend Ben is going to try to make a dance move on you. My feet are starting to hurt anyway. Let's go get another drink!" Jessica screamed over the music while keeping an eye on Ben as he fished through the crowd.

"Haha, let's do it," Kristin responded.

They weaved their way through the large dancing crowd toward the kitchen while trying to duck behind people to avoid being seen by Ben. What had the appearance of a clean home now reflected a drunken version of a cheap club. The floor was sticky from spilled drinks; empty bottles and cups were strewn on every available tabletop. Arriving at the kitchen, Jessica could see the boy that she had locked eyes with before. He was standing in a corner with his head down as a large, older-looking guy pushed him into a wall. Without thinking about it, Jessica approached the two.

"Hey, what's going on here?" she asked.

The older guy pushed the boy again in the chest with his fingers extended and rigid, then turning, he peered at her to gauge her intent.

"This kid got in the middle of my business. He took one of my beers, so now he's paying the price."

It was obvious the guy was just being an asshole, who enjoyed throwing his weight around. Jessica turned, went toward the fridge, and grabbed a beer from an area where John had told her she could.

"Here, have this one instead and leave him alone." Taking the beer, the older guy contemplated her for a moment. Jessica stood strong.

"Okay, but don't let it happen again!" the big guy said, getting a few last pokes in on the boy. "Your girlfriend might not be there to save you next time."

Once the older guy had moved away, the younger one said, "You didn't have to do that; he wasn't bothering me that bad."

"No biggie. My name is Jessica. Where do you go to school?" Jessica threw on a smile that could knock a man out.

"I'm—uh—my name is Drew. Yes, yeah. I am a student at Boston University," Drew stammered out.

"Oh, cool. I'm at Northeastern. I'm working on a degree in biology while fulfilling my pre-med requirements." Jessica had practiced that line so many times in the past year; it seemed that in college, everyone wanted to know what you were working on.

"Wow. You're going to be a doctor. That's wicked cool. I'm a criminal justice major, and, to be honest, I'm not quite sure what I'm going to be after that." Drew revealed a slight Massachusetts accent. There was a long pause as they just stared at each other. Drew opened his mouth to say something just as John made his entrance again.

"Heyyy, there you are. I have been looking all over for you." John casually walked up and put his arm around Jessica.

Drew looked like he got punched in the stomach. At eighteen, confidence was fickle and easily lost, something Jessica immediately related too. Jessica tried for a moment to ignore John, excited that the conversation with Drew might go somewhere interesting. Drew started to speak when he was completely cut off.

"Hey, so your friend asked me to give you this," John said and lifted up a large red solo cup filled with a red fruit punch. Jessica hesitated a moment, looked up, and saw Kristin drinking out of a similar solo cup, talking to another boy she did not recognize. John turned to face her, effectively cutting Drew completely out of her view.

"Thanks." Jessica took the fruit punch timidly.

"Let me show you something cool." John grabbed Jessica around the waist, spun her around before she could even refuse, and walked her out of the kitchen toward the back of the first floor. She gave an apologetic glance over her shoulder to Drew. She hoped he'd still be there later when she was done seeing whatever it was John wanted to show her.

"What are you showing me?" Jessica was getting nervous as John guided her up a long hardwood staircase to the second floor. Her gut began to turn with unease.

"Have another sip of your drink. You can trust me; my dad is a chief of police, and you are really going to like this." John squeezed her slightly. "It's just around the corner. My buddy doesn't allow drinks up here because he doesn't want to stain these floors, so let's chug ours."

With that, John tipped up the bottom of his cup and downed the liquored punch. Jessica followed by forcing down the unnecessarily strong punch. John watched with a smile on his face. Jessica was stretching out her lips, scrunching her face, and breathing in and out quickly. Her mouth seemed to swell with water, and she had to fight off the feeling that she needed to puke.

"You good?" John said, smiling. Jessica just nodded, insinuating that she would make it once the feeling subsided.

"Soooo, what did you want to show me?" Jessica said as they were still standing awkwardly in the hallway at the top of the stairs. Still smiling and looking at her with a weird expression, John put his arm around her waist.

"Just give it a minute," he said.

Just then Jessica started to feel almost like she drank way too much.

"I feel weird," she muttered out. Tunnel vision began to narrow her sight, and the room began to spin. This was the first time that she had more than three beers in the same night.

This must be what being really drunk feels like, she thought. She felt as if she were floating and her head was too heavy for her neck to support it. Even her eyes were tired, floating aimlessly from side to side, creating tunnel vision. *Are those my feet.* She thought, watching her legs dragging on the floor.

"Oh, I think I need to go," she tried to say out loud, but it came out as, "Uh, I neep top-gooo."

"You don't feel good?" John said. "Let me find you a place to lie down."

Her thoughts were loose and wild, screams of danger popping up to be suddenly replaced by thoughts about how weak her arms felt.

John was dragging her down the hall, which was causing the floating sensation she was experiencing. He opened a door, walked her to a bed, and dumped her semi-lucid, limp body onto it.

"What's going on?" Jessica tried to get out.

* * *

"You'll be safe here," John said, bending over her, checking her eyes to see if they were dilated. Taking her arms, he stretched them out toward the headboard, then grabbed her feet to unzip and remove her boots, pulling her legs to straighten her out on the bed.

"Hey, man, what are you doing?" a harsh, authoritative voice said from the doorway. John whipped around, slightly panicked.

"Nothi—ahh, you asshole."

Devin, whose parents owned the house, stood in the doorway, laughing.

"Haha, looks like you picked a cute one. You gotta love fresh meat. Maybe when you're done, you can tag me into that," Devin said, high-fiving the air to gesture an athlete being tagged into a game. John turned and regarded the semi-lucid Jessica, eyes still open, staring up at the ceiling, virtually unaware of what was happening around her.

"These roofies work fast, bro," John said as a matter of fact.

"Yeah, buddy. Way better than that batch we tried last weekend. Those girls got home before they even kicked in," Devin responded.

"She won't know what hit her in the morning."

"Can you play goalie with her friend downstairs? Tell her that Jessica went home with me," John said as he hooked his fingers into the waistband of her leggings, one hand on each hip, and slid them off her, exposing her panties.

"Mm-mmm, that is silky smooth. Tower, this is Ghost Rider. Roger that. I got you covered," Devin said, licking his lips as he made a reference to the recently released *Top Gun*.

"I'm gonna take her right into the danger zone," John replied as Devin shut the door to the bedroom.

* * *

Early the next morning, Jessica awoke to the sun piercing through the shades and burning into her eyes. She was completely naked, save for her socks. Next to her lay John, fast asleep with his naked, muscular butt exposed by a lapse in the sheets.

"What happened last night?" Jessica whispered to herself. She had a pounding headache; all of her muscles seemed to be sore. She slipped out of bed as gently as she could to avoid waking John up; she wanted nothing to do with him and had no idea how she ended up in a bed with him. She collected as much of her clothing as she could find and stumbled quietly out of the room.

A sick feeling overcame all her senses. Something was wrong. She felt violated.

"Oh God. Jessica, what did you do last night?" she half-cried to herself, trying desperately to keep it together.

"I have never felt this terrible. How many drinks did I have?" Jessica continued to question herself on what was going on. People were passed out in the hallways, the bathrooms, almost anywhere they could slump themselves. Picking up a phone in the kitchen, she called a taxi. While she waited, she wondered where Kristin was.

"How could she leave me here?" she said to herself.

* * *

Jessica wiped the fog from the bathroom mirror just after her morning shower. She viewed her neck, inspecting the bruising that extended from her ear to her collar bone.

"What the hell happened to me?" Jessica spoke with a total look of disgust in her eyes. It had been exactly twenty-four hours from when she was picked up from the party house by a taxi. In that time, more and more bruises popped up around her body. Her neck, legs, hip, groin, right butt cheek, even her back wasn't spared. Something was seriously wrong.

"Why, why, why? Why would you drink that much? God I swear, please help me through this, and I will never, ever drink again."

Drew – 2014

"It is a sad scene today by the Charles River. Early this morning, the Massachusetts State Police pulled the body of a man out of the water. Reports coming from the scene indicate that the body was that of a man in his twenties. We spoke with a representative from the DA office who stated that the death does not appear suspicious. They have not identified the body yet, but investigators will be following up on the case. We will continue to update you on this story as more information becomes available. Coming up after the commercial break we will cover our top ten places to eat in Boston. Don't go anywhere."

The TV spat out the news as background noise in a busy household. It was just past 6 a.m. on a Friday morning where the Law family was up, getting ready for the day. Elizabeth, or Lizzy as she was called by her family and friends, was rushing to get out of the door to school when she bumped her dad, who was staring at the TV from his seat at the kitchen table. This jostling caused him to spill his first and only cup of coffee of the day onto his knees.

"Ah, Lizzy, be more careful, would yah?" Drew groaned, controlling himself. He was still wearing his running shorts. He got up at 5 a.m. every morning during the week for a three-mile jog, although it was normally closer to a sprint. A fit guy, standing six-three and weighing about 205 pounds, he spent forty-five minutes at his local gym every day to keep toned. At forty-six, he was in pretty good shape.

"Sorry," Lizzy spoke back with a weak reply.

"Yah lucky I haven't dressed for work," he said sarcastically. His Massachusetts accent seemed more pronounced at home than out at work or anywhere else.

Drew had been born and raised in Massachusetts. He had grown up in Dover, a wealthy town twenty miles south of Boston. His father, Jeff, had made his money working his way up the food chain in big oil. He had worked hard enough so that he had the means to retire at fifty and could focus his time on his family. Jeff had met his first and only wife, who was ten years younger, later than most and, in turn, had started a family relatively late for the times. They had four children in total. Drew was the first, then came Elizabeth, Sarah, and lastly the baby of the group, Theodore.

Elizabeth had died in a car accident at twenty, a bad head-on collision on Route 3 with a drunk driver who was heading the wrong direction. She was on her way to New Hampshire for a three-day camping trip on Lake Winnipesaukee. Drew had been in the car with her and had been lucky to have walked away with only minor injuries. That was, to Drew, the hardest time that he would ever have to endure, or so he hoped. Of the siblings, Drew had been closest to her; her death had crippled him emotionally for months, and left an emotional tarnish for years. Later, he would name his daughter after her as a tribute.

Sarah now lived in New Hampshire with her own family, a wealthy husband and two kids who were reluctant to leave home. Sarah worked as an advanced math teacher for the local high school—she enjoyed shaping young minds and liked to keep herself busy. Advanced math was the only subject she would ever teach. In truth, she hated putting up with teenagers, but the type of students in her class always seemed to be the "good" kids.

Ted lived in London. He was the only member of the family to follow in their father's footsteps and pursue a career in big oil. Like many families, they didn't connect nearly as much as they should or used to, something Drew regretted periodically.

"Yah know, Lizzy, if you get up a little earlier, the mornings wouldn't be so rough," Drew said as he was wiping his legs off by the sink with a rag drenched in warm water.

"I know. That's why my alarm clock goes off for an hour every morning. I just can't get up though," Lizzy said with a smile on her face.

"Can't play the snooze game forever." Drew had done well with her. She was his only child, yet she didn't act like a typical only child. When she was young, they would spend a lot of time with her cousins in New Hampshire for summers on Lake Sunapee, where Sarah had a two-season lake house.

"Dad, can I drive your car today?" She knew the answer already.

"Nope," Drew replied.

"Please, Dad? My car is acting up, and I don't want to be late."

"Well, at this rate you'll miss school anyway." Drew was looking at the clock on the wall in the kitchen; it was now just past 6:15. Lizzy followed his eyes to the clock.

"Shit!" she spat, rushing out of the door.

* * *

The big hand on the kitchen clock now pointed to 9 a.m., a full hour after he usually got to the office. Drew had planned to be in the office this morning, as usual, working through old emails, photos, and social networking sites, looking anywhere, reviewing everything, to put together as true a story as possible. That's why people hired him; his storytelling was better than that of others, and, more often than not, it was the truth. Being a self-employed private investigator afforded Drew the ability to get to work whenever he wanted. Today Drew decided to take advantage of that.

"It's an easier drive from home into the city than the office," he quipped, assuring himself it was ok to stay home and avoid a full-morning work schedule.

He had been hired, not even a week earlier, by the family of a young man that had been pulled out of the river the previous March. The police officially labeled it as an accidental drowning. The young man, Josh, had been out drinking at a local dive bar, alone, on a Friday night. Witnesses say he left the bar with a sway in his step. Two weeks later, he showed up in the river. There were no signs of trauma on the body to indicate a struggle. Water in his lungs came back positive as that of the river water. But the family would not accept accidental death as an answer. They wanted more—where was he for two weeks? The police told the family that the cold February waters had made time of death difficult to determine, and they were lucky they found him.

Probably the truth, Drew thought, but he was paid to double-check and put all the details of Josh's life under scrutiny, as far back as he had access to. Interestingly enough, Drew had received a phone call early this morning, just before Lizzy came bursting through the kitchen, from a friend on the Boston PD that changed Drew's day.

"Another body!"

Drew paused as he thought about his friend's statement, those words echoing over and over all morning in his mind.

"Found just one mile downriver from where Josh's body was pulled. It's probably nothing." He rolled over the facts and scratched his chin, then ran his hand over his head.

Drew noted that both were young men in their twenties, white males, found within a mile of each other. That was enough to keep him interested. Soon after he had received the call about the body, he called his assistant and told her he wouldn't be in until the afternoon. Drew then called another friend who worked in the morgue to set up a time to view the body of the newest victim of the Charles.

June 9th, 2003

Drew had worked on the Boston police force for fourteen years, four of those years as a homicide detective. Prior to that, he had been in college at Boston University, where he had completed a Bachelor of Science in criminal justice. He had joined the Boston PD at twenty-one, as soon as he had left college. It was right around this time that he had met his future wife and mother of his daughter, Nell. Nell Abel Smith, or Nell-a-bell as her parents nicknamed her growing up.

Nell was gorgeous, tall for most women at 5'11", with shoulder-length, wavy, dirty blond hair. She had hazel eyes that changed color depending on the colors around her. Sometime Drew would see brilliant greens in her eyes with touches of deep browns swirling together, like a mysterious forest full of life; at other times, her eyes would glow back at him a mesmerizing blue, especially when light would hit the glowing blue stone that hung from her neck, a necklace she always wore. She had lips that were large and inviting, with soft skin that made snuggling hard to ignore.

* * *

Drew and Nell first met in a sophomore-year chemistry class, way back in 1987, when Drew, a handsome guy with dark hair, great big brown eyes, all mounted to a tall, lanky frame, entered the classroom. Naturally alert, he scanned the room and his future classmates. Immediately spotting Nell in the front row, he made sure to sit next to her and introduce himself.

"Hi, my name is Lew—ahem, haha—I mean Drew. My name is Drew Law." Drew had dyslexically mixed up his names due to nerves. Nell loved it; she giggled at his clumsiness and his awkward, goofy look.

"I'm Nell." They locked eyes, and Drew immediately knew he was in trouble as anxiety filled him.

"I really like this necklace you're wearing." Drew reached over and lifted the heavy necklace off her chest and examined it. He realized later that it might have been too bold of a move, but his anxiety in situations like this often led him to make poor decisions; luckily, Nell didn't think twice about it. The necklace was silver with a thin long bar setting that led to a beautiful, heirloom sapphire stone minimally set with tiny prongs.

"This was my grandmother's," Nell said with pride. "I always wear it. She gave it to me when I was six."

Admiring the stone, Drew thought it must be worth quite a bit. "She must love that you wear it often," he said, letting the stone drop back to her chest.

"Yes, she did." Nell picked it up with sad eyes.

Drew and Nell became close friends over the next year or so and then became romantically involved toward the end of their junior year. Initially, Nell had been holding on to a relationship from high school, but Drew didn't care; he knew exactly what he wanted, and he was willing to wait for it. As soon as Nell became single, Drew started to make his move.

Drew had always been a little rough around the edges. You could rely on him to tell it straight, and this attitude was there when he told Nell they should, in his words, "hook up." Drew married Nell soon after college and Lizzy followed soon after that.

Straight out of college, Nell pursued a degree in corporate law from Harvard Law in Boston, while Drew went to the police academy. After graduating top of her class from law school, Nell joined OpacOne, a company that served to promote the interests of a group of oil giants such as British Petroleum, Exxon Mobil, Royal Dutch Shell, and more. Nell was hired in as an associate legal representative to support OpecOne's chief legal officer, Ronald Spak. Ronald was a rough man both in looks and attitude.

Drew often thought Ronald might be the ugliest man he knew. He was stocky, shorter than Drew, with a large square face that featured a large nose, big uneven eyes, large protruding ears, and what seemed like scarring on his right cheek. It could have been from acne as a young man or maybe a physical altercation. Drew thought it best not to ask. You could also tell Ron was bullied in high school just by looking at him, and the opposite occurred now.

Nell always complained that Ron had a superiority complex that made work a challenge for everyone on the legal staff. Drew only met Ron a few times over the years; each time Ron said nothing, stood silently staring at Drew with his dark eyes, which always creeped him out. Despite having a difficult boss, Nell could not justify changing jobs because her salary was almost double that of her peers and what others were willing to pay.

* * *

It was a beautiful Saturday morning in June when Drew and Nell got out of bed together to prepare for a wonderful day. It was one of those summer mornings where you felt like nothing could go wrong. They were planning to take Lizzy on her first trip to the Boston Museum of Science. Nell was exceptionally beautiful that morning with the soft summer sun making her hair and skin glow. During breakfast, Nell got a call from her office, a call that made Nell immediately upset. Nell rushed into her home office to finish the call. When she emerged, she had her large purse hung over her shoulder.

"I love you two." Nell kissed both Drew and Lizzy on the foreheads. "I have to go into the office for a few hours; I'll call later when I'm on my way back, and we can do the museum later in the afternoon, okay?"

Without waiting for a response, she moved toward the door in a rush and said, "Drew, look for the box, baby." A tear streamed down her cheek, which she wiped away quickly.

"What box?" Drew had turned to her at the door. "What are you talking about?"

Before he finished asking his question, Nell had already disappeared out of the house.

Drew waited by the phone all day. Instead of Nell calling to say she was on her way home, Drew got a call from the Merrimack NH Police Department.

"A car was spotted by a passerby in the Souhegan River. Apparently, she lost control of the car coming around a corner, crossed the double yellow lines, and exited the road on the opposite side to smash through small brush, rolling into the river." The officer spoke with sadness and sorrow. "When first responders arrived on the scene, they pulled Nell from the car, but it was too late; she was dead."

Drew listened, his eyes wetting from the words as they rang through his ears.

Her death was officially ruled an accident by the medical examiner, and no investigation was ever launched. Cause of death:

drowning.

Drew was devastated, the pain equaling what he had felt when he had lost his sister. He took a leave of absence from BPD in order to "focus on healing." In truth, he wanted to take the time to properly review Nell's accident as he was not convinced that that's all it was.

"Maybe I'm just a grieving husband," he would tell himself when reviewing details of the case. Lizzy was just eight at the time, a very difficult age for anyone to lose their mother, and Lizzy would need Drew there more than ever. Nell Abell had died on June 9, 2003.

One year after the accident, Drew took everything he had put together on her death and locked it away in a storage facility. He had yet to convince himself it was just an accident, but, at the same time, he had not found any information saying otherwise. He still had a lot of unanswered questions, such as "Why was she in New Hampshire?" and "Who called her from the office?" Drew was never able to figure out what she had meant about the box. *Did it mean anything? Was it a clue? Could I have stopped her from going into work? What fucking box?*

Drew decided that after a year of fruitless pursuit, it was best for him and Lizzy to move on. Lizzy had been acting up at school, getting into trouble more frequently, and her grades were slipping. Drew felt he needed to be there for her without the distraction of Nell's death on his mind 24/7. He officially retired from the BPD that day, spending the next year focusing on Lizzy, helping her with her grief, her school work, and more. When Lizzy started to show consistent improvements in her behavior, Drew decided to open up his own PI practice.

This was an exciting moment for him. He was emerging from what seemed like a coma, starting out on something new.

"A fresh start," he whispered while looking at the classic wood-framed door with *D. Law, Private Investigator* etched into its glass window panel. He did not start the practice for money. The insurance payout from Nell's death was enough to keep him comfortable for the rest of his days and likely Lizzy's. He wanted to start the PI practice to help others, and telling himself, "One day, when Lizzy is independent, I can revisit Nell's investigation with a clear mind."

Business was slow for the first couple of years. Drew had started out taking jobs from the bitter and paranoid, such as men wanting to catch their wives in an affair or vice versa. As his success increased with each job, and as he gained a reputation, he was able to pick which cases he wanted to work on. For some reason, he found he had an interest in missing person cases, maybe because he was in a strange state of denial about Nell's death, his heart wishing her to be a missing person, someone he could find.

Due to his connections with the BPD, he was personally recommended by the Boston police chief as a PI to help out in the disappearance case of Scott Drowd's son, David Drowd. Scott was a candidate to become a senator for the State of Massachusetts at the time. This would normally have been treated as a high-profile case by BPD, but Scott pleaded with the commissioner to help keep the story under wraps and to limit the knowledge of the case to only a select few for fear of a media leak turning the story into an exposé on his son, a drug addict.

Scott hired Drew for his experience, skills, intelligence, recommendations, and because he could be trusted to be discreet. It took Drew two days to track down David; he found him in an abandoned warehouse in Springfield, MA with a needle in his arm, but alive. After the successful conclusion of the case, Scott made it his business to make sure Drew's name came up at any opportunity someone needed a gritty, discreet investigator.

Boston Morgue – 2014

It was around one o'clock in the afternoon by the time Drew was allowed to see the body. He had been waiting in the lobby of the Boston chief medical examiner's office for more than an hour.

"Drew, how are you, old buddy?" Dr. Kelly Courtney said joyfully as he entered the lobby of the morgue.

"Kelly, you old bah-stad," Drew replied, giving him a hug. Drew and Kelly had been friends for years; they'd been teammates on a Boston-based beer-league hockey team.

"I've been doing good, keeping my self outta trouble at least. What about you, looks like the good food of Boston has been treating you well." Drew patted Kelly's large belly. He had put on at least forty pounds since the last time Drew had seen him.

"Yeah, well it has been six years or so, and I don't play hockey anymore," Kelly replied, obviously uncomfortable about the comment. "So, you want some time with, *and* information on, our most recent floater? John Doe 2199?" Kelly was referring to an unidentified body – by giving the last four digits of the BPD case number. "I should have told you to go fuck yourself, hahaha!" Kelly laughed at his own vulgar comment. Kelly had a poor sense of humor and a boisterous laugh, so boisterous, it sounded fake and annoyed most people.

When he got no reaction from Drew, Kelly said, "You working a case?" They talked and walked toward the access door for the main offices of the medical examiner. Stopping, Kelly pointed at a reception desk just past the door that led to the lobby. "Sign in here for me, will you, Drew?"

"I have been here before, remember, old man?" Drew replied and reached down to sign in. "A body of a young man came through here last March. Officially ruled an accident, so no investigation was done. The family hired me to look into it."

Drew finished signing his name on the dotted line. The sign-in sheet asked for his name, the date, the time, viewing name or last four digits of the case number, escort ID, phone number, and signatures of both the guest and escort. Drew scanned the page for the day, spotting that another guest had signed in to view the same body. *Ashley Tinder* had signed in about an hour earlier to view case 2199.

"Anything wrong?" Kelly had picked up on Drew's pause.

"It looks like someone else had interest in this body?" Drew asked as Kelly moved in and filled in his escort ID on the sheet.

"Looks that way, hmmm," Kelly mumbled as he signed the sheet. "Ah, yes, that ID belongs to Dr. Jack Jefferson. Whoever this Ashley is, she's connected, because Jack doesn't do 'Jack-shit' without being told to do it from the top. Seriously, that dude is a 'Jack-ass,' all he does all day is 'Jack' —"

"Off!" Drew cut in, annoyed with the joke. "I get it. You don't like the guy."

Drew took one more peek at the information on the sign-in sheet and grabbed a small notebook from his back pocket, feverishly scribbling down *Ashley Tinder* and her phone number.

"That is frowned upon around here," Kelly said as Drew was slipping the notebook back into his pocket.

"Tough." After a pause, Drew continued sarcastically, "It'll be fine . . . as long as no one else around here complains as much as you." With a deep breath, Drew said, "Let's see the body."

This part he never enjoyed. He liked his job, but seeing a dead body was always tough on him. He would always think about the person, who they were, or who they could have been. The younger the person, the harder it was.

"You have to accept their fate, look at them from the perspective of science and ask yourself, 'What can I learn from them now? What problems can they help us solve?'" Kelly would say, objectifying them.

They entered examination room 1B from the main hallway. The room was larger than Drew remembered it, a rectangle about forty-five feet long and twenty-five feet wide. It had four rolling, stainless-steel carts that supported large rectangular plastic trays that sat at a slight adjustable angle. That way, when a body was placed on the tray, it could be tilted toward the sink so that fluids could run from the head toward the feet and then into the sink, with a three-inch lip to catch any solid objects that might run down the tray. The trays were long enough so that they could hold most men and wide enough so that large men could be rotated from lying on their front to their back.

The tray itself was ribbed on the bottom to promote fluid flow, while restricting solids. Each cart was rolled up to a bench station so that the small lip of the tray hung just over a sink. The sink had a normal faucet, one you would expect to see on a utility sink. Two long hoses hung on each side of the sink and could be easily extended the length of the tray. To the sides of the sink were perforated stainless-steel counters and more hoses hung over these counters for use in cleansing objects and the counter. Over the cart was a large circular light that was attached to an arm not that different from what you would see at a dentist office, only larger. The arm allowed a technician or pathologist to position the light as needed to perform examinations. Lastly, each station had a digital scale with a basket on top; these were placed next to the sink and are used to measure the weight of organs and objects removed from bodies during examinations.

John Doe 2199 lay on the first tray from the left wall, opposite from the entrance. While the "toe tag" was still in use in many morgues, this morgue used red plastic bracelets that contained all the same information as a toe tag, such as name, case number, date of death, time of death, cause of death, height, weight, race, sex, and an internal ID number used by the morgue for record keeping.

Drew looked at the bracelet and noted down its information in his notebook. Name – John Doe, Case # – 2199, Height – 6'1," Weight – 185lbs, Race – white, Sex – male, and MID# – 100628998. All other fields were blank as a full examination had yet to be performed. Drew caught himself crossing his arms, trying to stay warm in the near freezing temperature of the room.

"Are you making corp-sicles in here? It's freezing," Drew shivered out.

"Ah, well, if you look to the right, just outside the door here, you can grab a spare lab coat. They're insulated to help take off the chill. We lowered the temperature in here a couple of degrees over the past few years to increase the longevity of the bodies . . . and to prevent stank," Kelly informed him.

"You could have mentioned that before we came in here," Drew chided Kelly.

"I was hoping to see you shiver." Kelly laughed. Drew went outside and came back moments later, swinging a full-length lab coat over himself.

"Who's scheduled to perform his examination?" Drew asked Kelly as he walked around the cart to John Doe's left side.

Kelly shrugged his shoulders. "Beats me. That hasn't been set up yet."

"You guys are starting to slack off here," Drew smirked. He liked to rip on Kelly whenever he got the chance.

"Ya know, you can leave now if you want. We have a strict no asshole policy here," Kelly replied sarcastically, then said, "Handsome guy," as he peered at the body.

Drew rolled his eyes but thought the same about John Doe—he was handsome, albeit he seemed a little swollen. John Doe had a good head of dark brown hair a few inches longer than Drew liked to cut his own. Other than his head and his genitals, he had no hair on the rest of his body.

"Help me here? I want to take a look at the back side." Drew slipped on a pair of latex gloves and started to wedge his fingers under one side of the body. They lifted the body up slightly on one side so Drew could take a quick look.

"No tattoos . . . there seems to be a small bruise here at the back of the neck." Drew was talking out loud, almost to help himself remember what he was seeing.

"You're lucky it's almost winter. In the summer these things swell up fast in the river. It is common for their eyes to pop out from gases, and, boy, do they stink something special, like a—"

Drew blocked Kelly out as he took a closer look at John's face. His eyes looked fake, like they were made out of plastic and wax. They were flatter than they should be.

"Brown eyes," Drew said, cutting Kelly off. Drew opened John's mouth and peered around, then moved down his arms and hands, checking his fingers. Drew pointed, his eyes moving up to match Kelly's. "It looks like he's missing a fingernail?"

"Hmmm, it's tough to say what might have caused that. See the bruising around the proximal nail fold? He lost his nail before he went an' died. Maybe it happened as he fell into the river? Maybe when he was struggling against rocks to swim? Or maybe it was unrelated altogether. His other nails don't show signs of fungal infection," Kelly said, inspecting each finger on John's right hand. Drew quickly glanced at John's genitals and moved on to his legs before finishing his visual inspection at the feet.

"Where are the belongings that were found on him?" Drew asked.

"Let's take a look." Kelly began opening up cabinets around the station. "Here we are!"

Kelly pulled out a large Tupperware container and a five-gallon bucket from a cabinet next to the sink. With tongs, Kelly pulled clothing out of the bucket, stretching them on the perforated countertop. The bucket contained a thick gray winter sweater from the Banana Republic, Lee jeans, a button-down shirt from the Banana Republic, blue Calvin Klein boxer briefs, black Calvin Klein ankle socks, and a black beanie cap with the New England Patriots logo on the front. Drew looked over the clothing closely, flipping each item over, looking for anything out of place.

"Have a look at his personal items?" Kelly questioned, holding out the smaller Tupperware container. Without responding, Drew grabbed it, along with small tongs. Inside the container, there was only a watch and a key to a Mercedes-Benz, a newer Mercedes-Benz by the look of it. The watch Drew recognized as a Burberry.

"From the look of things, this guy had access to money," Drew said as he looked at Kelly and held up the watch over the Tupperware container with the tongs. "This is it? This is all they found with him?"

"I don't fill the boxes," Kelly replied. "What you see is what you get! I'm surprised that watch is still here, even after going into the drink."

"Are you getting redundant around here?" Drew smirked. He played around with the key to the Mercedes. "It seems this key is missing an insert."

Drew spun the key around to show Kelly. The fat side of the key had a thin slit in it that would fit a backup key to the keyless entry system.

"I don't know what to tell you there; maybe we'll get more information about that when we ID him and get a chance to speak to his family."

Drew sighed at Kelly's response. "Can you send over the official report to me after the examination has been done? And let me know as soon as you get an ID." Drew ordered bluntly, not asking. As a retired detective, old habits die hard, and this was an old habit.

"I'll tell you what, you give me your on-ice Bruins tickets for a game this coming season, and I'll send you over anything you want."

Drew hadn't been a season ticket holder since Nell's death, but he played around with the offer nonetheless. After a moment, he extended his hand. "Sure thing, you'll have tickets for the season opener."

"Then you have a deal. As soon as this report is complete, I'll send it over to you." They shook hands to consummate the deal. Kelly walked Drew back to the lobby, going on about what happens to the body in salt water vs. fresh water, but Drew had tuned him out, lost in his own thoughts.

"Sorry Kelly, my mind is swirling around Ashley. Who is she? How is she connected to this?"

Kelly stared back at Drew for a moment before responding. "You're the detective." Then he turned around, leaving Drew at the door.

Last Lesson – 1995

"Where are you? Jessica? Where the fuck you hiding, woman?" John's yells could be heard throughout the house as he entered from the garage.

John was not large, standing five-nine and weighing about 170lbs after dinner, but he was a hard, controlling, and intimidating man. He owned his own successful construction company. At the tail end of completing a local contract to build two new streets with forty-five homes, he had reason to drink more than usual, excessively. Truthfully, John could find any reason to drink. On most days, he would drink on the job site, come home half in the bag, demand dinner, and then pass out watching TV in the living room.

Some nights he would come home angry. Jessica never understood why, but she would take anywhere from a slap to a full beating for almost nothing, depending on John's mood. She married him to pursue the dream of becoming a happy husband and wife raising a child, while he married her at the demand of his devout Irish Catholic father who wouldn't have it any other way.

"Mommy, why are we hiding?" the boy asked. She was heartbroken hearing this.

Jessica was hiding in a hallway closet with their eight-year-old son, Jack, on the top floor of their three-story home.

"Shh, please whisper. You know how your father gets some nights. If we hide, we give him time to calm down." She tried to speak without showing her fear. She had talked to John on the phone earlier that night, and he had said something to her that reminded her of one of her worst nights living.

"I've got something for you. You're gonna learn. I know what you're up to, woman."

"Fuck, fuck, fuck. He knows," she muttered to herself.

She thought back to the last time John had used those words, when Jessica had spent all afternoon making a sirloin-tip steak roast with a side of seared Brussels sprouts and red potatoes. She had planned the roast to be ready for when John typically got home, around 6:30. Unfortunately, John decided to stop at a bar for a quick extra drink. When he got home at 7:30, the roast was colder than John thought it should be. Something must have put him into a mood at the bar because as soon as he came in, he was already giving her an aggressive attitude. After complaining about the temperature of the meat, he took a metal spatula from a kitchen drawer and placed it on top of the hot stove until it began to turn an orange-red color.

"What are you doing with that?" Jessica cried out.

"I've got something for you. You're gonna learn!" he responded, saying it with calm certainty. John put on an oven mitt on his left hand, picked up the spatula, and approached Jessica. "You'll learn to keep things warm!"

As John approached, Jessica put up her hands and began pushing at an invisible wall.

"Please—please don't," she begged. She had no idea what he was thinking, but she knew it was bad. "John, please don't do this!"

She saw a look in his eye she had never seen before, a look of pleasure, like he was enjoying what he was doing and was pleased with himself causing her fear.

"Stop joking around. You're sick," she screamed out. John reached over and grabbed her by her hair, pushing her head down toward the floor.

"Ahh, please no—no!" She screamed so loud her neighbors might have heard if they were home. With her head down toward his crotch, John dragged her to the kitchen table and forced her to bend over the table, a table that had been bolted to the wall as it only had two legs supporting it.

"You stay just like that, or I will put this thing in your mouth," he told her calmly as he held her face violently to the table with one hand and the burning spatula so close to her forehead she could feel it's painful, radiating heat.

Jessica started to cry, but she didn't dare test his threat. He moved away from her face and began fiddling with her skirt. She was sobbing now, bent over the table with her face squished against the cold marble top.

How could this get any worse? she thought. Then it did, as she looked out of the kitchen. She could see her four-year-old baby, Jack, watching; just his face was peering around the edge of the entrance to the kitchen. Jessica tried to wave Jack away covertly; she didn't want him seeing this. She couldn't say anything, fearful John would turn his rage on him if he knew he was there, spying.

She closed her eyes and began to pray. John had already managed to pull her skirt up over her back and was peeling her pink panties down to her ankles, exposing her soft, white, blemish-free behind. John next unbuttoned his pants, unzipped them, pulling them down with one hand. John was hard, harder than he'd been in months.

"You're fucked up—you're sick," she said back to John when she realized what he was doing.

"You'll see; you'll learn!" he said to her. John spat down into his right hand and began rubbing her.

"Is this what it takes to get you going? You're sick; you know that!" Jessica yelled back again.

"Here we go!" he said like he was about to ride a bull. John then put his right hand at the base of her back to keep her still. Then he took the hot wide-end of the spatula and placed it against her soft left butt cheek while he entered her and began thrusting, violently. Her skin began to sizzle and smoke, and she screamed out in terror and pain; she wasn't expecting to be branded. She tried to wiggle, but it only seemed to make it worse. She tried to kick.

"You keep that up, and I'll do the other side," John said immediately. She then tried to keep the screams in, for Jack's sake. She bit her tongue, closed her eyes, and tried to imagine this was all a nightmare she would wake up from. John kept thrusting hard, making the burn worse with every stroke.

"That oughta teach you," John said when he finished. He threw the spatula toward the sink and pulled himself out of her. "You clean up, and if you tell anyone what happened tonight, I will go a second round, but with Jack."

"You're a monster; how could you even say such a thing? About your own son!" she yelled back.

Pulling his pants up, John ignored her. He stumbled into the living room with his dinner plate, mumbling about how bad the food was. Jack had already disappeared back upstairs. Jessica went into the bathroom to attend to her burns while John turned the TV on and acted as if it were a regular night after work. She first applied burn spray then taped over the wound with fresh sterile-gauze from a first-aid kit. Her left butt cheek had already swollen to almost twice its size, and a large blister was forming. She wanted to tell someone; she wanted to get help, but all she could think about was Jack having to go through what she had just endured, or worse, and that could not happen.

Jack is only four.

From that day forward, Jessica felt as if she were a prisoner, a prisoner of fear. She plotted her escapes, she considered murdering the son of a bitch; more often she fantasized of a rescuer. But relief never came, and she continued to stay with a man she hated because she was afraid of what would happen to her son.

"Jessica! Hiding will only make things worse!"

John's screams startled Jessica out of her flashback.

"Shh, don't worry, baby. We won't be here for long," she whispered to Jack to help soothe him, reminding him to stay quiet. She could hear John downstairs swearing as he stumbled through different rooms in the house in search of her. She had built a small wall of blankets in the closet so that there was space for her and Jack to huddle behind. If John opened it, it would look as if it were just a closet full of blankets and sheets.

"Goddammit, Jessica! I'll fucking kill you if you don't come out now!" John's yelling was getting closer; he had moved his search to the second floor. The thought of calling the police had crossed her mind, but what would he do to her if they didn't hold him? What would happen to Jack?

No, this is the last time. She had been sending her sister money to save for her just in case. *Fuck, that's what he figured out, oh god please help me.*

"Keep quiet baby. We are going to leave here forever, soon." She spoke softly, trying to keep Jack from giving them up.

She comforted Jack as she snuggled with him. John had now reached the third floor and was going door to door. She started to panic. *What is he going to do this time?* Without knowing it, she began to squeeze Jack.

"Mommy, you're hurting me," Jack said to her. She didn't hear him, because she was fully focused on John, who was now just outside the door. Fear overwhelming her, Jessica began to squeeze tighter. John opened the door to the closet, looked in, and then shut it. For a moment Jessica breathed, thinking she had won this game of hide and seek.

"You think, bitch, I don't know your plan? I know you've been sneaking money to your sister so that you have a honey pot when you want to leave me!" His voice was loud and booming. Her body shook from the stress of his voice reverberating her soul.

"Mommy, you're hurting me!" Jack said a little louder this time.

It was loud enough. John opened the door again and kicked the pile of blankets.

"You think you're a clever bitch?" John said as he grabbed her by the collar of her shirt and pulled her out of the closet.

"Run and hide, Jack!" she screamed.

"You stay and watch, boy. You might learn something!" John bellowed over her. Jack followed them out of the closet, obediently.

John was carrying Jessica by her belt and collar, dragging her. She was in full panic mode, trying to punch John, but never landing any substantial blows. He dragged her to the edge of the staircase and propped her up straight on her own two feet, facing down.

"This is your last lesson, bitch. I have had enough of your goddamn shit." John stuck his left foot out in front of her legs and gave her a good push. She reached out for a railing, but there was none. John had removed the railing the prior weekend to re-stain the wood. Jessica rolled down the stairs. Her body contorted in ways that seemed impossible. Her arms and legs twisted around in the most unnatural directions before it was over. At the bottom, Jessica opened her eyes and was looking up at the ceiling. She felt warm. *I must be dying.* In reality, a bone had ruptured through her right arm and was spilling warm blood out over her torso. She couldn't move, and she closed her eyes, wishing for it to end.

Opening her eyes again, she saw John looking down at her. Fear started to fill her heart. His hand came toward her head; she could see the calluses on his palms. Palming her forehead like a basketball, John lifted it up, and with all his strength, he smashed her head back down into the floor. A large pool of blood immediately formed around the back of her head as her life drained out of her. John went back upstairs where Jack was peering down.

"If anyone asks you about what happened to your mother, what do you say?"

Jack looked at his father and didn't reply.

"Repeat after me, 'Mommy fell while Dad was at work. It was an accident.' Repeat after me!"

Best Friends – 1996

"Hey, punk, you know what your face looks like?" ten-year-old Chris Pall snickered at Jack. Jack ignored him and just kept eating his lunch. Jack had moved from Massachusetts with his father, John, to a small town in New Hampshire in August and had struggled to establish new friends. He had been in his new school for almost two weeks, and there had yet to be a day in which Chris and his goons let him eat lunch without harassment.

"Haha. Your face looks like a mountain range! Do you wash your face with pizza?" Chris bellowed and laughed with his friends, referring to Jack's early onset of acne.

Jack continued to ignore the jokes. Typically, they would run dry, and Chris would find a seat to eat his own lunch. Today was different though; Jack was sporting a fresh black eye. A black eye he earned from his father after he had burned popcorn in the microwave. Jack told everyone that he had hit his eye on his own knee jumping on a trampoline.

"Did you get into your mom's makeup? Cause that looks fake," Chris told him. "Or did your daddy beat you for being so dumb? Hahaha!"

Chris bellowed out the high-pitched laughter in front of the whole cafeteria. Jack's face started to turn red, his blood boiling at the truth in Chris's joke.

"You'll learn someday," Jack said through mad, squinting bright blue eyes.

"Hey, Chris! Your mom just called and said not to forget to change your diapers," Dean Balk yelled out, and after a slight pause, the joke continued. "Cause its full of shit, like you!"

As Dean approached the tables, he appraised the situation before sitting at the lunch table next to Jack. Having been held back a year, Dean was a little older than everyone. His parents owned one of the only active farms in the town. Routinely, they kept him out of school to help with the farm during the busy season. This had caught up to him, causing him to struggle with his classes. The school and his parents had thought it would be best that he stay back a year to give him time to catch up. Dean's family was of Irish-German descent with all of the siblings sporting red-blond hair and baby faces.

Mumbling something, Chris walked away with his goons. Dean had a reputation in the school of being a "tough guy," at least as tough as one can be at age twelve in a rural New Hampshire middle school.

"Hey, don't let him push you around like that," Dean said to Jack. "Chris has always been an ass, but he falls apart if you give it back to him."

Jack didn't say anything; he wasn't used to someone being on his side.

"My name is Dean, and you're Jack, right?"

"Yeah, I'm Jack. Thanks for sticking up for me. Here, have this." Jack pulled out of his bag a red keychain that he had found earlier that week; it was shaped like a baseball and had the logo of the Red Sox across the front.

From that day forward, Chris never bothered him again. Dean and Jack became inseparable best friends. Dean had a great sense of humor. Always trying to get people to laugh, Dean constantly joked with everyone, something that eventually rubbed off on Jack. When he needed to fart, he would sit down and pull his legs up toward his head; then he would light his fart on fire. One time he did this, and his pants caught fire, much to Jack's delight. Jack liked to spend as much time at Dean's house as possible to avoid his father.

The Balks had always liked Jack; he was always polite if not quiet. Dean's mom, Tracy, was a very pleasant, attractive, motherly woman who always cared for Jack when he was over at the house. At times, Jack even thought of her as his own mother. When he got a little older, he fantasized about her sexually. Confusion about his feelings and emotions toward her led to Jack being shy around her more than almost anyone else.

Often times Jack would stay at the Balk's house for dinner and hang out with Dean's two younger brothers and older sister. Sometimes he would be there hanging out even with Dean not around, a test of the trust developed between Jack and the Balk family.

After a few years of growing friendship with Dean and his family, Jack began to develop feelings of resentment toward Dean. He was jealous of Dean's place in the Balk family—a place Jack would never really have. He began to have visions of violence, of hurting Dean.

These visions started sometime when he was thirteen or fourteen years old. Jack would think about hurting people, animals, and other things. He tried to quell these urges; the Balk family was a positive influence that went a long way in doing so.

* * *

"Happy birthday to you. Happy birthday to you. Happy birthday, dear Dee-ean. Happy birthday to you!"

Everyone was there for Dean's sixteenth birthday. Jack was sitting with Dean's siblings. Dean's parents were cutting a cake that they had made for the occasion.

"Happy birthday, baby," Tracy said to Dean and kissed him on his forehead.

"Thanks, Ma!"

"I have something special for you!" Tracy said as she left the room. A moment later, she came back in with a large, awkwardly wrapped rectangular package. Laying the large package in front of him, Tracy said, "Hopefully this is exactly what you wanted."

Wearing a fake smile, Jack watched, full of jealousy—a mother's kiss on the forehead, a birthday present, all things that were void in Jack's life.

"Ohh, yess!" Dean yelled out with excitement. "A snowboard! It's a snowboard! Exactly what I wanted," Dean bellowed as he pulled it out of the box that it was crudely fashioned in, bindings already attached. Dean got up, placed it on the carpet, and strapped his feet into the bindings, pretending to snowboard right there in the middle of his birthday party.

"That's awesome. Congratulations, so cool," Jack blurted out, trying to be polite even as his face turned red. Courtesy was something that his mother had always pressed him on when she had been alive.

Jack got up and walked to the bathroom to work out his burning sense of jealousy. He hated that his best friend had everything he didn't. He hated that Tracy loved Dean more, that Tracy looked at Dean with eyes only a loving mother has for a firstborn son. Jack was feeling desperate. He washed his face in the sink with cold water. Gazing in the mirror with water dripping off his face, he reflected on his own family—and it reflected back.

Jack saw his dad in the mirror staring back at him, and it made his mood worse. Pacing around the bathroom, thoughts of anger flooded his mind. Emotions were taking control of his thoughts, manifesting into physical pain. Jack was sweating, his hands gripped into fists. Sharp pain clawed at his chest and arms.

"Why, why," Jack kept repeating, not making much sense if anyone had heard him. "Errrrrrr."

Jack whipped around at the sound of the bathroom door creaking. The Balks lived in an older home. Almost everything creaked—the stairs, the cupboards, the doors—and almost nothing shut properly. Jack saw that Kittles, the Balk's ten-year-old cat, had nosed his way into the bathroom and curled around the door as to scratch his own side. Kittles rotated and curled around the door in the other direction, switching the side he wanted to scratch, meowing softly. Jack picked up Kittles, petting him gently down his spine. Jack had liked Kittles, a very friendly feline indeed.

Except Jack was not Jack tonight—he was John, or some twisted version. He looked up in the mirror, again seeing his father. He stood silently holding Kittles, staring into the mirror. Images of his mother's death began to plague him; the pain in his chest began to increase, stifling his breathing. He thought that he was on the threshold of passing out. He walked back toward the door and shut it, this time making sure it would not pop open again.

Jack approached the toilet and looked down into the still water in the bowl, again seeing his father looking back up at him in the reflection. He got down onto his knees, his actions robotic, as he forced Kittles' head into the bowl. Kittles fought, scratched, pleaded for his life in ways only a cat could. Jack's eyes were wide open and focused. His eyes showed calm and peace, as if his anxiety had been lifted.

The expression on Jack's face told a different story than his eyes, though; his lips curled up, exposing his teeth, breathing through them. He looked like a plumber having to stick his hands in a dirty toilet for the first time. Jack could feel the life leave Kittles as he became motionless in his hands. The water had turned a brownish-red color from blood and fluids mixing in the bowl. Jack felt relief. The pain in his chest began to level, as his heartbeat returned to normal; he even felt high as if he had taken a hit of marijuana, and aroused. Jack got up, leaving the cat in the toilet. He tried to flush it, his mind clouded by the endorphins charging through his brain.

Moving to the sink to wash his hands, he realized he had been severely scratched by the cat and was bleeding. He took a few wads of toilet paper, applying the compress to the scratches to try to stop the bleeding. He looked back into the toilet bowl to throw away the blood-soaked paper and realized the cat didn't go down with the first flush. Oddly, there was no panic in him. He pulled Kittles out, holding the dripping, slumped corpse over the bowl. Jack looked around the bathroom for a place to hide it temporarily.

No, that won't do. Looking under the sink, he thought, *they could go in there at any time.*

He lifted up the cover to the toilet tank and forced the cat inside.

"An upper decker, I think they call this," Jack joked with himself. He flushed the toilet to both get rid of the bloody paper and to make sure it would not jam up immediately on the next user. He then dried the seat, the toilet tank cover, and around the toilet bowl where water had spilled out. He stood for a moment to collect himself. Washing his hands one more time, as if they were instruments of evil that he was ashamed of, Jack shoved his hands into his pocket. He wanted to hide the scratches the remnants of guilt that he felt. Looking in the mirror again, Jack no longer saw his dad—he was back to being Jack. He turned and left the bathroom to rejoin the party.

"Hey, Jack, I'll let you ride it," Dean said as Jack entered the room with his hands in his pockets.

"Great, thanks. That will be awesome," Jack replied. Jack wanted to leave, but instinct was telling him that it would be less suspicious if he stayed and tried to act as normal as possible; he needed to find a way to take care of Kittles. Walking by Dean and the family, he went into the first-floor closet where his winter coat, hat, and gloves were. Putting on the winter gloves, he grabbed a pair of ski goggles that were hanging in the closet. Returning to the room, Jack pointed at the snowboard with snow gloves on and ski goggles over his eyes.

"Hey, can I give that board a try?"

"Haha. That's great. Get into it," Dean said back, referring to Jack's attire.

"I'll wear these gloves all night, all night long!" Jack exclaimed.

After Jack had finished playing with the snowboard, he went into the kitchen and grabbed a couple of trash bags.

"I'll help you clean up the mess in there, Mrs. Balk," Jack said as he went under the sink for the bags.

"You are so sweet, Jack. Your mother would have been so proud of you!" Tracy replied.

Leaving the room quickly, Jack jammed one of the trash bags in his pants. He walked around the living room picking up empty paper plates from the cake and empty solo cups that were spread about. He found a plate that still had half of a piece of cake left on it. He reached for it, loosely grabbing the back of it so that the cake would fall onto his pants, smearing frosting down his leg.

"Oops, dammit," Jack said out loud as an intentional ploy that came off as accidental and innocent. "Let me go change out of these pants."

Jack had a sleepover duffel bag with him as he had planned to stay the night at the Balk's. He grabbed his bag before bounding upstairs to the bathroom again, pulled a clean pair of pants out from his bag, and set it on the floor near the door, placing his gloves on top.

These should stay dry here, he thought. He then pulled the plastic trash bag out of his pants and lined the sink with the bag. He reached into the cabinet under the sink; grabbing an extra hand towel, he rubbed the cake off his pants with it. Jack then pulled off the toilet tank cover. Peering inside, Kittles was still there, eyes open and swollen, with its teeth out as if it went into death smiling. He reached in, pulled Kittles out, and dried him with the hand towel as best he could. Telling Kittles, "I can't have you soaking through my duffel bag."

After Kittles was sufficiently dried off, Jack placed him into the trash bag in the sink, squeezed as much air from the bag as possible and tied the bag into a knot. Kittles then went into his duffle bag where Jack wrapped him with other clothes, zipped it up, and went downstairs.

"Mrs. Balk, can I put my pants and this towel I used to clean up into your washer?" Jack asked.

"Oh, hun. You have perfect timing. I have a load in the washer ready to go. Just drop it in and let it soak with the others; I'll finish it for you," Tracy responded off-handedly, as she was finishing cleaning of the kitchen counters, multitasking as only mothers can do.

The very next day, when Jack could get away from the Balk's house, he went home and pulled Kittles out of his duffle bag.

"Gross," Jack said aloud as he dropped him into a utility sink. Fluids were dripping out of its mouth, and Kittles was starting to smell. Jack grabbed a pair of wire cutters from his dad's toolbox. He didn't know what he was going to do. His first thought was to cut Kittles up into pieces; making it easy for him to scatter the remains in the woods, but that seemed like too much work, and *really gross*.

Why not just bury it? It's just a cat. At that very moment, a feeling of pleasure began to pulse in him. He felt good, really good, looking at what he had done. Jack felt powerful, standing taller and stronger. Jack reached down and put Kittles' left ear inside of the clippers. He wanted to keep a memento of what he had done. He started to cut, and just as the blades of the scissors began to meet the skin, he paused.

"This is stupid," he said out loud to himself. "If anyone ever found a cat's ear—"

He imagined the consequences from his father. He wanted to remember this, yet keeping something from Kittles had risks. He pulled the clippers away and then put Kittles back into the plastic bag, found a spot in the backyard of his house, and tried to bury Kittles. Unfortunately, the ground was too hard this time of the year because of the cold. Jack decided to throw Kittles into a nearby river and let that be the last of it.

A couple of weeks after Kittles was killed, Jack found himself again with another cat, this time a neighbor's cat. Jack had placed a bowl of milk on his porch to lure the feline.

"I won't do this; I will not do this," Jack told himself as he watched the cat drink milk on the porch. He understood his fantasies were wrong and immoral, a gnawing shadow of guilt at the edges of his consciousness. This made him want to hide these urges from others, but he could not hide these fantasies from himself. There was a constant desire in him to feel as he did the first time with Kittles. He wanted to feel powerful again; power, he learned, was the root of all the other soothing emotions that would flood him. The cat came and went for a few days while Jack wrestled internally with himself, placing a fresh bowl on the porch each day nonetheless.

Then one day, "I won't do this," changed to "I can do this. I won't hurt it, though. I'll just hold onto it." Jack convinced himself to get his feet wet in hopes that the act of grabbing the cat alone would soothe his needs. Jack bagged the cat in a pillowcase and tied the opening. He brought the cat inside and put it, alive, into his closet. At first, Jack tried to use the cat in his closet as a means to stir fantasy, like people imagining winning the lottery after they buy the ticket. He hoped that he could keep it just that—a fantasy—and never a reality. Unfortunately for the cat, fantasy alone could not provide the relief he needed.

"Why aren't you at your friend's house, boy?" John spat.

When John came home from work that very night, he reached back and, with a drunk stumble, put his weight into a backhanded strike that put Jack onto the floor.

"Yes, sir." Holding his cheek, Jack got up and rushed up to his room. Jack knew better than to answer his drunk father with anything other than "Yes" and "Sir." The pain was coming to his chest and arms; all he could think about was drowning that poor cat in his closet. Emotions once again flooding through him, Jack started to pace again.

They never seemed to have been this bad before. He thought of the anxiety attacks, the emotions of being a broken teenager. His ideas of good and bad, limits of right and wrong, were unraveling Jack at his core as he focused on all the bad in his life.

"Why is it I only have bad shit in my life?"

His muted, tortured question compounded his anger. Like a young drug addict, Jack didn't like the feeling of doing something bad alone. He wanted to feel normal. He wanted someone else to enjoy what he enjoyed, and he yearned for a partner in crime. *Dean.*

"Dean likes just about everything I like," he said out loud.

With every step toward justifying why his best friend would also enjoy the power trip, Jack's anxiety attack seemed to lessen. Jack picked up the phone and immediately called Dean without even thinking of the consequences should Dean reject him.

"Hi, Mrs. Balk, is Dean there?" Jack asked for Dean as he normally would.

"Yeah, he's right here working on his calculus homework. Have you finished your homework yet?" Tracy asked.

"Yes, I did," Jack responded, not lying. Math had been very easy for him, requiring little work and practice for him to achieve success. Evidence to this fact was that both Dean and Jack were in advanced placement math at their high school.

"Wazz upppp?" Dean shouted as he grabbed the phone.

"Wazzzz uppp," Jack responded.

"Haha. That movie was funny," Dean said.

"Yeah, it was great. What are you doing today? Want to come over to my house and hang?" Jack asked.

Dean was silent for a moment. In all the years they had been friends, Jack had never asked him to come over his house.

"What? Definitely, buddy. I think I've only been over to your house like twice since we've been chillin'," Dean responded.

"First I have to finish my calculus homework. You know I need to learn this so I can find the tangent line at any point on the curve of

Kimmy Park's boobies. Haha!"

Kimmy was considered one of the hottest girls in school. Jack and Dean often idealized about her between them.

"Ha, nice. I'd like to find her limits!" Jack poked back.

"Haha, that's awesome. All right, I'll finish up; then I should be around your house in an hour or so."

Dean showed up on his classic Mongoose mountain bike that he'd been riding for a few years. Jack and Dean only lived a mile from each other, which made hanging out only a quick walk away, and a quicker bike ride.

"Hey, man, what are we doing today?" Dean said as he pulled up. "You want to go for a ride through the backwoods?"

"Yeah, I was thinking we could go chill by the river too," Jack replied.

The backwoods trails were accessible directly from Jack's backyard, leading to an intricate network of riding, walking, and horseback trails. It was October, and the temperature was in the high forties; it was just warm enough that they didn't need to wear gloves. Jack and Dean jumped onto their bikes and plowed into the woods.

"You going to work on your calculus out here?" Dean said, glancing at the backpack slung over Jack's back.

"Yeah, maybe." Jack tried to let the topic slip. They both biked hard through the brush, hitting stumps and drops. Dean rode first, as he was the better rider. They cranked through a narrow path that could only fit one bike at a time, branches flanking them on both sides made it necessary to duck and shift to avoid getting cracked in the face. At the end of the path was a remote beach along the river. Jack and Dean knew the spot well; they often came here to take a dip in the summer to cool down. Jack caught his first fish at this very spot when Dean took him fishing a couple years ago. Dean propped up his bike against a tree; pulling his bottle from the bike frame, he took a long drink.

"Ahh, so good," Dean said, wiping his mouth with his sleeve.

Jack had already jumped off his bike, just letting it tip over into the rocks. He walked to the water's edge and looked around to see if there was anyone else on the river. Not seeing anyone, he turned to Dean.

"Hey, I want to show you something." Jack took his backpack off. He placed it on the rocks before bending down and pulling out a pillowcase.

"What do you have?" Dean said with obvious curiosity.

"This thing attacked me earlier, so I caught it," Jack lied, but he figured Dean would have an easier time accepting this if he thought the creature was pure evil. "This thing is literally pure evil! It's going to get what it deserves. It's gonna learn!"

Jack had a look about him that Dean had never seen before, a look that made Dean uncomfortable.

"What is it? A rat?" Dean asked.

Jack didn't respond. He was starting to turn into an addict that needed his fix. He was so close to it that he began to anticipate it. His eyes were wide open with excitement. Dean walked closer to Jack to try to get a look.

Before Dean came over to the house, Jack had taken the pillowcase, with the cat at the bottom, and banged it into the doorframe a few times until the cat stopped meowing. He did not want Dean to hear a meowing cat on the ride out to the river. Jack squeezed the bulge at the bottom and could feel it was still moving around gently in the case, so it was alive.

"Perfect," Jack said aloud, now ignoring that Dean was present.

Jack stepped on a few large rocks that extended out into the water, he kneeled down, forcing the pillowcase under the water with the cat inside. Feeling the cat wriggle, he closed his eyes. He was swimming in the rush of endorphins again, imagining the look on Kittles when he had snuffed him out. A smile of pleasure began to form on his face. Dean shuffled uncertainly, knowing his best friend was killing something, and worse, enjoying it.

"C'mon Jack, let it go," Dean said. "This is not like killing ants. Just let it go! I'm sure it won't bother you again."

Dean's pleas went unheard. Jack was finishing what he had started. After Jack was sure the cat was dead, he pulled the pillowcase out of the water and threw it back on the rocky beach. He went to his bag and pulled out a pair of needle-nose pliers.

"What are you doing?" Dean said, looking at Jack as though he were a stranger. Ignoring him again, Jack grabbed the bag, brought it to the edge of the water, and pried open a wire fastener he had crafted to use as a tie for the case. Dean stood on the other side of the bag, curiosity making him want to see what was inside.

"Next time you can do it," Jack said as he opened the case.

"Wha, wha, what is that?" Dean asked, ignoring Jack's previous comment. Looking inside, it looked like a wet pile of fur and skin.

Jack reached in and pulled out a long-haired, young gray cat, no more than two years old. Jack was holding it by the back of its neck so that its facial skin was pulled back, revealing the cat's eyes and teeth. Dean turned around and immediately gagged.

"A cat!" Dean managed to get out between chokes, then berated Jack. "Jack, what the fuck man? Are you sick? Did you hit your head? Why would you do this to a cat?"

"It's just a cat, Dean!"

"I'm outta here. I can't believe you." Dean was disgusted.

Jack was surprised—he was sure that Dean would get into it. He didn't understand Dean's outbreak.

"Don't be a little bitch, Dean!" Jack said sternly, as if nothing about killing a cat was wrong.

"Dude, fuck you, man. My cat has been missing for two weeks. Did you kill Kittles, too?" Dean raised his voice even louder.

Jack's lack of response was all that Dean needed to know the truth.

"You fucker. Goddamn you!" Dean said, putting his hands in his pockets, looking for something.

At that moment Jack pushed him square in the chest. Dean went to take a step back to balance himself, his hands still in his pockets, but he instead caught his heel on a rock and toppled backward like a tree. With nothing to break his fall, Dean tried to get his hands out to brace himself, but it was too late.

Crack.

His head had contacted the top of a sharp rock protruding just outside of the shallow water. Jack stood still for a moment, taking in the sight of his best friend gurgling and coughing. Dean's eyes were open, but he lay motionless, his head just slipping in an out of being underwater with a streak of blood flowing downstream with the current. Dean's right hand was caught under some rocks. Jack reached down, the needle-nose pliers still in his hands. Bending over him, Jack took a long look at his best friend, a friend that had rejected him and made him feel hollow.

"You'll learn," Jack said to Dean just as he put the bottom of his shoe onto Dean's neck, forcing his head underwater. Jack watched Dean's horrified eyes as they wavered with the rippling water. When it was done, Jack felt immense; he was a god—no—he was God, deciding who lived or died. His shoulders never felt so square, so broad; the feelings he had experienced from dispatching the cats were amplified tenfold.

Jack cleaned up the area to make sure it appeared as if Dean were alone.

It just has to be believable, Jack thought. Jack went to open Dean's hand so it would be consistent with reaching out to grab something. A red, roughed up baseball-shaped keychain was hidden in Dean's hand.

"You held on to this thing?" Jack said. "Why would you hold onto to this?"

At that moment, Jack's moral emotions rushed over him. He began to cry.

"What am I?" he said, realizing what he had done.

Jack walked back to his house and called 911. He told the first responders that they had split up in the woods and that he had found Dean lying in the shallow waters. Dean was declared dead at the scene. A preliminary investigation concluded that it was an accident. The report stated that Dean had fallen backward off his bike near the river, hit his head on a rock, rendering him unconscious, directly resulting in his drowning in four to six inches of water.

First Love – 2014

Lizzy was sitting comfortably, holding a warm cup of coffee, ignoring the commotion around her. Tom was watching her through the Starbucks window as she pleasantly enjoyed the steaming coffee with a smile. She was squeezing the mug close to her breasts. Lizzy was witty, smart, feisty, and cute. She'd be graduating this coming May with an associate's degree in biotechnology and planned to transfer to the University of Massachusetts to pursue a bachelor's in biochemistry and molecular biology.

She was wearing black leggings with an oversized cream-colored shirt that fit slim to her body perfectly. She had a long winter jacket propped behind her on the seat and was wearing tall heeled black boots.

"I really love this girl," Tom said to himself.

Lizzy saw Tom enter the front of the Starbucks, and her smile lit up the room. She had one of those smiles that would show just about all her perfect white teeth, a smile that was contagious to others around her.

"Hey, babe," Tom said when he got close, leaning in to give her a kiss.

"You're late!" Lizzy belted out. "I have been waiting at least fifteen minutes."

Lizzy was being playful; she truthfully didn't mind a moment alone with a fresh cup of coffee.

"Well, you know, my other girlfriend kept me longer than I expected," Tom said sarcastically after picking up on Lizzy's playfulness. "I'm going to get myself a coffee. Did you want anything else?"

Lizzy shook her head, still bursting forth with a brilliant smile. She was a typical nineteen-year-old, grasping for independence while still unable to let go of the security of home and her father's umbrella. For Lizzy, her taste of independence was twofold: one was dating an older guy against her father's wishes, and two was working as a waitress in a small diner just across the border in New Hampshire.

Drew had always hated the idea of Lizzy working while in school; he told her that if she needed money, he would give it to her while she was finishing her degree. As tempting as the offer was, Lizzy yearned to prove to him and herself that she was a capable, independent woman. The money at the diner wasn't great, but it had presented her with the opportunity to meet a lot of new people while putting a little extra cash in her pocket.

"Are you going to visit me at work tomorrow?" Lizzy asked, batting her big grayish-green eyes at him. Tom looked back at her, shaking his head as he sat down across from her with his own cup of coffee.

"I can't. I told Mark I would go out with him to that stupid rally. It's going to be an all-day event."

Mark was one of Tom's best friends, although Lizzy had yet to meet him. Mark was a libertarian that liked to try and recruit others to follow his political beliefs. A popular politician was coming into town to throw a rally, and it was rumored that he might be announcing his candidacy for the upcoming presidential election as an independent. Mark really wanted to go but hated going alone to events, and Tom had agreed to accompany him on what was sure to be a boring day.

"Well, don't go all crazy on me hanging out with those kooks," Lizzy said. Anyone who wasn't a Democrat, which is what her father was, was a kook to Lizzy. In all truthfulness, she was as far from politics as palm trees were from snow. It's not that she didn't care, it was more ignorance of the effect politics actually played on her life. She only voted because her father told her to and the true positions and beliefs of the different political parties were more work to learn about than Lizzy was willing to put in, a view on politics similar to most.

"So do you have to dress up for this rally? Or are you going to go looking like a bum?" Lizzy was pointing at Tom's stained sweatpants, oversized hoodie, and beanie cap.

"I might. I doubt these libertarians would care. They're all a bunch of bearded hippies anyways. Haha." Tom was smiling and chuckling to himself.

Lizzy looked at Tom. He wasn't the prettiest guy, but he did have a rugged, handsome look about him. His humor was intelligent and playful, all the while having a personality that was goofy and brutally honest, and he always spoke his mind. She first met him four months ago at the diner when she was just in training. She found him a pleasant release from the typical townies crowding the restaurant on any given night. He would stroll in, and his blue eyes, brown hair, rugged look, and mysterious aura stole her attention. In a way, Tom reminded her of her father, although she didn't want to think about that.

Eww, would be her thought if she found herself comparing her man to her father.

"You know my dad wants to meet you?"

Drew was a protective father and a guy that liked to look others in the eye to make a judgment on their character, something Lizzy was afraid of. Lizzy wasn't a virgin when she had met Tom, but Tom was the first guy that she had the sensation and feelings of love toward. They snuggled on couches for hours, and Lizzie enjoyed the constant warmth and comfort of being against his body. She felt this was intimacy at its finest. She had "puppy love," as Drew constantly told her, warning her that it may not end well. Her father's efforts to sabotage the relationship through warnings and ridicule only made her fall further into Tom's arms. After six months of dating, this was the first time Lizzy entertained the idea of having Tom meet Drew.

"I'll meet your father," Tom said confidently. "I mean who wouldn't like this?" He sarcastically shook his head and pointed to himself.

"Don't go blowing your top on me with that ego, and don't try to be clever in front of my dad," Lizzy responded seriously while failing to stop a smile. Tom's goofy attitude had a knack of keeping her smiling. "My dad is no joke. He is seriously badass and will not hold back sending you packing with that high tail of yours between your legs."

Putting on a southern accent, Tom said, "What, me? A big ego? No, can it be? My dear, you must be mistaken. I am the most level man you have ever known."

Tom tried and failed at the accent. Lizzy put her hand in her pocket, pulled something out, and poked at the air around Tom's head.

"Psss, you hear that? I just deflated your ego. Why don't you come by this weekend to meet my dad then?"

She was now tilting her cup up in front of her face to hide her worry at his answer.

"Get your hands out of your face!" Lizzy could hear Drew yelling into her head. It was a nervous habit she'd had for as long as she could remember. She brought the coffee down too fast and crashed the cup into the table. *Whack!*

"Mrrrr, Hulk smash," Tom spoke out in response.

"Ha, sorry. I misjudged the table. So, are you going to come meet my dad?" she pressed.

"Yes, of course, I will," Tom smoothly replied.

Meeting Dad – 2014

Two days after convincing Tom to come over, Drew was witnessing something he had never seen in his life before. It was 9 a.m., and Lizzy was bouncing around the house, cleaning. Drew grabbed her by the shoulders, gave her a light shake, and yelled at his daughter's forehead. "You're cleaning? *Cleaning?* On a Saturday morning? What happened to my daughter? Lizzy, are you in there?"

"Dad, stop, stop it, I have a lot of stuff to get done."

Drew was smug, happy with himself. "Well, I am conflicted, honey. Now that I know what motivates you to clean, I can't say that I'm totally psyched about it."

He knew the day would come when she would fly from the nest, but he didn't have to be happy about it. And Drew was definitely not happy that his baby girl, his only girl, was introducing him to a "serious" boyfriend.

"Tom is coming around noon for lunch. I want this place to be spotless, and I still need to take a shower!" She said that last part with frustration in her voice, as if she were running out of time.

"Honey, calm down. You have three hours. If you're in the shower that long, I, seriously, will shut the hot water off on you." Drew put his feet up on the ottoman with his laptop on his lap.

"Dad, please tell me you have never done that. I can recall a few times where the water went cold on me, and you said it was because of 'a small water tank.'"

Drew pretended to ignore her, but he couldn't hide the sly smile stretching across his face.

"I'm going to take your silence as an admission of guilt." Lizzy picked up the last random sock that she found in the living room. "And how is it that I find your socks all over the house?"

Lizzy didn't wait for an answer; she had already hurried off to the basement to start a load of laundry.

* * *

Knock, Knock, Knock. The front door was barking.

"Honey, I think Tom is here. Are you going to let him in?" Drew was trying to finish getting his notes into his laptop. "Has it been three hours already?" He spoke out, rhetorically.

Knock, knock, the door continued, and Drew continued to ignore it.

"Dad!" Lizzy said as she rushed down the stairs with her hair frizzled out; obviously, she was still getting herself together.

"He's not my friend," Drew responded, and with that, he received a darting, "You behave" kind of look from her. Lizzy took a deep breath and opened the door. Immediately Drew could tell his daughter had really fallen for Tom as her mood swung to that of an angel. She stood, leaning against the propped open door, trying to look as cute as ever, and her eyes had grown wider than he had seen in a long time.

"Hey, babe," she greeted Tom and invited him into the house. "Would you like anything to drink? Water? Soda? Beer?"

"I am all set right now, thanks." Tom stood in the entryway of the house, trying to stand tall and confident.

In truth, he was thirsty, but there was something about meeting a girl's father for the first time that makes a young man remain conservative, such as possibly needing to run at any moment.

Meanwhile, Drew was thinking, *Dammit, why do I already hate this guy?* Drew narrowed his eyes, stood up from the couch, and puffed out his chest. Drew was a good five inches taller than Tom, and he let him know it. Instead of shaking his hand, he wrapped his arm around Tom's shoulder.

"Come, Tom, let's have a seat." Drew half-forced, half-ushered Tom into the living room and pushed him into a sofa seat. Drew sat down on the couch directly across from him.

"How old are you?" Drew said with a straight face.

"Dad," Lizzy objected to the question.

"It's okay, Lizzy. That's a fair question." Tom made an attempt to try to stand up to Drew while also trying to earn points with him by being frank, honest, and open. "I'm twenty—"

Just then the phone in the living room went off. Drew immediately turned for the phone.

"I need to take this; I'll be back in a few minutes. Hello?" Drew answered the phone and headed into his office.

"So that didn't go so bad." Tom looked at Lizzy; she reached over and grabbed his hand, giving him a reassuring squeeze.

"Well, I'm hungry; what did you plan for lunch?"

Lizzy smiled at the question. "I think you're going to love it. You know, I spent hours trying to figure out what to make us, what we would all be happy with, and well, I ordered D'Angelo steak and cheese subs." Lizzy shrugged, giving an "It's no big deal" type of expression. "My dad loves them, and I know you like them, so, I figured why not make this a little easier for everyone."

Tom put his fist into the air, and when she responded with a fist bump back, Tom said, "That sounds awesome. I just want to let you know, though, I have to be outta here before two. I have to meet up with Mark again."

"Brave. You think you're going to make it that long around my dad?" She knew her father to be one of the toughest characters to please. Even Drew's friends seemed to tiptoe around him to avoid his wrath. His best friend Nick used to tell Lizzy, "Your dad could beat up Wolverine in a fight," referencing the ever-healing Marvel comic character. It was a statement she loved so much growing up that she had actually made a t-shirt. The front read, "My dad beats Wolverine in a fight 9 outta 10 times," and the back read, "1 outta 10 times my dad forgets to show up."

Lizzy found the back caption especially appropriate, as her dad had a history of missing events. Her father completely spaced out on her seventh-grade ballet recital; Lizzy needed a ride home from a teacher after waiting until 9 p.m., two hours after the recital ended. Lizzy didn't let Drew forget it. At the time, Drew was working the Scott Drowd case; he was getting close to locating the Drowd son, and everything else in the world seemed to vanish as his focus narrowed. Drew liked to think he had redeemed himself. Since that time, he hadn't missed one of Lizzy's events; he didn't think he could deal with her nagging if he did.

As 1:45 rolled around, there were two empty aluminum foil-type D'Angelo wrappers on the kitchen table and one unopened sub, cold by now. Drew had gone into his office for a call from his friend at the medical examiner's office and never came out.

"So, what does your dad do?" Tom and Lizzy had retreated upstairs to Lizzy's room where they turned the TV on and snuggled on her bed.

"He used to be a cop, and when my mom died, he decided that he wanted to help people in a more personal way. So he became a private investigator. It has its ups and downs. Sometimes he has no cases, so he just mopes around the house; other times he'll take on four or five cases at a time, and I barely see him for weeks."

This was the first time that Lizzy had opened up about her mom. Tom had gathered that her mom was not in her life since she never talked about her.

"I'm really sorry to hear about your mom." Tom didn't know what else to say, but he still wanted to be sympathetic.

"It's okay. It happened a long time ago when I was, like, eight years old."

They both got up from the bed and began to make their way downstairs. Lizzy looked down as they reached the front door. It was one of the few times Tom had seen her sad side, where her smile dissolved and her eyes grew dark.

"I think your dad is awesome," Tom said, trying to divert the conversation to a more pleasant topic. "I mean, I'm freaking out that he was a cop. But on the plus side, he didn't tell me I couldn't date you."

"Ha, trust me, he doesn't want us dating. I know my dad." Lizzy stood at her doorway on her tiptoes to kiss Tom as he left. "Thanks for coming. Sorry my dad didn't really hang out."

She looked at him, and a sense of warmth rushed over her that felt like she was being wrapped in a blanket near a wood stove.

Tinder – 2014

Drew hung up his office phone and ran his hands through his hair as he leaned back in his black leather office chair. It was a stress habit— some people bit their nails, others chewed on their inner lips. Drew would stroke his thick, wavy, dark brown hair so often that it looked as if he were trying to sport a combover. Thinning hair wasn't an issue for Drew; he had come from a family of thick hair that turned white before it fell out.

He reached into his pocket and pulled out his small notebook, looking at the name scribbled on the last visited page. *Ashley Tinder.* He had just gotten off the phone with Kelly. The body he had examined at the morgue was just officially reviewed by Dr. Jack Jefferson, and the cause of death was classified as an accidental drowning, which meant that no follow-up investigation would be performed.

No toxicology screen would be processed beyond the generic blood alcohol check. Drew thought about Kelly's words. Kelly had sent over a copy of the report via email and walked him through the details over the phone. Nothing new had surfaced except a name; a positive ID came back on the body. The young man's name was Frank Doherty.

"I still don't like it. Something stinks here," he said aloud to himself.

"Knock, Knock. Hey, Dad, I heated up your sub for you in case you were hungry." Lizzy was peering around the door to his office holding a soggy sandwich.

"You're the best, babe." Drew called almost any female that he was close to *babe*, something he picked up from his father. "Is your friend still here?"

"He left hours ago. I would have brought the sub in earlier for you, but I could tell you were still on the phone . . . it sounded important." Putting the plate down in front of him, Lizzy sat on a corner of his desk. She gave him a wry smile, shrugging her shoulders to signify she was guessing. After a brief pause, she headed for the door.

"Oh, and I'm going out tonight, and I may not be home until late. Love you, Dad!" She was already shutting the door by the time Drew processed what she had said. He had too many things on his mind; his brain had started a queue, and Lizzy's words were being delayed like she was the last person in line for a carnival ride.

Being a private detective was frustrating work that required patience. You had to be the type of person who enjoyed solving puzzles and the time that it took to solve them. Usually, the people who didn't like puzzles were not people who couldn't solve them, but the people who disliked the time it took to solve them. Ironically, Drew hated puzzles. For him, being a private detective was all about uncovering the story. Drew was meticulous with his work; he was the type of person who would board himself up in his office and forget about the time, and before he knew it, he had pulled an all-nighter, a trait his late wife, Nelly, would have said was one of the worst things to deal with as a wife and partner of a detective.

"Ashley, hmm. It's not much of a lead," he said aloud to himself, shaking his notepad in one hand, lightly tapping it against his desk. Letting out another long sigh, he leaned way back in his chair and stretched his arms upward. "I need to take a break, or I'll go crazy."

He was staring up at the ceiling again, running his left hand through his hair. He never liked phone calls, making them or taking them. He was that person who always seemed to be in a rush on the phone, and any time he had to call a woman who wasn't a family member, he would feel like he was back in high school—struggling, trying to figure out what to say if she picked up, only to have her mom answer and tell you she wasn't home. He leaned forward abruptly, reached for the phone, and punched in the number from his notepad for Ashley.

"Hello?" A soft, feminine, yet sharp, voice answered the phone.

"Is this Ashl—" Just as he was asking his question, Ashley's voice cut in. "Hello? Oh, I am sorry. I am not able to get to the phone right now. Leave a message after the beep." Ashley's voice became more playful toward the end of the recording.

"Really?" Drew said with a chuckle of disbelief. He couldn't believe people made voicemail recordings with the intent to trick callers.

"Ah, hi. I'm looking for Ashley. My name is Drew Law. I had some questions for you about Frank Doherty. Give me a call back at 617-333-6222."

Drew hung up the phone, his eyes lingering on it for a moment.

The phone number he had for her was a Boston area number, but nowadays anyone could get a number for just about any area code.

"Let's see what we can find on Ashley."

Drew pulled his chair closer to his desk and pulled up a new browser window. He watched his fingers as he typed, "A-s-h-l-e-y T-i-n-d-e-r" into Google. The first results that popped up were links to profiles on Facebook. He went to click on the link, then hesitated a moment, lingering on the next link in the search result.

"The creeps you meet on Tinder," the link read, referring to a "hook-up" dating app that had grown in popularity over the past couple of years. He had heard about it in the news and even pursued some leads on the app in the past when he was working a "cheetah" case.

He thought he was clever, often making up names for different types of cases he took on. Cheetah was for cheater, a case in which he was hired to investigate whether or not a spouse or loved one was remaining loyal within a relationship. Another name he had invented was an "Elsa" case, taken from a Disney movie in which the main character, Elsa, goes missing. These were cases for missing persons. He always chuckled when he said, "I'm heading out to work an Elsa," although Lizzy would tell him that his humor was highly inappropriate and that a missing person case needed to be treated with more sensitivity. Of course, he never used those terms outside of his tight circle of friends and family.

Drew clicked on the Facebook profile links, which presented him with a large number of results comprised of girls and women with the same name. He let out a long "humph," as the name was more common than he thought it would be. He had never known a Tinder, nor an Ashley for that matter.

"Too young, too young, probably not from Russia."

He scrolled through the results filtering out girls with braces or women who claimed to be from other countries. His mouse made a noise as he spun the center wheel to scroll.

"What do we have here?" He stopped abruptly and clicked back up two profiles. The image was of a woman who looked like she was in her twenties but with charisma that led him to believe she was in her thirties. She was attractive, with wavy light brown hair that was pulled back as if she had just rolled out of bed.

"Narragansett, Rhode Island," he said, reading the "from" information listed under her photo. He was leaning back, staring at her photo. *I hope this isn't her.*

Ever since Nelly died attractive women intimidated him, and this woman had a face that belonged on magazines. Sliding over to a black-framed Rolodex, he started to flip through the names. Drew had a cell phone with a complete contact list, but the name he was looking for wouldn't be in there as he hadn't spoken to him since the early nineties.

"Here we are." He reached out for the phone and dialed, half-expecting the line to be dead.

"Yah?" A man answered with a gruff voice and more of a Massachusetts accent than Drew.

"Hey, Davy. It's Drew Law."

"Drew! Yah fahking bast-ad, how yah been?"

Davy had been in the academy with Drew. They both started on the force at the same time and had grown a frat-house sort of relationship, which meant they didn't have a whole lot to talk about while sober but loved to play drinking games and get loud at the bars together. Davy had a boisterous personality with a sense of humor that was rough around the edges.

Davy "left" the force just after his fifth year on the job. In truth, he was given the option to leave or be terminated after a conduct hearing. A woman had accused him of lewd behavior during a traffic stop. At the time, that sort of thing would have amounted to a smack on the wrist, but the woman was the daughter of a powerful industrial chemical manufacturing company CEO, who also happened to be the largest donor to the Democratic party in Massachusetts. Davy left without a fight and became an investigative journalist in Providence.

"I've been good. How long has it been? Ten? Fifteen years?" Drew scratched his head as he spoke.

"Yah know, I think more like eighteen years. Hey, I heard about your wife. I know it's been a while, but I never got the chance to pass on my condolences. Hell of a thing losing your wife that young."

Feeling a little uncomfortable at the comment, Drew hesitated before saying, "Ah, thanks, Davy. It was a tough time in my life, but I've been able to move forward from it."

"I'm glad for yah. So what's this call about?" Davy was a clever man and knew right away that if Drew was calling it wasn't to chat.

"I'll get straight to it." Drew cleared his throat. "I'm working a case and am trying to gather some information on a person that's in your neck of the woods."

"Well, can you tell me more about the case?"

Drew had to be careful here; Davy was a journalist, and a good one; his pieces often got front page placements in the local Rhode Island papers.

"I can't tell you much just yet. I'm still in a discovery phase."

"Shit, Drew, yah know how this wa-hks. This business is give and take."

Drew took a moment to think about what he could offer. "What do you want? Can I pay you?"

"Ff-ack, Drew, I have no interest in the amount of cash you would pay for this. Tell me, what kind of case are you wah-king?" Davy was making another attempt to get information from Drew, to measure if the story was worth anything.

"I can't tell you right now," Drew responded firmly. "But if you can get me some pie, I can guarantee you'll be the first person to get a crack at the story."

Pie, personably identifiable information, was a term used often in the investigative field. Pie was any information that could be used to contact or locate a single person, or to identify an individual in context.

"Hmm." Davy considered the offer. In truth, Drew didn't need Davy; he could go down to Narragansett and work out Ashley's pie on his own, but he knew Davy had to have contacts in the local PD that would make quick work of this type of request, saving him hours, or having to pull other favors from more expensive resources.

"Yah, all right, I'll see what I can do. I ain't promising yah anything though."

"Awesome, what's your email address there? I'll send over what I've got." Drew wrote down Davy's email directly on the card in the Rolodex. "All right, I got it. I'll send over the information after we hang up. What kind of timeframe do you expect?"

"If my sources have any information, I should have it for you tonight or early tomorrow."

Drew couldn't hope for anything better. "Great, all right then. It was good chatting with you, Davy, and I look forward to your response. Next time I'm in your area we should plan a day for you to show me around."

Davy agreed.

When Drew hung up the phone, he wrote a brief, concise email with Ashley's information and sent it to Davy.

Broken Windows – 2008

"Step up, and double punch. Nine, eight, seven, six, five, four, three, two, one. And now jab, jab, jab, cross, jab. Okay, step up. One, two, three, four, five! Again, jab, jab, jab, cross, jab! Ash, you can join us anytime!"

Ashley had dazed off and had shamefully attempted, if not completely missed, the past three routines. Juan, her instructor, had noticed and tried to turn her attention back toward the class. She put a determined look on her face, emulating a focus which was not there.

"Shake it off, just shake it off," she told herself. Alvaro Delgado Araya had chosen to go by the name of Juan when he had moved to the United States at eighteen. He thought it was easier to say, plus he wanted to be named after the famous Spanish libertine, Don Juan. He was a dark-skinned, handsome man with long black hair and a fitting five o'clock shadow. He wore a typical martial arts, Gi-style uniform that was solid white with black accenting on the edges.

Ashley had been attending his classes for the past six weeks in hopes of improving her self-defense skills. At the same time, she found it was improving her figure and toning muscles she hadn't known existed. Juan was maybe an inch taller than her, which usually would cause her to lose interest in a man right away or never develop an attraction to begin with. She typically liked her men to stand at least 6'2". But his dark skin, thick accent, and thrusting hips in class helped her overcome his height deficiencies.

It was around the third week of classes she started to think his lessons would be useless in a situation that called for self-defense. It was the style of kickboxing developed more for fitness than actual fighting. The only reason she kept coming to his classes was for the opportunity to flirt with him. She wasn't interested in it going anywhere beyond "teacher-student," or at least that's what she told herself. But who knows what would happen if circumstance had them share a late-night drink. Her work had become stressful as of late, and the 6 p.m. kickboxing class was the only place she felt a positive human connection, Juan being a major part of that.

"Okay, very good," Juan yelled, his Spanish accent prominent. "Let's take a five-minute break time."

Panting, hands on her hips, Ash was pacing in circles as if it were easing her body. She could feel the warm rolling beads of sweat stream down her face and back.

"Ash, whatz up?" Juan asked as he was walking up to her, accentuating the "p" with a pop. "You've seemed distracted recently in classes."

She took a deep breath to steady her voice.

"I'm sorry. Work has been really stressful recently." She tried not to meet his big brown eyes, which made her feel gooey and weak at the knees.

"You should be in here twice a week at least. Only this will help you," Juan replied with a smile as he gave her an innocent whip on the shoulder with the towel he was holding.

She shook her head at the mats. "I wish I could find the time to take two classes per week."

"Come as often as you can! Your work life will settle down, and you will still have—" Juan made a punching motion with his right hand while smacking his right bicep to mimic the punch landing.

Ash didn't get the gesture. Juan thought it was clear he was insinuating strength. She laughed lightly and gave him a quirky look.

"Okay, let's get back to class and work on our front kicks!" Juan yelled enthusiastically for everyone to hear.

Ash watched the clock; the class usually ended around 7:40, which was ten minutes later than scheduled. Typically, she would stay until the end, but not tonight. She had too much on her mind, her head spinning with thoughts of work.

"Kick, kick, kick," Juan yelled in her direction when he saw her half-assed front kicks. She snapped back to class and glanced up to the clock. It read 7:31.

I'll give it five more minutes then I am gone, she told herself.

For what must have been the first time ever, Juan looked up at the clock and yelled, "Great job, everybody! That's it for tonight. I want you all to get home safe. Remember to practice your jabs, crosses, and kicks at home!"

Not in the mood to chat with Juan or the other students, Ash moved quickly. There was this guy, Bobby, who had always dropped the worst pickup lines on her any chance he got. She was almost certain he was a professional banker. He was always well dressed, like he shopped directly out of GQ or Maxim. He had brown, medium-length hair that seemed to be too wavy to be natural. He was handsome, but he had lines like, "Hey, why are you learning to kickbox? Soon you'll have me at your side, and I am all the self-defense you need," or his most recent line, "If your bra gets tired, I would be happy to step in and hold those beautiful girls up." Ash was sure that the last one was him just testing how inappropriate he could be around her. She had almost slapped him. She was certainly in no mood for zingers from Bobby tonight. Grabbing her bag from a locker cubby, She quickly skirted out of the door hoping to avoid conversation.

As soon as she stepped outside, she felt the light cool drizzle of the night's rain on her face. It felt good after the kickboxing class. She put her chin down into her scarf and moved quickly toward her car, shuffling in her gym bag for her keys. She got halfway to her car when she stopped and opened up her bag wider.

"I remember putting my keys in here somewhere," she said to herself, a light panic bubbling up inside her. "Dammit."

Ashley started pulling all the contents out of her bag one at a time, shaking them, just in case the keys were tangled inside. When she realized her keys were not in her bag, she turned around to head back into the dojo.

"Ahh," Ash screamed out briefly and grabbed her chest. "Bobby, you scared me."

In the midst of her searching for her keys, she didn't realize that Bobby had come from the dojo behind her.

"Sorry? I guess," Bobby said hesitantly when she didn't respond. He restated his unheard question, giving her a wry stare. "What's wrong with you?"

"Ugh, I lost my keys somewhere. I'm going to head back into the dojo to look for them." She had started walking as she stated her intent.

"Well, I'll stick around in case you need a ride."

Ash ignored him as she headed back in the dojo. Used by everyone, the lockers were in a nook just off the side of the dojo. She first looked in the changing room. *Maybe it fell out when I changed?* Unsuccessful, she then headed to the lockers. She opened up the locker she had used—nothing.

Juan came over just then. "Ash, whatzz up?"

"I lost my keys!" It came out louder than she had anticipated.

"Wow, calm down and take a deep breath. Think of yourself in a happy place."

She chuckled a little when Juan said this, as it made her think of the movie *Happy Gilmore*.

"I just can't do this tonight! Errrrr!" After checking everywhere she could, the car, outside, inside, even in the toilet, Ash was starting to show her frustration.

"Rawrrr, I like a girl that growls," Bobby said as he came back into the dojo while making a clawing motion with his hand. He followed this inappropriate comment by tipping his chin toward his chest and raising one eyebrow above another while he winked at Ash. "Seriously though, I do."

"Juan, any chance you can give me a ride home?" She looked over at Juan after rolling her eyes away from Bobby.

"Ashley, sweetie, I cannot. Tonight I am doing in-home private classes that I cannot miss." Juan shrugged apologetically.

"That's right. Bobby's here for you, baby." Bobby was shaking his head up and down with a look of victory on his face.

Taking a deep breath, Ash closed her eyes; everyone else had left for the night, and her phone and purse were locked in her car, which was limiting her options.

"Fine, Bobby. But, please, I am not in the mood for your cheesy lines. God, you sound like a bad movie." Bobby started to respond to her when she put her hand up in a stopping motion and cut him off. "In fact, please just refrain from talking."

Luckily for Ashley, she lived five minutes from the dojo just to the east of the College Hill district of Providence. When she sat down in his luxury BMW M5 sedan, she immediately switched on the radio and turned up the volume in an attempt to keep Bobby silent, which worked for the most part. Ash lived on the bottom floor of a multi-family; she owned the entire three-unit building, which she had inherited from her grandmother. The top two floors were nicer; because of that she rented those room out, thereby maximizing the rent. In fact, the two units above her made enough to cover all expenses and provide quite a bit of passive income. Pulling up to the street in front of her house, Bobby turned off the car.

"What are you doing?" Ash said sharply with a hint of disbelief. "You are not coming in."

"I have to walk you to your door, Ash; I wouldn't be able to go on should something happen to you on my watch."

"Bobby, I'll be fine. My front door is fifty feet from here. Look, you can just about see it." She gave him a tilted look. Bobby reached for the door and stepped out without taking in her comments.

"I must, Ash. Besides I want to see how you get in without keys!" he said defiantly with an excited eyebrow raise.

Her hands balled into fists in front of her, and inside she was screaming with frustration. The night was not going how she envisioned after a long day at work.

Ash made her way up the two flights of long but low angle stairs to her front door as her home sat on a slight hill. She realized Bobby was right; she was locked out without her keys. The entryway to her part of the house was not shared, and the only other key to get in was a two-hour drive to Peabody, Massachusetts where her mother lived. Swinging around to vent her emotions at Bobby, she saw that he was in the bushes to the right of the front door. She made her way down the front steps to get a better angle at what he was doing.

"I'm checking your windows to see if you left one open."

Ash stood there, a bit in shock, pleasantly surprised. *This guy actually thinks, and isn't just a fancy block of wood,* she thought. While Bobby made his way from one window to the next, Ash was silent, letting him do his thing, hoping that he could get her inside.

"Is this supposed to be broken?" Bobby said, as soon as he turned the corner of the home.

"What's broken?" She squeezed through the two juniper bushes that decorated the front of the home then made her way around the corner. The top middle window pane of the bottom window had been smashed out, with glass littering the ground in and outside, mostly on the inside. The window was jarred up as if it had been recently opened.

"That is definitely not right," she said, shaking her head back and forth.

"It's okay. These things happen." Bobby tried to keep things positive. "I don't think we should go into your house. Do you want to call the police and wait for them?"

Motioning her away from the home, Bobby walked back toward his car with Ashley in tow. Waiting inside his BMW, they used his cell phone to call for the police.

"What is keeping them? Someone could be dying inside, and they are taking their sweet time," she spat out. Bobby shrugged.

Thirty minutes had passed since they called 911, and the police had yet to make an appearance.

"Well, I'll tell you what; I would like to be inside—"

Bobby was most certainly going to drop an inappropriate one-liner when a cruiser turned onto her street and cut him off. Ash let out a sigh of relief. Passing them, the cruiser made an immediate U-turn, parking behind the beamer. Out stepped two officers, one of whom was a younger woman officer, looking like she had just joined the force. Her uniform seemed overly crisp with lines like it came directly out of the package. The other officer was an older man, probably in his forties, with a plump belly and thinning and graying hair that was slicked over to one side. Subtle stains spotted his uniform, clearly from eating fast food in the car while on duty.

"Are you Ashley Tinder?" the male officer said with authority as he approached Bobby and Ashley.

The pair had eagerly jumped out of the car when they saw the cruiser pulling up.

"Yes, thanks for coming! It appears someone has broken into my home." She felt a little helpless yet relieved the police were there. She wasn't overly fond of police. Ash had not been the best behaved as a teenager growing up. She had been the tipsy, loud, and obnoxious party goer in high school. When the cops had shown up to break things up, she would tell them, "You have no jurisdiction here," or "My lawyer is going to have a field day with you."

"Is the door unlocked?" The officer was already walking toward the house, breaking Ash from her high school flashback.

"No, I actually can't open the door. I lost my keys. That's how we found the broken window. We were checking to see if I left a window unlocked."

Nodding to the younger female officer, the elder officer grunted, while directing her toward the rear of the car. Obviously used to the lack of respect for a rookie, the young policewoman doubled back and popped the trunk of the police cruiser. She reached down and, with a rough moan, heaved out what looked like a solid pipe of steel that was about thirty inches long, five inches in diameter with handles fifteen inches apart, offset toward the back. Walking by Ash, the female officer carried the ram up the stairs.

"Shit, you keep that in your car?" Bobby scoffed out at the ram.

"Not ordinarily, but you're in luck. We had brought it out for an earlier call on an abandoned warehouse that needed a wellness check."

"You're not going to use that on my door." Ash was truly alarmed.

The male officer looked at her with a look that a principal in a high school might give a young student who was about to be disciplined.

"Do you want us to check the home for you or not? We are not crawling through your window," he said matter-of-factly. "The damage can be claimed on your insurance . . . probably."

Ash took a moment. "What about calling a locksmith to get me in?"

The officers looked at each other, both seemed to be communicating via telepathy as they turned in sync and started to walk back to the car.

"Wait, where are you going?" Ashley was aghast.

The male officer paused to say, "You can call a locksmith, but around here, at this time of night, it will be at least an hour before someone gets here. I never really know what a locksmith is doing, and they take forever making trips back and forth to their vans, tinkering. You can give us a call back once you're through all that. We'll send someone out again."

"Wait a minute!" Bobby said as the officers were about to place the battering ram into the cruiser. He turned to Ashley, obviously with something in mind. It was then that she noticed how tall he was, a sneaky 6'3".

"You are actually taller than I figured," she said, noticing his height for the first time.

"Well, I slouch—something my grandma would scowl at me for." He winked at her, ready to unveil the thoughts he was harboring. Turning back to the cops, he let loose: "I can crawl in from the already broken open window and unlock the door to let you in. Will that work?"

Stopping in his tracks and turning back, the policeman considered the proposal.

"And if the perp that originally broke in . . . is still there?" the male officer responded.

Bobby looked over at Ash and smirked.

"You'll owe me dinner either way?" He said it part-statement, part-question, a look stretched on his face waiting for a guarantee.

"Okay, yes. I will go on a dinner date with you. I just want to be in my house."

At that moment, Ash realized that while part of her wanted to get in to see what the damage was, there was another side of her that felt violated—and fearful.

"All right. Let's do this!" Bobby pumped himself up. Motioning toward the battering ram the cops had leaning against the car, he said, "If I yell, then just smash the door with that thing and save me and don't listen to Ash."

The four moved back up to the house and moved around in front of the broken window. Ashley offered a handhold to give Bobby a lift up.

"Ughh." Ashley let out a moan. Bobby was much heavier then she had expected, bulkier as well.

"Hold still. I can't climb in with you wiggling around." Bobby had two hands in the window, slowly pulling himself in headfirst. He exclaimed, "Why is your window so high up?"

Ash was leaning against the concrete wall of the foundation, just below the frame line of the house with her hands out between her bent knees as she tried to act as a stepping stool. Bobby's weight was causing her hands to wiggle from side to side, making it hard for him to jump in.

"Just be a man and pull yourself in already!" Ashley pleaded, the two officers enjoying the exchange.

Bobby finally managed to get the center of his body over the window frame, his stomach and waist being strained, squeezed, and pinched against the metal flanging of the window. Then he reached in, grabbed part of the couch that was in front of him, and with a pull, thumped into the house. His feet were uncontrollable for a moment as he tried to right himself. During that moment, something large had hit the ground and broken into a bunch of small pieces. Bobby turned around to take a good look, wincing at the mess; he then poked his head out of the window, looking at Ash.

"Sooo, did you hear that?"

She had clearly heard.

"I broke your lamp, sorry!"

"Oh, and I suppose if I had not heard, the burglar had broken it?" Ash shook her head, asking the rhetorical question. "Try not to break anything else on your way to the front door. And don't snoop!"

Ashley spoke hastily as Bobby had already turned away, making his way to the front door. The officers came in and walked through the house while Ash and Bobby waited outside. It took no more than ten minutes.

"Your back door was open by the way," the male officer said with a look of humor on his face as he thumbed toward the back, he was shaking is from side to side in disbelief.

"You have a back door?" Bobby looked over to Ash, realizing his heroic exploits could have been avoided. Ash felt a little embarrassed. She had completely forgotten; it was typically locked.

"Shit, I never use the back door. In fact, it has two deadbolts, and I don't even have a key to them. I never could get in through that door from outside."

"It was prahbly tha perp. Leff tru da back door and nevah locked up," the female officer stated. Looking at her partner, she motioning toward the door. "Less-get-outta-he-ah."

She has a deep accent, Ash thought, something in between Boston and New York, with a thick splash of Italian. Ash was surprised. Since moving down to Rhode Island for college, she had not run into as many thick accents as she had expected, but, when she did, Ashley had to stop and listen carefully to make sure she understood them.

"Okay, we're going to file a report, but you should do a good look through the house. Once you got all the details come down to the station to report anything that may be missing. It will need to be stated in our report for insurance." The male officer stopped and gave her his contact card.

Ash glanced down at the card before looking back at the officers. "When do you think you'll find out who did this?"

"Hun, unless some big item is missing, this is where our investigation stops. Most of the time, these things work themselves out. Maybe one of your exes or a crazy secret admirer, maybe an ex of your new boyfriend here?" The cop turned around and chuckled under his breath. With that, both officers got in their car and left.

"Hey, ah, sorry about your evening," Bobby said with sincerity. The sleazy wise guy voice was gone. "I know tonight sucked. You lost your keys only to come home to find that someone had smashed their way into your house. Then some sleaze-ball cracked up what was probably your grandmother's lamp."

Ash cracked a smile, shaking her head and looking up at the ceiling. "It was my great-grandmothers lamp."

"I picked it up, and I think I can fix it." Bobby had already cleaned up the mess while she was talking with the officers. He had put the lamp in a plastic shop-n-go bag by the door to bring it with him.

Why can't he be like this all the time?

"Seriously, don't worry about the lamp. You helped me out tonight." She put her hand up as to wipe something from his face, then stopped short, realizing she was about to try to wipe a birthmark.

"I never saw that before, haha. I was just going to wipe your face." Putting her hands in her pocket, Ashley giggled.

"My mom gave me that. My grandma had one just like it actually, skipped a generation and landed on me. It reminds me of my mom though—every time I look in the mirror."

Ashley sat back and thought, *Bobby was actually charming when he wasn't trying to send one-line zingers at her.* She walked him down to his beamer and thanked him for helping out all night.

"You're sure you'll be all right?" he said with his window down before pulling away. Bobby then started to contort his lips, ensuring a one-liner was on its way.

"Don't ruin the moment, Bobby!" Stopping the ribald comment in pre-flight.

"Ok…" Bobby looked down at his steering wheel, trying to control his bad habits.

"Yeah. I called a friend, and she's coming over to stay with me tonight." Ash continued. Pausing a moment, second-guessing herself, she half-stuttered, "Ah, I guess I owe you a dinner date."

Bobby looked up, beaming, and without hesitation said, "How about Saturday night?"

Option One – 2001

"How did I get here?" Jack wondered as he sat in a plush black leather sofa chair. The end table to his left was solid maple with a Pumice finish; on top of it was a metal bin with ice and bottled water. The nice woman who escorted him up to the twenty-eighth floor told him that he could take one. Jack considered it, then thought, *Maybe it's a trick? Maybe they want me to take one? But the correct answer is to say no. Maybe they want to poison me?* After a moment Jack reached out and took a bottle from the basket. *It's just* water. *Why would they want to poison you? If someone wanted you dead, you would probably be dead.* He took a deep breath, half-confident in his assessment, twisted the plastic top off. Taking a big gulp of water, Jack paused, giving his stomach a moment to tell him if anything was awry. Moments later, the nice woman returned with a wicker basket, stacked with assorted snacks. Jack grabbed a bag of Lay's potato chips.

"He'll be with you in just a moment, sweetie," the woman said, revealing an honest, soothing smile. Jack beheld the strangest, yet prettiest, set of eyes he had ever seen. They were off color. Her left eye was a glowing chestnut brown while the other was a vibrant yellowish-green. She spun around, leaving just as quickly as she had come with the snacks.

Jack was nervous, but not as nervous as he thought he should be. In fact, he was calm for someone who had just been caught murdering his best friend.

What gave me away? Jack had been trying to figure out what he did wrong for the last three days. *How did they know?*

Standing up, Jack walked over to the massive floor to ceiling window. Pondering his situation, he looked out at the city of Boston. Although he knew it was Boston, he had a tough time figuring out exactly what he was looking at. Jack squeezed the side of his face against the window, trying to get the best possible viewing angle to the ground.

"Ahem!" A pleasant but firm voice spoke out as if to correct him from doing something wrong. "Sorry to disturb you from the view. But he will see you now. Follow me."

Jack followed the woman, the same one who had shepherded him up and offered him snacks. She was attractive, wearing a blue suit. She had wide hips that seemed to extend from elbow to elbow, then her body slimmed up, quickly heading toward her chest, an hourglass figure at its finest—much different than the girls he was used to in high school. She had long silky brunette-black hair that extended halfway down her back. Her skin was a natural tan-brown. He followed the hair down where he found himself staring at her backside, thinking about her sexually. He quickly looked away.

"Not now! Think of something else," he said to himself, trying to prevent a boner from forming on his teenage body.

Turning toward the door, she stopped abruptly, putting her hand on his shoulder; Jack was taller than her already at his age, which made him feel good.

"Sir, your ten o'clock is here." She gave Jack a firm push and quickly shut the door behind him.

"Come in, my boy, come in. Take a seat here." Jack hesitantly stepped forward until he had crossed the massive office space—ten steps to the desk, Jack had counted. The dark brown leather chair had wood armrests with leather tops. Jack looked at the seat for a moment, trying to decide if he should take it.

"Sit!" the man said sternly. Staring at the man, Jack took the seat. The man turned his back to Jack to peer out of his office window.

"So little, everyone seems so little from up here. You know what the truth is? It's that they are little," the man said, speaking softer now. "That's one of the reasons I bought this building; every morning I go to the top floor to just look down at everyone as they scurry to work, shuffling to get on with their pointless, little, lives." The man had emphasized *little* more than any of the other words, changing his tone on the word.

"There are two types of people, my boy, no matter how you slice it. There are producers and consumers, or to put simply, there are big people, then there are little people. Who do you suppose you are?"

Jack didn't answer at first, unsure how to.

"Well, speak up," the man said impatiently.

"Um, a little person, sir."

"Smart boy. Ha, ahem, huaaa."

The man laughed, then coughed mid-laugh, followed by excessive swallowing as he held his fist up to his mouth. He cleared his throat. "Do you know why you're here?"

If there was one thing his father taught him, it was to always hide information. "Keep people on a need-to-know basis, and even then keep the people who should know in the dark," his dad would say.

Jack kept quiet. In response to Jack's silence, which he interpreted wrongly as hesitancy, the man didn't move or say anything. He just continued peering out of the window.

After a long moment, he calmly said, "Hmmm, that's good. Keep your mouth shut." His eyes seemed to be locked out on some distant object or person on the ground.

Jack remained silent.

"So tell me, when you killed that poor boy, did you look him in the eye?" The man's voice grew violent; Jack felt fear trickle down his spine, the hair on his neck standing, his heartbeat speeding and his sight narrowing, yet he maintained his silence. He had indeed watched Dean's eyes through the water as he perished.

"It's irrelevant at this time, I guess. Make sure you look 'em in the eye in the future. Give them the respect to know who is sending them to the next life. He was your best friend, I'm told. Was it over a girl? It's always over a damn . . . ."

The man continued saying something, but he mumbled off under his breath, and Jack couldn't make it out.

"You must be sitting there, wondering how it is with certainty that I'm claiming such things?"

Jack still remained silent, continuing to watch the man carefully.

"Why won't you look at me?" Jack said out of nowhere.

"Boy, I have already looked at you plenty."

The air seemed stale now. Jack's breath shortened unwillingly. They both remained motionless and quiet for what seemed like five minutes.

Jack began wondering what he meant by that comment. "Looked at me plenty?"

"Let me tell you what actually happened. You pushed your friend, and he hit his head on a jagged rock." Jack could feel sweat starting to form on his body.

Must be a lucky guess, Jack told himself silently.

"Then you walked over to him and put your foot onto his neck. Without any further to do, you intentionally kept him underwater until he drowned."

Jack's eyes widened with stress. "How?" Jack didn't even realize that he spoke out loud. Shock was twisting his reality.

"You were sloppy is how." The man took a deep breath. "And you got lucky. You see, I employ one of the detectives that was on the scene of your friend's death."

Jack was totally confused.

"When my agent arrived on scene, he accidentally discovered a camera that was hidden in a bush just off the edge of the river, ahem, hack-huaa." The man went into another brief coughing fit before continuing. "A hunting camera had been placed just off the side of the river. It was pointing directly at you and your friend. They call it a trail cam or some such shit."

The man seemed to be getting tired as the conversation continued. He was older with white hair, at least what was left on the back side of his head. At least forty pounds overweight, he had a wide frame that hid it a bit. Jack would have guessed he was in his late fifties, then again it was tough to guess someone's age accurately. He was wearing a boxy charcoal gray suit and shoes that seemed to have been crafted from alligator skin. He coughed again.

"My agent is in place to feed me information, anything he can get. I have guys in almost every state trooper outfit in New England." He was boasting, his voice projecting power; Jack was absorbing it, sensing that this was a man in control, like the emperor from Star Wars.

"When my deputy came across this camera, he wisely decided to take it with him and have the film developed on his own. When he discovered what was on it, he called me."

Jack didn't know what to feel. He felt helpless, confused, scared, and happy all at the same time.

"You know, you're quite poised for a boy of fifteen. You'll want to keep that quality as you get older."

The man moved to his right toward a strange-looking table that had clear bottles with fancy tops on them. The man opened a cupboard that was under the table; pulling out a short but wide glass, he poured brown fluid from one of the bottles. Taking a deep look into the glass before tilting his head back, he downed the half-poured glass at once. "Well, you have two options, boy."

The pace in his words was picking up, like he was refocusing.

"You can work for me now, and going forward; you do what I tell you to do. That's option one." His index finger extended into the air.

Then he extended a second finger. "Or two, I can have those photos sent on to the police."

Jack did not like limited options and felt his legs shuffle in the seat as he squirmed.

"Which do you prefer? Number one or number two? Neither option is easy, boy. Let me warn you, option one is a far more difficult path."

Mrs. Balk and Dean's siblings flashed into Jack's mind. He was picturing them when they found out what he had done, the looks on their faces, Mrs. Balk rejecting him, pushing him away. That was the only thing he wanted to avoid; he didn't concern himself with the consequences.

"One, I'll take option one," he declared instantly.

"Are you sure you want that?" the man asked again. Jack didn't even hesitate; he had made up his mind.

"Yes, I'm sure."

The man turned slightly away from the corner, moving away from the liquor table, never fully revealing himself to Jack. Facing the windows once again, he finally stopped. "You will go home after this meeting. You will do your best to forget that this meeting took place. Aheeem."

The man coughed a long and wheezy cough.

"You—" He continued to try to clear his throat and nose. "You will not kill anyone or anything unless you are told to do so. Do you understand?"

Jack looked toward his feet, a feeling of guilt overwhelming him. "Yes, sir."

"Good. You will never try to contact me. It may be days, weeks, or years even before I bring you on board. I am told you have excellent grades in school. I want you to continue in school. You must keep up your high academic performance; after high school, you will go to college. Do you understand what I am saying?"

Still looking at his feet, Jack nodded in acceptance.

"Boy, do you understand me?" Jack forgot the man was refusing to look at him and couldn't have seen the accepting head nod.

"Yes, sir," he responded with a quivering and beaten voice.

"Lastly, if you ever tell anyone of this meeting, I am afraid it is you who will end up in the river. Tell me, boy, do you want to become a mystery of the Charles? Another poor sap floated and bloated?"

"No, sir." Jack knew dangerous men when he met them from growing up with his father, and Jack knew this man was a very dangerous man. His father was a carebear next to this guy, he could sense it.

With that, the door opened, and the lovely woman who had escorted him through the building appeared. She smiled at Jack, who had turned in his seat abruptly to face the door.

"Sir, your eleven-thirty is here." Jack was stunned. *Only a half-hour?* He felt like he had been in that seat for hours. His tired hands were sweaty and sticking to the leather tops of the armrests. He must have been holding on to the chair with all his strength.

"Come on!" The woman waved at Jack to get up and come to the door. "Let's go," she said when Jack just stared at her.

The man said nothing, and Jack wondered how much the woman knew. "Probably nothing," he suspected. As he got closer, she revealed that wonderful, genuine smile that seemed to remove his pain. Shutting the door behind him, she pushed him along quickly into the hall.

"I know he can be intimidating, but it's for that very reason he is a very successful man," she said as she walked him to the elevator.

When the door opened, they squeezed into the full elevator and kept quiet for the ride down. When they reached the lobby, she pushed him out first.

"You know, it's not every day that he brings someone in, let alone a fifteen-year-old. In fact, from what I can remember, he has only ever once before brought someone into this building that was under twenty."

Awake – 2014

"Aww, fuck me."

My head was pounding in pain, every thump of my heart was like a hammer cracking down against my skull. *Thump, thump, thump.*

"GODDAMMIT!" I heard my voice echo when I yelled. I felt as though I had just recently been punched in the throat. It was hoarse and dry.

"Jack! What kind of joke is this, dude?" My voice cracked as I spoke.

I was sitting in a cold metal chair, an old 1950s Harter office chair that seemed to be built entirely out of steel. My wrists were bound to its arms with what felt like zip ties.

"Jack, are these fucking zip ties on me?"

I tried to wobble the chair loose, but I didn't get so much of a creak out of it. Clearly, the chair had been bolted to the floor. I had to get this bag off my head. The same dark stinking bag that Jack had wrapped me up in was still on my head with the exception that the closing tie had been loosened so I could breathe. I stuck my tongue out. Maybe I could bite a hole into the material. I could just reach the bag. It was damp, like a ski mask that had been worn for too long on the slopes, the humidity of my breath soaking the fabric.

"Fuck, where the fuck am I?" I screamed out to no one. There was a long silence as I wriggled and twisted in an attempt to free myself.

"You're not going to get loose," Jack said; he was close to me.

"Have you been here the whole time? Dude, just let me outta this shit, man; I thought we were on the same page." I could feel my heart beating quicker, my nerves on edge. "Ahh, what happened to the girl?"

"You don't have to worry about her anymore," Jack said assertively.

"What do you plan to do with me?" My voice cracked again, this time from fear; it was hard to ask the question. I was getting more and more terrified by the second.

"You know, I told someone where I would be tonight—that I

would be hanging out with you," I lied.

"Who did you tell?" Jack responded; I could tell he was doing something other than just chatting with me. I could hear clinks and clicks—ratchet clicks; he was working with tools on something.

"I told a friend."

"Who?" he responded quickly.

"My friend Jim."

There was a long pause.

"That's funny. I had a look through your phone, and you haven't talked to a friend named Jim in some time."

The asshole, how did he get my password?

"I emailed him on a separate email I have set up."

Again, there was a pause then a deep breath from Jack.

"Ben.grabble@gmail.com,   Bengrabble@gmail.com, bengrabble@yahoo.com, bengrabble@hotmail.com, and my favorite sexyben1990@yahoo.com. Did I miss any?" Jack had found every email I had ever owned. "Before you put yourself further in the rabbit hole, you should know that I placed a 'key-logger' spyware on your computer and your cell phone, allowing me to monitor all of your electronic transactions including emails, browsing, and financial."

"No way; I don't believe you," I said flatly.

"Really? Let me see here. August fourth at nine twenty-nine p.m. you logged onto bankofamerica.com, entered a user ID of bengrabble90, then you entered 'spokySpock90' as your password. This was rejected, of course, because you misspelled 'spooky' as 's-p-o-k-y,'" Jack said, spelling it out. "You re-entered your password, 'spookySpock90,' and you were in."

Fuck. I sat silent, unsure of what to say next. I continued to sit there in awkward silence, with the only sounds coming from the tools Jack was working with. I swallowed, carefully; I was worried he would hear me swallowing and see it as a sign of fear, which it was. I was fucking terrified.

"What are you working on?" I choked out.

Whoosh. Jack had walked over and pulled off the bag covering my head then returned to a workbench across from me. I appeared to be in an unfinished bathroom. I was bolted down, as I had suspected, to a raised platform where it seemed a shower should belong. With all the restraints, my head had limited movement, so I strained my eyes in all directions. There were these strange, heavy-duty, Y-shaped clips to the right and left of my head, seemingly attached to the steel headrest of the chair. I was sitting in the dead center of a square plastic shower base with a drain located just to the right side of my chair. The walls were uncovered, unpainted, with nothing but mold-resistant drywall that was waiting to be taped and mudded. The bench that Jack was standing over was none other than the frame for a long, double sink, except the sink basins had yet to be placed into their spots. To the far right of me, where I would guess the toilet would belong, instead housed a large plastic tank, which had a line with "100 gallons" marked on it. The tank was about two, maybe two and a half, feet wide and about three feet high, sitting on a dolly.

Looking back at Jack, I tried to talk, but I couldn't. What would I say? Jack was standing over this large contraption. It was old looking, with a rusty metal frame. The core of the contraption looked like an old diving helmet like the ones you see in movies that are connected to an air supply on the surface, only this seemed much too large to be practical. It had a large single glass port on the front about the size of a basketball. I could see large rivets wrapping around a seam at the base. There was a hose attachment on the top, which was supported by another external-skeleton-type frame that reminded me of bars people put on their windows to prevent break-ins. On both sides of the helmet were long ridged bars that extended from past the base up to the top of the helmet. The contraption was lying on its side, and Jack was working on something on the base.

I sat there in silence, watching him work. My mind was racing with what was going to happen next. After what seemed like an hour of silence, I spoke out.

"Are you going to kill me?" My voice cracked. The thought terrified me, but I needed to know.

"Don't worry. I will tell you soon exactly what is going to happen."

I needed to figure a way out of there.

"I can help you get another girl if that's what you want? I won't tell anyone." I was getting desperate; I needed to gain an angle, any angle. Jack remained silent. Putting on some sort of strange safety glasses, he began welding, glowing speckles and sparks shot up from what he was working on.

"Hey!" I yelled to make sure he heard me over the sizzling sound of the welder. "Hey! I can help you, man! Let me go, and we can go grab another one. I have her all staked out already, and she's better than the first."

I made it sound as convincing as I could, like my life depended on it. Jack continued to ignore me. His silence was painful. Every moment of it made me want to talk more.

"Please, man, just let me go. You don't have to do this!" I begged and begged all the while Jack was leaning over his contraption. With some effort, he picked it up and stood it on its base with a loud thump so that it was right side up. It was obvious that it was quite heavy. He stepped back, admiring his work.

"I think this will do just fine," he finally said, turning and walking toward me.

He was wearing his welding glasses still. His hair was sticking straight up, caused by the band of the glasses. The glasses themselves were white, and each lens was linked together across his nose by a thin piece of leather. The frames were completely round with tinted lenses, making it hard for me to see his eyes. Guards stretched from the lenses toward the side of his face. They resembled glasses that pilots used to wear in an open cockpit plane. His black t-shirt read, "If you're reading this, it's already over," on the front. He was wearing Timberland work boots; the color had darkened a bit from heavy use in sooty environments. He was so close I could smell him; he smelled of chemicals and grease. Jack began working on the clips to the side of my head.

I realized I was taking in big, rapid breaths. *How long have I been doing that? Oh my God. Oh my God. Calm down. Everything will be all right.* I shut my eyes as I talked to myself, wishing I would just wake up from this nightmare.

"So."

Jack's voice shook me out of my state of meditation. I opened my eyes. Still wearing those glasses, he stood in front of me, completely still. Jack was more frightening now than I had ever seen him. He was glowing a terrible glow of mal-intent. Pulling the stool from the makeshift workbench closer to me, he sat down.

"I am going to tell you something, and you may decide you want to scream. But if you scream, I am going to use this to take something from you. Do you understand?"

What is happening? Is this really happening to me? I thought while he waved a large set of pliers in front of me.

Jack stood up quickly.

"Hey!" he yelled, his deep voice rumbly and violent. Jack cleared his throat and sat back down, composing himself. He was excited; it was clear the outburst was driven by him losing his patience because

I didn't respond to him. With more calm, he asked, "Do you understand?"

I weighed him, trying to judge what type of person he was. *Is he lying to me?* I wanted to believe he was, but his demeanor told me he wasn't. I nodded that I understood.

"Good," he said quickly. He took a deep breath and cranked his head slightly to one side. He said matter-of-factly, "You're going to die tonight."

My body shivered; I felt a warmth rush over me. My breathing quickened again, and the back of my neck tickled with fear.

"Don't scream. Nobody can hear, so it's pointless. You'll only annoy me, and I start clipping and pulling when I'm annoyed."

When he snapped the large pliers in the air, I nodded, eyes wide.

"We all have to die someday; you knew this was coming. In your bed at night, you thought about death, pondering what, where, and when it would happen. What did you think would kill you? Cancer? Yeah, that's what everybody says. Fucking cancer!"

He continued talking, not letting me answer. He was leaning back with his hands gripping the front of the stool in between his legs and staring up at the ceiling.

"Although, I once had a guy tell me he expected to die in a plane crash. Do you know how unlikely that is? Something like one in eleven million."

I had never heard Jack talk this much—apparently, death was a topic he was passionate about.

"What do you think is the probability of being killed by a serial killer?" Jack was looking at me now, a look of truth coming from his eyes. He gave me a brief moment to answer, but my mind was completely blank, denial and disbelief lingering. *This can't be happening! I'll be okay; this is some kind of joke.*

"About one in six million. Yep, well, that makes you the one."

Jack got up and approached his makeshift workbench. With a big grunt, he picked up the clunky helmet and lugged it toward me. With an even louder grunt, lifting the heavy helmet up, he placed the base neatly onto the Y-clips near my head.

"We are almost ready."

With a couple of loud snaps, the helmet slid down on rails into the clips where he twisted on a hand screw that locked the helmet to the chair.

"There we are."

Jack sounded like a dentist trying to reassure his patient. I could see the inside rim of the helmet as it hovered above my head, slightly in front of my eyes. Jack moved to the right side of me, leaned down, and began turning something that lowered the helmet on the ridged bars. With every turn, the helmet inched down, encasing me.

"Oh my God, please." I didn't realize I spoke out loud; then I was yelling as loud as I possibly could.

"HELP! HELP ME! SOMEBODY! ANYBODY HELP!"

Jack stopped cranking the wheel as I pleaded for someone, hoping upon all hopes someone would intervene. I could hear Jack move, casually it seemed, as he walked to his bench.

"Ugh, please don't do this—please." My pleading was a cry now; water was rushing from my eyes, and I was turning into a blubbering mess.

Jack looked at me through the glass portal that was just above my eyebrows, as the helmet had not yet found its final footing.

"I told you not to yell. It annoys me." Grabbing my right hand, he slipped the tip of the pliers under my thumbnail and locked down the tip.

"Please, please. I'll do whatever you want—anything. I have money. I can give you money!"

He ignored my pleading. He gave the pliers a couple of light tugs, testing to see if the grip would remain. Jack then pulled, slowly, and the pain shot up my thumb first, then into my arm.

"AHHHHHHH!" I screamed, and my crying picked up. I heard a tiny pop as he was pulling the nail from side to side just as it tore off. My thumb was now throbbing, although the pain wasn't as bad as I thought it would be. The sheer shock of the experience was worse.

"I can do this all night. It's up to you how you want to look when you go. Next, I'll take your ear off."

Jack returned the pliers to the bench and continued lowering the helmet again. The helmet was just over halfway down when Jack paused, stepped off the platform, and sat down on his stool opposite of me.

"Do you know what's coming?"

"Please, Jack. Jack, you don't have to do this; Jack, you can let me go, and I won't tell anyone anything. I swear!"

My desperation now was all I had left. Any ounce of toughness was gone. Any hope I had left disappeared instantly. Jack didn't look amused.

"You are going to drown." His voice was dark again, rising with excitement. "Do you know what happens when someone drowns?"

I stared at him, not knowing what to think. My mind again was a blank slate.

"It's not like the movies. The first thing they get wrong is the time. They make it seem that death happens in a matter of seconds. But this is far from the truth. I once had a guy that I swear took five minutes before he lost consciousness. The second thing is the violence of drowning is always sugarcoated in movies. Drowning is one of the most violent ways a person can go out, period. Especially if done right."

Jack was spinning back and forth on his stool, a nervous habit perhaps, or maybe a sign of excitement in anticipation of what he was expecting to come next.

"You see, there are a few things that can happen. As you hold your breath, which is what most people try to do at first, you may reach a point of blacking out before you get to experience drowning. Don't worry. I won't let this happen to you. Another thing that could happen is that your body automatically swells up your larynx and voice box, attempting to block your lungs from water. They call this a dry drowning. That one happens more often than you think."

Jack sat quietly for a moment, letting me soak in the words.

"You're sick," I said, looking him in the eyes.

"Yes, I suspect that to be true," he said with an accepting wince.

Standing up, he continued to winch the helmet down over my head. I felt claustrophobic all of a sudden. I had never been claustrophobic before. The bottom of the helmet had a rubber flap, which also had a similar closing tie to the ones from Jack's custom head bags. When the helmet was down, he reached back; I could hear snaps. He must have been creating a seal with the back of the headrest from the chair. He then pulled the string on this specialized head bag, and I could feel it tighten around my neck.

"The last thing that can happen, which you have about a ninety percent chance of going through —" He paused a moment and began again by dragging on the start of his next words. "Innnnn my experience at least. I must admit it's my favorite to watch, so I may help it along." Jack spoke with a chuckle.

"That is, water enters your lungs, and your natural response is to cough, which in turn forces more water into your lungs. Eventually, your stomach will also fill as your body tries desperately to find other places to put the liquid. Then you will begin to throw that up, and re-inhale and re-swallow it again until you go into cardiac arrest or pass out. The look in your eyes when this happens, is, well, unlike anything else in the world. I have played with fire, knives, guns, pliers, and even ropes. Nothing delivers fear in a man's eyes like water."

Jack spoke almost reverently. Satisfied that he had set the psychological stage with his victim, he got up. Grinning at me, Jack pushed a white tube, hooked it at the end, down through the top of the helmet.

"You're going to want to suck on this," he said as he hooked the end toward my mouth. Jack then reached behind the water tank to my right and pulled out a standard water hose that seemed to be screwed into the back of the tank. He placed the open end slightly into the top of the helmet where he wedged the metal ring against the side of my head and helmet then reached around the back of the tank.

Click. Jack must have flipped a switch. A low humming sound came to life; the hose coming from the tank began to shake and slither. I could hear a low whooshing sound coming from the hose as water made its way up to the helmet. I immediately bit down on the white tube, inhaling through this fragile life line, as I felt icy-cold water fill the suit from my neck up. The water was cold, yet my face and body were sweating. My heart began to beat heavier, with more force than ever before, each lub in the lub-dub rhythm felt like being punched, making my breathing more difficult. I bit down harder on the white tube, sucking frantically in and out.

I breathed through my mouth, desperate to hold on. What else was I to do?

Why the tube, Jack, why give me an out? I thought as the water was passing my eyes. I closed them at first, afraid the water may hurt or damage them. I could feel the water quickly reach my scalp; then I was completely submerged. I could hear Jack turn off the pump as the low-pitched hum quit. I then felt a tapping on my right shoulder.

"Hey, open your eyes!" Jack yelled, his voice wavering under the change from air to water. He said again, "Open your eyes!"

I ignored him, sure that giving him what he wanted would only quicken my demise. Then, I felt cold metal against my pinky finger. It began to tighten. *Fuck.* He was locking vice grips down on my finger, not enough to cause damage, just enough to get my attention. I immediately opened my eyes; all I needed was to lose a finger.

As I opened my eyes, they began to sting slightly. As I forced myself to keep them open, I could feel my eyelids tighten up. I looked through the greenish, murky water and could make Jack out, smiling as he stood in front of me.

"That's it," he said, pleased, as if he were nursing me along.

Jack then went back to the bench to grab a dusty half-empty bottle of whiskey. He pulled off the top and walked over to me. Sniffing the whiskey, he gave a disapproving shake of his head, saying, "Ugh, I never drink this stuff."

I watched him step up onto the platform that my chair was bolted to. He looked down and said, "Bottoms up." Jack reached over the helmet; I could feel the white tube in my teeth vibrate as he pulled it toward him to reposition the hose, straightening it.

"Get ready for a drink."

He started to pour the whiskey into the tube, slowly. I had to hold my breath and chug to avoid choking. The fluid was gross and burned as it went down, but I kept chugging. Taking a step back, Jack looked at the bottle. It was nearing empty. Jack shrugged his shoulders, reached back up, and poured the rest down. Coming down at me faster than the first, I choked on this last chug. A little bit of the whiskey had made it into my lungs, searing them. Luckily, I was able to keep the tube in my mouth with my teeth as I made it through the coughing fit, while I tried to force the whiskey into my stomach before I inhaled more.

Jack leaned in and stared directly in my eyes, sending a chill down my spine. His eyes had changed from a bright blue to a fiery black. At least he had removed those hideous glasses.

I am going to die right now. No one is going to stop him; no one is coming to save me. What did I do wrong? Why did I even agree to hang out with this guy? Please God, please stop this. I'll do anything. I'll become a better man tomorrow; I promise, just please. I will dedicate my life to your cause if you get me outta this. My thoughts were coming at me faster and faster.

"Hold your breath!" Jack spoke to me as he reached up and began tugging on the white tube. I shook my head from side to side, begging with my eyes. He yanked the white tube from my teeth. I tried to bite down as hard as I could to hold onto it, but I had no leverage to hold on as the plastic material was smooth and slick. It was gone in a blur. I began holding my breath, thinking about what Jack had told me on how I might go out. *Just hold your breath until you pass out!* It seemed to be the most pleasant way to go.

"I know what you're thinking!" he yelled at me as he tapped on the glass on the front of my helmet, no doubt mocking me. "Not going to happen on my watch."

He placed his fist just under my solar plexus where my rib cage split. Then he geared up, winding his punch back as far as he could.

Fucking asshole. Don't breathe in. Don't breathe in, I thought as I watched his fist approach.

His fist slammed into my stomach with the force of a baseball bat. I breathed the instant he struck me; how could I fight nature and expect to win? Cold water began rushing down my throat, into my lungs and stomach. My lungs seared and screamed in pain. The water turned brown and red as the whiskey and other contents of my stomach came screaming, scorching back up through my nose and throat.

* * *

When it was all over, Jack had gotten exactly what he wanted. He leaned back and shut his eyes, trying to re-live and memorize the moment. His body was drunk with endorphins. He felt high and lightheaded. He decided he would put off cleaning up until the morning, then wandered blissfully to a couch in the next room. Feeling like he had just had sex, he plopped down; his eyes fell shut as soon as his head hit the cushion.

Cute Jen – 2014

Drew had been in the car for just over an hour, long enough that he was starting to feel muscle cramps in his left foot. Being a tall man had always made it uncomfortable for him to sit for long periods in a car, partially cramped, all his limbs bent in awkward positions. Drew didn't much care for driving, and he took great interest the driverless future that awaited, a future where people wouldn't even own cars anymore. If you needed to get somewhere, you would pull up an app on your phone to make a request, and within five minutes a community, driverless car would be there for you with more room to stretch, sleep, video game, or whatever.

"How many lives would that save?" Drew said aloud as he rubbed his left eye, which was starting to itch and dry from focusing on the road for too long. If people stopped driving, deaths due to car accidents would likely be a thing of the past, like automation in the commercial flight industry. When the change to fully automated flights happened in the eighties, the safety record improved by fivefold.

Beeeeeeeeeep.

Merging sharply onto I-95 South, a car barely missed crashing into another car that was in front of Drew. Drew could see the second driver, pissed, holding up his middle finger in frustration to the vehicle that had made the poor merge.

"I can't believe we still drive." Drew shook his head.

Drew had made multiple unsuccessful attempts to reach Ashley by phone over the past three days. Davey had come through, emailing him back as he said he would, the following day. The only thing Davey could come up with was her address. Unable to reach her by phone, he had no choice but to knock on her door and figure out who she was face-to-face. He figured she might be a medical student doing research on bodies submerged from rivers or maybe a journalist writing an article on the dangers of rivers. He was getting anxious, the same feeling he always got when a case slowed to a crawl. How many times could you look at the same information and continue to glean value or make connections? Drew had emails, access to Facebook accounts, Twitter accounts, he had Josh's computer, which he had spent weeks pouring over, looking for anything out of place. Josh's parents had called yesterday, asking for progress on the investigation.

"These things take time," Drew had told them. "We must be patient."

In truth, Drew was not very patient; he felt this case was going nowhere. The only similarities, up to this point, between Josh and Frank sitting in the morgue together was that they were both young men, which was hardly a connection.

"Why am I even doing this?"

He bumped his palms against the steering wheel. Drew had hit an investigative wall; there was no evidence of foul play. Josh likely got too drunk and went for a disastrous walk near the river. Drew imagined the situation with Josh standing up on the riverbank wall, leaning over the side to stare into the water, pondering life when "oops!" he had leaned over the wall a little too much for his uncoordinated, drunk body to handle. Losing balance, he went front first, arms flailing, into the river. The water temperatures in March were just cold enough to make swimming difficult when sober, let alone drunk. Imagine trying to swim to a break in the river wall while every muscle in your body fired off at the same time, trying to generate heat.

"It was just an accident." Drew sighed. This was a very dangerous thing for a PI to do, starting to accept the report in which he was supposed to be scrutinizing. Yet, everything had pointed to such an event. The family had hired out for a second autopsy—complete with toxicology tests. The preliminary tests showed alcohol in his blood and stomach. Drew hadn't been able to find any rifts, tensions, enemies, or anything that could be a motive for murder.

"This is it—if Ashley turns out to be nothing, then I'm closing this."

He pulled up into a driveway to a large square-shaped home with brown siding. *Multi-family*, he thought, looking up through the windshield. It had a staircase leading up three steps to a wooden deck with a single door. On each side of the door was a metal mail bin, blackened with "b" on one and "c" on the other. Drew pulled out his notebook, checking the address he had scrawled down from Davy's email. There was no letter in the address he had.

Drew sighed and knocked a few times on the door without any answer. He took a look down at the doorknob; without hesitation, he turned it, hearing a click. The door was open. Not wanting to startle anyone, Drew opened it slowly and wedged the upper half of his body into the door.

"Hello! Is anyone here?" The only thing Drew saw was a staircase leading up at an awkward angle, which ended at an out of place wall that was abutting the stairs. "Hell—ooooh!"

Leaving the door open, he walked inside and up the stairs, slowly listening for sounds. When he got halfway up, he could see a door off a hallway paralleling the stairs, which read "b." His nervousness settled down as he realized this was some sort of entryway for the two units. When he reached the door, he looked to his right, seeing the hallway extend and then turned toward another set of stairs that sat over the first. "C" must be the next flight. Drew knocked on the door. Getting no answer, he knocked again, this time with a little more force, but the results were the same.

Deciding to try the next apartment, he moved his way up to the next floor, and as predicted, there was a wood door similar to the one below that read "c." Drew knocked. A moment passed without any answer. He put his head down and went to knock once more.

Suddenly, he heard the sound of a chain being connected then the door being unlocked. The door opened to the extent that the chain would allow, and a young woman, who must have been in her late teens, early twenties, peered through the crack.

"Can I help you?" she said with a slight "why are you bothering me" attitude.

"Hi, sorry to intrude. You wouldn't happen to be or know an Ashley Tinder?" Drew scrunched his eyes a bit when he said Tinder, not a hundred percent sure if he was saying it right.

The girl looked at Drew a moment. "Why are you looking for Ashley?"

Drew took this as a positive sign. "So you know her?" he asked.

"Yeah, I know her," the girl said, still giving him an attitude.

"I'm a private investigator working a missing person's case and needed to ask Ashley a few questions." Drew thought it would be easier for the young women to hear "missing person" rather than a "death case, murder, suicide" or anything similar to those.

The girl gave Drew an up and down look. He was wearing light gray khakis that had a skinny fit. He had on a blue, slim-fit blazer that accented a blue and white designed button-down shirt. On his feet, he wore brown leather boat shoes.

"You're hot for an older guy," the girl said with a wink in her eye. Then she shut the door on him. He was about to knock again when he heard the chain being pulled off. The girl opened the door all the way. "Come in; I'll help you out."

Drew didn't even hear her invite him in. She was standing there in a see-through white t-shirt without a bra on. She had reddish-blond hair that was pulled up into a ponytail, brown eyes, and a choker tattoo that was stitched around her thin neck, depicting a vine. Her small nipples were cutting through the t-shirt, surrounded by faint dollar-coin-sized areolas. She was wearing long socks that were pulled up almost to her knees. Thinking about his daughter, Drew realized that he had been staring.

"I said come in."

Drew looked up half-ashamed. "I'm sorry. I don't know . . . " He trailed off when he realized it would be better to move on from it. He cleared his throat for effect rather than necessity while surveying the room. Putting his eyes anywhere but on her, he said, "So, you know Ashley?"

"Yeah, I know Ashley." Reaching up, she rubbed her left eye. "You woke me up. I was at a party late last night. Sorry if it's a mess in here."

There were clothes everywhere. The kitchen sink was filled with dirty dishes, waiting to be put in a dishwasher. Otherwise, it looked like a fairly clean college apartment without any damage; the walls looked fresh and sharp. On one wall in the living room, there was a large tack-board with what looked like hundreds of photos. Drew took another step in to improve his angle on the wall of pictures. He could now see they were pictures of her with other people. There was a section that seemed to be marked out for party photos. Each shot had its occupants holding some sort of alcoholic beverage.

It seemed to Drew that the woman was being seductive intentionally. When he brought his eyes back to her from the wall, she had her chest propped out even more than before, and her head was tilted to the side; her eyes wide open with a puppy look.

"Wow, ah, I have a daughter. Ah, you know?" Drew burst out in an attempt to dissuade her from any sort of sexy or cute action.

She paused briefly, putting on a confused look. "That's nice. I'm sure she's wonderful. Hold on a sec; I'll be right back." She turned around on the spot and began a hop-walk toward the back rooms. Her shirt was just long enough that it mostly covered her behind. Drew could see the perfectly plump lower quarter of her butt—the soft curve crest moon created where her legs met it—bouncing slightly as she walked away.

Thank God. She's getting dressed, Drew thought.

He felt guilty being in an apartment with a half-dressed college girl probably the same age as his daughter. It did not help that she was showing herself off. Drew was used to women making moves on him, but usually, they were fully dressed, over thirty, and proposing a nightcap. Taking a deep breath, he moved into the living room area, leaning closer to the wall to take in the photos. They mostly appeared to be selfies, where she was squeezing her cheek up against other people. Some people had looks of surprise and others appeared enthralled.

"So, you have a badge or something?" She emerged back from her room again, carrying her cell phone, and to Drew's dismay, she was wearing less. She had removed her socks.

"Ah, I'm a PI, not a cop. I have a certificate, but not on me." Reaching back, Drew pulled out his wallet and slipped out his business card.

Grabbing the card from him, she shrugged. "Will you take a picture with me?" she asked politely.

Drew hesitated. "Am I going to end up on that wall?" He pointed behind him.

"Maybe, only if you get voted up," she said.

"I have no idea what that means, voted up?"

She smiled. "Yeah, haha, well, I run a website to pay for college and part of it includes this thing I like to do. I take pictures with almost everyone that I meet, and I let my users vote on them. The ones in the top hundred or so go on my wall."

Drew took a moment to take it in.

"Seems like a weird hobby, but I guess as long as you don't attach my name to it, I'm okay with it."

She bounced a little with a smile and put her hands together. *A look of pure happiness,* Drew thought. He wished Lizzy was as easy to make happy. She rushed next to him, put her arm around his back, and motioned him to lean down. Drew didn't get the message as he almost never did selfies, only when Lizzy snuck them on him.

"Hey, big guy, you need to bend down a bit so I can be in the same frame as your face."

He sighed and was a little astonished that he was going along with it. She had a bubbly, happy type of personality that just made you want to smile with her.

I need to get out of here as soon as possible, before she starts asking to borrow money . . . because she'll probably get it from me.

She squeezed her cheek next to his, put on an authentic smile, and half-closed her eyes for the shot.

"You can check out my site if you want. It's easy to remember, cutecamjen.com," she said quickly as she threw her phone on the couch. "Ashley actually set up the website for me. She's pretty awesome—didn't charge me anything for it. I just had to pay for the cameras; those weren't cheap though."

Finally, the conversation was going in the direction he needed. "Don't you use your phone as your camera?"

Momentarily, she gazed at her phone, slowly taking it in, then smiled and looked up quickly.

"No—I mean, yes—for those types of photos." She pointed at the wall. Almost shyly, she continued. "But that's not all my site is about, silly. I'm an adult film star. Well, not exactly what you're thinking. You can pay a monthly fee on my site, and you always have access to my bedroom, living room, kitchen, and bathroom cameras. Basically, my entire apartment."

Drew's eyes widened, as a wry grossed-out smile crossed his face when he started thinking about what happened in bathrooms.

"Your bathroom? People are into watching that?"

"Believe it." She nodded, seeming to bounce at the topic. "It started in my bedroom, of course, but I got a lot of requests for more cameras, and the second one went into the bathroom by popular demand. I'm up to almost three thousand active subscribers for the single bedroom camera. A thousand for the bathroom and six thousand for a subscription to all cameras."

"So, just about ten thousand users?" Drew said aloud as he was doing the math. "If you don't mind me asking, what do you charge?"

"I don't mind." She smiled. "You could always go to my site. Check it out and join! It's four ninety-nine a month per camera, except eight ninety-nine a month for the bathroom cam. I charge more for that. Oh, and you can get access to all cameras for twenty-nine bucks a month." She spoke fast, clearly a pitch she had given a number of times. Drew took another deep breath as he thought about the numbers.

"You can pay for more than college with that type of income."

"Yeah, I put most of it into savings actually. Once I finish my degree, I want to stop and move on to a regular job. I realize I'll probably not make this kind of money again, but it's a difficult job, attracts the wrong sort of people. It's almost impossible to have a serious relationship. They end up not wanting to hang out here after a little, and well, it's my job to hang out here. It's actually a stressful job. Sundays and Mondays I turn the cameras off. Tuesday is topless night. Wednesday isn't special, but the cameras are on. Thursday I do popular requests. Friday I put on a two-hour show that's labeled Wet And Wild, and Saturday is no panties day."

Drew had to move the conversation in another direction. He could feel the blood surging to a certain organ in his body when he realized it was Saturday morning.

"Are the cameras on? Right now?" He looked around nervously; he was certainly not comfortable being recorded on a porn site.

"Well, I turned off the mic when I went to my room so you can speak freely, but yes you're on the internet." She shrugged like it was not a big deal.

He hesitated a minute, considering leaving.

"What the heck—tell me about Ashley, and I take it you're Jen?" he finally said, waving his hands. Moving around the side of the couch, she sat down, patting the cushion next to her. Avoiding her beckoning, Drew moved to the opposite couch that was against the photo wall.

"You *are* a detective! My name is Jen! And Ashley is —" she sucked in air between her lips and teeth, "amazing, super smart, ultra sexy."

She paused, pointing to herself. "Even I've tried to sleep with her. But, for real, Ashley is amazing. I haven't seen her nearly as much as I like, but her husband went missing last year, which was super tough. Oh, who are you looking for?"

"What?" Drew responded, forgetting that he told her he was investigating a missing person case.

"Your missing person," she said.

"Ahh, that! Sorry, I was wrapped up in a thought about what you were saying. Yeah, a young guy, his name wa—is—his name is Josh." He had to correct himself mid-sentence from referencing Josh in the past tense."

"Well, you seem really good, so I think your gonna figure this out." She put her head down a bit and frowned. "Ashley is my landlord. She lives downstairs, although you have to go around the building to get to her front door. She has a side door also but never uses it. She works from home usually, but I actually haven't seen her for a few days. I tried calling her today too, and she didn't answer. Should I be worried about her?"

"No, no, I'm sure she is fine." Drew waved his hand in a crossing pattern. "I found her name attached to a list associated with the last place Josh was seen at."

Drew stood up and made a line for the door.

"Thank you for your help. I'm going to try Ashley downstairs. And good luck with your business. Oh, why the selfies?" Drew was halfway out the door when he asked the question. He was curious why she liked taking photos with strangers.

"I just love people." She smiled. "I think everyone is amazing; I love making a physical connection with as many people I can. It started as a hug-a-stranger-a-day thing; then I realized that face-hugging was a little more intimate and really makes people feel good."

A soft look of caring and happiness overtook her as she spoke.

"Well, you made me happy," Drew said as he left. When he got back down to the outside deck, he thought, *What a nice girl, but I would kill Lizzy if she worked in porn.*

X's and O's – 2014

Bzzz, bzzzz, bzzzz.

Drew pulled his phone out of his pocket to check the caller ID, a number but no name.

Hmm, who do I know from 401? Drew thought a moment, realizing he had been leaving Ashley messages at a 401 number.

"Hello, is this Ashley?" Drew piped into the phone as he stood outside her house.

"Haha, someone's excited. It's only Jen. You just left my apartment a second ago." Drew shook his head, remembering that he had given her his card. "I wanted to let you know that you left a notepad up here."

Drew reached into his pockets, felt around to find his notebook, and realized it was gone.

"I must have. I'll run back up and grab it." Drew was heading toward the door when he heard a third-story window open.

"Hey!" Looking up, he could see Jen extended out of the window. "I can just toss it down. That way you don't have to come up."

Drew opened his hands in a catcher's position, as she tossed the book. It flailed around in the air with its pages flipping, as if some would tear off, but it held true and landed a few feet from Drew. Picking it up, he straightened it out, then looked up, holding the pad up in the air.

"Thanks!"

"You're welcome, Mr. Law. Next time you're in the area, you should stop by and say hi." With that, dipping back into the house, she shut the window.

Drew put the notebook back into his pocket. Standing back, he took in the whole house in one glance. Not wanting to block anyone from their spot, he pulled his car out of the lot and parked it on the street. Returning, he gave the house another good look over, wanting to get the dimensions of the house down. It was in decent shape with brown perfection siding and a Mansard roof, the kind that angled up from all four sides then flattened out at the top.

He moved toward the direction Jen had said Ashley's door was. The lawn was mostly weeds; he could tell landscaping was an afterthought. When he found the front door, he hit the doorbell but didn't hear any type of *ding* in the house. Figuring it was broken, he gave the door a good knock.

As soon as his fist touched it, the door creaked open. Drew's eyebrows lifted. On quick inspection, he could see that the door frame had been fractured so that the bolt no longer had any wood to lock itself against. Someone had taken a crowbar to the door, professionally done too.

A clean job, Drew thought.

"Hello? Hello? Ashley? I'm coming in the house." He cautiously moved into the house and pulled out his phone, dialing 911, holding his finger above the dial button. *Just in case.* He wasn't licensed to carry a firearm in Rhode Island, but he did carry mace with him no matter where he went. He pulled out the small canister from his pocket. It was a miniature single shot car key canister no more than an inch in length. He gave it a twist to unlock the trigger and held it at the ready. Drew looked to his right. A comfortable dark red leather couch was pushed up against the windows with end tables on either side. He was a bit puzzled by a lamp sitting on the far end table that looked as though it had been smashed, but put back together with super glue and duct tape.

He gave the lamp a second look and saw what looked like a picture frame below it. He moved closer, curious to get a look at Ashley, of whom he had spent a better part of the last week trying to get a hold of. It was a wedding picture in a black frame. The attractive woman looking back at him had brown hair, done up elegantly with curls falling out to the sides. Her eyes were wide and smiling; her lips curled as if posing for a model shoot. It was the same Ashley he had found online when he started looking for her, pretty as ever. She was standing next to a tall, goofy-looking younger guy.

This guy scored above his level, Drew thought, looking at the lanky guy with brown hair and thin facial features. The picture frame had the wedding date on it, July 19, 2011. Drew backed away from the picture and moved toward the kitchen in the back. It was spotless. There were no dishes in the sink; the glass stove top was clear and streak free. Drew opened the fridge, peered inside; it was mostly empty except for condiments that expired last year. He stood there, staring off into the fridge for a moment, losing himself to his own memories of the weeks following Nell's death.

He felt sorrow and loneliness drawn from his own grief, then shook himself out of his flashback. He felt he could relate to Ashley losing her husband.

No sign of kids. Not sure if that makes it easier or harder— probably harder. He pulled open the cupboard that was under the sink; there was a wastebasket but no bags or trash. *Hmm, no luck.*

As a PI, trash was typically an information gold mine to tell you all you needed to know about someone, oftentimes providing too much information. Drew felt more and more comfortable as he moved through her house, yet a concern for Ashley was slowly bubbling higher in his chest. Besides the door jam, he could feel something wasn't right. Drew finished checking the single-level two-bedroom apartment. He was about to leave when he realized there should be more space in the apartment. He recalled his earlier visit to Jen's apartment and the awkward abutting wall to the stairs leading to the upper floors.

There has to be another room. Drew went back into the kitchen toward the back of the apartment; he looked over to the side door that was bolted in three places. Moving to this door, he went over to check the locks.

"This thing hasn't been opened in years."

He looked outside the window to get his bearings on where he was in the house, standing straight up. The wall he was looking at was one of the walls that paralleled the stairs. The modification to the original home was done well. With the open floor space and large archways between rooms, the apartment felt larger than it was. In fact, he might have never realized the wall hid a staircase for other tenants had he not come in from the other side where he met Jen. Walking to the corner, Drew stopped. Following the wall, he counted his steps.

"Eleven," he said aloud as if to help him remember the number; as he reached the end of the wall, he turned to his left and opened up the closet, more as a sanity check. Looking up, he could see the framework of the stairs. *Using the space under a set of stairs as a coat closet is a perfect use,* he thought. Drew shut the closet door and continued, hooking around left down the hall. He began counting his steps again as he walked. This hall had two doors from where he stood, all on the right of him. The first door led to a somewhat cramped bathroom, followed by the second bedroom that was used as an office with a guest room. When Drew reached the end of the hall, he put his hands on the wall, looking it over, then saying, "Eight, what do we have here."

Drew entered the second bedroom, the second time he had been inside this room. In the far corner was a closet door, which he walked straight over to, opening its double doors. The closet was filled on the right side with shoes and purses, and on the left side, it had an assortment of men's clothes, including shirts, button downs, and spring jackets. Reaching in, Drew pushed the clothes as far over to the left as he could. He looked over the wall inside the closet, but it was just a wall. Pulling his phone out of his pocket, he turned on its flashlight.

"I'll be damned!"

It was hard to catch, but from a knee-high angle, there was the slightest of gaps that could be seen between the bottom of the wall trim and the floor. The trim seemed a little high. It would have been very easy to miss had he not been looking for a missing space. Drew was on his knees with his face planted against the floor as he tried to guide his phone light under the wall to see what might lie behind.

"Table feet—there's a damn table in there. How do you get in there?"

Standing up abruptly, Drew started looking around the closet. He began pulling the purses and shoes out, throwing them on the guest bed. He emptied the entire closet to find no entrance whatsoever. "Dammit."

Drew paced the bedroom, double-checking the walls and floor, when he stopped suddenly. Pulling out his phone again, he dialed Jen back.

"Hey there, good-looking, I didn't expect you to call me back so quickly." A playful Jen answered the phone after the second ring.

Drew talked right through her chatter. "Do you know, does this place have a basement?"

There was silence for a second. "Do you mean my apartment?"

"Yes, your building," Drew said quickly. He felt like he was close to something and his excitement was showing. He was starting to get uncomfortable; he had just emptied a stranger's closet onto their bed.

"There sure is, but it's hard to get into cause it's like a crawl space entry."

"Where? Where can I find it?"

Jen suddenly became less playful as his tone became demanding.

"Is Ashley home? Are you in her house?"

Drew didn't want to play this game. He needed to get her on team Drew and quickly.

"I think she's in trouble. I came over to her place right after I left your house, and I found the door broken in by a crowbar." He paused a moment. "Then it appears that her office has been tossed by someone looking for something."

Why not use the mess he made to his advantage?

"Oh my God. What do we do? Should I call the police?"

"Not yet, we will, but why not let us have a chance to try to figure out what happened before the police force us out of the place."

"I'll be right down."

"No, just—" Drew sighed as she hung up. He was not interested in having to deal with her again. Moving into the living room, he heard Jen storming down the staircase just above him.

"I'm definitely in the right spot."

Moments later, Jen came bursting through the door that was slightly ajar.

"You probably had time to put clothes on," Drew said nonchalantly.

She looked down at herself, still wearing the same semi-see-through shirt. "What's wrong with this? I did put panties on."

Drew gave her a fatherly, disappointed look.

"Whatever, Ashley's missing!" she stated defiantly, taking a look around, expecting the apartment in total disarray like in the movies. "It doesn't seem so bad in here."

Drew put up his finger and motioned her to follow him into the office. She took one look at the mess.

"Oooh, Ashley!" She put her hand to her mouth in shock. "Is this—you're like a cop—is this bad?"

Drew looked at the mess he made on the bed, a wry smile pulling on the left side of his face, away from Jen.

"It's really bad," he said with a depressing tone on his voice. "How do you get into the basement?"

Jen put on a look of confidence. "Follow me," she said, walking into the kitchen.

Moving toward a tall cabinet next to the back door, which Drew had just been standing next to not twenty minutes ago, she opened it up and pulled out the three bottom shelves that weren't storing anything. Getting on her knees, Jen leaned into the cabinet, her butt popped into the air, exposing her entire backside and everything underneath, and before he looked away, he could see a well shaved set of lips snuggled around a thin string.

"Ahh, dammit, Jen. Those aren't panties. That's dental floss."

She looked over her shoulder at him, smiling. She shrugged. "I'm a working girl, and promiscuity is my marketing plan."

Drew looked up at the ceiling, moving his lips without speaking. *You have a daughter her age. You have a daughter her age*, he repeated in his mind.

At the sound of hammering, Drew looked back, ignoring the skin this time. He could see Jen was using her fist to pound down on a wooden floor in the cabinet. She said with strain, "It—" *Bang.* "Just sticks sometimes. Ahh, got it."

Giving one corner a pull, a sheet of plywood popped out with finishing nails sticking out. Drew gave her a gentle push out of the way and peered down. It was obvious from the enlarged holes where the nails had been that the board had been pulled up and put back a great number of times, each time loosening the holes where the nails went. There was a ladder, just under the floor line, that went down. Drew could feel cold air coming up from the dark endowed with a musty smell.

"How did you know about this?" Drew said, looking up and then away quickly as their eyes locked.

"Well, haha, that's a weird story. But I had a stalker who was getting a little violent, and I really needed to hide. And well, Ashley, she, like, totally saved my ass."

"You went down there?" Drew gave her disbelieving look.

There was a brief pause, like she was deciding to be truthful.

"Well, no," she said quickly. "Ashley tried to send me down there, but I made her put the board back, and I just stacked the shelves and hid in the cabinet."

Crouching into the cabinet, Drew fished around with his feet to find the rungs. He wasn't sure if he would even fit. The hole was about three feet by two feet wide. He turned his phone flashlight back on and pointed it down with one hand. He began a slow and careful descent into the darkness. The ladder was longer than he had thought; he counted six rungs before he reached the bottom. Each rung was likely twelve inches apart. Conveniently, he could stand without hitting his head on the ceiling, while the floor was smooth with dry concrete. He had imagined a dungy, rocky, slimy, short basement, but it was the complete opposite. He could hear humming and, in the distance, see flickering lights. His cell phone light wasn't strong enough to illuminate that far away to totally make out what was against the wall.

"There's power down here. There must be a light switch. Look around up there and flip random switches," he yelled up to Jen. He remained in the same spot, with his head tucked and shoulder scrunched, like a wrong step would trigger a deadly booby trap.

A large elongated fluorescent bulb came to life above him, filling the large basement with light.

"You got it!" Drew yelled up then the light turned off again. "Hey, Jen you had it. Flip that switch back on again." There was a pause.

"What did you say?" Jen yelled back down into the hole.

"I said, you got it! The last switches you just flipped—flip them again and leave them."

The light took another second but, sure enough, lit the basement once more. There was a single half-rack of blade servers sitting in the far corner of the room with twenty servers, computers built for serving up websites, humming along. Next to it was a medium six-rung ladder folded against the wall, and next to that, stairs to the bulkhead.

He yelled up to Jen incredulous, "There's bulkhead access?"

When he got no response, he thought, *Maybe this is where Jen's site is hosted from?* He looked around and didn't see any other ladders or stairs leading back up. He tried to get his bearing, but, from his experience working on houses, you're never where you think you are.

He walked back over to the ladder, yelling, "Hey, Jen!"

"Yeah?" she responded promptly.

"Can you go into the closet in the office and tap on the floor?"

Drew could see her. She was leaning into the cabinet, staring down. Having become undone, her red hair was falling softly around her face.

"Sure," she said, pushing her hair to the side.

Drew could hear her walking across the room, turning left at the hallway. He followed her steps as she moved along. Then she stopped and began tapping on the floor above with the tip of her toe. Drew looked up, trying to avoid the falling dust from hitting him in the eyes. Then he saw it. Another loose, thin board, lightly nailed up hiding another entrance.

"What are you hiding?" Drew said suspiciously.

He walked over to the server rack and grabbed it, rolling it over a few feet out of the way. Revealing a ladder, he guessed to be six feet tall straightened out.

"You can stop. Hey! Jen! You can stop!"

This time Jen heard him, and the tapping stopped. Her footsteps began moving back toward the kitchen. Drew used the ladder, stopping about halfway to work on the board. Reaching up, he pulled the wood with his fingers. The board fell out immediately, ceiling dust raining down on him. He coughed a few times at the dust settling in his throat.

"You okay?" Jen called down.

"Yeah, yeah, just dusty." Drew turned his phone flashlight upwards with one hand, his other holding the board. He could see a light switch at the top.

As he stretched up for a closer look, the wood board slipped from his grip and crashed onto the floor below.

"What was that?" Jen yelled down, but Drew was now too interested in what he was finding to hear her.

"What the hell? Homeowner hack job?" he pondered at the setup.

He began a slow ascent up into the hidden room. When he reached the top of the ladder, he was able to shift his upper body onto the floor and slide in a bit until he could get his legs up. He reached out and flipped the light switch; a single incandescent bulb immediately lit the room. A small table against the far wall filled most of the thin room. That wall was most definitely separating the room from the office closet. On the wall, pinned up with flat metal thumbtacks, was a map of Boston that spanned from, going left to right, Harvard Stadium to Jeffries Point in East Boston, and from top to bottom, East Somerville to Lower Roxbury.

"Back Bay," he whispered as he reviewed the locations.

The map had little red X's marked all along the Charles River and little blue O's scattered around Boston.

Each one of the X's and O's had a corresponding number attached to them. A single X had a "1" then he found a single O with a "1" and so on. Drew counted through each O, making sure to match it with its counterpart. Numbers 1, 2, 3, 5, 8, 21, and 29 were missing an O counterpart. Some of the X's had a little check mark next to them.

"I wonder why that is," Drew said as he moved his hand along the map, taking it in. There didn't appear to be any pattern to their placement, at least none that he could tell.

Drew was focusing on the map when a sudden loud thud came

from behind him. Turning around quickly, he pulled his hand up into a defensive position. Drew was an excellent grappler. He had studied the art of Hapkido, as well as other fighting techniques, religiously for many years growing up and into his late twenties. He had competed in tournaments and competitions, always placing on the podium, although that was twenty years ago. Even though he wasn't active in a gym now, he still practiced his forms on a weekly basis. For Drew, forms were a technique of active meditation where focus was tuned to the sequence of moves and the execution of those moves. The better the mental focus, the better the results; clearing your mind of distractions was a must in order to succeed.

"Whaaa?" Jen screeched as she saw him. "Slow down, karate kid!" she said, using a movie reference Drew thought she was too young to be using. She started to elegantly raise herself into the room, like pulling herself out of a pool. Then her grip slipped, her body swung forward, and her head met a stud protruding from the wall with good force.

"Essss," Drew breathed in between his teeth, relating to the sting of how that must have felt. "Are you okay? Let me take a look."

Drew moved in and pulled her hands down away from the forming bulge just above her left eye. He gently held her head as her brown eyes glowed back at him. He rubbed from side to side lightly over the bump.

"Ahhhh," she squealed when he put pressure on a sore spot.

"Well, you're not bleeding, and you probably didn't break anything."

She looked at him helplessly. "Thanks, doc, too bad you're not here to do a physical." She winked at him jokingly.

Drew smirked, shaking his head. "Are you always like this?" Shuffling, he started rubbing his hands on his hips, as if to cleanse them.

"Only with the cute ones." She continued the flirtatious tone. That's when she noticed the map on the wall. "What is all this?"

Drew looked over to the map he'd been closely inspecting prior to Jen's painful entrance.

"I think it's a map marked with locations of where bodies have been recovered from the Charles River." He said it with certainty.

A disgusted look washed over Jen's face as she counted the marks. "So many of them . . . ." She trailed off at the end of her statement. "How do you know?"

Drew pointed to the map, on the north side of the river, just south of the MIT campus and east of where Massachusetts Avenue crossed over the river; his finger came to rest on a little red X with a check mark next to it.

"This is where Josh was found. And this X was where Frank popped up," he said frankly.

"Found? Wait, Josh's body was found?" Jen responded. "I thought you were looking for Josh?"

"This is where he was last seen alive, at a bar." Drew ignored her and pointed to another mark, a blue O a few blocks north of the river.

"But I thought you said that Josh was a missing person?" She had an incredulous look on her face.

"Sorry about that. I didn't want to scare you when we first met. I'm trying to figure out what happened to Josh in his last moments of life." Drew went on to tell her how he had been following multiple drowning deaths that all had a similar pattern in the Boston area. She looked down at the floor when she heard the truth, mumbling slightly to herself.

"So many, why so many?" She looked back up to Drew and the map. "How the hell did you figure that out looking at this mess?"

Drew shrugged. "I've been on this case for a little while now, and these marked locations just popped out at me. I could be wrong. I hope I'm wrong."

Pulling out his phone, Drew began taking pictures of the map, questions whirling in his head. *Are there connections between all of these? Did Ashley know who all of these X's and O's were? How far back is being represented here? Is this real? Did Ashley know about this map?*

"I really need to find Ashley," Drew said out loud with worry in his voice.

Trigger – 2005

"K three," A slight pause ensued. "Fff, ee, see, two, oh four, three time three, H two Oh."

Jack was saying the formula out loud as he wrote it, copying it from a lab worksheet to his lab assignment. Jack was in his second semester in the Chemical Engineering program at MIT.

"Fuck," Jack yelled out as he picked up a white eraser, erasing half the page. The paper was thinning because he had already started over on three previous attempts, and it began to tear from the voracity of his erasing.

"Fuck, fuck," he swore, each iteration more intense than the last. Picking the paper up, then crumpling it into a ball, he tossed it in a blue recycle bin that was conveniently placed next to the desk. It was 7:30 p.m., and he was sitting in the engineering library by himself working on a lab that was due twelve days from now. Ever since Dean's "accident," Jack had become more isolated than ever, alienating himself as best he could. He was in constant conflict, a part of him holding on to the only sliver of his mother he had left, a part of him that his father had carefully crafted over the years with un-ending violence, leaving a monster behind.

Frustrated, he stood up, picking up his backpack. Jamming his school books and worksheets into the bag, Jack fought his demons. He was always mad, tension boiling up and constantly spilling over into his life. Trying to keep a mellow mood, he put on headphones as he began his twenty-minute walk to his off-campus housing. Jack walked with his head sunken, hands in his pocket, locking his eyes on his feet. His mind had been teetering in this state of frailty ever since Dean's death. He felt guilt and sorrow for killing his friend. The look of horror on Dean's face seemed to become more menacing every time he thought about it. His mind had manipulated his memory, constantly changing events of his death with the slightest tweaks. Just as quickly as that guilt swarmed him, it would disappear. Afterwards, the feeling of excitement and lust would replace it. He wanted to do it again, but he would talk himself out of it. He knew it was wrong. There were two unique forces at work in his body: emotions and lust butting against logic and morality. He often wondered about this. Law would tell him that he was sane; his actions were not a result of insanity due to his ability to discern right from wrong, yet that made no sense.

"I am one fucking crazy bastard."

Jack reached his apartment and climbed the two stories that hung on the outside of a colonial home. He rented a single-bedroom apartment that sat on top of a larger three-bedroom unit rented out by three graduate students studying clinical psychology.

Ironic. If they only knew they had one hell of a case study living directly above them.

Every day seemed like a repetition of the last. He would wake up, hitting snooze upwards of five times, which would assure that he missed his morning class. When he finally got out of bed, he would skip a shower, grab a granola bar, and start his walk back onto campus. It was Friday today; his second class was calculus, which he always made. He liked calculus. It was multivariate calculus, a subject he excelled at. He also liked this class because he was obsessed with a particular peer whom he only shared this class with. Like every morning, he sat down directly behind her. Immediately he began to wonder what it would be like if he drowned her. Would he let her know what was coming? Would she beg? What would she offer him for her life? Her name was Anne Nalow, a plump, cute, smart brunette that always sat in the front row. She was the student in class that constantly answered the professor's questions mid-sentence. Even the professor seemed to get annoyed with her. Over the course of the semester, he had daydreamed about the different ways he could end her—naked in a tub or bound and gagged on a bed. Maybe he would use a knife? Or maybe just a rope? Awkwardly, he caught himself getting hard as he daydreamed—about her eyes glossing over, the look of shock etched into her face, her mouth open.

No, no, no. Not again. Jack looked swiftly out the large window. Moving stiffly in his seat, he put his baseball cap on his groin area to make sure no one would see the growing mound. *Think of birds. Think of flowers.* Jack tried to dissuade the situation. It was working. His heartbeat was slowing, and he could feel things begin to soften. He wondered how long he was going to be able to keep himself locked up. Who was going to be the next one? He knew it was not a matter of if, but when. When was he going to snap?

As soon as class ended, Jack rushed out of the room. Onlookers saw a young man who was socially awkward, shy, and always in a rush, which was not that different from many young men in an engineering program. Truly, there had been only one thing that kept him from unleashing his murderous urges, and that was the sweet words of his mother telling him how much she loved him. Those words rang in his head, blunting down the darkness in him. Those words made him think about the people in Anne's life, the people who loved her, the mother who loved her, and how her death would cause so much pain to them. Now that Jack had a better understanding of who he was, he valued his mother's voice more than ever. It was a speck of light, keeping the dark from consuming him.

"Soon enough they will bring me on board and permit me to be who I am. I shouldn't mess this up," he told himself, also reminding him of his employer's demands.

Jack was walking between buildings when a feeling of concern brushed through him. He stopped in his tracks and spun around immediately, which caused a young freshman girl to bump into him. The collision was soft, just a brush. Her head was down with her attention on her iPod. Stepping to the left at the last second, avoiding a much larger collision, he shook his head. The girl didn't even realize what had just happened. "No clue, no fucking clue," he muttered to himself. Jack looked around for anyone who might look out of place or suspicious, something he realized was hard to spot on a college campus where diversity was high. There were dozens of students walking behind him. There was one older guy who looked a little out of place—but he was probably a professor. Jack took a deep breath and turned around slowly, continuing on his path.

Just then, a strange sound and feeling came from his pocket. He reached down to find a buzzing mobile phone, unlike any he had ever seen. It was black, sleek, and thin with a screen on the front that displayed "Unknown." Puzzled, he looked at the phone, wondering where it had come from.

The ringing stopped. He rotated the phone in his hands, inspecting it. He could tell it was a flip phone, a type of phone that had been available for a couple of years, although he had never seen one so thin. The phone began to vibrate again, and again the word "Unknown" was splashed on the grayscale screen. He flipped the front of the phone up, exposing the keypad. Another screen lit up. He slowly brought the phone to his ear and said, "Hello?"

A female voice responded promptly, "Who is this?"

Jack was clearly confused. "Uh, I'm Jack. I found this phone." Jack had assumed it was in his jacket on accident.

"I know who it is. The phone was meant for you, Jack. Check your pocket. You should have a charger for it." Jack reached deeper into his pocket; sure enough, there was a battery charger rolled up and tied together with a Velcro strap.

"Ah . . . I don't—I think you have the wrong Jack." His right hand rubbed the back of his head, a nervous habit.

"Do I?" she said sarcastically. "Put your right hand down, Jack. You look nervous." Jack froze. Slowly lowering his hand, he began to look around.

"You can see me?" There was a brief pause.

"Of course. I came here to see you. Let's not dwell on this, Jack. Meet me tonight at Belly's Café at eight p.m. Do you know of it?"

Jack took a moment to think.

"Do you know of it, Jack? It's off campus in the center of town," she said hurriedly.

"Ah, yes. I think I know where that is. It's next t—"

She cut him off. "Oh good, see you then." *Click.*

He hung up the phone and stared at it for a moment, then slipped it back into his pocket. Surely he would have time to play with it later.

"Is this it? Is this the contact that the mysterious businessman said would come, his recruitment?" he muttered to himself staring off into the distance. Worry and excitement surged through him at the same time, a feeling similar to one that you get waiting for your first date. He started to walk, increasing his pace as he went. Without realizing it, he passed the building his next class was in. School was the last thing on his mind. Jack had one place he needed to be, that was Belly's Café at eight. He was anxious, needing to get home to prepare. He could only guess what was going to happen next, but that in itself was exciting. Suddenly, his future didn't seem so predictable, so repeatable. He had convinced himself that the businessman was never going to reach out, a small part of him hoped he wouldn't, the part his mother still held. As Jack's apartment came into view, breaking into a jog, he hustled up the stairs, skipping steps with each stride.

Into the Fold – 2005

Jack arrived in front of Belly's Café at exactly 7:15. It was more of a burger joint than a café. It had a white sign over the entrance that read "**Belly's Café**" in bright, bold red ink. The cursive made him double-check it to make sure he had read it correctly. *Why have a sign that's hard to read?* Jack thought as he pushed the glass door, entering the café.

"Hi, Hun! We'll be with you in just a moment," a waitress said politely as she walked by. Jack looked around but didn't see anyone waving to him or signaling him. He decided he would sit down with a good view of the door and order a starter or at least a coffee. Having barely eaten all day, he could feel his stomach turning. A different waitress came out from behind the counter.

"Just one?" she said between long chews of gum. She reached for the laminated menus and paused, waiting for him. He was unsure how to respond.

"Ah, I'm meeting someone," he replied unconfidently.

"So two?" she said with a smile, her eyes squinting as she was seeking confirmation.

"Yes, two, that should be fine, thanks," he replied. Turning, she walked him between the rows of bench seating.

"Here you are. Can I get you water or anything to start?" She was still chewing her gum with her mouth open, which bothered Jack.

"A coffee and a water, please." Jack took a seat at the bench so that he was facing the door; he had a hard time taking his eyes off of it. He pulled his phone out to check the time, 7:20 p.m. He put the phone and his wallet on the table, sliding them toward the wall. Every time the door opened, he found himself looking up promptly.

After forty-five minutes of painful waiting and holding off the waitress, the door opened. A slim woman with wide hips stepped in. Her dark brown hair was tied up in a ponytail, and she was decked out in a tight-fitting gray suit and teetering on three-inch high heels.

Definitely out of place in this diner, Jack thought. As she walked toward him, he realized that he knew her, behind black rectangular glasses her eyes were glowing at him in different shades. She had once shown him into the office of the mysterious businessman a few years back. He recalled her as kind.

Approaching the bench across from him, she slid down as elegantly as she could while placing her purse on the inside of the bench. Having anticipated this meeting for some time now, the waitress came over hurriedly.

"Can I get anything for you to start, sweetie?" the waitress said. She was the type of waitress who took pride in her ability to remember orders, eliminating the need to carry an invoice or pad. The woman sitting down adjusted her glasses and looked up.

"Yes, please, soda water with a lemon."

Jack was waiting to speak, unsure what to say to her, realizing then that he didn't know her name.

"Did you eat?" she said looking down at the menus.

"I waited. I wasn't sure who I was supposed to meet here," he said calmly as he watched her.

She reached up pulled out the hairband that was holding her ponytail together. Her wavy dark hair fell to one side.

"Ahh, that's better," she said as she next unbuttoned her jacket and the top button of her blouse. She was very pretty with a strong jawline and olive glowing skin, but it was her eyes that mesmerized Jack.

"Let's order something. I'm starving." She put her hand up to let the waitress know that she was ready to proceed with her order, assuming Jack was ready as well.

"Yes, I would like your build-it-burger, medium rare with lettuce, tomato, mayo, and cooked onions, and French fries are fine." She paused a moment, then looked up at Jack, signaling to him that it was his turn.

"I'm going to have your spicy mac 'n cheese bowl."

Reaching out, the waitress took both menus from the table. "I'll put that right in for you," she said, then walked away.

"Jack, it's good to see you!" She reached out, touching his hand briefly with a smile. He felt a warmth shiver through him, and his hairs stood up as if on alert.

"How has school been?" she continued excitedly, as if they were close friends.

"Good, I guess." He took a deep breath as he tried to judge the situation.

"I hear you're doing quite well with your studies. Dr. Leaon speaks very highly of you."

How did she know who Dr. Leaon was? He was Jack's college mentor, a person who he rarely talked about and few people even knew about. How long had she been spying on him? How long have *they* been spying on him? The feeling was uncomfortable.

"Wait, what is your name? I don't even know who you are," he blurted out.

"Elle," she responded. "Pronounced like the letter 'L.'"

"Oh." He paused, taking in the name; it was not quite what he had expected. "Elle. Tell me something. Why now?"

Taking in a deep breath, Elle leaned back. "Jack, how old are you now?"

"What difference does that make?" he spat back quickly, his anxiety starting to snarl up.

"You're nineteen, Jack." She ignored his response. "You see, Jack, our employer has been in business for a long time, and, well, he has been very successful. He sets the rules, and the one rule is that we don't start training recruits until at least nineteen."

"Here you are," the waitress said rolling her "r" at the end of the sentence as she swapped out the empty glasses for full ones.

When she was gone, Jack said, "Recruits?"

Everything seemed so strange. His gut was telling him that he should get up and leave, ignore this woman and her mystery, ignore the man behind her and his lure, just ignore all of it and go back to his life. Sure, he had anxiety and depression issues, but he had been able to deal with them without hurting himself or, more importantly, someone else over the past few years.

"Yes, that's what we call our pending associates." She paused, then said, "Our employer seeks uniquely talented individuals, and we identified you as having a unique skill set."

Jack started to feel his stomach turn. He knew exactly what she was referencing. How could she call that a skill? Without noticing what he was doing, his face coiled and twisted as if he had just bitten into a lemon. She let him wriggle in his seat uncomfortably for a moment.

"Oh, please. Just relax. You had an accidental outburst. Trust me, that won't happen again." Just then the waitress returned with the food.

"Here we are—oh, is something wrong?" She put the plates down, noticing the lingering look of disgust on Jack's face.

"He's fine. I just shared a gross joke with him I heard at work today." Elle moved the conversation along.

"Can I get you anything else then?" She was still chewing gum loudly, watching Jack.

"I think we're good, thanks," Jack said, looking down at his plate.

"Enjoy your food," Elle said as she looked at Jack, one side of her mouth curled into a smile.

Wow, she is pretty, Jack thought.

The two ate in silence. Conflicting emotions flooded his mind, driving away his appetite; he only picked at his food. Elle, on the other hand, had a very large appetite. The burger she ordered must have been a half-pound slab of meat, and she ate it as if she were in a food-eating competition. By the time Jack had pushed his half-eaten plate away, she was just finishing up her fries, meticulously dipping them in a side dish of mayonnaise.

"How many recruits are there?" Jack asked.

Elle finished what she was chewing on before answering. "Well, right now there are three others, but that number changes often." She picked up another fry, analyzed it, dipped it into mayonnaise, and continued to eat.

"So." Jack looked down at the table. "Are the others monsters too? Like me?"

Reaching out, Elle grabbed his hand, pulling him in closer to her and the table. She stroked his knuckles sensually.

"Look at me. Hey, look me in the eyes." His eyes glanced up. "You are not—*not* a monster. They are not monsters. Do you understand?"

Jack began to look down again, and she shook him. "Hey, tell me you understand." She wasn't letting him get away that easy.

Jack looked back up at her. "I understand," he said, almost dejectedly. She held on to his hand for a moment longer, finally giving it a tight squeeze before letting go.

"Now that we cleared that up, like I said, there are three others, each very different from the other."

Jack took a sip of his water; his throat felt dry. "What are their names?"

"I can't tell you their names. That's against our policy. In fact, it's doubtful that you'll ever meet them. The work you recruits do for us is more like, well, it's more like you're independent contributors."

Pulling up her sleeve, Elle checked her watch. Suddenly stretching her arm out, she lightly touched the arm of the waitress as she walked by. "Our check, please?"

"Of course. I'll be back with it in a minute."

Elle began cleaning up around her plate, brushing spilled food into a napkin. Slipping her right hand into her purse, she pulled out a dark red lipstick and locked eyes onto Jack as she spread it on her lips.

"It was a wonderful dinner, Jack. Thanks for being my date," she said between pops of her lips. "We will do it again, soon." After she paid, in cash, they both walked together to the exit. A town car limousine was outside, the driver already holding open a propped door for her.

"That's it?" Jack said, a little flustered on the whole evening. She shut the door before rolling down the window.

"Oh, this is most definitely not it. I just wanted to have dinner with you before we begin our work together. Remember, you're a very special and talented man. I'll be in touch." The limousine rolled away.

The Death Map – 2014

Drew walked the police through Ashley's apartment for a third time, describing everything he had discovered when he first entered, leaving out his discovery in the basement. Drew figured it was best to keep the "death map," as Jen took to calling it, to themselves—at least for the time being. Jen had been sent back to her apartment before the police arrived. Drew figured it was the safest play, keep her out of the picture and reduce the risk that she would say something that tilted the police in the wrong direction. "We need to keep the police focused on the task of finding Ashley," he had told Jen before sending her up.

"So tell me again, how do you know Ashley?" A younger detective with a square jawline, excellent dark blond hair, and a thin beard said as he was gazing at the wedding photo of Bobby and Ashley.

Drew wasn't ready to tell the real story of why he was looking for Ashley, so he made up a story, with the intent of making it seem so bogus that everyone involved knew it was bullshit.

"I'm investigating a missing puppy case for a wealthy family from Boston's North End," Drew said before the detective cut him off.

"Yes, yes, I remember. As you say, a witness puts Ashley around the scene of its disappearance, in front of a café. Okay, say I believe your friggin' puppy story. Why are you so worried about Ashley? Isn't it possible that she could walk in at any moment? That the door was broken accidentally or as part of a completely separate event?"

Drew gave the detective a sly smirk.

"Look, you got me out here for a reason. You'll have to share with me sometime what dirt you have on my captain 'cause I can never get her to do anything. But here I am. On direct orders from the cap to be out here looking into your missing Ashley." The detective was a sturdy looking man with an athletic build, and Drew pegged him as a man who could handle himself in a scrum.

Drew shrugged his shoulders to the statement. He had, in fact, not known the captain, but he had made a call to a former client with ties to the political arena, a former candidate for senator of Massachusetts who had once been a selectman in Providence and was extremely close to the current mayor. The request to help find Ashley had propagated down to the captain from the mayor.

"You don't want to tell me, fine, but don't expect much from us," the detective said, waving his hand in the air as he turned toward the door. "C'mon, boys, let's get outta here." The other two officers in the room followed him as he exited the house. Drew walked out behind him.

"You will put out an APB for her?" Drew asked to the detective's back.

"Yeah, we can do that, and we'll send an officer by again later to check for her."

"Don't go. You can't leave!" a high-pitched screech belted down to the officers. Drew rolled his eyes. "Some crazy murderer is after her; you have to find her! The Charles!" Jen was yelling out from around the corner.

Stopped in his tracks, the detective gave Drew a look, tilting his head toward Jen and smirking while keeping his eyes on Drew.

"A murderer, you say?" Breaking his gaze on Drew, the detective began to walk toward Jen. Drew gave her a look that was clear. *Shut. The. Fuck. Up.* She caught it in time before the detective blocked Drew from her sight.

"I'm Detective Trenhon, who are you?"

Jen seemed hesitant now, pausing before answering, "Oh, I'm sorry. I don't even know what I'm talking about. I just am scared about Ashley, you know, her missing."

The detective stared at her for a moment. "What's your name? Do you have identification on you? How do you know Ashley?" Pulling his phone out, he began tapping around on it while waiting for answers.

"Ahh, my name is Jen Elision, and my license is upstairs in my apartment. I rent from Ash—"

"Jen, you don't have to answer him." Drew stopped her mid-sentence. "I think that's all the information you need." Walking up to Jen, Drew put his arm around her, pulling her close.

Ignoring Drew's interference, the detective asked, "What was that about the Charles, Jen?" He continued tapping notes onto his phone.

"Um, I . . . ." She trailed off, glancing between Drew and the detective uncertainly. "I am sorry, Detective. I can't help you."

Drew sighed with relief. He needed to keep the map under wraps until he had a chance to take a deeper dive into what it all meant. Keeping the circle of knowledge to as few people as possible was the best chance he had at figuring everything out, then when facts have been found and suspicion validated, he would loop in the authorities. *Well, not these authorities.* Drew would go to the people he trusted.

"We are not able to answer any more of your questions. I think it's best for everyone, Ashley included, if you put out your APB and start looking for her car," he said to the detective.

The detective analyzed the situation, staring at Jen, weighing his choices. "Okay." Shoving his phone into his pocket, he turned around abruptly, heading back to his unmarked cruiser.

"That was unexpected," Drew said out loud as the cruiser pulled away.

"What do you mean?"

"Well, I was sure that he was going to give us more of a hard time about your comments." Releasing Jen, Drew walked back toward the front door to Ashley's apartment. He pulled on the door, trying to shut it as tightly as he could.

"I'm sorry. I didn't mean to yell like that. I don't know what happened. I just saw them leaving and, all of a sudden, I was terrified."

Drew turned to her. "Hey, don't stress out about it. No harm done. It wouldn't have been the end of the world if this detective knew about the death map." Drew paused, looking at Jen before continuing. "He should be focused on finding Ashley, and what value would that map really provide him in that search?"

"You're right, you're right! That would probably just distract him." She shook her head from side to side. Drew could see that she was scared and anxious.

"Hey, why don't we go grab some lunch together? What's your favorite place around here to eat?"

Jen looked up, a smile broaching her cheeks. "Stonewalls!" she yelled out without any hesitation. "Can you give me like a half-hour? I have to explain to my customers that I won't be accessible today and redirect the feeds to some stored vids."

Drew didn't even want to ask.

Asset Unleashed – 2006

Raising his arm, Jack wiped his nose with his elbow. He'd been fighting a cold for what seemed like weeks, a typical head cold giving him a stuffy nose, sneezes, a slight headache, and muscle aches. Sitting up in bed, he looked at his phone: 4:27 a.m.

"Dammit." Jack had already been up three times previously, the last no more than thirty minutes earlier. He rolled restlessly in his bed back and forth, searching for a comfortable position, finally giving up and whipping off the covers.

"That's it. If I can't sleep I may as well do something." Stumbling into the bathroom, he looked at himself in the mirror. "Still handsome," he said to his reflection. Jack was a confident young man now, one hundred and eighty degrees from the torn, identity conflicted boy from just a year ago. He had just finished up his sophomore year with a perfect GPA, and his girlfriend was supposed to be coming over tonight, which always made him a bit restless. In reality, she was not his girlfriend, although he liked to think of her that way. They had only hung out a handful of times, but she took his virginity and made him feel like he was a king. She helped him accept who he was. Drying his face off, Jack headed into his living room, plopping himself on his couch.

Pulling out his phone, he stared, as he often did, at his text message history. Every time he connected with Elle, she would contact him on a different phone number. While this constant change protected Elle and her business dealings, it was frustrating for Jack, never being able to reach out to her when he wanted. Flipping his phone closed, he slipped it onto the coffee table.

"I'm going to tell her that I have to see her more often. I need to tell her how I feel." He was experiencing the kind of puppy love that normally one experienced in one's early teens. But Jack spent most of his life having little to no contact with the opposite sex. His mind was swollen with obsession, longing, lust, and questions. He tried to force her out of his mind, but it was useless. The only way he had found to keep Elle from occupying his life was to do busy work. During the semester, it was easy. He could dive into his studies and fade into another world where everything dissipated. Sitting up on the couch, he turned on his Xbox 360 game console, hoping that time in Cyrodiil could help him pass the time in Cambridge.

His phone buzzed on the coffee table. He was so engrossed in the game he almost didn't look. He put down the controller and reached toward the coffee table. "It's three thirty already," he exclaimed, half-surprised. He flipped open the phone, and there it was, a text from a number he had never seen before.

UNKNOWN NUMBER

NA – See you at 5, see you soon 😁
Today@3:27pm

It was Elle; she always seemed to flirt to him in her messages, and he liked that. Turning off the TV, he went straight to the bathroom to take a shower and clean up. After his shower, he tidied up around his apartment like a twenty-year-old bachelor would—straightening his sheets on his bed, putting dishes away, pushing piles of clothes into his closet, and giving surfaces a quick wipe down. When he sat back on the couch, his phone read 4:30 p.m. He would continue to watch his phone until Elle knocked on his door.

Knock, knock, knock. Jack was already waiting near the door. He had spotted the town car parked across the street and Elle being let out by her driver. He paced the apartment frantically.

"Stay cool. Stay cool," he told himself. Excitement drove his heart into a heavy, fast-paced rhythm.

Knock, knock, knock. He reached for the door and stopped. "One more time—I'll let her knock once more, keep her waiting as not to seem desperate." Jack stood, holding his breath, waiting for another round of knocks. His phone buzzed in his pocket. It was Elle. "Here" was all it said. Jack reached out and opened the door.

"Hey, sorry, I—"

Walking straight in, Elle kissed him mid-sentence.

"Mmm," she said after the kiss, tasting her lips seductively. "Let's go to the bedroom." She didn't waste any time to get to it. Jack froze, watching her walk into his apartment and toward the bedroom.

She was wearing glasses that took attention away from her off-colored eyes and a white button-down shirt with a thick three-inch collar that snuggly wrapped around her neck. The blouse rested untucked on her hips, just covering her waistline. Her navy-blue linen pants clung to her, hinting at her feminine features. Jack followed her into his bedroom; he watched her spin and land backward on his bed. She pulled up her legs and undid large zippers on the inside of her high-heeled shoes, aggressively pulling them off. With a glance to the left, Elle found a good spot for her shoes, throwing them toward the nearby wall.

"I need this, Jack. It's been a long day."

Pulling her knees up, Elle twisted them anxiously, seductively.

"Won't you come to bed?"

Jack stood in the doorway, peering into the room with a throbbing in his pants. This was faster, more aggressive sexual behavior than he had ever seen from Elle before. He liked it. It felt dirty, risky, and it peaked Jack's sensations. Stepping up to the bed, he looked down, his mind drifting off into fantasy.

Opening her legs, Elle pulled him to her, wrapping her legs firmly around his waist. She started a slow grind. Feeling moisture in his pants, he was already beginning to cum. She reached up, pulled her glasses off and threw them toward a nightstand, barely landing them. Her eyes glowed aggressively at him, and he felt as though he was the only man in the world. She unbuttoned her blouse completely, leaving the collar tightly bound around her neck. Her perfect C cup breasts fell out immediately as she expertly slipped off her bra. Jack was merely a leaf on the water, the river taking him wherever she wanted. She pushed him back hard until he fell into the wall, almost crashing through the plaster. She kicked out her feet at him.

"Pull them off," she demanded. Reaching down, he grabbed the ends of her pants and pulled. Her pants slipped right of with ease. Jack found that she was not wearing panties. He could smell her, a warm, tangy-sweet scent. She gestured for him to come in close. He peeled off his pants and boxers as he no longer resisted moving toward her. Looking at him, she kept eye contact as she moved her face toward his crotch and wrapped her lips around him, smoothly stroking with the sound of slight choking noises here and there. Lying back, Elle pulled him into her, guiding him inside; reaching up, she grabbed his hands and put them on her throat.

"Squeeze," she said as her fiery eyes pierced him.

Jack didn't need to be told twice. He wanted to choke her; it felt natural to him. He felt power and strength overtake his body, a familiar rush, similar to what he had felt before when he had taken a life. Elle could see in his eyes that he had traveled somewhere else now. As his mind began to go blank, the thrusting of his body became completely involuntary. Thought itself seemed to slip away from him. He was suddenly squeezing as hard as he could. He was going to kill her if he could, and he didn't even realize it. His body was overtaken by something else, some other lust.

Elle reached out, grabbing his backside, aiding his thrusts, encouraging him.

"Harder."

Her voice was rough and scratchy. Jack leaned in now, putting his weight into choking her, the stress of the action was showing at his seams. Showing his teeth, he breathed heavily. His senses were dulled from the emotion as the world around him was foggy and distant.

Coming inside her, he stopped thrusting, his body naturally controlling him without his mind catching up. Elle looked into his eyes. It was no longer sex for Jack; he was trying with all of his strength to snuff her out. She started to pull on his hands, grasping, scratching, clawing—she looked desperate—taking empty gasps for air. Jack didn't relent. The struggle seemed to add motivation to his pursuit. He could feel his arms, wrists, and fingers starting to sour and build soreness from the effort, but he shook it off and doubled down. Shaking her head by his grip around her neck, he picked her up and violently slammed her back down as if trying put more and more pressure on her airway. Closing her eyes, Elle then opened them, showing him the fear he lusted to see. This continued for minutes, Elle slapping at him and crying, as Jack tried to get a stronger and more dominant position on her. He grunted and winced, his face contorting from strain.

His hands became so tired that he could barely squeeze anymore; his arms felt tight and curled. He began to emerge from his fantasy, his eyes slowly returning to normal from anger and lust. He suddenly let go of her and stepped back, as if realizing what he was doing was wrong. Gasping, she moaned as she gulped air. Moving her hands up, she caressed her neck.

Jack looked at her in horror, a look of someone who just realized they made a massive mess of things. Reaching out, she grabbed his hands, looking deep into his fearful eyes, and pulled him back in close, thrusting him back inside of her and putting his hands back on her neck.

"Keep trying," she whispered into his ear. "Don't stop." Her hands slid down his back, each hand grabbed down again around his backside cheeks, she pulled, making him thrust. Jack couldn't comprehend what was going on. One moment he was certain she would hate him from being so physical, the next she was pleading for more. The monster again overtook him as he repeated the previous cycle, trying with all his strength to end her, although his hands had become tired, and it took longer to climax.

After they were done, Jack laid next to her, staring at the ceiling, his body in a complete state of euphoria, but it wasn't sex that brought him there.

How is she not dead? he thought as he felt his hands throbbing. He was certain he would kill her; he had put all his strength into crushing her throat. Spinning his head around, he looked at her, half-expecting a slap for what just took place. But she only rubbed his chest and told him how strong he was, and that they would have to do that again.

Elle's phone began to ring. "Arrg, terrible timing," she said. Rolling toward her Coach bag, she pulled out her phone. Wearing nothing but her blouse, still buttoned at the collar, she stood up and walked to the bathroom, holding Jack's underwear to her crotch. Getting up, Jack looked around the room.

"How did we make such a mess?" He scratched his head. One of the nightstands—not the one with Elle's glasses on it—was tipped over on its side. The lamp on it was now on the floor with the bulb in pieces. The bed was stripped of sheets, exposing a stained and dirty mattress. There was a fresh heel-sized hole in the drywall next to his bed. He must have stepped into the wall accidentally when he was dragging Elle about, attempting to get into a position with more strength.

"Hey." Elle popped back in the room with her blouse fully buttoned and started to put on the rest of her clothes. "I have to head out. Something has come up with work."

Jack didn't know what to say; he didn't have anything to say. His mind was reliving the time he killed Dean and the similar emotions that had overwhelmed him then. After she was dressed, she put her glasses back on and straightened her hairpin, which miraculously stayed in during everything that had happened. Sitting on the bed, Elle pulled her purse to her chest; reaching in, she pulled out a file.

"I need you to take care of something for me, Jack. We need to make use of your skills." She looked up at him, her eyes cold and focused. He could see she was all business now. "Are you ready to join the company?" she said before handing him the folder. "I need to know you're ready."

Jack looked at her, already knowing what she wanted him to do. The folder may as well have been transparent. Feeling excitement again growing in him, he immediately reached out for the file.

Pulling it away from him briefly, Elle said, "If you take this file, Jack, there is no way out. You either work for us or—" She paused for effect. "Or your name will be in a similar folder." Jack didn't even hesitate. He knew what he wanted, and it was no longer Elle.

He took the file.

Getting up, Elle went to kiss him, but he didn't pay her any attention. His eyes wide with greed, his focus was entirely on the file in his hand. His early ambitions to demand more time with Elle had vanished.

"Contact me on this number when you're done." She was waving the phone she had on her in the air. Not saying a word, Jack nodded, closing the door on her.

* * *

Elle stood a moment on the stairs outside of Jack's apartment and composed herself. When she returned to her car, her driver was already waiting with the door opened. Plopping onto the leather seat, she adjusted herself as the driver shut the door. Unbuttoning her collar, she flipped it up, revealing a three-inch metallic collar, perfectly manufactured to fit her throat, with a gel coating surrounding the metal. The collar was underneath the whole time, perfectly interlocked. She leaned over to the man sitting in the back with her. Reaching in, he helped her unlock the metal collar and pulled it off her. She then pulled out the fancy hairpin, revealing a four-inch shiv, placing it into the center console.

"Everything went as planned?" the older man asked. Elle threw the fake glasses she was wearing into the console and shut it.

"Yes," she replied. "The asset has been tasked. Your profile on him was accurate. He had no idea I was wearing a collar. Emotion clouded his senses." She spoke with a tone of pure business. The man continued to stare at her, looking for any sign of weakness or uncertainty. She was sure.

After a long period of silence in the car, he said, "Yes, very predictable. The boy has parental issues that we can leverage." Pausing, he rubbed his nose. "We needed a strong feminine influence to help break any of his emotional holdouts he might have aligned to his mother. It seems you played your part well, as always. We have to monitor him closely."

Elle looked out of the car window, her face stressed, lines appearing in her perfect skin. She hated this part of the job—no, she hated everything about the job.

You're Drooling – 2014

"Hahaha! You are drooling." Jen laughed aloud.

"Careful you don't choke," Drew quipped back. Jen was giggling as she took the next bite of her steak and cheese sub.

"Soo, what—mmm—do ya think?" Jen spoke as she chewed her food. Her brown eyes looked bright as she gave Drew a long, suggestive stare that made him uncomfortable. Jen had continued to show her interest in him; she was relentless.

Looking away, Drew said, "Well, I have to admit this is one of the best steak and cheese subs I've ever had, although I can't imagine that it's any good for yah." Drew had ordered a large steak 'n cheese with mayo, grilled onions, mushrooms, and peppers, with extra American cheese, lettuce, and tomato. Using sliced sirloin meat, the cook had taken extra care to chop up the steak on the grill into smaller bits that blended especially well with the melted cheese. Drew was a fan.

"I fucking told you it was the best!" Jen yelled out triumphantly. On the ride over, Drew had given her a hard time that there was no way he would find the best steak 'n cheese sub in Rhode Island in a dingy diner.

"All right, relax. I'll give it to you. This is a great sub. Maybe, I said maybe, even the best I have had. I'll have to come back again before I can give it that title. Consistency is what makes things great."

"Hey, J!" A man carrying a slight belly, wearing a dark gray sports coat, tight jeans, and black square-rimmed glasses shouted as he squeezed himself into the bench next to Jen. Drew got the feeling the glasses were for aesthetics only and not an aid for seeing.

"Who's this guy?" he said frankly, pointing to Drew. Jen slapped his hand down.

"This, Jeffrey, is my newest friend. Drew. Drew meet Jeff, my very first and longest paying customer." Drew reached out his hand to be polite, offering to shake, but the gesture went unanswered.

"Ahh, a new friend, huh? Well, I'm not quite sure I like him, Jen. I think he's too old for you." Jeff spoke as if Drew wasn't even there.

"Although, I have seen you with worse. He does have a bit of a ruggedly handsome look to him, doesn't he? I see why you like." Jeff spoke with heavy mannerisms, waving his hands about, even reaching across the table to poke Drew's chest. "And muscley. Okay, I like him." Drew had a look on his face that was a mix between *What the fuck?* and *thanks.*

"Tell me, Drew, are you going to be spending the evening with our mutual friend here?"

Straightening his shoulders, Drew cleared his throat, bringing his fist to his mouth. "I don't think so. I was hoping I would be heading back to Boston today."

Jeff twirled the ice in the water glass a waitress had filled up for him. "Well, that's unfortunate. I think I would have enjoyed watching you rail on Jen. That would have made for interesting TV tonight."

"Ahem." Drew choked on his water, spitting back half a mouth full into his glass.

This guy seemed more and more obtrusive by the minute. *No wonder Jen is having men problems in her life.* He shook his head, detesting the comment.

"Jen, Jen, my dear. It's been fun as always. Be careful with this brawny man. He doesn't seem to want to play." With that, Jeff stood up. Taking his glass with him, he strolled past the diner bar and into the employee-only section.

"I'm sorry about that. He can come off a bit obnoxious. But he's actually very sweet. And he's gay, if you couldn't tell."

"I suspected as much. Your friend had some flamboyant hand twirls that mostly gave it away. It's curious that he's your longest customer. I mean, I imagine some of the appeal about being your customer is seeing you in, ah, in ah—a sexual way." Drew moved his hands up and down in an hourglass motion to outline her curves.

"It's actually a story. I used to work here. Jeff's been there since I started cutecamjen.com. He was my manager at the time, and when I told him what I was doing for work when I decided to stop here, you know, he promised that he would support me for as long as I did it." Looking down, Drew shook his head again as if to shake off the uncomfortable nature of the conversation.

"You can stay with me tonight. I would turn the cameras off for you. And I mean on my couch," Jen said honestly.

"Ha, I don't sleep on couches. I'm not sure what I'm going to do tonight. I was hoping that I would be home by now." Sliding his hand on the table for his glass, Drew sucked down a couple of gulps of his iced tea.

"You can't leave tonight. You have to help find Ashley, and you can't do that from Boston."

"I'm not sure I can do that here either. I don't have very much to go on, and the last place I know where Ashley was, was in Boston yesterday at the city morgue." Looking up at the ceiling, he ran a hand through his hair.

"Why was she at the morgue? In Boston?" A puzzled look stretched across Jen's face.

"She had signed in to view a body. That's what has me here in Providence to begin with. I was trying to track her down."

They both sat in silence for what seemed like five minutes, contemplating where Ashley could be., what it was that she was involved with.

"Okay, I'll stay in Providence tonight. But you're going to need to guide me to all and any of Ashley's hangout spots. Where she goes to the gym, shops for groceries, has a drink. Where is her favorite food spot, any place you can think where she might be. Then I'll head back to Ashley's home in the morning and give it one more walk-through with fresh eyes to be sure I didn't miss anything."

Jen clapped her hands together in excitement. "Yes! I really like that we'll be hanging out! I'm going to use the girls' room. Don't go anywhere without me."

While Jen was in the bathroom, Drew put his hand in the air to gesture the waitress.

"What can I do for ya, sir?" she said as she was approaching.

Drew made a signature motion with is hand. "Ah, can we get the check, please?"

"Sir, you are all set. Jeff said that your meal is on the house and that you can come back anytime." With that, she kept on walking past. Coming out of the bathroom a few moments later, Jen motioned toward the door with a hop in her step.

"Let's blow this joint! I know the first place we should look."

Jumping in the car, she slammed the door with so much force Drew was surprised the windows didn't shatter.

"Jesus, take it easy there." Shaking his head, Drew glared at Jen, as he turned the car over. "Where are we headed?"

Jen was already signaling him to pull right out of the parking lot. "That way!" Drew followed her directions, and just as he pulled onto the road, she said, "Okay, here, this right. Now!" Jen led him out of the diner parking lot, onto the road, only to pull into the parking lot of a Shaw's grocery store, which was connected to the diner.

"Why did I have to pull out of the diner. The parking lots are connected!"

His question went unanswered.

"This is where Ash shops for food. What do we do now?"

Drew pulled into a spot toward the back of the lot, turning the car off. Pulling out his phone, he looked to see if he could find that photo of Ashley.

"Is this a recent photo of Ashley?" Drew spun the phone toward Jen. She squinted a bit.

"Mmmm." She leaned in. "It's her, but she's not brunette anymore. I don't think I have ever known her with brunette hair. She's blond now."

"Damn, this won't work well then. You don't happen to have any recent photos of her?"

A big "of course I do" smile broached her face.

"I sure do. I'm Facebook friends with Ash." She reached into her pocket, pulled out her phone, and within three touches had Ashley's face blowing up the screen. Taking the phone, Drew analyzed the image. The picture was her, but the dirty blond hair was enough to make him look twice. Without knowing what to look for, he might have walked into her and not recognized her.

"This is great. Is there any way to send me a copy?" He handed the phone back to Jen, and within a few seconds, his phone buzzed.

"I texted you her photo."

"This is what we're going to do at these places. We walk in and politely ask any employee we see if they have seen this woman. Simply tell them that she has not been seen recently, and her family is worried. Got it?"

Puckering her lips out, Jen nodded her head. Together, they strolled into the market, wandering from employee to employee without any affirmative responses. Having spent a full hour walking, asking employees to give the photo a good look. They seemed to get the same response, everyone gave the pic the same squinty look, jogging their memories, a faint sense of familiarity by almost everyone. Unfortunately, Ashley had that type of look—a charismatic smile, familiar face, soft eyes, and a girl next door look.

Oddly enough, as they left the store, Drew found himself starting to open up more to Jen. He caught himself flirting back with her. *Whatever, she's a very fun woman. She's an adult, for Christ's sake,* he thought at times, his barriers crumbling. Picking up on this change, Jen adjusted her pursuit, becoming subtler with her attack, but steady and persistent.

Her car door slammed again, and as they entered the car again, Drew looked over at her.

"Oops, sorry." She dragged out the sorry as she said it.

"Please don't slam the door, and just when I was starting to think you were all right!" Drew winked as he said it, thinking, *I have to stop. What would Lizzy think?*

Separating Drew from his thoughts, Jen blurted out, "That was fun, but . . . I feel like we're in the same position we were, like, two hours ago? Is this how your PI work usually is? 'Cause that seems a little boring." Kicking off her shoes from the heels, Jen put her feet up on the dash, pulling up her yoga pants and showing her glowing skin.

"Ahh, yes. Yes, very boring. It's usually worse than this. You typically don't have someone to talk to. Where are we off to now?" Rubbing her toes for a moment, Jen leaned back, making sure that her perky breasts blossomed visibly against her thin shirt.

"There's her gym, Papi's Bar, her work—but I don't really know where that is. What about trying to reach her family?" Jen said triumphantly. "She probably saw her shit was jacked and decided to stay with family. That's what I would do. Or with friends, I guess." Drew had already thought about visiting her work and family but was confident the police would be able to make more effective calls there. He had on good authority, should anything about Ashley come in on the PD side, he would get a call.

"Let's leave the work and family to the police. That's standard procedure for them. It's probably best if we keep looking where they won't."

Jen nodded, again affirming Drew's thoughts. "That sounds like a good plan. If we go on the best route, I think we could hit up her gym and her friend Shelly's house. Shelly is a stay-at-home mom so there's a good bet she's home. Then we could go to her bar slash late-night food spot at Papi's Bar."

After a series of lefts and rights and near accidents caused by Jen's penchant for giving turning directions at the very last second, Drew found himself in front of a kickboxing gym.

"She kickboxes?" Drew said aloud.

"Yeah, and she is like, so hot too when she does it. I came a few times with her. Oh, and it's no joke." Jen was punching the air from a prone position. "Kickboxing is as serious of a workout as it gets. She has literally been coming here for twenty years or something. Okay, maybe not twenty, but a long time. She met her husband here, and the instructor is a very good friend. Totally gay, just to warn you." Drew gave her a look. He didn't need to be warned about gay men.

"Please don't do that anymore. It doesn't matter to me."

As they entered the studio, a flamboyant tanned man approached them. He had long dark brown hair, a scruffy graying beard, and walked with a little hip shake that seemed telling.

"Hello, ahhhhh, my cute Jen!" he screamed as soon as he saw Jen. "Who is this handsome man you have brought me?" He pointed at Drew, then wiggled his finger, pointing from Drew's feet to head and back down before extending his hand. Reaching out, Drew gave him a firm handshake. "My name is Juan, and I own this establishment. Are you looking for a dojo?"

Drew picked up an accent but couldn't quite place it, although he knew it was of Spanish origin.

"Drew. Nice to meet you, Juan, and no I'm not here about the dojo. We're here about Ashley."

A concerned look crossed his face. "Ahh, my dearest Ashley. You know, she has been my favo-rito student. But I am worried. She has been making crazy requests recently and ever since her husband went missing, she has not been to a single class. I have called her a few times, and no response. Please tell me you have good news?"

Drew gave Jen a look to stay mute. "Well, it's not bad news. I'm working with local law enforcement to help locate Ashley. It's no big deal. A break-in was reported by Jen here, and we wanted to do our best to reach her and discuss it."

Juan had his hand to his mouth, aghast. "Is she okay? Was there blood? Did it look like a fight happened? Trust me, you would know. She is feisty as hell that one." Coiling up, Juan gave the air a fierce punch, while spitting out: "PAAA!"

Drew was puzzled, not sure why everyone associated with this dojo liked to punch the air. "No, no, nothing like that. In fact, we doubt at all that she was home during the break-in. When was the last time you saw her?" Drew reached into his back pocket to pull out his notepad when Jen grabbed his hand.

"I got it!" Smiling, Jen flashed her phone. She had been recording the entire conversation.

"You know it's illegal to record conversations in some states without telling all parties present that they're being recorded?" Drew said, looking at her. She glanced at Juan, putting the phone out in plain sight.

"You are being recorded, Juan. There, now that's outta the way." She looked at Drew with a "You happy?" head nod. Drew pulled out his notepad anyway and began to take notes despite Jen.

"Well, let me see. She did come in once last week for sure. But it was strange. She was not here for class, no, no, no. She came early last Sat—yes it was Saturday—before I had any classes. She asked if I had any weapons."

Interest perked, Drew looked up from his note pad.

"Weapons? What kind of weapons?"

Juan looked at Jen uncertainly. "Oh, ahh, you know, just normal weapons."

Drew shrugged. "I don't know. Tell me what are normal weapons?"

Juan took a step back. "Ahh, I am not sure if I should be telling you this."

Drew took a step forward. "Ashley might be in trouble, and any information you have may help us help her. Do you understand?"

Juan nodded. "I can't keep secrets. Everybody knows that. She wanted brass knuckles. Which I don't have. So she asked if I had a switchblade. Something easily concealable."

After a brief moment, Drew raised his eyebrows.

"No! Of course not. I don't have switchblades. The only thing I have is pepper spray, and she took that."

Drew scribbled more notes into his pad. "Did she happen to say why she needed these weapons?"

Juan shook his head to the question before speaking. "No, no. I asked what was going on. But she said it was best if I didn't know anything."

Drew bounced his pen upside down for a moment on his notepad. "You said she made a crazy request recently. Can you tell me about that?"

Juan gave him a puzzled look for a second before yelling out, "Her asking for weapons is crazy!"

Drew figured as much but never wanted to lead an interviewee to an answer. "Thanks, Juan, this is helpful," Drew said as he presented his hand for a farewell shake. Juan reached out with both hands, grabbing Drew's.

"When you find Ashley, please tell her to come see me." Juan hugged Jen and gave her a single kiss on both cheeks. "Love you, Jen." They turned around to leave when the door swung open.

"Fancy finding you two here." Detective Trenhon walked into the dojo, confident as ever. "I had a feeling that our paths would cross again." He gave Jen a not-too-discreet once over, pausing at her chest before continuing his gaze down. "You're in different attire. I like it; it suits you. Do you really have eleven thousand followers?" He had looked her up, and what he had found had changed the detectives' attitude toward her. He was acting demeaning now. "You know, I bet there are a bunch a pervs out there who've recorded everything you've ever done. I'm sure I could find it, and well, find something on you to put you away." He was playing the bad cop now. He wasn't here for the dojo; he was here for Jen. As soon as he found out she was a cam girl, he immediately pegged her as vulnerable. That was information he could use to push her into telling him the story.

"Jen, go to the car," Drew said, handing out his keys to her. He wanted to put a stop to this before the conversation went further into disarray. Drew had seen these conversations before. Hell, he had been the detective pushing buttons, threatening, manipulating would-be witnesses or suspects.

"We will talk soon, Jen. I guarantee I'll be seeing you." The detective winked.

Once Jen was gone, Drew said, "I know what you're doing," straight-faced.

"You know, I have a class starting very soon. I would appreciate if this conversation no longer took place here." A nervous Juan motioned toward the door.

Ignoring Juan completely, Trenhon said, "What am I trying to do, Drew?"

"Ahh, wait that's right. You *were* a big shot detective. I guess you know exactly what I'm doing. My friggin' job!"

Drew really didn't have a response. He was right, in a way.

"Tell me, Drew, what do you know about all this? Really? You tell me so I don't have to embarrass that whore out there more than she already does to herself."

Drew felt his face start to burn up. When he was a child that feeling was an indication of a fiery temper tantrum sure to follow.

"Jen is not a whore. She happens to be quite pleasant," Drew responded calmly.

"You can watch her poop! On the internet!" Trenhon put his hand on his head at the outrageousness of it. "What the f-ahk?" The detective raised his voice, shaking his hands to emphasize how crazy the idea was.

"She makes more money than you do, bub. Everyone does what they can to provide themselves with some financial security. She isn't hurting anyone. She isn't breaking any laws." Drew began to take a few steps toward the door. The detective stepped in front of him.

"That doesn't mean I won't use it to get information from her. You know as well as I do that some part of her knows. She friggin' knows it's taboo. And that, right there, gives us all we need to open up that can." He made a can opening motion with his hands.

Looking him in the eyes, Drew said, "If you want to keep your financial security, I suggest you stay focused on finding Ashley and leave that girl alone. I can assure you she has no information that will help you." He didn't like doing it, and he was unsure if the detective would call the bluff, but Drew had to try. He was certain, even with his friend, that there was no way he could have this man fired or reprimanded in any way.

"I wondered if you would throw that card. You got dirt on my captain. Did you date her?" Trenhon's mood changed, from combative to friendly, like they went way back, jock buddies from high school. Tapping Drew on his chest a few times, he said, "Ahh, yeah, you and the cap were—no—*are* doing it! Shh-ite. I knew it. I'm sort of jealous, man."

Figuring his comments were positive reinforcement that Trenhon would leave Jen alone, for now at least, Drew said, "I have to go," quickly and marched out, thinking it best to leave Trenhon wondering.

Training Day – 2006

Jack opened the envelope slowly, being careful with a blade as to not accidentally slice any contents. Spreading open the envelope, he could see two thick documents inside and a strange wire with two handles. Slowly, he tilted it over his coffee table until the contents slipped out. The first document was a welcome letter.

Welcome! You have been selected and recruited into one of the most lucrative and successful organizations in this world. All of our 3002 employees are multi-millionaires and are often permitted to pursue their passions in any way they like. This package contains information about your first assignment. Before you proceed, there are some ground rules.

New Hire Rules – 1BG2

1. *Your employment contract is for life. Only the organization decides when you will no longer provide value, only then allowing you to retire.*

2. *You are never to share any details about your employment with us—to anyone. Breaking this rule would result in the termination of yourself, your family, your friends, and anyone else who you may interact with who the company deems necessary.*

3. *Your recruitment has been in the works for many years. From our identifying your skill sets, to your college scholarships, and finally your acceptance into the organization. We*

expect this effort to be rewarded with loyalty. Any sign to the contrary will result in immediate termination.

4.   Any and all documentation you receive from us must be destroyed by incineration immediately after you have completed the reading. You must memorize all content. Failure or inability to do so will result in termination.

5.   Your position requires you to maintain an athletic body type. You must be able to manage your own endurance, weight, strength, and stamina so that you could compete with the most serious of athletes. Failure will result in termination.

6.   Your position requires you to develop more advanced skill sets over the next 2 years with a schedule of your training to be sent in a subsequent package. This training will include self-defense, weapons training, flight training, dive certification, forensic science, and criminal justice courses, and more as you become specialized in what you do. Failure to complete and maintain these skill sets, and remain qualified for your role, will result in termination.

Jack sat down on his couch, re-reading the welcome letter, wondering what he had got himself into.

Who the hell are these people?

He pondered the word "termination" and how distant it felt to him. Like any other twenty-something-year-old, the thought of one's own death seemed unreal, an aura of immortality seemed to glow around the thought of it. Even though he had caused the immediate death of someone, the "it's not going to happen to me" attitude was there. Flipping the card on the floor, he pulled the next one towards his face.

Joseph Trainer—3 Valley Street, Manchester, NH 03101

Target Info

Desc: Age – 22, Height – 6'3", Weight – 220lbs, Hair – bald, Eyes – brown, Skin – white, Race – white
Marital Status: single
Occupation: unemployed

Package Contents

Item 1: Garrote

You must terminate your target without alerting anyone. You have been supplied with a garrote, one of the most effective assassination weapons ever conceived. Simply hold one handle in each hand, loop the double wires over a victim from behind, and pull in and toward your chest. Many will exchange the handles from one hand to the other so that the right hand is holding the handle on the left side and the left hand holding the other. This hold provides better leverage for tightening the garrote. The garrote can be used effectively on victims up to 3 times your own weight with minimal noise.

Your victim is an amateur MMA fighter who participates in many underground competitions in the New England area, making your task difficult should your victim gain any advantage. We do not typically provide you with any information on the reason for your assignments, but in this case, we are making an exception. Joseph is an employee who failed to maintain one or more of the conditions of his employment with the organization, resulting in this termination assignment.

Your target will be at the provided address in 2 days, at approximately 11:45 PM. We expect him to be alone and to enter the building from the back. This will be your opportune time. As he approaches the building through the unlit parking lot, you will have plenty of coverage between parked cars. If you suspect or see anyone else, you are to abort and re-attempt at a later date.

Contingency

There is no contingency plan. At this stage of employment, your failure in following directions will result in termination.

Bonus

Successful: $20,000

All other outcomes: TERMINATION

Picking up the garrote from the table, Jack noted the handles were smooth and ergonomic for his fingers, aiding a more comfortable grip. Connecting the handles was a thick guitar-string-like wire. Jack tried both methods of holding the handles that were suggested, settling on the cross-handle configuration. He practiced all night, wrapping the wire around random objects in his house—pillows, stools, lamps, nothing was safe. Anything that he could swing it around was fair game.

Jacked up on anticipation of his first assignment, he paced around his apartment all night. He wanted to leave right away to get started, maybe watch the parking lot for the next couple of days, but he decided against that. *Best not to raise any suspicion or give anyone the chance of seeing me before the kill.* He re-read the assignment document again and again, making sure he could recite it blindfolded. Finally, he put the document in his metal kitchen sink, opened up the kitchen window, and placed a small fan blowing air out of his apartment. Placing the other documents in the sink, he lit them on fire with wooden matches. The papers immediately burst into flames and disappeared within seconds—coated with some sort of accelerant, no doubt. There was less smoke than he had expected.

* * *

Elle looked at her buzzing phone. The contact read J-team2.

"Yes," she answered in her normal business tone.

"Sir. Ah, I mean ma'am," A nervous voice sputtered on the other side.

"Never mind formalities. Give me your report," she responded as if she didn't have the time to deal with these people.

"Yes, ma'am. Of course. The target remained in his apartment all evening, and most of this morning, practicing his technique with the weapon. He has also memorized the program and destroyed the documents as instructed."

Elle looked to a wall in her office, a wall dedicated to Jack. Strings extended from one side to the other, a timeline of Jack's life with major events highlighted and notes tacked to the wall.

Elle was a recruitment specialist, handler, and point of contact for the organization. The wall was her way of organizing so that she could visualize everything about that recruit. She would likely keep up Jack's profile for the next two years while he worked through his training assignments. In fact, all assignments over the next two years were considered low-value assignments where his capture or failure would have little to no impact on the company. Their purpose was to introduce tools and techniques to him in a manageable yet challenging way.

"Tell me, have you scrubbed the film from my visit yet from your recordings?" Elle always asked them to destroy any evidence of her being in Jack's apartment. Even though she knew it was standard procedure for them to do so, somehow asking them made the importance of completing that procedure higher in her mind.

"Yes, ma'am. We deleted it yesterday as soon as management reviewed the interaction, and adhering to your instructions." Elle took a deep breath, cringing at the thought of her actions.

"Good. Keep up the good work."

The entire apartment above Jack no longer held any students. The students who lived there when Jack moved in were offered a new, nicer residence and cash to move out. It was now rented out as an operation of the organization. A monitoring team was tasked to record, listen, and watch everything that Jack did in his apartment. This was standard on all recruits in their first two years of service, possibly longer depending on the types of assignments that they received. For Jack, and the type of work he was to perform, it was likely that he would be monitored his entire career. To minimize exposure of any other employee in the organization, Elle would remain his point of contact for as long as his career lasted.

Number 6 – 2008

Jack was sitting in a black leather reclining chair, sipping his morning coffee and staring out of his top-floor three-thousand-square-foot apartment. He was no longer in Boston but living in a quaint city a little over an hour south of Boston. The last two years had been busy, to say the least. Having completed his degree at MIT, he took a job with a front company named Falcon Consultants that had been set up under fraudulent paperwork. He didn't care. It didn't matter who started the company with a seven-figure salary right out of college, and, with performance-based bonuses, Jack had more money than he needed.

He blew lightly, hissing at his coffee to cool it down. Most mornings, he would be downstairs at this time, in the building's gym, getting a quick morning workout in before his day, but today was special, a day he waited for excitedly. He felt like a child on Christmas morning, staring at presents, wondering what wonder lay beneath. About six times over the past two years, Jack would get a package delivered to him, a small box, approximately twelve by twelve by four inches. This was one of those mornings. The courier had come and rang his bell at 4:30 a.m. to deliver it.

Putting his coffee down on the table, he slid the box closer to himself. The envelope was sealed with a special white tape, making it tougher and more difficult to open than normal packing tape. He had opened four identical to it, and one, his first assignment, had been packaged in an envelope. With a red box cutter, he gently slit the tape. As he pulled up the folds of the box, he had a feeling of wonder and tingles. Excitement stirred his imagination; he loved getting new missions. Inside the box was a stack of pictures, the first a picture of a woman in her late thirties with a fair smile, average features, dirty blond hair, and a homely smile. Taking the pictures out, he placed them on the table. Behind the picture was a document printed on board paper:

Kat Bundell – 686 Pine Street, Wellesley, MA 02481

Target Info

Desc: Age – 41, Height – 5'9", Weight – 138lbs, Hair – blond, Eyes – brown, Skin – white, Race – white
Marital Status: Married – 2 Children (Beth and Harrison, 2 and 4 years of age)

Occupation: Chief Operating Officer

Employer: Pic Tech Enterprises

Spouse: James Bundell

Spouse Desc: Age – 44, Height – 6'1", Weight – 189lbs, Hair – brown, Eyes – brown, Skin – white, Race – white
Household Gross Income: $458,200

Package Contents

Item 1: Chloroform jar - assumed dose for knockout of spouse within 60 seconds. Apply to rag immediately prior to use and cover both nose and mouth for best effect.

Item 2: Spouse workout clothes

Item 3: Suicide Letter

Item 4: DNA prevention kit, razor, bleach wipes.

Your target must be terminated within the next 2 weeks. It should appear to be a murder-suicide. The husband James ideally will murder the family, including children, with a kitchen knife prior to cutting his own wrists. Item 1 includes the necessary amount of chloroform to disable the spouse. The clothes included belong to the spouse, and you should be able to fit in them. It is suggested that you kill the target and the family on a weekday at 5:15 PM. The spouse should arrive at 5:25 PM. On his arrival, disable the spouse and change him into the bloodied clothes. The spouse must be awake for 40 minutes before slitting his wrists to allow the chloroform to become more difficult to detect with standard tests. A suicide note has been written and will match the spouse's handwriting. Leave note on kitchen counter.

Contingency

Should there be a failure in proposed plan, masking the murder as a failed burglary attempt should be your contingency.

Bonus

Successful: $600,000

Successful - Contingency: $300,000

All other outcomes: $-200,000

Putting the document down, Jack pulled up a piece of cardboard that was covering more contents of the package. Immediately below the cardboard was a small envelope containing the suicide letter, and below that was a Styrofoam box insert that had two square sections. The left side contained workout shorts, shirt, and socks that were neatly folded and vacuum sealed in a plastic bag. On the right side was a small square with a jar of liquid wrapped in a rag.

Probably from the garage of the Bundell's, he thought. In case something went wrong, it was best to keep evidence contained to the Bundell's property. Picking up the pictures again, he leaned back in his chair and took a long look at the children. He had never done kids before. He thought he might have some sort of emotional friction to the idea. But he felt "meh" about it. *They look like anyone else, just smaller*, he thought.

Picking up the box, he noticed another letter on the table.

"How did I miss you?"

The letter was different than any other he had received. It was written on smaller notepad paper, and handwritten.

Jack, to continue employment with our firm, it is a requirement that you take a wife. Please begin courting as soon as possible.

The short note was signed E. He leaned back, thinking about the demand. *A wife? A fucking wife?* He had not dated, been with, or even attempted to be with a woman since Elle delivered him his first mission package.

"Why do I need a fucking wife?" Crumpling up the paper, he tossed it in the trash, flustered by the demand.

"Fuck me, no, fuck you," he yelled, this time pointing to the trash can. How could they ask him to find a wife knowing who he was, what he was?

Jack paced around his apartment for most of the day. To refuse would result in loss of employment, which in his company meant he would end up on someone else's coffee table in a tightly packaged box. Picking up his phone, he sent a message to Elle, asking for a reason why. He felt betrayed, powerless, like a chump, as if he were owned. Frustration made him want to hunt Elle down and make her face the knife. He took a few deep breaths; letting his anger subside, he allowed his frustration to drift away. Then he tried to work through it logically.

They have always wanted me to appear normal. Go to college. Get my degree. Join a company and live a normal-looking life. This is just another aspect of that. He convinced himself that it was for the better. Maybe they had information that his real identity was at risk and that recruiting a wife would help reduce that risk. *God Damn-it.*

Bar Prep – 2014

"Tell me, what do you think about our customers?" A short man with blond hair and blue eye asked as he swayed back and forth on a spinning bar stool.

"Um, well, I can't really say. To be honest, I've never been in here before," Lizzy responded nervously. The man looked down at his notepad. It was more of a nervous motion than anything else. He was just as nervous as Lizzy was being interviewed for her first bartending job.

"Uh, that's okay. Describe to me how you might handle a rude customer. Our customers are generally pretty good, but every once in a while, we can get someone in here that's a bit out of control. How would you handle that?"

Lizzy quickly racked her mind of any similar scenarios that she'd experienced waitressing. "One time, while waitressing, I had this guy that got really handsy with me." The man gave her a questioning look. Picking up on the response, Lizzy smoothly went into detail without him having to ask. "Yeah, I was carrying dishes, bussing them back to the kitchen, when this creep of a guy grabbed my arm as I was walking by." Lizzy gave an arm wave motion.

"It was lucky I didn't smash a bunch of dirty plates all over the place. He pulled me in, uncomfortably close to him, then with his other hand, he reached around and copped a feel of my, ah, my backside.

"I slapped his hand so hard away from me. Looked him straight in the eyes and said aloud so others could hear, 'Sir, your wife likes to eat in here with you on Sundays. Does she know you're also a pervert?' He looked me in the eyes with a 'you bitch' sort of look. After that, he didn't even look at me the rest of the night. In fact, I never saw him in there with his wife again."

The man interviewing her nodded. "I like that you stand up for yourself."

"I sure do. I try not to let anyone bully me around. My dad always says that the best way to handle someone disrespectful is to call them out publicly about it. Because even the lowest, most revolting people understand right from wrong. When given a choice of exposing that immoral behavior in a social context, typically they will take the high road to avoid ridicule."

The man just stared at Lizzy, a somewhat blank look on his face. "Oh, uh, yeah, I guess that makes sense," he finally blurted out. He looked back down at his notepad of pre-written questions, almost halfway through them.

"What would you do if you knew that you were going to be more than an hour late to work?"

Lizzy was quick to respond. "I would call in, as soon as possible."

"That's good. You wouldn't just leave us hanging then?" he responded rhetorically before continuing. Setting aside his notepad, he said, "Well, I think you would be a good fit here. You would be working as a waitress here every Thursday through Saturday night. Our waitresses typically average thirty dollars an hour." He was padding the number a little bit. But to Lizzy, anything more than what she was currently pulling in as a breakfast waitress making less than ten dollars an hour would be awesome.

"But I can get you behind the bar one day per weekend as a floating bartender and barback. You'll get to learn how to make some drinks, how to keep up with the customers, and it pulls in more money, so all the girls around here like it."

Lizzy really liked the sound of that. The thought of bartending was causing her eyes to widen with excitement. Trying to sound normal, she said, "That sounds great."

"Awesome, welcome aboard!" the man said, stretching his hand across the bar toward her.

"Janet, our lead bartender, arrives for work in about ten. Why don't you hang out until then, and she can give you a walk-through of the place."

Lizzy nodded her head eagerly. "Definitely, I can't wait to meet her and get started."

"All right, well, uh, on your first day next week, make sure to bring in with you two forms of identification, and be prepared to fill out some paperwork. Tax stuff, ya know," he said as he stood up.

"Oh, yeah, no problem. I had to do something similar for the job I'm at currently." *He is an awkward sort of guy,* Lizzy thought. This part of the job he seemed not to enjoy, the people managing part.

"Great. Just hang out here until Janet gets in then, and, uh." He paused awkwardly as he was backing away from her. "Yeah, so again, welcome aboard."

He walked off toward the back, leaving Lizzy alone at an empty bar while other employees were flipping chairs down from the tables they had been stacked on the night before. The restaurant was small. The main dining room had about ten tables, which Lizzy guessed could serve between thirty and forty people.

The bar was long and U-shaped, with a long stretch of beer taps on the left side farthest from the entrance to the bar. This was where Lizzy was sitting as she waited for Janet to show up. She was excited. *A new job!* she cheered internally. She really wanted to get out from early morning breakfast shifts, as well as have the opportunity to make more money.

Pulling out her phone, she opened up her texting app and responded to the message she had waiting for her.

TOMMY

Tommy – Hey Sexy! How did the interview go? Ping me when you get this! 😄
Today@11:38am

Awesome!!! I GOT THE JOB!
Today@11:44am

Tommy *is typing...*

As Lizzy was waiting for Tom to finish his message, an older girl walked in, letting the door slam behind her. Looking up, Lizzy tucked her phone into her pocket, not wanting to seem busy on it. The older girl was wearing large leopard print sunglasses. She had black hair that was tightly braided and pulled back, wrapped into a bun on the back of her head. Lizzy thought she looked confident. She was wearing white jeans with a loose-fitting beige t-shirt that had an orange graphic stretched across the front. The shirt had an extra wide neck hole, so large that it exposed her left shoulder while her right remained covered. A dark jacket was draped over her left elbow. She had taken it off as she entered the restaurant.

"Hey, girl!" Reaching out, she pleasantly squeezed Lizzy's

153

shoulder as she walked by and rounded the open end of the bar. Lizzy was a little taken aback by it; she rarely met anyone that friendly.

"Hi, I'm Lizzy. Are you Janet?" Stopping, the girl looked at Lizzy, pulling off her sunglasses, looking puzzled.

"Who the fuck is Janet? There ain't no Janet here, honey." A rush of uncertainty flooded her at the girls' response, and her nervous posture magnified.

"Ah, I—uh," Lizzy sputtered.

"A-ha!" The girl started laughing, grabbing Lizzy's right hand that was nervously cupping her left on top of the bar.

"Girl, you should see your face! Yes, damn right I'm Janet. I couldn't help myself, you laid that up there. You had such a smooth look on you I had to throw a rock in that pond."

Lizzy tried to play it off cool with a couple of forced laughs. "Gary said that you would give me a tour of the restaurant today, before you start your shift?"

Putting her stuff under the bar, Janet looked back at Lizzy. "Of course he did. He always has me giving the tours to the newbs. What did you say your name was? Liz?"

"Lizzy—well, actually it's Elizabeth, but my friends and family call me Lizzy."

Janet gave Lizzy another inspecting look while she pulled baggies off the beer taps. "All right, babe, why don't you wiggle that cute ass of yours around this bar and let's get to it."

Janet walked her through the bar, showing her where all the glasses were located, the sinks, trash, and the organization of the coolers under the bar. Janet then walked her through the dining room, giving her a diagram of all the tables and their numbers.

"You'll wanna get real familiar with this layout," she said, pointing to the tables. Lastly, she took Lizzy through the kitchen area and employee-only section of the restaurant, showing her how to clock in and out at the start and end of shifts, where to pick up paychecks, and where to look up her weekly schedule and table assignments when they were posted.

"We typically will have one or two people in the dining room all day up through the dinner rush. On weekends, I've been needing some help behind the bar, so you might be helping me out there every once in a while."

Lizzy nodded, not confident to discuss more about the schedule, just accepting of whatever she was given at this point.

Turning a corner of the kitchen near the dishwasher station, they stopped. There was a skinny older guy with long hair and a goatee beard already washing dishes left over from the bar the previous night. He looked up, noticing Lizzy and Janet were standing there, and gave a wry smile.

"That's Mark. Do yourself a favor and stay away from that guy. He's bad news." She gave Lizzy a serious look. "Got it?"

Lizzy didn't need to be told twice. "Don't worry. I don't think I'll have any problems keeping clear of him." Shaking her head, she gave a concerned smile. After the walk-through, Janet let Lizzy hang out behind the bar for another hour or so while she took orders, rolled utensils into napkins for dinner, and stacked warm, recently cleaned glasses.

"Hey, it was so nice to meet you, Janet!" Lizzy extended her fist, looking for a fist bump in return.

"Yo, girl, any time, sweetheart," Janet said, returning the fist bump. "This place ain't a bad place to work. For the most part, we're a tight crew. I think yur gonna like it here."

As soon as Lizzy shut her car door, she pulled out her phone and looked immediately at her recent texts from Tom.

TOMMY

Tommy – Hey Sexy! How did the interview go? Ping me when you get this! 😉
Today@11:38am

> Awesome!!! I GOT THE JOB!
> *Today@11:44am*

Tommy – Congrats! I knew you would, who wouldn't hire you? 💚💚
Today@11:46am

> You're the best, see you soon! 💚
> *Just Now*

Lizzy stared at the hearts for a few seconds, a nervous smile and happy eyes taking over her face. She felt, for maybe the first time, he just might be Mr. Right, Mr. Forever. She caught herself staring into the distance of the parking lot, suffering from a quick daydream. She shook off the notion.

"Better to let things be rather than set up any sort of expectation."

Turning on her ignition, she began to pull out of her parking spot when a van marked New England Rental smashed into her rear right quarter panel. While the accident was not that bad, her body trembled from shock. A sudden feeling of despair and worry struck through her.

She stepped out of the car. Leaving her door open, she ran around to the other side of the car where the impact happened. To her surprise, the other car's bumper had no indication of an accident. Her car only suffered a broken taillight and a slight dent in the panel. Surely her dad could get this fixed up for her. A man stepped out, a stocky man with a look of impatience on his face. He didn't say anything, just walked around the front of the car to assess the damage, then shook his head at her disapprovingly.

"Might be good if you looked before pulling out," the man said as he went to get back into the rental van. "These guys would kill me with fees if there was any damage." The man pointed toward a sign in the strip mall. *NEW ENGLAND RENTAL, Vans, Cars and Trucks!* Lizzy had no idea it was there, the business right next door to her new restaurant.

"I'm so sorry, sir. I don't know what I was thinking." She took full responsibility for it, as she was still trying to shake Tom from her mind when the accident happened. Waving, the man pulled away.

The Esplanade – 2008

"How the fuck? I mean seriously, how the fuck do they expect me to find a woman to marry?" Taking a shot of whiskey, Jack looked up, raising his head slowly, dragging his eys.

The bartender shrugged at him. "I don't know, man, sounds like you have a shit employer, making you get married? Is that legal?"

Jack shook his head, then his shot glass, silently asking the bartender for a refill.

How did this happen? What happened? Was this a typical procedure for the company? Or just for me? What choice do I have? His mind questioned their orders.

Returning, the bartender filled up his shot glass with another pour of whiskey. Jack really didn't care what it was. He just asked for a shot of strong stuff. He slugged it down as soon as it was full.

"Hey, bud, you're not driving today, are you?" The bartender tried to perform his due diligence in preventing a DWI.

"I'm taking the train. Just pour one more, and get me a glass of water."

He had hoped his latest assignment in Wellesley would help him cool off a little from the news that he would be required to find a woman. It had not. Instead of going to Wellesley, he continued on into Boston. He had already hopped through a couple of bars in the Boston University and Kenmore area. This wasn't like Jack. He was usually calm and cool. He hadn't had such instability since his early years in college. There was something about being forced to marry another person that scared the shit out of him.

"Why couldn't they just arrange something? Why do *I* have to find a woman?" Looking up at the ceiling, he rubbed his eyes. The alcohol was starting to affect his vision, and the world around him was blurring just a tad.

"Here you are." The bartender came back with his water, and after seeing Jack take a good sip, he went ahead and refilled his shot.

After Jack drank the last shot, he looked around, seeing the bar was made up of mostly twenty-somethings. The bar was L-shaped, and he was sitting at the far end near the opening. Looking to his right, his eyes stopped on a girl at the other end of the bar. She was sitting in the corner of the "L." On her right was an empty bar stool and to her left there was another man having a drink. Jack watched her for a bit and decided it was clear that she was there alone. He concluded that the guy next to her was not with her, leading him to consider her for a moment.

Probably the right age, close to mine, I would guess.

The girl had glowing red hair, hazel-brown eyes, a friendly face, and a large bust. He liked that.

That's not too bad. I have to start somewhere?

With another sip of his water, he got up and walked over to the busty redhead, plopping himself down to the right of her. Unused to this type of stalking, Jack decided he needed to be a bit smoother, when coming up on his potential prey. She might have been considered a little large for some, but Jack needed a wife.

Now what do I do? he asked himself. Boldness was never a problem for him, but smoothness was. The redhead looked at him half-puzzled. Just sitting there, Jack waited for a few moments, contemplating his next move. Finally, he decided he should offer to buy her a drink.

He turned toward the girl, and at the moment he was about to speak, she said, "No, no thank you. I'm all set." The redhead stopped him in his tracks. His hesitation and awkward motions while sitting had done its work to creep her out and there was no recovering. A moment later, she took her drink and skirted off to another part of the bar.

Dammit, I suck, he thought, bobbing his head in disappointment.

"Nice try, dude," the man to his left said. Jack tried to ignore him, but the man sat up and shifted his seat over to where the redhead vacated, getting closer to Jack.

"I wanted to say something to her but you beat me to it. Oh, don't get me wrong, I'm sure she would have rejected me worse."

Jack didn't want to talk to this guy, but he couldn't help himself.

"Yeah, I figured why not? Don't know unless you try, right?" Jack spoke as if he were a professional, then took another sip of water.

"Let me buy you your next drink. My name is Geoff." Geoff waved to the bartender, signaling to him that he wanted to put in another order for drinks.

"Get me another V and T, and get this guy whatever he is having." Jack didn't offer his name but decided it was harmless to have another drink. It's hard to turn down a free drink when you're in a drinking mood.

"I'll have what he's having," Jack said to the bartender.

"You sure? You may have already had enough," the bartender snapped back at Jack.

"Here!" Jack threw down a twenty-dollar bill on the counter. "You keep 'em coming, and I'll keep throwing you these." The bartender snatched up the twenty, nodded, and moved off toward the other side of the bar to make the drinks.

"How do you talk to women?" Jack asked in a rhetorical sense.

Geoff nodded up and down. "I hear ya, man. Sometimes it seems easy, and at other times it's pulling teeth." After a brief moment of silence, Geoff continued, "I always find the easiest way is to say hi. Or maybe, sometimes, use a movie line on them. You know, that gets their attention."

Just then the bartender came back with the drinks. "Here you guys go. Enjoy."

Geoff looked at Jack. "You have to find something that you can relate to with these chicks." Then he took a deep sip of his drink, letting his own words stir. "Guys like us don't pick up girls in bars. It's just not gonna happen." He took another sip, watching Jack.

"Na, the best thing we can do is find things that we enjoy doing that chicks like to do. Like cooking!" He pointed toward the food that another patron was eating at the bar.

"I bet you if we took some cooking classes, there would be some sweet pussy in that class, and we would probably be the only guys in there." They both looked around the bar, peering from girl to girl, taking stock.

"I got to hit the pisser, man. I'll be right back." Getting up, Geoff headed to the bathroom. While he was gone, Jack reached into his pocket and pulled out a small white envelope. He carefully pulled apart the sleeve to expose four white pills, then grabbed one pill and placed it on the stool between his legs. Refolding the envelope, he put it back into his pocket. Using the side of his cell phone, he crushed up the pill into a fine powder, losing part of it as it spilled over the seat. He then brushed the powder into his palm, pulled his drink down under the bar and dumped the powder into his own drink. He stirred it thoroughly, making sure to squeeze every drop of lime juice from the wedge on the edge of the glass, then pushing the lime wedge toward the bottom of the drink.

"Hey." Geoff was back from the bathroom.

"How did it go? Pick up any numbers while you were gone?"

Geoff looked at Jack for a moment before breaking out into a brief laugh. "Ahh, you are bad at jokes, aren't you?" Geoff reached for his drink and slurped what was left of it. It was just about empty, and the cocktail straw was sucking a mix of air and water.

"Here, have mine," Jack said, reaching over and handing Geoff his drink.

"I haven't had a sip. I just realized that a V and T was vodka, and I can't drink it anymore, not after a *real* bad night back in college, you know what I mean?"

Geoff looked at him, hesitating slightly.

"I'll get Jack and Coke. Here you take this. You paid for it, and I would hate to see it go to waste."

A smile crossed Geoff's face. "Sounds good. I can't see a good V and T go to waste. I'll need to slow down though; this will be my sixth." Just as Geoff was about to take a sip, Jack called for the bartender.

"Bartender! Jack and Coke!" Jack yelled out, and the bartender nodded, confirming that he got the order.

"Ah, you're lucky you didn't drink this. It's bitter as shit." Geoff shook his head as his face contorted from the bite of the drink.

"You need me to find someone else to drink that?" Jack said, mocking him for complaining.

"Nah, I'll drink it. You kidding me?" Geoff took another, bigger sip this time. Jack watched with his blue eyes burning into the straw with focus.

"Wow, mans, I am getting drunk." Geoff's eyelids began to droop, and his speech was slurring. He began to lose balance in his seat.

"Yeah, man, me too. Fucking hamma'd, man." Jack played it off like he was just as intoxicated.

"Say what, we should get outta here and watch the chicks on the esplanade."

Swaying in his seat, Geoff had no idea what Jack was talking about. His judgment and all of the warning signs that your body would be screaming went amiss from the alcohol and codeine he had consumed.

"Yeah, that would ble awesome." He slurred his speech.

"Although, I don't know if I will make it long. I'm starting to get tired." He nodded his head up and down.

"You got this, just a little longer, and you can sleep all you want."

Paying their bills with cash, Jack helped Geoff to his feet. He waved to the bartender, and with Geoff's arm over Jack's shoulder, they disappeared into the evening.

The air outside was warm and muggy, with thunderstorms in the distance. Jack and Geoff looked like a couple of old buddies that had too good of a night out on the town. Jack half-dragged Geoff slowly toward the esplanade. The Charles River Esplanade was a state-run park that ran along the river on the Boston side, for about three miles, supplying a leafy waterfront walkway with fitness stops and benches. As they got closer and closer to the water, Jack was starting to get the feeling of anticipation. Over the past couple of years, Jack had been good. He had only worked his assignments, never indulging his own interests.

"Well, not anymore. Fuck them. They want to force me to marry someone, they can deal with me getting something for me!" Jack yelled out, thinking out loud, realizing that fact too late.

"What are you tal-laking about? Who's making you get hitch—*hiccup*."

Jack ignored the question. He could see the water now and started to drag Geoff along at a faster pace toward it.

"There's probably no chicks here at this time. I think I should go home." Through the fog of codeine-fueled alcohol, Geoff's body was finally getting alerts to his brain, telling him something was wrong. Geoff began to try to resist Jack. He pulled on his right arm, but Jack was all that was holding him up, and he fell to the ground, his knees making contact first then his palms. He was unbalanced, dizzy, and lightheaded, but he was able to hold himself up on his knees. Turning over his palms, he saw little lines of blood caused by tiny pebbles that punctured his skin. Jack grabbed him again and pulled him up. His body having been programmed his entire life to stand back up after a fall, Geoff naturally went with Jack.

Jack moved him closer and closer to the edge of the water. They could hear the soft turns of the river.

"I don't want to do this, man. I don't want to-la go."

Ignoring his drunken words, Jack looked around. Unable to see anyone in either direction of the walkway, he knew he had a moment or two alone.

"Geoff, you know that drink I gave to you? The one you offered to pay for?"

Geoff was kneeling at the edge of the water, on the rocky riverside. He looked up at Jack, a look of betrayal in his eyes.

"Yes, that drink. I have a confession to tell you." Jack pulled on the back of Geoff's shirt quickly to keep him from falling forward.

"I crushed up a large dosage of codeine and put it in the drink."

Just then a jogger ran by, blatantly ignoring the scene.

"You see that—that guy there who just ran by—he knew there was something strange happening here. But he didn't care. That's the thing about people nowadays—as long as it's not their business, they keep to themselves. Hmm, where was I?" Jack pulled on Geoff again as Geoff tried to crawl back toward the walkway.

"That's right, do you know what the effect of consuming codeine with alcohol is? Basically, you get really, *really* disoriented—weak, dizzy, drowsy, and you lose your judgment. Sound familiar?"

Geoff looked up at Jack, his head swinging wildly. "C'mon, I just want to go home now."

"Why do you think I drugged you?"

Geoff stared at Jack, fear and uncertainty swelled in his eyes at the questions, unable to comprehend it.

"You're going to have an accident tonight, Geoff. You're going to drown in this river." Jack looked up at the Charles, a rush of adrenaline and endorphins flooding his mind, bringing him physical pleasure.

"A jogger just like that guy who ran by will find you in the morning. The cops will write you up as another drunk asshole that took the wrong combination of drugs and alcohol and wandered too close to the river." Kneeling, Jack looked Geoff in the eyes. "Disastrously close, and now I am going to teach you your last lesson." With that, he gave Geoff a push, and his body went into the river head first. He was only in a few feet of water, but with Jack keeping a hold of his feet, he was unable to straighten out and stand up.

Splashing, Geoff fought with his arms, flailing to keep himself afloat. As he began to tire out, barely keeping his face turned to the side to allow himself to breathe, Jack pulled him in toward the shore so that his body was parallel to the shoreline. He reached out, putting his hand on the back of Geoff's head, then forced it underwater. Geoff's body flinched a few times, contorting and twisting; his body understood what was happening, but his brain was too fogged up to do anything to prevent it. It was over in a couple of minutes.

Reaching over to Geoff's left arm, Jack raised it slightly out of the water. He turned his wrist and admired a black polycarbonate-cased watch with white-green accents, and the letters *nite hawk* written on the face. Undoing the watch, he slipped it into his pocket—a memento for himself. It was a rarity that he took things from a victim. He stood up, in the darkness, and peered down toward the water.

You could hardly see the body from here, never mind the walkway. Surely you won't be found until morning.

He stood there for at least a half-hour, watching the dark outline of the body slowly rock and drag along the shore. Something was amiss, though. It wasn't quite the same as he remembered it. He enjoyed himself, no doubt, but it was not nearly as pleasing to him as when he had killed Dean. What was missing?

Jack snapped his fingers.

"His eyes—I didn't get to look into his eyes!" Jack looked around as the thought crossed his mind to try to pull Geoff out, resuscitate him, and give it another go.

Fuck, don't be stupid! Do you want to get caught? The thought lingered a moment longer. *It's never going to work.* Convincing himself out of the urge to satisfy his obsession, Jack turned around and disappointingly walked back toward the city.

First Contact – 2014

"What the shit! Arrg!" Jen was punching the dashboard of Drew's car and flipping her hair about as she jerked her head in angry movements.

"Hey, calm down! Christ. And I thought I had a temper problem. Is this a typical flair up for you?"

Slamming back into her seat, Jen crossed her arms then blew her hair out of her own face, looking angry and mischievous before grunting out, "Sorry, I just, I hate that shit."

It was at that moment Drew could tell her light was turned off. That spark of happiness and pop had been crushed and kicked to the curb and replaced by anger, lack of confidence, and shame. *There must be more history there on the topic,* he thought.

"You okay?"

Jen didn't respond, and Drew couldn't take the silence.

"I can't imagine some of the shit you have to deal with." Drew could see that her lower lip was beginning to quiver. After a moment, she slammed her face down into her hands and started to cry.

"Hey, you're okay! Everything is going to be okay." Reaching over, Drew rubbed her shoulder with the hopes that it would help soothe her.

"I just—sssp, I—sssp—just can't take assholes like that." She was sucking in tears, drool, and snots as she spoke. "I've had to deal with guys like this before. Sssp." She wiped her nose and eyes on her forearm. Her mascara was beginning to smear and run down her cheeks.

"These guys, they think that, because of my work, because of the job I do, they think that they can *march all over me* without any consequence. Well, FUCK THEM." Her voice screeched louder, and she had her hands pointing toward the dojo with both middle fingers out.

After a few minutes of crying and letting out steam, she finally seemed to be starting to calm down.

"If it makes you feel better, I told him I was going to get him fired if he didn't leave you alone." Drew was finally able to get her to crack a smile.

She looked up at him, a little giggle slipping out.

"Aha, I knew you couldn't hide that smile for long!" Moving his hand on to the keys, Drew turned the ignition, starting the car. Looking back over at Jen, he reached his open hand out and cupped her cheek, wiping away a mascara stain with his thumb.

She closed her eyes at his touch then reached up with her own hand and cupped his, holding his hand there. Something about the contact felt good to Drew, but strange, driven by a sense of taboo. His conscience was at war over the morality of his actions, of letting himself enjoy this moment with a significantly younger woman. He pulled his hand back to the steering wheel. "Where to next?"

Jen continued to wipe away the leftover snot from the crying fit, but she was mostly returning to normal. "Well, we have Shelly's house and the bar. I think Shelly is closer." She finished by pointing toward the exit of the dojo.

Putting the car in drive, Drew looked left and right before making the turn out of the parking lot. Hearing a buzzing sound, he looked down into the console where his phone had lit up from an incoming message.

Jen scooped up the phone. "Who's Lizzy?" she demanded with a hint of jealousy. "And why have you ignored her messages from yesterday. You know your phone is going to keep telling you that you have unread messages. Right?"

"Lizzy is my daughter. And I saw enough. I'll have a talk with her when I see her." Pulling over, putting the car back into park, Drew reached out for his phone. He was not particularly fond of someone reading his texts.

Pulling the phone toward herself, Jen moved her body toward the passenger door. "It says . . ."

Jen read the text messages out loud, opened up the keyboard, and began to write.

LIZZY

Lizzy – I didn't tell you but I got a new job!! This weekend is my second weekend working. I didn't tell you before because… it's bartending. Don't hate it.

Lizzy – So... I won't be home tonight or tomorrow night. You should see me Sunday. Love you!
Yesterday@3:08pm

That's great news honey 👍I think bartending is awesome!
Just Now

"I responded for you. You start driving." She slapped his hand toward the steering wheel. "Drive! I will take care of this for you."

"What did you write? What did you send her?" Drew pulled back onto the road while reading the texts that Jen was sending in the passenger seat to his daughter.

"Oh, fuck's sake, relax. I just told her it was great news." Jen dropped the cell phone back into a cup holder in the console. "See, I wasn't going to steal your phone. It's back where I found it."

Drew frowned momentarily at her. "I don't want her bartending. I will deal with it later and without your input." Drew gave her a playful scowl. "Are we even going in the right direction?"

Jen squinted her eyes a bit to take in where they were. "No, nope. We are not going in the right direction. You need to turn this boat around. Like full U-ey now." Jen was twirling her right index finger in the air. Drew pulled up to the next set of lights and obliged.

"One thing I should tell you about Shelly." Jen paused a moment. "She doesn't exactly like me. So I might have to stay in the car."

"I can't wait to hear this story. Please tell me, what did you do?"

Jen rubbed her hands together nervously. "Well, she caught her husband on—"

Drew cut her off from finishing, "Stop! I take it back. I don't need to hear this story."

"Oh, no, no! It's not what you think. No! Gross. Let me finish. It's just that she caught her husband on my website. And let's just say he was a committed member."

Drew didn't know what to say to that. It made sense why Shelly might not be a fan.

"I had no idea, by the way, if that's what you're wondering. Mostly my customers are totally anonymous to me."

"How did you find out then that he was a customer?"

Jen opened up her eyes wide to the question with a "You really want to know?" look. "Well, it's fucked up and was super awkward. I had actually never met Shelly before, then this one day Ash invites me

166

to come with her to have wine with her friend Shelly." Tossing her hair out of her face, Jen paused a moment. "I had, of course, heard of her. She's one of Ash's best friends. So, I'm like, 'Yes!' I show up with Ash, and Ash has been there a thousand times so we just walk in. And I shit you not, Shelly takes one look at me and drops this massive fucking bottle of red wine on the floor." Jen motions an explosion with her hands.

"Fucking wine bottle explodes, place looks like a scene outta *Dexter*, with red splatter everywhere." She whipped her hands in a brush splattering motion.

"Shelly does not care, totally ignores her feet marinated in Cab Sav. You could literally hear the wine bottle burp at her feet as it spilled out." Jen paused to let Drew take in the story.

"She just stares at me. Finally, after like this weird tense minute, she just says, 'I have had enough of you in my house' and points to the door to get out."

Drew tried to visualize the scene.

"I find out later from Ash that he was one of my fully paying customers and Shelly caught on to the billing on his credit card. Not only that, he was one of those fetish customers I was telling you about, buying up old panties and shit from me."

Drew scowled. "Yikes, yeah, okay, I'll just go in and talk to her alone. You stay in the car. We don't need to trigger any domestic violence issues tonight." Drew shook his head at the unbelievable story. "What's Cab Sav, by the way?"

"Uh, I'm sorry, you're too old to get slang." She tapped him in the chest jokingly, laughing. "It's short for Cabernet Sauvignon."

They pulled up to a nice cul-de-sac neighborhood southeast of Providence and parked at the curb of a fair-sized colonial home. From the looks, Drew figured it was built in the early 2000s.

"Okay, Shelly is one of Ash's best friends," Drew said out loud as a verbal cue to prep for his approach to the home.

"Yeah, we covered that already, Sherlock," Jen spat back.

"I'll be back soon." Drew left the keys in the car for Jen.

"Ok, Shelly, Ash's best friend, I'm Drew," Drew muttered to himself as he walked the brick path toward the front door.

Bzzt, Bzzt. Feeling his phone buzzing in his pocket, Drew stopped walking to pull the phone out, and saw *Kelly* on the screen, a call he immediately answered.

"Kelly, what do you have for me?" Drew spoke fast, unsure about having a conversation on the doorstep of some stranger's home.

"Drew, fuck if I care about your afternoon either." Kelly snorted before continuing. "I won't hate yah for it. I have some news. We got another floater." Turning, Drew headed back toward the car. Shelly would have to wait.

"Yeah, I'll be there in a couple hours. Make sure if anyone else shows up, you stall them as long as you can. Uh, huh, yep, thanks, Kelly! See you soon." Putting his phone back in his pocket, Drew hastily made his way into the driver seat.

"We have a real lead to follow!" he said triumphantly as he started the car. He looked over to Jen. "Any chance you can Uber home from a gas station?"

She crossed her arms and legs defiantly. "What, no! You will not leave me at a gas station."

"I'm sorry, I have to get back up to Boston A.S.A.P."

"What is so important you need to get back to Boston for?" Jen inquired.

Drew wasn't sure if he should tell her.

"Come on. We're basically partners now. Soon I'll be on your payroll."

"Ha, really?" That comment amused Drew. "I have a friend up in Boston at the city morgue. Another body was found in the river. Just came into the morgue not ten minutes ago."

"Shit, holy shit. There is something seriously wrong. That's like thirty bodies or some shit if Ash's map is right. Is your friend Kelly trustworthy?"

Drew ignored the question.

"Seriously though, Drew! Holy shit! Are we hunting a serial killer? Or is this normal? I mean do all cities have thirty or so bodies pop up in the river over a few years?"

Her questions were valid. In fact, Drew had done a little research on drowning deaths in port cities similar to Boston in the U.S. and Europe. The drowning rate per capita in Boston was twice that of any other city, a significant number.

"That is a good question. I'm beginning to believe that Boston has something else going on. Maybe even a serial killer." He turned briefly to Jen, their eyes locked with the same concern and fear.

"But now you know why I need to get to Boston." Jen nodded her head up and down, agreeing.

"Let's go. I'll go with you, and when we're done, we can come back and continue looking for Ashley." Drew didn't like the sound of that; he didn't want to be responsible for her. Plus, what would Lizzy think of him hanging out with someone just a few years older than her?

"I don't know, Jen. It might be best if you stay here. Besides, I'm planning to hang out in the lobby of the morgue in case Ashley comes in to inspect this body like she did the last time."

A defiant look crossed Jen's face. "Oh, now I am definitely not getting out. You're going to have to accept this, Mr. Law. Besides, don't worry about me. I'm like a mouse. I can sleep on the couch, and you'll never hear me."

Drew really didn't like this. "Fine, but if I say to do something, you have to promise you're going to do it exactly as I say." He pointed at her with authority, which she slapped down playfully.

"Yes, you can tell me to do anything. I'll play the sub," she said with a wink.

"No, Jen, no, I really need you to promise, no joking around. Promise that you are going to follow my directions when it matters."

"God, yes. I promise you that when you tell me to do something, I will do it. There, happy?"

Peering at her briefly, Drew nodded before putting his attention back on the road.

"Next stop Boston then. And buckle your seat belt."

Kelly's Long Stare – 2014

Kelly put his cellphone down once Drew told him he was on his way. Picking up his half-eaten vending machine pastry, he peeled the wrapper down in an attempt to keep his fingers clean. For a man of medicine, he seemed to lack some self-control around all the things that a typical doctor would recommend against. He had a terrible diet, stopped any exercising years ago, and smoked cigars daily as an after-work escape. His office was small, maybe one hundred square feet. On one side, it had floor to ceiling file cabinets. His desk was just small enough that he could sneak around the end of it and the wall opposite the filing cabinets into his chair.

Kelly finished his pastry, opened up the wrapper, and licked every last crumb before throwing it out into the waste bin. His eyes once again drifted to his phone. After a moment's pause, he picked it back up and pulled up a contact, *Tinder*, on his phone, and pushed the call button.

The phone rang a few times, then went to voicemail. "Yeah, hi, this is Kelly, the medical examiner in Boston. Ahh, yeah, well, we got ourselves another floater coming in. Like you asked, you wanted to hear about that." He paused, thinking about what he could or should leave on a voicemail.

"If you're willing to make the same contribution as last time, I can get you in for a viewing to help us in the identification process. We are expecting the body here in an hour or so, and I expect I can get you in for a visit in about two hours." Kelly knew that his old friend Drew was looking for Ashley, and he didn't want to tell Drew directly that he had a working phone number for her. She had said, after all, "Don't give this number out." He would also prefer not to tell Drew that he was accepting cash from other people interested in the same case as him. What he could do for his friend was try to control the timing of Ashley's visit to that when he expected Drew. If they were to bump into each other, well, that might work.

"I will see you in two hours then."

Hanging up the phone, Kelly put it back on his desk. He pulled out his car keychain and spun a few keys over until he came across a smaller rounded key, which he then inserted into his lower right desk drawer. Unlocking the drawer and opening it, he stared long and hard. Inside were stacks of money bound together; On the top was a note with the total handwritten. *$128,304.00*

Staring at the cash had become a ritual of his after any negotiation, a time for him to reflect on his unethical actions over the years, allowing anyone willing to pay to come in and view a body. Sometimes, he took more money in exchange for altering reports or looking another direction when performing an examination of his own. He never spent any of the money for fear that it would lead to him being uncovered by co-workers. Instead, he figured the money would come in handy when he retired. It would be easy to spend untaxed cash in retirement with gambling, women, traveling, and, hell, on any other cash items he might need. He stared long and hard at the contents of the drawer, contemplating the ethics of it all, a slight bubble of guilt rising in his stomach.

"There's no turning back now. Besides, if it wasn't me, it would have been someone else." He told himself lies to help smooth over the guilt he felt, to help him justify his actions. After a few more minutes, he shut the drawer, locked it, and put his keys back into his pocket.

Leaving his office, he headed toward the elevators, then stopped, looking at the wrapped pastries in the vending machine. He decided one more couldn't hurt. Kelly didn't know it, but he was suffering from emotional eating, a disorder that has its sufferers consume high-carb, high-calorie, sweet foods with low or no nutritional values. This eating was a direct response to a vast number of emotional triggers. For Kelly, it was stress, guilt, and anxiety, among others.

Convergence – 2014

Drew pulled in and parked on the third floor of a large downtown parking garage. He peered over at Jen, who had a look of excitement on her face.

"You are staying here," he said, pointing to her sternly.

"What? No way, no fucking way."

Shaking his head, Drew raised his eyes. "You promised that you would do exactly as I say. And right now I'm telling you, you are staying here." He did not want her to be anywhere near the morgue or dead bodies. "I can drop you off at the bus station and buy you a ticket back to Providence if you'd prefer."

She crossed her arms defiantly but slouched back into the seat in defeat.

Reaching across her, he opened up his glove box, pulled out a pair of handcuffs, and dangled them in front of Jen.

"Don't make me put these on you."

"Drew, these have seriously been in your glove box this entire trip? You can put these on me any time." Reaching out, Jen grabbed them. Then she raised her arms up toward the ceiling of the car and crossed her wrists as if they were handcuffed. Closing her eyes slowly, she let out the slightest whisper of a moan.

Shaking his head, Drew got out of the car, shutting the door hard behind him. "Fuck me," he mouthed.

For the second time in the past week, Drew walked into the city morgue, asking for Kelly by name. A feeling of déjà vu hit him. He reached across the reception desk and grabbed the sign-in book, skimming through it for any entry that started with an "A" or "T." Not seeing any, he began filling it out. The door swung open loudly as Kelly came busting in.

"Oh yeah!" Kelly yelled with his arms out wide, a Kool-Aid Man reference. Drew ignored the act.

"Kelly, bud, sign this so we can get started."

Walking over, Kelly looked down at the sheet. "Sure thing, sure thing." He paused for a moment, looking at his watch.

"You made better time?"

Kelly was right. It had taken Drew about one and a half hours since they spoke on the phone.

Kelly stared at the sign-in sheet. "Oh, yes. Let's see."

"Here." Drew pointed impatiently at the signature line. Kelly leaned in and signed, then picked it up and began scanning through the sheet.

"Let's get on with it then, shall we?" Kelly said, placing the sheet down and motioning toward the entry. "Now what was that case number again? Drew, follow me to my office to grab the number, then we can pull that body out."

Drew was incredulous. "You knew I was coming? Right?" Drew said sarcastically. Drew took one look into Kelly's office and decided it was best if he waited in the hall. The room permeated a foul smell of BO and past-due food.

"Aha, two two zero two—Drew, remember that for me, would ya?" Kelly yelled from the office.

"I need another couple minutes to find out what cooler he's in." Kelly knew already exactly where the body associated with case 2202 was. Having already pulled him out, he placed him in examination room two, a smaller room than the room Drew had previously visited.

After a few minutes of Kelly clicking away at a keyboard, he muttered, "Uh-hum," "Yep," and "Here we go!" This vignette replayed a few times before he said, "I have it—cooler number two. Now we can have the boy pulled into an examination room."

Drew was getting irritated. He pulled out his phone, looking for any messages to try to temper himself. Stepping out of the office, Kelly motioned back toward where they had come.

"After you," Drew stated, his voice stern, making it apparent that he was displeased.

As they walked past the door that led back to the lobby and toward the coolers, a man was walking toward them with a white doctor's lab coat. He saw Kelly and belted out. "K, what's with the body in examination room two?"

Kelly looked over at Drew briefly. "Shit, that's right. Yes, Jack, we are on our way there now." Jack gave Kelly a look of disgust and continued walking in the opposite direction.

Before Drew could say anything, Kelly said, "Shit, sometimes I forget things. The rate I'm going, I'll have to retire sooner than later."

He elbowed Drew in the side. "How's your memory these days, Drew? Any signs of age hitting you?"

Drew felt bad for him, believing Kelly's memory was as bad as he was making it appear.

"Yeah, you know how it goes. That's why I write everything down." Drew flashed the notebook from his back pocket.

"You do know they have these smartphones that could replace that pad for you, and you don't ever have to worry about losing it because everything gets backed up to the cloud." Kelly went silent for a moment; just before Drew was about to ask what the cloud was, Kelly blurted out, "Whatever the hell that means."

As they entered the examination room, Drew instinctively pulled out his notepad and pen. Looking up at the clock on the wall, he noted the time, room, and case number, *4:14 p.m., examination room 2, case-id: 2202.*

"Do you have an ID on this guy yet?" Drew looked at the body lying naked on the stainless-steel cart. He looked as though he could still be alive. His body was in significantly better condition than the other victims.

"We do, but we're waiting for verification from next of kin. We believe his name is Gabe Caple, born May 12, 1990." Kelly looked down from his file at the body. "Poor kid." He looked back into his file. "We have called his family. They're coming in tonight to verify."

Walking up to the body, Drew immediately noticed its fingers. "He's missing a nail," Drew said out loud with suspicious concern in his voice. The body was pale, cold, and stiff. His eyes were foggy and appeared slightly larger than normal, almost bulging. He had a tattoo of a pocket watch on his right forearm. Drew had to slightly roll his arm to make it visible.

"Was this used at all in the identification?" Drew was pointing to the tattoo. It's common to identify criminals based on their tattoos and was standard procedure to photograph them at prison intakes.

"Yes, that helped. But not what you're thinking. It wasn't prison. One of the techs here said he had seen this tattoo before on the wall of his ink shop. We called over there, and sure enough, we got a name." Pausing a moment, Kelly flipped a page in the file he was reviewing. "His time of death has not been officially established. But we think he went into the water sometime last night."

Pulling his phone out of his pocket, Kelly looked at the screen. Looking up, he nervously played with the papers he was holding.

"Drew, you, sir, are going to owe me big." A wide smile broached Kelly's large face. "I told the lobby that if anyone came in here by the name of Ashley Tinder, that they needed to page me immediately." He flashed his phone up in the air. "She's here, in the goddamn lobby. Want me to go get her and bring her here?"

Drew thought about it a moment, pacing toward Kelly. "Wow, perfect timing. You think she's interested in this body? Must be, right?" Drew said.

"Gotta be." Kelly paused a moment, then said, "This room is soundproof, so anything you guys say here will be private." He motioned toward the walls as he spoke.

Drew nodded, liking the idea. "Okay, go get her. Let's find out exactly who Ashley is." Drew looked in a mirror hanging over a sanitary sink; it was instinct to make sure he was put together before meeting a good-looking woman. Kelly left the room, smiling.

Questions whirling around his mind, Drew paced around the body.

What's up with the death map? Or the weird secret room? Why did someone break into her house? Drew stopped in front of the mirror again.

"Pull yourself together."

He ran fingers through his hair, then reached out and turned on the cold water in the sink below, splashing his face. As soon as he dried up, the door swung open and in walked a chatty Kelly, who stopped mid-sentence when he saw Drew, pretending that he did not know Drew was there.

"Excuse us. I didn't realize someone else was using this room." Kelly winked, almost obviously, at Drew.

"Ah, yeah, yes. I'm reviewing case two two zero two." Drew reached into his pocket, pulling out his PI business card from his wallet, he flashed it without explanation. Kelly proceeded into the room with Ashley in tow.

"That works out. It looks like we're all here for the same case." Kelly sort of shrugged his shoulders at Drew.

"I forgot a file. I'll be back in a few minutes." Kelly used his hands as signals, telling Drew he had ten minutes before he would return. Ashley stood in the room confused, looking at Drew warily.

"Is this typical? Is it safe?" She spoke to Kelley, but he left the room without responding. She turned to Drew. "I am so sorry. I should probably leave and come back." She seemed genuine to Drew, honest, with a caring look on her face that she didn't want to intrude.

Ashley was shorter than Drew had imagined, standing around 5'8" to 5'9", although she was still as pretty as the old photo he had found of her. It seemed she hadn't aged a day. As Jen had said, her hair was a dirty blond now with a hint of red. It was wavy, almost tangled, and thick. By the looks of the size of the bun, it was also long. Her eyes were big, blue-green, with long natural eyelashes wrapping them. Her lips were petite and a soft pink color. She seemed to lack a little color in her skin, and her eyes looked tired and darkened at the edges, almost as though she were battling the flu.

"Please, don't leave." Reaching out, Drew grabbed her hand, pulling ever so slightly, gently. "I'm sorry, I didn't mean to grab." He paused a moment. "My name is Drew. You have been a hard women to find, Ashley."

She looked up at him sharply when he said her name. Fear filled her eyes, as she backed toward the door. Drew immediately picked up on her mood.

"It's okay. I just have some questions for you. I'm working with the police, looking to stop a murder." Drew threw out a dart, hoping it would land on the board.

Looking at him, she continued to walk backward, putting one hand on the door slowly.

"Jen came with me. You know, your tenant? Cutecamjen.com? She's outside in my car right now." Drew figured that might help push her to stay and at least listen.

"Jen's here?" She had a puzzled expression, but her hand fell from the door, taking a step forward, moving back into the room.

"It's a long story. She was worried about you."

She looked over at the body on the cart. A tear trickled down her left cheek. "Poor kid." She spoke softly, her sadness seemed personal, and it seemed to swallow her. "Do you ever get used to this?" she asked Drew, assuming he had been in morgues more than a normal person should be.

"No," he responded starkly. "No, you don't. At least, people like us don't."

Walking over to the counter closest to the door, Ashley put down her large purse after pulling out a flip-style notepad and pen. She walked toward the body, visibly shaking herself into composure.

"Why have you been trying to find me?" Ashley spoke as she wrote notes, peering at the body.

Drew ignored the question for the moment. "They believe they have an ID on him." Drew was trying to play into her investigation, give her some useful information in hopes that there would be natural reciprocity.

"It looks like Gabe," she said without hesitation. Drew was shocked. She figured that out quickly.

"They suspect so. Who else might it be?" Drew wanted to ask questions that resulted in Ashley talking, divulging, opposed to leading questions and giving her an easy out.

"I wasn't sure at first; I'm sure it's Gabe now." Pausing, she moved in on the right forearm of the body. Ashley knew exactly where to look.

She has a profile on this guy; who's the PI here? he thought.

"It's definitely Gabe." She pulled the skin on his arm with her pen to better expose the tattoo. "Why have you been looking for me?"

"I'm investigating the death of a young man for his family. He had drowned in the Charles last March, and his family wanted more answers as to what happened."

"Josh, right? His mom told me that she had hired someone."

Who the hell is this chick? Drew was annoyed with her seemingly know-it-all attitude.

"You spoke to Clair?"

"I did, yesterday, in fact." Ashley looked up from her notepad, giving Drew a fast smile. She knew she was impressing him. "It was the sign-in sheet, right? I knew someone might notice that." Ashley shook her head.

Stepping closer to her, Drew pulled the pad down from her view. "Yes, that's exactly why I was looking for you. Imagine my surprise when I find a weird map in your home, marking the exact location where my boy Josh's body was discovered among what I am assuming is roughly thirty or so other bodies?"

Dropping her notepad to her side, Ashley pointed the tip of her pen into his face. "You've been in my home?" she said aggressively, eyes squinting with disapproval. "You have no right. Do you have any respect for privacy?"

Her voice was rising. Drew could tell he hit a note. "Oh, I've been in your home. And whatever else creepy thing you can think about; well, yeah, I did it," Drew responded sarcastically.

"But I don't think I should be the one answering questions here." Drew spoke fast to prevent her from getting a word in until he got his point across. "I am not the one with a creepy, hard to get to office room in the basement—a basement that is only accessible via a hidden panel in a cabinet." Drew turned around, wailing his arms about to emphasize that she was the creepier person of the two of them. He turned around dramatically. "And, to boot, it's you that has a very odd map in said creepy room, a map that happens to have the location of where a bunch of dead people were found."

"Basement? Why did you go through the basement? Come on now." She started laughing at Drew. "There's a bulkhead right there, and the wall in the closet can be pulled out to access the room. Ever since I had my kitchen redone, well, before that there used to be a staircase, but I got rid of it to make more space for a larger kitchen. When I renovated, I had them remove it and put in an access panel."

She poked him in the shoulder with the pen. "Did you even fit?"

Shrugging his shoulders, Drew sucked in his gut. "Yes, of course, I could fit. And stop poking me with your pen."

She gave him a coy look. "And the, quote, creepy, end quote, room, is a gun room. There's a locking mechanism in the bedroom that allows you to swing the wall out, where guns and other items could be stored, preventing theft in the event of a break-in." She looked down to the floor, hiding her eyes.

"My husband installed it, and a—well, when he left, I sold the guns. Something I regret doing now." She looked back up, looking into Drew's eyes. "Look, I've been doing this." She motioned around the room. "I mean, I have been on this case for months now. It's best if you stay out of my way."

"Was your husband a victim? Is that why you're working this case?" Drew watched her for a reaction. Her eyes began to redden and swell with water. Drew had touched a sore subject. He regretted the question instantly; he'd had his fill of crying women for the day already. "I'm sorry, I guess I already knew, and there was no reason for me to ask that."

Turning away from him, she rubbed her eyes.

"Look, I know you've been working this for a while. But I'm an investigator. This is what I do. I'm being paid to do this, which means that if you're also working this case, then there is no way for me to stay 'out of your way.'" He walked slowly around to position himself in front of her so he could look her in the eyes again.

"Why don't we work together? The great work you've been doing these past months, mixed with my investigative experience—I will even split my payout from Josh's family with you if you want." He paused to let the proposal settle in. "You don't have to do this alone."

His words struck home. Closing her eyes, Ashley took a deep breath. When she opened them, Drew had his hand out for a handshake.

"Partners?"

She looked at his hand a moment. Taking a deep breath, she reached out and grasped his hand firmly. "Partners then."

Gabe – 2014

"Now that we have that out of the way. Who is Gabe Caple?" Drew pointed to the naked, slightly bloated body that lay on the stainless-steel cart. Ashley took a deep breath; he thought that he could see color returning to her skin. Stress was a powerful thing on the human body, known to cause physical ailments and disease. Perhaps the stress of working this case alone was more than Ashley had given it credit for.

"Gabe," she paused to take another breath, "was found this morning. He is twenty-four years old, six feet tall, and one hundred sixty-five pounds. He lives on Wayland St, just off the northwest side of the BU campus. He was born in Newton, Massachusetts, where he also lived with his parents until he was nineteen." She spoke fast, as if she had his profile memorized.

"He has two sisters, Jade and Joanna, both younger." Walking around him to his right arm, she reached onto the counter next to the cart, grabbing a set of latex examination gloves and handing the box of gloves to Drew after. Reaching down, she rolled over Gabe's arm to expose a marvelous tattoo that stretched across the whole inside of his forearm from wrist to inner elbow.

"He has here an elaborate tattoo of a pocket watch." Finally, she managed to get the arm to stay facing up, showing the tattoo. It was a complex piece of art, complete with a chain, faceplate, and stop. The center of the watch was exposed, showing the internal workings with mechanical gears coming together. On the top rim of the watch, there was an engraving. "GCI."

"Gabe Caple the First." She brushed over the initials with her fingers. "You see, he was named after his grandfather. This tattoo was a memento, a tribute to his namesake. His grandfather loved watches." She looked into Drew's eyes. "Gabe was a sweet boy growing up. His parents tell stories of mischief and laughter. He was a trouble maker in high school like so many of us, but deep down he had a sweet and gentle heart. With a penchant to get mixed up with the wrong crowd." They looked at Gabe a moment in silence, both paying respects mentally.

"Well, here we are!" A loud and boisterous Kelly finally returned to the room with a folder. "What did I miss in here? Should I even allow the two of you in here at the same time? That may be against the policy of the building." Nodding at Kelly's words, Drew decided to play along with his charade for now. "Yes, Doctor . . . ." Drew trailed off, rolling the "r," raising his eyebrows, and extending his hand as to meet for the first time.

"Kelly Courtney." Reaching out, Kelly took his hand, winking with his right eye at Drew.

"Can you tell me anything about Gabe here? What was the cause of death? Any toxins? What do you have?"

Kelly opened up the file. "We don't have the full drug report yet, obviously, but he did have a point zero five blood alcohol content when he died. Initial C-O-D is drowning with no obvious signs of a struggle." Kelly flipped a page in the report. "Mmm, interesting." Using his finger as a guide, he read aloud a note from the intake exam.

"There are two notes of injury, his missing fingernail appears to have been torn out." Dropping the paperwork, he looked up at Drew. "Hey, didn't we see another body that lost a nail recently?" Kelly asked.

Twisting his lips in a confused way, Drew eyed over at Ashley, wondering if she heard Kelly speak. She was focusing on writing something in her own notes and hadn't heard him.

"Oh, yes, that's right, and moving on." Kelly brought the papers back up to continue reading. "There is a bruise on the back of his neck that is about one-sixteenth of an inch thick and runs parallel to his hairline. Shall we spin him over and have a look?"

Drew and Kelly positioned themselves on the right side of Gabe.

"Okay, on the count of three, we are going to pull and roll. Pull and roll!" Kelly repeated himself. Drew was positioned around the upper thighs of Gabe, while Kelly had the upper torso and shoulders. Putting her notepad away, Ashley stood at the feet.

"One, two, and three." With a couple of strained grunts from Kelly, they were able to flip the body squarely on the cart with Gabe's back pointed into the air.

"Let's have a look at this bruise."

Kelly and Drew peered at the neck, just below the hairline. Sure enough there it was, as described. It appeared as a straight line that extended around the back of his neck.

"What do you make of it?" Drew asked, looking at Kelly. Ashley walked around to the opposite side to have a look for herself.

"Could it have been a t-shirt, getting caught on something?" she asked out.

"Seems a little too high, but I suppose it's possible," Kelly responded.

Drew felt like he had seen this before. He pulled out his phone, stepping away from the cart.

"I think I've seen this before." After a minute of scrolling through emails, he said, "Here we are. The Ryans had a second autopsy performed as they wanted to make sure nothing was missed by the city's examiners." He gave Kelly a quick and uneasy glance. "I guess they didn't believe your group here did a good job." Looking back down to his phone, he continued talking.

"It wasn't noted in the city's report but was found by the subsequent examination requested by the Ryans. It notes, 'At the base of the skull meeting the upper neck, across the splenius and trapezius muscle is a one-sixteenth of an inch bruise, measured two inches long, running parallel to his hairline. Identification of the cause of the bruise was inconclusive but would not have attributed to cause of death and is not reflective of a sign of struggle, origin unknown.'"

Reaching into a drawer built into the counter, Kelly retrieved a tape ruler. He placed the flexible ruler on the back of Gabe's neck.

"Two point two five inches; I would conclude this is not coincidence. We might want to pull the medical examination reports on all drowning victims to see how many of these we might be able to connect."

Running his hand through his hair, Drew paced the room. "Is Anna online yet?"

Kelly looked at him with a frown, shaking his head. "No, not yet. The engineering team had some setbacks on the install. It probably won't be available until next year."

Throwing her hand in the air, Ashley asked, "And who is Anna?"

"A-N-N-A-I, the 'I' is silent, stands for Advanced Neural Network Artificial Intelligence for the explicit use of analyzing all case data on multiple crime types. The justice department teamed up with a few cities on the east coast to pilot an A.I. system that would be capable of constantly reviewing new and old case files for the PD and justice department. Kelly here was interviewed by the engineering team when they were investigating use cases for the system. Their hope was that information from autopsy reports could be used as a major source of data. Ultimately, the team believes that they will be able to identify connections between cases that would remain unseen due to the sheer amount of information that would need to be reviewed in the first place to make those connections."

Shaking her head, Ashley raised her eyebrows at them. "You two—you are friends," she said accusingly.

Kelly picked up when Drew stopped. "They have some promising ideas, categorizing and connecting is just the start of it. They think A.I. will be the future detective, naming suspects with the use of personal data brought in from the major cell phone, ISP, and DNA heritage companies. I love how Americans just let themselves be completely owned by crooked politicians and greedy corporations. You know, a few years ago most of that information was protected! Now anyone can buy it. America has created a market for data about people, fucking Christ, America made a hacker market!"

Ashley and Drew stared at Kelly—he was like that overly obsessed uncle at family parties that couldn't help himself bringing up a conversation around politics when a choice subject arose.

"I can see that being useful. The A.I. sounds promising," Ashley said, eyeing Kelly as though he might start in again at any moment. "But do we really need that here? Now? I mean, I was able to patch together a map of connected victims."

"A death map," Drew cut in.

"Yeah, sure, whatever you want to call it. I used old-fashioned victim profiling, you know, males eighteen to twenty-eight, under a hundred and seventy-five pounds, drowned in or around Boston." She waved at Gabe's body. "And I assumed everyone that met that profile was a victim." She paused a moment. "I mean, it took me six months to get all the news clippings together and access to police case files, so I guess I could have used Anna, like back then."

"Yes, exactly, imagine that Anna could make all those connections in six minutes! And, without the need to be triggered to do so!" Kelly said it as a matter of fact, even though he had no idea how long any process might have taken Anna.

"Triggered?" Ashley asked, unsure what he meant.

"Yes, in most investigations there needs to be a trigger to cause the investigation to start. Here it was you or Josh's family refusing to accept the initial report. Well, if Anna was online, she would have been looking for connections to every case ever, without the need to be triggered to do so."

Ashley took a step back, nodding in understanding. "Yes, that makes complete sense." She spoke softly before Kelly continued.

"She finds the connections you probably missed. Maybe even names the killer!" Kelly put his hand up in a stopping motion. "But wait, hold up. What is this death map?"

Drew and Ashley looked at each other, silently deciding who was going to fill Kelly in.

"Our mutual friend, Jen," Drew pointed between himself and Ashley as he spoke, "named a map that Ashley here put together. A map that highlights the locations of all drowning victims found on the Charles."

"Twenty-nine bodies spread across five towns and cities. With twenty of those found in Boston and Cambridge alone," Ashley said.

Kelly's eyes widened at the striking number. "The police don't know about this?" He asked the obvious question.

Ashley looked at Drew for a response. "I'm sure they've noticed a high number of bodies turning up in the river, but from what I've seen, they've all been labeled as accidental drownings. I'm not aware of them linking this to a killer, and with the friends I have in the local PD, if there was someone on this, I expect I would know about it, especially with the questions I've been asking them."

"I went to the police in Providence, and they told me it was out of their jurisdiction." Ashley spoke passionately, making it clear that she did not have a pleasant experience.

"So I called the BPD and left a message for a detective I was referred to, and I never heard back from him. After leaving three messages!" She shook her head, her expression showing her displeasure.

"Did you say why you were calling? In the messages? Because detectives get messages all the time, it can be hard to call everyone back if it's not directly associated with an active case. I was once a BPD detective and can tell you we got a lot of crazy talk type of calls."

"Well, Drew, yes, I was very clear. 'I think we have a serial killer!'" Ashley replied with a harsh, escalated tone.

"OK, I'll give them a call and see if I can probe my network there. We could use some help on this. If the police aren't on it yet, we might be able to get them to assign a couple bodies to the case. That would help in trying to connect some more pieces, looking for connections, and trying to identify other possible victims that you missed." Ashley nodded her head as he spoke.

"Oh, it's more than likely I missed people, and it's possible some of the victims I tagged are not connected," Ashley added.

"Sounds like we're in agreement. I'll set something up with the PD this afternoon to discuss what we have, what we think is going on, and how we can all work together on this." Drew walked over to Gabe's body, looking at it. "We will find out what happened to you, I promise."

He then looked up at Kelly. "You'll send me the full autopsy report when you have it? I'll also want to know what was found on him."

Kelly nodded in acceptance. "You will remember our agreement? Front row?"

Drew rolled his eyes.

"You guys don't know each other. Right. I believe that, calling your bullshit right here." Ashley pointed to herself, looking at them expectantly. When they didn't say anything, she said, "Whatever, guys, be children." She then looked over to Drew. "Where to next? Partner?"

As they left the building, Drew pointed at Ashley. "I think it's time you and I sit down and go over everything. I mean, I want to know everything you know."

"Okay, yes, I'll tell you what you want," Ashley snarled back defensively.

"Did you drive here?"

"No, I've mostly been using the T and buses."

"Okay, I'm parked over here. Jen is supposed to be waiting there for me." Drew signaled in a northerly direction from the building.

"Can you tell me . . . why Jen is here? And has she molested you yet?"

Drew looked up at the sky. "Oh God, not yet. But not for lack of trying on her part. Has she always been like that?"

Ashley laughed at the comment. "Yes, haha—oh my God, yes. Anyone attractive and friendly, she gets really—" Shrugging up her shoulder, Ashley held her hands out, squeezing the air. "She gets handsy, touchy-feely?"

"All those sound about right," Drew said in response.

"She is actually a sweetheart though, and contrary to what you might think, she's an amazing person. A lot of that is just a show; it's like she's in constant character for her brand."

"I got that sense as well." It was true that he had become quite fond of her over the past day. "She was really concerned about you. We found your door was broken and thought something might have happened to you." Drew looked at Ashley for a reaction.

"Yeah, I saw that too. Maybe I'm paranoid, but I think someone might have noticed me asking questions and digging into things that they might not want me digging into."

"Did you notice anything missing?" Drew asked.

Ashley shook her head. "Hell no. I'm on the tail of a mass murderer, psycho, and as soon as I saw my door like that, I backed away literally yelling, 'NOPE,' in my head. Didn't even go inside."

Drew saw her point. "Makes sense. That's how we found your death map though, looking inside for you."

Pausing, Drew took a deep breath. "When I went there looking for you, my GPS brought me to the other side of the house, which is how I met Jen. And well, I haven't been able to shake her since."

Ashley smiled. Having someone else to share the burden of what she was doing seemed to be having a positive impact.

"Thanks for working with me," she said, reaching out and touching his hand.

Drew shrugged it off. "Don't thank me just yet. I may turn out to be an awful investigator that does nothing but delay you in your pursuit," he joked.

"Even if it takes me twice as long to find these people, I think I'd rather not do it alone."

Drew was about to ask what she meant about, "these" people when he heard screaming coming from a nearby car in the parking lot. His heart jumped.

"JEN!" he yelled, thinking the worst, bursting into a full sprint. He deftly skirted a couple of tightly parked cars, and one foot hopped the hood of another, landing squarely in front of his car in a defensive stance, where Jen was screaming.

"Help me! Get me out of this car! Fuck!"

Drew was ready for anything, but what he saw made him start laughing immediately.

Jen stopped screaming when she saw him. "Finally! What in fuck's sake took you so long?"

Drew walked around to the passenger side. He could see that she had indeed handcuffed herself to the door handle on the inside ceiling of the car.

"I had a feeling—I seriously had a feeling you might go and do something stupid." Just then Ashley had caught up and was peering in from the driver side.

"You handcuffed her to your car?" she asked with concern in her voice.

Drew looked up shaking his head. "Oh no, this is all her. Some sort of sexual fetish thing."

"Ash? O-M-G, Ashley, where on shit's Earth have you been? We have been worried sick, running all over the place trying to find you."

"We can all catch up soon. Let's first get you out of those cuffs?" Ashley said, looking at Drew, waving her hand toward Jen.

"I can't, I mean, I don't have a key with me."

Jen turned red. "You don't have keys? Why the hell would you give me handcuffs? For which you have no keys?"

"I didn't put them on you, did I?" Drew responded.

"Ah, hello, have you met me? There was a one hundred percent chance I would put these on as soon as I knew about them."

Drew shrugged it off. "Yep, well, I think I have a key in my office at home. You're just going to have to hold out for a half-hour or so. Should be a fun ride through traffic."

"Aaarrrg," Jen screamed out in frustration before calming her voice again. "Ashley, seriously though, it's so nice to see you. And not all chopped up or something. Or I guess all bloated and floating in the river."

As she got into the back seat, Ashley seemed to be mixed about seeing Jen. "Jen, you should have stayed home. Why did you get yourself involved in this?"

Jen looked at her, eyes widening. "I was really, really worried about you is why?" Her voice squeaked slightly.

"You really wanted to try to get into Drew's pants, didn't you?"

Jen, pretended to be shocked at the accusation, continued with the off joke. "Okay, yes! But also, I was worried about you."

Drew tried to ignore the banter between the two as he pulled the car out and headed home.

Second Week – 2014

"You have been doing so great, hun!" Janet tapped Lizzy on the shoulder as she walked by. They had Lizzy doing barback and busboy duties for the first few weeks, that is, assisting Janet with cleaning glasses, restocking, wiping down the bar, cleaning up bar tables, rolling silverware, and other mundane things.

"This is the best place to start. Don't you worry none. You'll learn the ropes and soon Gary will have you taking orders, waitressing, and all that good shit." Reaching up, Janet grabbed a glass hanging from a rack above the bar.

"That's where you can really start making money," she said, her eyes widening. The bar was not particularly busy. It was a typical cold early fall night that kept most New Englanders home to stay warm. *Probably a good thing,* Lizzy thought. The previous week was the complete opposite. The bar was swamped until 11 p.m.; she could barely catch her breath trying to keep up with the work. Her feet were sore. She was clearly not used to the amount of walking and standing.

"Janet, did you start here as a barback?" Lizzy asked as she stacked pint glasses into a cabinet under the bar.

"Oh, hell no, sweetie." She waved her finger in the air. "Uh-uh, no, no way." She walked to the other side of the bar where she replaced one of the only customer's beers with a fresh one.

"I was a waitress over at TG's for a couple years; I also filled in as a bartender there on multiple occasions. You know, I had experience." She paused to update the order in the computer.

"When I first came here, I started as a weekday bartender. I was working jobs here and at TG's, then one day the guy that was the lead bartender left. And I took his job and ditched what I had going at TG's; this place makes way more money!" she said with pride.

"I have the choice on the nights here too, which TG's didn't give me. I had to rotate weekends with someone else."

Lizzy wasn't sure about Janet yet, and after every conversation, Lizzy felt put down at the end of them. Janet had planted her flag in the soil, making sure Lizzy knew who the real boss was.

"That's awesome, Janet. Seems like having that experience was really good for you." Lizzy tried to stay positive and engage with caution. She didn't want to ruin relationships with co-workers on her second week.

"Ah yeah, girl, you know it. You'll get there, babe. By the way, you can probably leave around ten tonight, a little earlier than last Friday. That's nice, right? Getting out early on a Friday?" Janet asked the questions rhetorically as she walked off as soon as she finished. Lizzy nodded her head.

"Yep, super nice," Lizzy whispered to herself sarcastically. In fact, she had been a bit disappointed in the new job. Keeping her on a tight leash, Janet treated her as an assistant rather than a peer. Lizzy understood that she lacked the experience, but there were better ways to treat people than Janet did, just her attitude toward her was belittling.

I'm not a threat. Ignore it! Ignore it, Lizzy. It will get easier. Trying to convince herself to move forward, she worked to not let the little things bring her down. Janet was not all wrong; experience was something that would lead to the next step.

"Hey, next week I think I'm ready to waitress the bar tables, if that's okay with you?" Lizzy asked Janet, trying to push her own timeline.

"Um, yeah, hun, that might work. Let me run it by Gary later and get back to you." Even if Lizzy was not able to convince them to give her more of the work she wanted, asking would move her one step closer to it.

The end of the shift snuck up on her; even on a slow day she found ways to keep busy and keep herself from looking at the time.

"Janet, it's ten-thirty, and it seems to be really dead tonight. You said I could leave early, right?" There, in fact, were only two customers in the bar, regulars. A small quick snow flurry had come through around nine. It didn't leave any accumulation but was enough to continue to keep folks out.

"Oh, yeah, babe, definitely. You should get out of here." Janet shook her head convincingly.

"Should I call Gary or is it okay to take off?" Lizzy was not sure of the proper protocol for leaving early.

"Nah, it's totally fine. Just clock out, and you're all good."

Lizzy nodded. "Okay, awesome. Thanks for another night of

teaching me, you know, the ropes."

"Oh, you are too damn sweet, girl. It was my pleasure. Now go on and get going." Janet walked over and gave Lizzy a friendly slap in the behind, ushering her out.

Lizzy wrapped herself with a large scarf over the tight sweater she had on. It was warmer when she came into work, and she had left her jacket at home. Just as she was walking out of the building, her phone went off. Pulling it up, she saw that it was Tommy. He knew she would be getting out soon.

TOMMY

Tommy – Are you out yet? Are you coming over? I would love to see you tonight 🤍
Today@10:42pm

Yes!! Just waking out, thankfully. Working a slow night is super boring. 😵 🔫
🤍🤍 missing you
Just Now

Tommy *is typing…*

Just as she was waiting for Tommy to finish his response, she felt a scratchy cloth cover her, like being blanketed playfully as a kid. Her reaction was the same, she froze.

Is this is a trick? Is someone playing with me? Am I being hazed as part of a tradition with my new co-workers? She stood silent, not breathing a moment, waiting for it to play out. She felt hands around her legs and heard a *zip* sound. Her keys and phone fell to the ground as the bag tightened around her waist. She was barely able to move in the bag; it was stiff and constricting, almost like the bag was made with embedded strands of metal.

She meant to scream for help, but all that came out was a short screech, a result of her holding her breath and not taking the next one. Feeling herself being picked up off the ground, she began to kick and squirm, fighting, trying to do anything to stop it. Part of her felt as though it was a joke, a prank being played on her. She could sense two people working together to hold her. One was holding her by her arms and torso, the other at her legs. By the intensity of their grips, she could sense they were both men, with the one holding her shoulders being the gentler one.

"Please, stop—stop!" She was finally able to get a scream out, still convinced that it was a prank, as if asking them to stop would suddenly have them put her down, take off the bag, and snap a photo for Facebook. She was put down on what felt like a pad. The space was tight—she seemed to be unable to fit with her legs extended. The man who held her legs punched her behind the knees, forcing them to bend as he jammed them into the space. *Thunk.* She knew that sound—she was in the trunk of a car.

"What the fuck! Stop! Stop! You're freaking me out, guys!" she pleaded again more. "This can't be happening." She felt the car turn on and begin to drive.

"Fuck, fuck." She began thinking out loud. The ride seemed to go on forever. She envisioned everything from being murdered, raped, a prank, and even had visions of herself fighting for her life and getting away triumphantly. She thought of her dad and Tommy. Tommy would realize she was missing. After her dad found out, he would find her quickly, she knew it, he had too.

* * *

The box that Lizzy was in now was even tighter and less friendly than the trunk of the car. She had struggled as much as her 118lb body was capable of while trapped in an impenetrable bag with zip ties around her legs. The men were too strong for her to overcome in the position she was in.

She was scared—terrified—these people were going to kill her. She could sense it. Knowing the only way to survive this was to remain calm and be patient, she tried to talk herself down. "Remain calm. Wait for your opening."

"Jack! What the fuck, man?" She could hear the nicer one of her two abductors scream out, a shrill in his voice.

Were they fighting each other? She heard sounds of scrambling around, furniture being knocked over, and a couple of pleads from the nicer one, until finally there were no sounds. Lizzy remained quiet in her box. It was probably best that attention was not on her at the moment, and anything that delayed her inevitable destination was good.

Boxed up – 2014

The box smelled of musk and body odor.

Ugh, that's not me is it? Lizzy thought as she couldn't help but take in the smell. She didn't smell like that on her worst day.

He's had others in here before. Fuck this dude. She was unsure how long she'd been in the box but guessed it had been two to three hours by the feel of her stomach and her need to pee. Since the scuffle between the two men, all she had heard from outside the box was a couple of muffled sounds and squeaks. She most definitely needed to pee though.

Do I call out for help to let me pee? Or do I just piss myself? she contemplated. If she asked to use the bathroom, maybe he would oblige and at least she wouldn't have to sit in her own filth for the remainder of her life. On the other hand, maybe it would speed up that process of whatever was waiting for her outside of this box.

Shit, what do I do? What do I do? She didn't realize it, but she was grinding her teeth from terror. While she had been able to control some of her fear responses by meditating and convincing herself that remaining calm was the only way to survive, other parts of her body weren't on the same page. Her teeth were chattering, her hands were shaking by her side, and her back was tense and beginning to ache from the position she was in.

A door slammed violently from across the room.

"You fucked up!" Lizzy could hear a woman's voice screaming from a distance. Footsteps were coming down the stairs and into the basement. The box was virtually blacked out from her position, still stuck in a bag. There was a tiny bit of light coming from a hole just to her right; struggling to turn, she slithered about in the box to get into a better position to snoop. There was no way for her to get as close as she needed to the hole, but if she moved just ever so slightly, she could make out the bottom of the stairs through the grainy bag material that had meshed around the puncture.

"What are you doing here? We don't have a scheduled meeting."

A man appeared in her sight, from across the other side of the basement.

Fucking bastard, Lizzy thought. He was the one that had brought her here; she knew it.

"Help! Please! Miss! Fucker's got me in a box! Please help me!" Pleading, Lizzy kicked her feet, audibly trying to get the woman's attention.

"Help Me! Ahhhh!" Lizzy screeched out, a scream filled with horror, closing her eyes as she did it to squeeze out every last drop of terror from her voice. This was what she was waiting for, being patient for.

She stopped screaming briefly so that she could look again through the hole. She saw that they were moving closer to the box.

I'm saved, Lizzy thought. "Yes! Over here! Please get me out! I won't speak of this if you just let me go!"

As soon as they were near the outside of the box, the man violently kicked the box that Lizzy was pleading from.

"Keep it up, and I'll fill that box with gasoline and throw in a match," the man said gruffly, almost whispering, as he leaned toward the holes in the box.

Lizzy started to cry. She felt alone, abandoned, terrified, with wild scenarios of rape, torture, and murder cycling through her mind again and again, never ending.

"But, please, miss, you have to help." She spoke softly this time, sputtering, as if trying to whisper would appeal to the woman in the room.

"Oh, fucking shit. She shit herself," the woman said, standing almost directly over the box. When she heard the words, Lizzy's first thought was, *Who shit themselves?*

Sure enough, she could feel the warm bunch jamming in her pantie, pressing along her backside and hip as she was now leaning on her left side to try to look out of the hole.

Oh God, I did shit myself, she thought. She tried not to move around as motion made it feel like it was making it worse, squishing it farther down her pant legs.

Fuck, I pissed too. She felt her pant legs getting colder as the urine lost her body heat.

"You need to clean her up," the woman said with a long sigh. "Get her prepped for moving, break her in." The woman took another deep breath. "Make sure she's ready. We need her on the plane to Singapore in two days."

The man remained silent through the interaction.

Lizzy kept repeating the words. *We need her on the plane to Singapore. We need her on the plane Singapore.* Fear subsiding slightly, her visions of immediate torture and rape disappeared to be replaced by the more distant thoughts of being sold into sex slavery. She was sobbing at the idea of being dragged off somewhere, totally out of control and at the whim of some maniacs.

Break her in. She pondered the words. *What does "break her in" mean?* Their footsteps were soft on the carpet, but she could tell they had moved away from the box. Being locked in a box had a way of heightening senses; her hearing seemed sharp and ready to aid her survival. She took a deep breath and listened.

"What the fuck did you do?" the woman asked with the tone of a supervisor speaking down to an employee. Lizzy had to strain to hear the conversation now that the two had moved away.

"What do you mean?"

"Oh, don't play coy with me. You really want me to go back there in that room and see it for myself?"

Jack didn't respond for a few moments. "All right, you know what I am. You knew all along. That's why you hired me." The woman paced back and forth. Lizzy could tell there was tension in the conversation. She could tell by the tones of their voices that they knew each other well.

"Fuck, seriously fuck. My best goddamn operative is off in the clouds doing his own *fucking thing*." The woman lost her temper. Her voice raised with each word, gaining intensity until the last two words were screamed out.

Lizzy wasn't quite sure what she was talking about but thought it might have to do with the other man that brought her here.

"Okay, okay. Let's calm down. We can work through this. Here is what *you*—" Screaming, she laid into the words. Lizzy imagined her poking him in the chest as she said it.

"Here is what *you* are going to do. Get rid of him tonight. You hear me? Dump the body, bury the body, burn the body—I don't give a fuck. Just get rid of him. Tonight, I don't want him in this house." The woman didn't slow down to let him answer any question or put in any response; it was clear she was making demands with an expectation of execution.

"I can do that," the man responded calmly.

Lizzy heard the woman take a deep breath. "You're lucky I like you. If I were to report this—" There was a pause. "You know what that would mean?" There was another pause for effect.

"Get rid of him, and I don't want to catch you doing this again." With that, Lizzy heard the woman make her way back upstairs. The door opened and closed, and she was gone.

Soon after the woman left, Lizzy heard a door open very close to the box she was in. A squeaky wheelbarrow rolled by. Then maybe ten minutes later, it rolled back by her, but this time without the squeak, as if carrying something heavy was putting excess weight on the bearing, snuffing out the friction. The door closed. And Lizzy was alone again. She tried kicking the box, hoping that repeated strikes might be enough to break open a weak hinge or lock.

"Fucking bag!" she screamed in frustration, shaking. The box withstood her desperate attempts until all her energy was wasted. She dozed off, losing track of time, in and out of consciousness, wishing upon all wishes, that this was just a dream.

"It's just a dream. Wake up Elizabeth, wake up. Just wake up. You are Elizabeth Law. You are Elizabeth Law. There have been so many Laws before you, and they have all been tested. Wake up, Elizabeth." Speaking reminded herself who she was. For some reason, thinking about her family and those who came before, carried her name, gave her confidence. It gave her strength to prepare for what she thought was about to happen.

* * *

The car door shut with stiff intensity. Elle sat down in her usual town car, but today next to a man. He had silver hair, was in his mid-forties with a strong jawline, high protruding cheeks, and was well dressed in a casual slim-fit gray suit. He was stocky and long, probably standing 6'5" and 255lbs and could easily have been mistaken for a linebacker.

"Well, what do you think?"

Taking off her glasses, Elle rubbed them with a cloth, nonchalantly. After a moment she looked up into the eyes of the man sitting next to her. Her off-colored eyes were always enough to mesmerize anyone willing to stare into them. "Yes. He's burned. He has not stopped."

Taking a deep breath, the man looked forward briefly. He looked down into a mobile phone that had a streaming video feed of the basement, the bathroom, and every other room in the house.

"Do we let him continue? He's your best guy. And he did get the job done. I mean, you have to hand it to him, he used that man to help him complete the job that we assigned." The man chuckled a bit at his own musing.

"No, fuck that monster. He's put us all at risk with his continuous negligent actions. That shit is out of scope, out of scope!" She reiterated the words for effect while shaking her hands. "He's fucking sick, addicted to it. You should have seen the poor bastard he put out."

"You saw the guy die?" he asked with a raised brow.

"I watched everything; that's why I brought you with me. I wasn't sure how he might react with me," she said, disgust on her face.

"Clever girl. Do you want me to go in there and take care of it?"

Elle looked up for a moment, considering the proposal, but she knew he had an assignment, that she needed the silver-haired man in LA tomorrow afternoon.

"No, you should already be on the way to the airport. And we want the girl escorted to the strip on Sunday. You can't do both." She thought for a moment.

"Have we made contact with his clean team?" he asked her.

"Yes, they had gone dark about three weeks ago, but we recently made contact. They're currently evaluating his mess, seeing if there are others leaks that need to be plugged."

Elle considered the best way of handling it. "Okay, let's activate his clean team then. That's what they're there for. If we need to burn the deal on this girl—" She tilted her head back, not comfortable with dealing with the consequences of a failed deal. "Ahh, shit, so be it. If he's put the organization at risk, then we have no alternative."

The organization had three teams associated with every operative, agent, recruit, or employee involved in sensitive operations or assignments. Elle herself would have these three teams assigned to her, just like the man with silver hair sitting next to her, and even the man who oversaw northeast operations, a monitoring team, tasked with tracking, scanning communications, and randomly shadowing on operations the agent performs.

Then there was the clean team. This team was made up of one or many individuals, depending on the operative, and was tasked with eliminating the target on command and any potential leaks an operative may have outstanding—kids, wives, husbands, family, friends, and just about anything that might put the organization at risk. The guy sitting next to her had been a clean-agent in the past. When he had terminated his target, he had burned down an entire apartment building, killing twenty innocent people in the process. The only issue Elle had with a clean team was that depending on where they were embedded, it could be days or even weeks before the kill was completed to assure all leaks were properly identified.

Lastly, there was a handler team. That was a team of one or more individuals tasked with handling their operatives, keeping them on the company line, making decisions about agent actions based on the reports from the monitoring team, and making the call when an agent was burned. Elle was Jack's handler; she was responsible for him, and deep down, she felt pain for having been the one to unleash him in his current form. Sure, he had always been a monster, but she had made a choice to give him the tools and skills that made him a more efficient killer than even he could have imagined. She was the one who helped remove the last bit of humanity he had left. If she had simply gone with her gut and reported him as unfit to be an operative, then he would already be in jail wasting away.

"See if you can put a rush on that order."

She shook her head violently as she recalled her last sexual encounter with Jack. As they pulled away from the home, she held back a feeling of nausea and desire to vomit.

"Fuuuuuck!"

Profile – 2014

"All right, we are looking for a man, a hundred eighty to, mmm, say two hundred twenty-five pounds." As she spoke, Ashley wrote on a large whiteboard that Drew had on one wall of his office.

"Six feet to six feet two inches tall. White. Educated. Narcissistic." She turned around looking for additional suggestions from Drew and Jen.

"Fucking nuts! Crazy bastard!" Jen blurted.

"Sociopathic!" Ashley pointed at Jen as if she had helped her arrive to a notable point before flinging around to put it on the board.

Drew threw one in. "Strong, probably works out often." Ashley wrote it on the board. He tossed another out. "Likely from the Boston area."

"Hmm." Ashley bounced the marker against her lip as she stared at the board. "I still can't believe they're sending out a detective tomorrow. On a Sunday," Ashley said, spinning around, incredulous at the idea.

"Well, when you're a big deal," Drew joked, dipping his voice and spinning his eyebrows as he thumbed up to himself.

"Oh Jesus," Ashley said, rolling her eyes.

In truth, Drew was also surprised at the response time. He had called his old captain, now chief, asking for some resources to hunt a serial killer. The chief resisted at first, finally offering to look into it. Then about an hour later, Drew got a text message that a detective would be by to assist.

Jen pinched his thigh before massaging his leg up toward his groin, just slightly brushing and arousing him with her hand. A jolt shot through his body, forcing him to pull back awkwardly.

"You *are* a huge deal," she said slowly with some exaggeration, her lips slightly parted and her eyes wide. Drew looked over at Jen, then back at Ashley, trying to ignore what he could. The interest Jen had been working so hard to earn from him all day was disappearing now that Ashley was in the picture.

I like her, Drew thought as he checked out Ashley as she was turned and focusing on the board. She was beautiful, passionate, smart, talented, and easy to have a conversation with. Being closer in age was a big boost; he didn't like feeling like he was robbing the cradle. As the night had progressed, Jen could see the building chemistry between the two and instinctively was increasing the boldness of her sexual advances on him, trying her best to prevent the bud from growing with Ashley.

Shit, if I get a half-hour, hell, fifteen minutes alone with that man, I am going to strip down, pull his cock out, and stroke it until he loves me, Jen thought as stared off at Drew, the female competition triggering desperate actions.

"Hey!" Ashley yelled. Jen twitched her head, snapping out of her daydream, her hand still on Drew's thigh. "I asked you to tell me your thoughts on motive?"

Both Ashley and Drew were staring at Jen now.

"Ah—oh, sorry. Yeah, well, you know. I, ahh—got distracted for a second."

Ashley raised her eyebrows, glancing at Jen's hand near Drew's crotch. "We can see that," Ashley said with a snarky tone.

"How do you two get along? I mean, you are complete opposites. You realize that, right?" Drew was waving his hands in a crossing pattern, pointing in different directions as he spoke. Ashley and Jen looked at each other, eyes meeting.

"Opposites attract?" Jen asked out, still locking eyes with Ashley.

"Yeah, that's exactly right. We are very compatible." Ashley pointed to Jen with her marker, and all visual cues of discontent or disapproval washed away. Drew thought there was more between these two than he knew and made a mental note to investigate it later. *If you know what I mean,* Drew thought, being a bit of a dog.

"Motive is a tough thing to guess," Drew said, shaking his head.

"I mean, if it turns out that only two victims belong to the same killer, which is still a possibility, then maybe the killer targeted these two for a reason." Raising his hands as he got up, Drew paced in front of the whiteboard. "Maybe they were part of some group, online gang, hell, video game network. People are getting other people killed over video games nowadays with the swatting thing."

"Swatting?" Jen asked out.

"Yeah, some nerd gets pissed that he lost a game against you, somehow figures out who you are and where you live, and calls in swat with the local police on you," Drew spoke with frustration.

Drew paused a moment, taking a breath, before continuing. "Anyways, maybe he killed all these people, and he is just one sick f'n bastard."

Jen shook her head. "I hope they're not all connected." Her voice quivering, sadness mapped her face. "I mean, accidents, falling in the river drunk, or falling and hitting your head. Maybe there's a part of the river that's easy to slip into, right? And these two just slipped in the same spot, receiving similar bruises?" She took a deep breath and kept talking when the room stayed silent for too long.

"That's all, you know, sort of, okay, 'cause accidents fucking happen." Her eyes went from sorrow and pity to fear. "But if it really was a master serial killer, I mean, fuck. That sucks. Those poor guys didn't deserve that."

"So, let's go over what we have." Drew tried to move the conversation forward. "Besides this profile." Drew waved at the profiling notes on the whiteboard. "We have thirty victims, all men, all drowned in the river. All of them had consumed some alcohol prior to going missing." Standing up, Drew walked over to another wall where they had printed out the picture of the death map on eight sheets of paper, taping them together on the wall to form one large map. Drew thought it was a waste of paper, but Jen insisted it needed to be big.

"None of them weighed more than a hundred and sixty-five pounds, and the average weight of all thirty is a hundred forty-four pounds," Ashley added.

"Why is that important?" Jen said with a look of confusion.

Drew answered. "It's a tell, an upper boundary to his physical capabilities."

"Meaning, that he's targeting men that he knows he can handle," Ashley chimed in.

"Which is what Ash is using there to guess on our perp's height and weight." Drew pointed back at the whiteboard.

"I bet you the real profilers, no offense," he nodded at Ash without breaking sentence, "have an algorithm that they could plug in the height and weight numbers from the victims and would be able to narrow down the killer's weight to a five-pound gap."

Ash bobbed her head in an agreeing motion.

"We have those pictures that tie together at least two of the murders." Jen pointed to the whiteboard again. Opposite the profiling side, they had taped up photos of the two victims' necks, in which they had matching bruising patterns.

"I think this is our strongest piece of evidence." Drew sat back down, running his hand through his hair. "Shit, we need more. Two is coincidence. Three, four, or five—that's undeniable."

"I might have some more photos of other victims," Ashley said.

Drew looked at her inquisitively. "Why didn't you tell us before? Have you seen this same bruising pattern? How'd you get them?"

"I have been working on this for months. Everyone on that map that I was able to ID, fifteen or so, well, I tried to get ahold of the autopsy reports and pictures on them."

"But how? They don't let random civilians walk into police stations or medical examiner offices to poke around." Drew's tone changed from inquisitive to suspicious.

"Wow, relax, big guy. You know your friend Kelly there, with the Bruins tickets? Well, he's also dirty with civilians. He takes bribes. And for every one of him, in another office, there are two more guys with access to reports that will do about anything for a pretty girl." Twisting her hips, she rubbed down the sides of her torso, tightening her shirt so it gripped her figure in a skin-tight silhouette, her face dipping into a pose, like a model.

"Yup. Okay. Fair enough." Drew sat back down, totally convinced that would work. "Well, if you're asked again where the photos came from just say an anonymous source." It was no surprise that Kelly was taking cash for access to "otherwise confidential" information. Drew was giving him Bruins tickets. When you boil it down, ethically it's the same thing. He valued his friend and contact and would prefer his name not be dragged through the mud as a result of his investigation.

"Did you see any of these patterns?" Walking up, he slapped the photos they had on the board, showing the bruising.

"Ahh, no, you see, I haven't actually gone through the photos yet." She bit her lip, mouthing "sorry."

"I started to, a little bit, but I have autopsy and police reports on like fifteen of these guys. Each of them has like, hundreds of photos, at least." Drew and Jen stayed mum, letting Ashley continue to talk nervously.

"I started with the reports, and they are not easy to read, let me tell you. Lateral tear here, ulnar artery and nerve there, or mid-palm something." She pointed at her hands as she spoke.

"I pretty much needed to study medicine to make sense of it. And

you try looking at those pictures by yourself, on like, a Friday night."
She let out a breath. "I don't even know why I'm explaining myself
here. I don't need to be ashamed that I haven't finished reviewing
everything, and that this guy is still out there killing. I am one person,
and this is my first murder investigation."

Drew stood up, putting up his hand to help pull back the reins.
"Okay, we get it. I agree. It's not your fault." His hands made a
calming motion to help settle her emotions. She obviously was
carrying some guilt on the topic. Ashley was the type of person that
relied on herself to solve complex problems, as she usually did as an
engineer by profession.

"It's late. Should we get some sleep?" Since Drew had already
offered the guest room and Lizzy's bed to Jen and Ashley, he was
hoping this question would prompt action. He was tired from running
around all day and looked it.

"One a.m.?" Jen shouted out, looking at the clock. "Shit, it's
already Sunday."

The Detective – 2014

Knock! Knock! Knock! The door at Drew's house erupted with loud, hard cracks.

"The cop's here!" Jen jumped up with excitement. They picked up where they had left off the previous night, spending much of the day scanning photos, reading reports, and, in Jen's case, doodling on the whiteboard.

"Relax, sit down, stay here. I'll bring him, or her, in. And let me do most of the talking." The last part he yelled back as he left the room.

Drew opened up his front door, and to his surprise, there were two people standing at his door stoop. He knew both of them. The first man was dressed wearing a long black jacket with a detective badge hanging around his neck. Drew sized him up this time as if he may have to get into a hand-to-hand combat situation with the man. Detective Trenhon was a little shorter than Drew but very similar in weight. The other man at the door was a slender, shorter, younger man, that stood with a look of concern on his face.

"Tom, Lizzy isn't home. And it's not a good time." Tom put his hand on the doorframe, preventing Drew from shutting it.

"We need to talk. I'm worried about Lizzy," Tom said. The detective invited himself in the house, brushing past Drew, not interested in the conversation with Tom. Ignoring him, Drew turned his attention to Tom.

"What did you do? Did something happen?"

"Me, no, no, no—I didn't do anything. Lizzy was supposed to come over last night after she got off her shift. I got a really weird text from her, and—" Tom looked down at his phone nervously. "She didn't show up, and I haven't been able to reach her since. I think I know where she is." Tom paused, almost ashamed of himself.

"She's someplace weird in New Hampshire."

Drew thought about it for a moment. It was not uncommon for Lizzy to take off for a couple of nights without telling him where she was. Having family and friends in New Hampshire, she often escaped there when she wanted to get away. Drew had always been loose on rules, treating Lizzy like an adult after she reached age fifteen, more than he should have.

"I'm sure she'll show up. She's probably at another friend's house." Drew tried to relay the most likely scenario.

Tom shook his head. "I tried calling her friends. I don't think so."

"What did her text say?" Drew asked frankly.

"Um, I know this doesn't sound great, but trust me, it does not make any sense at all." Tom pulled up his phone, scrolled past a couple dozen unanswered texts that he had been sending her, then began to read the message.

"Tom, you are a complete douche bag. I don't want to see you anymore. Not tonight, not tomorrow, not ever!" Drew read the text from the phone. It surely was verbiage he had never seen from her before. Lizzy was almost always polite, even when she was angry. Then again she was texting this to her boyfriend. Who knew what kind of problems were really going on between them that Tom wouldn't want to share?

"Look, Tom, you seem like a nice guy, but—" Drew flashed an edgy, almost apologetic smile, "Maybe the text says what it means." Drew shrugged, trying to continue to lay it on soft and rushing the conversation without much thought as he had a *detective douche bag* to deal with.

"Look, just look at her earlier messages. She was excited to see me last night—and look, she hearts?" Tom pleaded for Drew to inspect the earlier messages.

"Give her some time. I'm sure she's fine. Okay? Give me a call if you can show me she's actually in trouble and not just ignoring you. Have a good night, Tom." As he shut the door, he could hear Tom mumble. "It's not Lizzy. This makes no sense. You need to come with me."

Drew was in a natural state of denial, ignorant to the reality, and unwilling to accept his daughter was anywhere other than safe and sound on a friend's couch.

Drew ignored him, shutting the door with his attention now on the other man from the stoop.

"Ahh, kids," Drew said to Detective Trenhon as he spun back toward the living room of his house. Eyeing the detective, he said, "What the hell are you doing? I was expecting a local." He was not particularly fond of the detective from their previous encounters.

"Please, call me Phil. It's a friggin' Sunday." Phil reached out his arms, shrugging, almost sarcastically.

"Truth is, I was already downtown." Phil was now walking freely through Drew's living room, looking at old family photos hanging on the mantle.

"Cute wife." He looked back, winking at Drew before continuing. "You see, I do my job. I do it well. Turns out our friend Ashley had been using her credit cards downtown and not once, but three times, she visited the same friggin' coffee shop." He turned from the mantle to face Drew again.

"I go there today, this café, not even two hours ago." Drew looked at his clock, almost 4:45 p.m.

"And, the guy working there, the owna, tells me she was there. Today!" He spins around again, facing the mantle. "Yeah, that surprised me too. He tells me, he seen her leave the shop at least twice and head across the street to the Boston medical examiner's office. Weird, right? What the hell is she doing at the friggin' morgue? Pretty thing like that?" He spins back around, facing Drew.

"All right, sure, so I follow the breadcrumbs, and the medical examiner's office gave me the logs of who came and went for the day. And guess whose name was on there, leaving at the same time?" Shrugging, he pointed at Drew, his head bouncing up and down. "You."

Phil raised his eyes. "Then, when I call some of my friends in the BPD to ask about you—yes, you're not the only one with friends in high places—I hear that you need a friggin' detective to help with some—" He put his hands in the air, using two fingers on each hand to create double quotation marks in the air. "Quote, serious, end quote, case you're working. Possible serial killer shhh-ite."

Drew figured the good detective was a family man. The way he had tried to avoid swearing, he probably had young impressionable kids running around the house at home.

"First thing's first, Mr. Law." Pausing, he had the look of an epiphany fall over his face. "You know you probably shoulda been a lawyer with a name like that."

Drew rolled his eyes and said, "I've never heard that before."

Ignoring him, Phil said, "Where the hell is Ashley? Is she okay? As soon as I get a chance to speak with her, I can close the book on that assignment. Tell my captain I did my job well done and, boom, move on."

"Okay, I know where she is, and I'll bring her to you. But you're going to leave us alone after. That's the deal. Period." Drew put out his hand, looking for an agreement.

"About that. You see. Your local department doesn't have the manpower right now to send you all the friggin' cops whenevah you want." Avoiding Drew's outstretched hand, he walked by a half-eaten pizza on the table in the adjacent kitchen.

"Pepperoni, that's my favorite. You don't mind? Do you?" he asked rhetorically, already walking through the kitchen and stuffing half a piece into his mouth.

"I'm friggin' Starving Marvin here." Drew didn't get the reference.

Drew was about to protest when the detective continued, mumbling as he chewed.

"You see." Phil paused to swallow. "None of my higher-ups here wanted to tell me anything about you. I had to broker a deal to get your address from them. Hey, don't look at me like that. They were the ones that offered to make the deal."

Drew gave him a disapproving look.

"Yeah, they were like, 'Nope, Drew. Great guy, yadda yadda, can't give you anything.'" Phil took another bite before throwing his half-eaten crust back into the open pizza box.

"Then just before this guy hangs up on me, he says, 'Well, if it's official business, in support of a request Drew himself made, I don't see any problem giving you his address.' You could tell this guy was spinning this around in his head for the entire call. I just had to keep him on long enough. But that's when he makes the deal. I stick around here for a few days, BPD will pay my overtime if I help you with some case you're workin', a case that you asked for some help on. Bam, he gives me anything I want about you." Phil now extends out his hand.

"Partner."

Drew felt like he'd been making too many partners recently.

"Goddammit. Greedy little bastard, aren't cha?" Drew couldn't deny it—the guy was pretty good, tenacious.

Just as they were shaking hands, Jen stormed furiously into the kitchen, Ashley following behind her.

"What the fuck is he doing here?" Jen demanded.

Phil looked at Drew.

"What kind of party is happening here?" Without waiting for a response, he said, "Mrs. Tinder, I didn't realize you were here. You look," he said, eyeing her up and down a little too slowly for Drew's liking, "very healthy." Taking his cell phone out, he snapped a photo. "Yep, that wraps up that case."

Ashley looked puzzled. "What case?" she said, looking at Drew for an explanation.

"You remember we called the cops when we found your door busted in? We also submitted a missing person report asking for help in locating you."

Ashley raised her eyebrows at Drew.

"We were worried after finding the map," Jen cut in, taking a break from the death stare she was giving the good detective. "But why is he here?" Flicking her fiery eyes back to the detective, she pointed directly at Phil's face, her finger not three inches from his nose. He batted it away instinctively.

Leaning in aggressively, he said, "Hey, sweetie. Don't blame me for your poor life choices just because I call you out on them. They were your choices."

"You don't have to be such a dick. Or does that come with the badge, pig?"

Stepping in between the two, Drew put his hands up. "Wow, all right, relax. Look, we're all going to be working together on this." He looked back and forth at the two.

Phil shook his head. "I'm not working on anything with her. What the hell kind of help is she going to be?"

Drew gave Phil a "shut the fuck up" look. "You don't even know what it is we're working on here," Drew pointed out.

"I know it's big, mass serial killer shit big. And I was told to find out if there was any credence to the claims," Phil swore.

Jen must be getting to him. That was fast, Drew thought. He couldn't believe Phil knew that much about the case they were on. He had only told his former captain, now police chief, what he was on to, and he'd thought he could trust him to keep a low profile.

"Here is the plan. We are going to bring the good detective here up to speed. We are all going to be polite and have nothing but respect for each other. Otherwise, you can go home now and forget about this." Drew motioned to the door. "If you stay, I don't want to hear about it." They both nodded silently.

Phil stepped back from Drew, taking a deep breath, the tension in his body ratcheting down a notch. "What kind of crazy shh-ite are you people in? How the hell did you all get involved in this?"

The Dump – 2014

Getting rid of Ben like this was not what Jack typically liked to do. His current ritual was to hold onto his victims for up to forty-eight hours. He would revisit their lifeless, rigid bodies and stare into their eyes through the glass of his makeshift, sealed helmet. He liked taking time to review the body for any evidence he might leave or sometimes even plant evidence. He knew that one day, someone would make the connection. The Boston area had more than double the drowning rates than any other port city in the country. If someone hadn't already figured it out, they would soon. All these men were not victims of drunken circumstance.

Part of him longed for it to happen. What would the media call him? "Killer of the Charles" or "The Back Bay Murderer" or "Murder on Charles"? He obsessed over his work being recognized. It had escalated in recent years, becoming a game he played with the system. How many more could he kill before they caught on? He had been intentionally clustering where he dropped his victims into the river, a subtle hint to the authorities. Yet, year after year and murder after murder, there was nothing on TV besides, "Another accidental drowning on the Charles."

I can't be caught, he thought often. A few times he even considered sending in a tip, nudging the media to make a connection; he even considered starting to sign his name the bodies.

"Not yet. I'm not ready. The next one, maybe, I'll leave some breadcrumbs," he would say every time he began to prep for his next kill. He would love to see the city paralyzed in the fear from his actions, and he knew it was just a matter of time before it came out.

"Fuck Elle," Jack said. He considered disobeying her directly and keeping the body around, but the safehouse he was using was not his. It belonged to the organization, and finding a new independent place would take time. It was, in fact, the first time he had indulged his personal pleasures on the organization's property and dime.

"Dammit," he murmured as he slowly dragged the body out of the open trunk of a white Toyota Sienna minivan.

The body slammed into the dirt with a muffled sound. He always thought that bodies were somehow heavier after they were dead. Leaving a wide mark on the slightly snowy path, he slowly dragged it to the water's edge. He had never used this spot before to dump a body, just under the Longfellow Bridge. The river had strong currents here due to changing widths in the canal. He finally reached the edge, peering into the familiar dark water. He paused to reflect on the many times he had been in a similar spot. His normal dumping area had construction going on. All the activity forced him to travel a little farther in.

He brought Ben's body parallel to the water. With a slight push, he was able to slip Ben in with barely a splash. The body bobbed, hooked on a rock for a moment, then whisked away out of sight, into the darkness of the night. Jack got back in his van, which was parked on Storrow Drive with hazards flashing, a brazen and uncharacteristic approach for him, but he didn't have time to pull together a utility truck or emergency vehicle. All he could do in short order was a white minivan. He walked around the van after waiting for a car to pass, waving as the vehicle skirted by, the driver never looking over.

He was amazed at the things he got away with, virtually in plain sight.

"People don't care."

Shaking his head, he stepped into the van. Getting back into the driver seat caused a sensation of safety and comfort to wash over him nonetheless.

His phone began to ring.

"Dammit, Elle, what now?"

Freedom – 2014

Her muscles ached all throughout her body. Her lower back the worst, stinging her as if a knife had been jammed into the right side, just above the buttocks. Her shoulders and mid-back had a deep throbbing pain.

A person was not meant to be confined in seventy-two by twenty-eight by twenty-eight inches of metal, Lizzy thought, guessing on the dimensions.

She had lost track of time. It could have been thirty minutes or twelve hours since the last time she heard the "evil bastard" man and his wheelbarrow by her box. She had given up the battle with her bowels, urinating on herself over and over.

What the fuck? I already shit myself in fear, she thought whenever the need to pee arose. *Fuck it. It just means they'll have more of a mess to clean and cover up.*

The one thing she knew for sure was that it had not yet been forty-eight hours. The woman said she needed to be on a plane to Singapore in forty-eight hours. She was most definitely still stuck in the foul shit-stained box and not on a private jet. She constantly drifted between a conscious and unconscious hallucinogenic state. Forcing herself to drift away mentally from her situation had a way of soothing fears and anxiety, only for her to be ripped suddenly back to reality, realizing where she was and that it was not a nightmare she could wake up from.

He has to come back to clean me up some time.

In truth, it had only been four hours since Jack left Lizzy so he could dump Ben's body, but a total of twenty hours straight crammed in the box.

The door nearest Lizzy's box opened as quietly as she thought a door could.

Fuck, he's back.

She began to hold her breath, instinctively, as if being quiet would hide her from him. She sucked air in heavily, gulping a few times, and held her breath again. Her heart began to race, her body beginning the fight response with adrenaline leading the charge. She heard him take quiet steps away from her to the other side of the room; through the silence she heard a squeak, followed by another moment of silence, and then another squeak. Someone was slowly, silently making their way upstairs. It didn't feel right to her. After a few moments, she began to breathe again. He had passed. He was gone for now.

What the hell is going on? God! Why is this happening to me? Lizzy was not normally a person found praying to God, but this situation pushed her mind to places she didn't think possible.

Bam.

Bastard snuck up on me.

He had practically kicked her box when he reached it, stumbling into it. She never heard him come back down the stairs.

She could hear his heavy, deep breaths.

Clink, clank, clink.

The words "break her in" rang loudly in her head like church bells as the lock on her box was being tinkered with.

The lid made an eerie noise as it opened.

"If it was not for this damn bag, I would fucking kill you right now," she managed to burst out, barely making out the silhouette of a person looking down at her from outside the box through the grainy material. She tried to get her eyes closer to the fabric so she could see her attacker but was unable to do so without a free hand. She tried to kick, forgetting that her legs were still bound together with zip ties.

"Lizzy!" a voice yelled back down to her. *A familiar voice.* Her mind washed over with confusion. It was a voice she knew so well, yet her brain full of adrenaline and dopamine wouldn't let her see who. Pulling her and out of the box, the man helped her onto her butt, propping her upright against the wall.

He said something to her, but she couldn't hear him, her mind overloaded from what was going on. Then for a moment, he was gone. When he came back again, he spoke some more, but she was unable to piece together the words.

Is he even speaking English?

"I'll get you out of this. Hold tight." Finally, words began to come together. Her heart was jumping with excitement.

"I'm free?" she shouted out, half-crying.

"Be quiet," he responded. "I don't know if anyone else is here." He spoke evenly, just above a whisper tone. He tinkered with the bag's locking mechanism for a minute before the sound of metal sliding against metal could be heard. He had twisted open the lock with a pair of pliers he had spotted in the back of the nearby incomplete bathroom. He released the cable, which released tension on her waist. She immediately felt soreness where the cable was tight around her body. That pain faded away as quickly as it came. Finally, pulling the bag off, her rescuer was revealed. Joy burst through the agony and trepidation that was contorting her face.

He stared at her neck for a moment, where a necklace he had bought two weeks earlier still hung. He meant to tell her what it was, but the word "GPS" failed to come out whenever he had tried. The way she lit up when she saw the gift or caught him looking at it he didn't want her to misinterpret his intention. She meant too much to him.

"Tommy!" Lizzy yelled again, ignoring his advice to be quiet. Snapping out of his daydream he shifted his eyes away from her chest. Her face was bright red, hair a tangled mess, and eyes watery and glowing from stress.

"You—" he paused, a sly smile crossed his face. "I think you pooped yourself."

Lizzy slapped him on the shoulder.

"You try being jammed in a box. How did you? How? I mean, where?" Lizzy had so many questions, all of them pouring out at once.

"I'll tell you later. We need to get out of here." He put the nose of the pliers around the zip ties holding her legs together and with one good twist, they were off. Grabbing her hand, he helped her to her feet, then pulled her through a glass French-style door into open air, a walkout basement. Lizzy looked back as she was led away.

Such a normal-looking home, she thought. *Nobody would guess it's a horror show in there.*

"Over here." He began to half-lead, half-drag her across a green backyard with the slightest dusting of snow. Lizzy felt dazed now, like she might pass out.

"Wait, wait. I need a second." She was desperate to leave, yet, her body had been spun in too many directions in too short of a time. Knees buckled, she hit the ground. Tommy held her up, like a parent yanking at the arm of a toddler learning to keep their feet, but she was too heavy, and her knees hit the hard semi-frozen ground.

"Ahhh," she moaned out as pain shot through her.

"I got you. I got you." Tommy leaned down to put his shoulder under her armpit. "Okay, I'll help you walk. But you have to try to stand and walk with me. Can you do that?"

When she didn't respond, he repeated, "Hey, can you do that? Can you help me?" He shook her to get her attention on the task. He would have carried her but for a hill they had to climb, which he knew would be too much. He needed her to help. Shaking her shoulder again, he said, "Are you with me?"

"Yes, yes!" Finally, she came back to him, her eyes gaining strength and focus. "Let's get out of this fucking place!" she cried out passionately, tears falling down her cheek, disappearing in the light snow below.

"Left, right," Tommy said, trying to help her remember her feet. "Left, right, left, right—that's it, and left, right, left." At the top of the hill, the land opened up to a large flat area, a driveway.

"Come on. This way." He led her across the driveway and into the woods away from the house.

They stumbled for a few minutes, over branches, rocks, drops, and ditches. Lizzy was a passenger, following whatever command Tommy barked out. All she knew was he was getting her out, getting her to freedom, away from that bag, and out of the box she was trapped in.

"Tommy, we need to call the police. These are bad people."

Tommy ignored her as they approached another clearing.

"Here we are." The woods parted to a wide dirt road.

"Shit!" Tommy screeched out as his car was not in view on the street.

"Dammit. It's okay," he said reassuringly. "I'm parked on this road. Just down here." After a quick walk, Lizzy could see a car, just off the road ahead.

"There we are. There we go," Tommy announced triumphantly. Pulling out his phone, he checked his service: one bar.

"As soon as we get to the car, we're calling 911." He put the phone back in his pocket. Lizzy was now walking mostly on her own. A few minutes of her body away from that shit hole was enough medicine to begin to restore her adrenaline and dopamine levels back into a proper balance. She was sore but could feel her wits coming back to her. She ran around to the passenger door, she got in, excitement screaming through her.

"Tommy, let's go! Let's get out of here," she yelled.

At that moment, she saw a shadow move silently out of the corner of her eye. She wanted to yell, but her brain handcuffed her. A jolt of fear almost stopped her heart. Having just sat down, he was closing the door when a latex-gloved hand reached in and stopped it from shutting. Tommy froze in a moment of shock. The door swung open, and the face of a man, a handsome man with brown hair and glowing bright blue eyes leaned in. Lizzy could tell he was tall by the way he had to crouch to make his way into the car. The man put his left hand on Tommy's left side temple, pushing his head up and away just slightly, into the headrest of the car. Then it happened. A silver flash in the moonlit car. A warm splash struck Lizzy in the face, a taste of metal on her tongue.

Opening her eyes, she saw Tommy with his neck split open, the mystery man's hand still holding his head back, blood bubbling out then being sucked down with desperate gasps of air. Shock and fear filled Tommy's wide open eyes; he looked at her, trying to comprehend it for a moment. Then his eyes flashed to the door. She felt something hit her lap. Looking down, she saw Tommy had managed to fling his phone from his pocket. Reaching down, grabbing the phone, she turned and ran from the car; the message from him was clear.

Run.

She didn't know where she was going, but she did it as fast as she could stumble, branches striking her in the face. Her eyes darted, looking down at the phone quickly and back up to avoid running into a tree. She used the unlock pattern that she knew by heart. She stopped to catch her breath, leaning against a tree before peeking back toward the road. She couldn't see anyone following her, but she knew he would. Tucking behind the tree again, she pulled up Mr. Law from Tommy's contacts and frantically typed a message.

"Hlp! Its Lizzy, Tom Dead. Ive been kidnapped!" She hit send, staring at the flickering service bar not sure if it would go through.

"Come on," she whispered, shaking the phone before putting it back into her pocket. Turning, she continued to scramble through the woods.

I need higher ground, she thought, hoping that a hill would help her get a better signal.

As she labored up the only incline she could see, her breaths became more labored and her chest started to sting. Nearing the top, she reached into her pocket for the phone, stopping dead in her tracks.

"No, no, no noooooooo."

She scrambled, her eyes looking around on the ground frantically while her hands went in and out of every pocket.

"No, God no." She began retracing her steps; somehow she had lost the phone.

"Gotcha."

She heard the voice of a man just before a thump against the back of her head struck home. She collapsed to the ground, struck by the butt of the knife that had moments earlier been used to split open Tommy's neck.

It's a Small World – 2014

"You know, you guys are all delusional. *Nom, nom.*" Phil spun in Drew's office chair as he spoke, chewing through another piece of cold pizza.

"I can tell you right now what connects all these idiots." He stopped spinning and pointed to a half-drunken bottle of whiskey that sat on Drew's desk.

"*That* kills more people than—" He paused. "Well, this shh-ite, it kills more people than drugs do. I can tell you that. And it's legal. And very delicious," he exclaimed loudly on the latter point as he spun the label toward him to inspect the brand.

Jen had mostly kept quiet since Phil arrived, hanging out in the corner, scowling at him whenever she got the chance. Now, she said, "You're the idiot."

Phil ignored her. "But seriously, these kids all had some alcohol show up on their tox screen." He put the pizza down on the left corner of the desk, saving it for later, picking up and flipping through dozens of papers that Ashley had printed from her collection of victim reports. He was sure to point out the mention of alcohol in each report.

"Alcohol, alcohol, alcohol!" He leaned back, letting his point settle. "I can see it happening. They go out to have a good time, and they drink a little too much." Standing up, he acted out the actions as he spoke.

"Then, on their way home, they stop at the water's edge to admire the beauty, and *whoopsie.* Boom, splash, in they go. Too drunk to recover, and gonzo." He sat back down in the chair after finishing his fake water splash.

"This is what happened, people. You're all just way too friggin' paranoid." Picking up his pizza, he worked on its conclusion, one bite at a time.

Pacing back and forth in front of the whiteboard, Drew responded. "It is possible, Phillip. But what about this bruising, that we have now found on eight, *eight*, bodies?" Stopping in front of a photo, Drew pointed to the bruise on the back of Gabe's neck.

"This makes your theory hard to swallow. What would be the odds of eight people having the exact same unusual bruise pattern?"

Phil didn't have an answer for that. He enjoyed playing the other side, forcing Drew to work and convince him.

"There's also another pattern." Ashley spoke up from behind a laptop screen. "I ran a machine-learning algorithm that is really good at interpolating data." She spun the laptop around to show a rudimentary bar graph, with a typical bell curve.

Phil stared at the visual for a moment. "I don't have any friggin' clue what you're telling me. Explain it to me like I'm five." He held up an open hand for her.

Ashley grunted and spun the laptop back around, putting it down on a small portable desk she had been working on. She then approached the whiteboard with a marker in hand.

"I used the longitude and latitude of all the victims' locations." She started writing on the board to help them keep track. "Where they were found, of course. That was my first data set. I then found that Boston University runs a website that tracks, year round, the water temperature and speed in which the Charles River moves at varying locations as vector charts." She had written all the data sets she used on the board.

"Then, I used information in the police and autopsy reports, telling me how long the bodies were in the water and how heavy they were." She spoke as she continued to write on the board.

A look of confusion and patience crossed Drew's face.

Seeing it, Ashley said, "Stay with me. What I then did was used this open source machine-learning algorithm that uses a naïve-bay."

Phil gave her a disgusted look before cutting in. "That's it, stop. Five! I'm five remember. This machine stuff is too much. Dumb it down." Putting the marker cap on, Ashley took a breath before turning and looking at him.

"I used this *magic* computer program." She waved her hands in an abracadabra wand motion. "Giving our *magic* program all this information, and it gave me back what it determined, using probab—" She stopped in her tracks when she saw Phil start to raise his hands. "The *magic* program gave us its best guess as to the distance it believes the bodies traveled." Walking over to her laptop, Ashley pressed a button. The printer next to Jen came alive and began to spit out sheets.

"Jen, would you be a dear and collect those for me?" Ashley pointed at the paper being pumped out. "Basically, looking at this map, most of these locations look pretty random, right?" She pointed to the death map on the wall and the scattering of marks.

"But," she said excitedly as Jen approached her with a stack of photos, "when you make use of all of the data that we have available, it tells a completely different story." She began to tape each piece of the new map on the wall, over the original, except this time, she had lines marking from each victim, with arrows pointing up river and ending with a bright red XX. Drew thought it resembled an NFL game-play analysis when the announcers line out all the different routes the wide receivers take on a given play.

"You see? They all went, well probably, went into the river in this area." She circled a stretch of river that engulfed part of the Harvard campus.

"What this bell curve is telling us is that ninety percent of the victims went into the water within five hundred feet of each other." Her eyes widened with seriousness.

After a long and awkward silence, Phil stood up uncomfortably. "Shit. Shit, Shhh-ite. Is this for real? You did all this over the past few hours we've been here? Why didn't you do it before?"

Ashley looked at the map. "It wasn't too difficult to do. Back in college, I used to do hackathons that would go for thirty-six hours, where I had to do stuff like this on short sleep."

Phil shook his head. "I don't like it."

Ashley laughed at Phil's comment. "What don't you like?"

Sitting back down, Phil pondered the question. "I don't like smart people. Period. You talk and talk, you hurt my head and make me feel like I'm not good enough to do what I do best," he answered frankly.

"I don't know, was that a compliment?" Ashley looked at Drew asking for his opinion.

"Sounds like it. But I sort of agree with Phil; I feel really stupid at the moment. But if this is accurate, we can't ignore it. Why haven't you done this before?"

Ashley pointed at Jen. "She gave me the idea earlier tonight."

Jen looked puzzled. "What did I do?"

"You posed a scenario: What if these guys slipped into the river in the same spot? Remember, back when you were contemplating these as accidents. That got me thinking. We had been focusing on my old map, which is where the bodies were found. We needed to do something about figuring out where these bodies went in!"

"Man—this is scary," Drew said. "This is like that Anna system that they're building out. And you put it together in a couple hours."

Ashley shrugged at Drew's comment. "I'm sure Anna is going to be really good. At a lot of things. With lots of security when it's finally done."

Rubbing the back of his neck, Phil stood up and approached the map, looking nervous as ever.

"This is sick. We have a serial killer here." He appeared convinced, thanks to Ashley's computer magic. "Yeah, this is friggin' nuts." Phil was almost bouncing with energy now. "It's like twenty people at least that this dude has killed. That has to be a record. We're going to be famous for breaking this open, double that if we catch him."

"Phil, please sit down before you hurt yourself." Drew pointed him back to his chair.

"I think we have enough to turn it over to the locals and generate a reaction. Phil, do you agree?" He peered at Phil, waiting for a response when Jen spoke up, one of the few times since Phil arrived.

"What would they do?"

Drew looked over at Phil again, who waved Drew on. "A task force is likely to be formed depending on how credible they take this. The FBI would be brought in to consult, and they would most likely take over this case and go through everything with a fine-tooth comb."

"*After* validating *everything*," Phil chimed in, looking at Ashley. "I have confidence that your magic software stuff is good, but they may want to validate it. *Magic* doesn't feel like an official term." Phil emphasized magic in that same way Ashley did when describing her work.

"Hey, you asked me to dumb it down," she quipped back at him. Walking up to the board, Phil looked at Gabe's face, the first face on a stack of faces that they had tacked to the edge of the whiteboard. Phil began pulling photo after photo off, exposing the face of another victim below.

"These poor kids. Look at them; they are all kids."

"Stop!" Jen yelled when the photo of a young, handsome, hipster-looking man was revealed. "What a small world." Craning her neck to look at the photo, she said, "I know this guy." She pointed at the picture, then turned to toward the rest of them with an aha look stretched on her face.

"I don't know, ah, or remember his name, but this guy is a

customer of mine. We have had some great one-on-one video calls. He's pretty laid back for the most part and likes, ahh, well maybe you don't need to know what he's into."

Phil raised his palms to the sky in a shrugging motion. "I dunnooo, I probably need to know this. For the case, of course." He paused. "Come on, tell us, or better yet, show and tell?" Phil was clearly being a dick.

Jen looked at Drew, who responded by tempering the request.

"Only if it is pertinent in helping the case. Which I don't see how it is," Drew responded, backing Jen.

Typing furiously at her keyboard, Ashley said, "I have an idea. Maybe we should have a look at the site logs and user sign-up data to see if any of the other victims are customers. We can cross-reference all of the victims with the site registration data." She squinted her eyes with a look of focus as she brought her head closer to the screen. "Should be able to find out pretty quickly if anyone else on the list likes watching you."

Phil shook his head at how quickly her fingers were tapping away on the keyboard. "One freaking day I won't have a job. It'll just be IT people like you doing everything. The hard work I went through getting here won't make a friggin' difference."

Ashley looked up with raised eyebrows. "You mean that day isn't here yet?" Smirking, she looked back into her computer.

"How long is it going to take? Should we pick up in the morning? It's starting to get late, and I need to get some stuff set up so you can all sleep comfortably tonight," Drew said.

Ashley leaned back away from her screen. "I'm done," she said with pride as they all looked at her, puzzled and shocked at the speed in which she got things done. "How many connections? What's your bet? I can tell you it's more than one and less than twenty."

Jen jumped in first. "Ten!"

Ashley nodded. "Not bad, but no. Drew?"

Bouncing his side to side trying to find a number, any number that made sense, he looked at her. "Uhh, fifteen?"

Ashley shook her head. "Both wrong, no winners. Four!"

"What about me? I don't get to friggin' play?"

Ashley ignored Phil like he was a child. "We have four victims that were also former customers of cutecamjen.com." Standing up, she grabbed a photo off the floor, one of the pictures that Phil had flung. She taped it back on the board, covering her crude scribbles of data sets used in the location analysis. She repeated the process until there were four faces staring back in a two-by-two ordering.

"Gabe, Taylor, Hank, and Evan." She pointed to them in clockwise order, starting at the top left photo. She spun on her toes, facing the rest of them. "Could there be another connection? Maybe we can dig into these four tonight to see where else they may be connected?"

Drew nodded his head up and down slowly to Ashley's question. "I'll make a pot of coffee then." He could see in Ashley's eyes, her nature was to keep going until the problem was solved, and there was work yet to do tonight.

"Well, this is a fun Sunday night," Phil sarcastically chimed in as he stretched his feet out on Drew's desk.

A Missed Message – 2014

"Any luck?" Drew wasn't asking anyone in particular as he stared at a stack of papers in front of him containing available police and autopsy reports on the four cases that they had decided to focus in on.

"*As a team,*" Ashley's words echoed in Drew's. They decided to dig deeper, looking for anything else that might connect the four. He looked at his watch, ignoring the lack of response to his question.

"It's twelve thirty. I might need to get to sleep." Looking up, he saw Jen was already asleep in her chair, head against the wall, her mouth wide open toward the ceiling and drool sliding down her chin. Phil looked up, eyes red and weary, but otherwise, he seemed ready to keep going.

"I might be onto something." Ashley spoke up, almost indifferent to the time. "It doesn't connect the victims, but—" Pausing, she smiled awkwardly before continuing. "It's weird," she said the words slowly and cautiously.

"I searched around for any reference I could find to Gabe's username from cutecamjen.com." Leaning back, she rubbed her eyes, pushing her hair out of her face.

"It popped up on Reddit and—"

"What's Red-it?" Drew had never heard of the website before.

"Reddit is a news, discussion, and social site that aggregates dialog between its members." She looked at Drew to make sure he followed. He nodded, pretending to understand.

"The site is very popular, and its user base is extremely diverse with discussion happening twenty-four-seven on probably every topic you can think of. It appears that Gabe was a Redditor, meaning he was a member, and he had a few discussions on some subreddits." She paused looking back at her computer. "His interests in girls online did not stop with Jen." She looked at Drew with her brows up, and her lips stretched wide, grimacing, showing some of her teeth before muttering. "Gabe was into some, ah—sketchy shit."

"So the guy had a thing for hot chicks on the internet. Tell me something we didn't friggin' know." Phil pointed to Jen passed out in the corner.

"Yes, but, it's even creepier than that. I pulled his password from Jen's site. I know, not ethical. And shame on me for using encryption only and not un-reversible cryptographic hashing algorithms to store it." She put her hand up in the air as if to stop the criticism before it came. Phil looked at Drew with a confused look. Clearly, no criticism was coming from them.

"I used his username and password from her site, and well, it logged me right into his Reddit account." She shook her head in disbelief. "I can't believe people still use the same credentials everywhere. So dumb. Anyways." She spun the laptop around showing his activity comment history. He had easily participated in hundreds of discussions based on photos of mostly nude girls. She then scrolled halfway down through the history and stopped, clicking on a link.

"This caught my eye because he commented on this thread five times more than anything else." She scrolled past the image of a young girl, maybe eighteen, with her finger in her mouth, posing for a seductive selfie. Stopping, Ashley looked up with her finger on the screen.

"He got into a discussion with another user about girls, well, maybe you should read this line for yourself." Drew and Phil crowded the laptop, leaning in to read the comment next to Ashley's finger.

Drew read it out loud. "'Sometimes I feel like I want to know what it's like to rape a girl.'"

Phil continued with the response from an unknown user. "'Yeah, I bet it's amazing, should we do it? Teach her a lesson?'"

A sickly feeling came over Drew as his eyes skimmed the thread.

"Ooh, that is weird." Reaching in, Phil took the mouse, scrolling up and down to read the entire sub-thread. "Wow, so Gabe here sorta had this coming huh?"

Drew looked at Phil with disapproving eyes. "Come on, Phil, no one deserves this. But it certainly seems strange," Drew said, but his voice was unconvincing.

Ashley took control of the computer again, turning it back to face her. "I don't know if they ever did it, but they go on talking about it. Then, after the conversation starts to get more serious, they decide to go to a different, private chat site."

Phil looked at her. "Well, can you get us in or what? Work your *magic* so we can read that?" he said as he pretended to type on an imaginary keyboard.

She shook her head. "No, I can't get those messages. They're end-to-end encrypted and only the actual devices they used can get the messages." She paused as Phil stared at her wide-eyed. "I would need their phones." Her face twisted into a stumped look. "I tried to find more information about this guy he was chatting with—" She peered into the laptop to read the name. "User underscore B, nine, A, Q, P, R, S, C. I'm pretty sure it's just a burner account. He has no previous history, posts, and comments. I think he's someone we should follow up on?"

Drew gave her a head nod in agreement. She straightened up her shoulders before shaking them as though she had chills.

"Eww. The way this guy writes, it's—" She paused. "It's—just—something is wrong with him. Put it that way. He gives me the creeps."

"Phil, any chance we could get a warrant for access to this user's records from Reddit?"

Phil shook his head uncertainly back at Drew then responds, "No way. It would take like a week at least".

"I don't see any evidence of a crime here either, which rules out an emergency, immediate warrant."

Ashley looked at Drew, obviously disappointed in what he was saying.

"What do you mean? They are basically planning out details to kidnap and rape a poor girl."

"I know. It's friggin' disgusting. But what some people talk about online and do are very different things." He paused a moment. "Unless someone is suggesting an act of mass murder like a school shooting, warrants are hard to get."

Ashley sighed. "Ugh."

Standing up, Drew stretched. "Well, I am going to set her up in a bed upstairs." He pointed to Jen, then turned to Phil.

"What are you doing? You're staying here, too, I take it?"

Leaning back, Phil rubbed his face. "Yeah, I'll catch a few z's on the couch I saw coming in." Drew gave him a thumbs up while walking toward Jen. He didn't feel like hanging around to help Phil get settled.

"Ashley, you can sleep in Liz's room again? I don't think she's coming home tonight either."

"Um, sure, that sounds great."

Drew got to Jen and gave her shoulder a little squeeze, then a not so gentle shake. "Hey, Jen, it's time to go to bed." He spoke to her softly, trying to be gentle.

Jen woke up fast. "Ah, what, shit, was I sleeping? What the fuck, guys, you should have woken me up." She stood up fast, wiping drool from her chin with her right sleeve. Drew ignored her and started pushing her out through the office door.

"Hey, one more thing." Standing up, Ashley leaned against the doorframe, her eyes glowing against the pale green paint Lizzy had insisted he color his office.

"I pulled up all usernames on Jen's site with a filter for randomized names. I figure, most people like to choose a relatable username, unless of course, they value anonymity like this creep might." She tightened her eyes. He nodded, thinking back to the usernames he created on websites, always a variation of his name like drewlaw, drew-law, dlaw, drewlaw1995, and so on.

"With our online creep, we know he likes to use anonymized usernames. Turns out, out of all of Jen's users, there are one hundred twenty-six that fit this. Of those, eight made requests to the site from the New England region, and lastly, one of those users had sent Jen a message. Even stranger, the message said, 'I am going to teach you a lesson!'"

Drew thought about it, unsure how to gauge the value of the lead that she was obviously excited about. It seemed loose.

"You have access to all the messages that have been sent to Jen?" Drew looked at her, thinking about the privacy concerns that some might have about that, especially for a site like Jen's.

"Oh yeah, I log all conversations with Jen. Sometimes they get creepy, and it's really good to have them available if we need them." Looking up, she rubbed her neck after speaking, then continued. "I know, probably nothing right? Not a great lead?" She reacted to the look on his face.

"I don't think I would say that. It's worth checking into, definitely. What do you propose?"

Ashley smiled, positive feedback on her work was something she clearly enjoyed. "I have two IP addresses that this guy used to access the site. One was out of Kentucky and looking it up, it belongs to a proxy service." Drew nodded, pretending to know what that was.

"People will use proxy and or VPN services in order to access the internet, more or less anonymously. When you access a website through these types of services, the site you access will only see requests coming from a pool of IP addresses that are shared by millions of people and look like they are coming from, well, maybe Kentucky or China."

Drew nodded. "That makes sense."

"One thing our guy didn't plan on is that I use an active polling feature on the site."

Drew shook his head from side to side.

"Basically, I send a request from the browser the user is on to one of Jen's services at my home, looking for updates every sixty seconds. While most of his requests came from the proxy service out of Kentucky, a few requests made it through to the service that the active poll hits." Her eyes began to widen with her smile of excitement spreading.

"He must have logged out of his account but never closed the browser!" Her voice seemed to jump, and she tapped him in the chest as she spoke the last word in a "gotcha" moment.

"It's actually a bug in my work that I've been meaning to fix. Even though he logged out, the active poll continues to make a request using his account until the browser is closed, which it shouldn't do." She shrugged off her own criticism. "But I can see it—he logged out of his account leaving the browser open, and he dropped off the proxy service back onto his local network. Bang. I have him." Ashley's smile had charm in it. Drew's mind jumped to kissing her before quickly shaking the thought.

Jen was rubbing her eyes from outside of the door. Phil sat quietly at the desk listening in.

"It's probably nothing, but what if it is this same creep from Reddit? And what if this is our killer? Finding targets in shady places? Sorry, Jen." Leaning around Drew, Ashley winked at a groggy Jen.

Drew nodded. "It's possible."

"Turns out that my bug gave us the real IP address of wherever he physically was accessing the site from." She paused, waiting for anyone to say something or ask questions. Drew was still trying to conceptualize what "active poll" was.

After waiting a minute, Ashley said, "He's in Dunbarton, New Hampshire. I don't have an address, just the town. We could probably fake a shooting conversation or something to get a warrant to figure out the address?"

Drew nodded. He wasn't even listening at this point, just nodding.

He realized that he was a man of few words in a conversation with someone who seemed so much smarter than he. She spoke so quickly that he could hardly keep up, needing a few minutes of mental replay to try to understand.

"We could also drive up there, and you know, check out the town. It's a small town with only nine hundred households. I bet we could drive around with a network shark to try to snoop in on people's routers, then check IP addresses from there."

"Okay, I know it's probably not that late for you youngins." He looked over at the sleepy Jen in the hall, although she was slowly getting livelier and her energy seemed to be rebounding.

"And I'm sure you passed out from boredom in here," he said as he pointed to Jen, not wanting to be the only one closing the case for the night.

"But this old man needs to get to bed soon. I really believe what you have found is super, super, wicked valuable information. But I'm afraid I need you to repeat it in the morning when I have a better chance at understanding."

Ashley put her hands up, offering an apology. "Sorry, I get carried away at these things."

"That's a friggin' understatement. You get hot for this stuff. Look at you, you're friggin' glowing, on your toes." Phil said it as he saw it.

"I really didn't miss anything else while I was asleep? Who is this creep she was talking about?" Jen asked as Drew put his hands on her back and guided her down the hall.

"Well, there was something with Gabe that was strange."

Jen cranked her head around to look at him. "Strange? What does that mean?"

"Ah, he was into some weird internet girl stuff."

Stopping, Jen turned to face him.

"Oh, no. I don't mean you." Drew didn't mean to say it like that. "I meant, like strange and illegal things."

"Out with it, Mr. Law. I want to know what was our friend, my customer, Gabe into?" Walking her upstairs, Drew brought her up to speed while he got the guest room together for her for a second night.

"So, Gabe was a fucking rapist? I could have been next!"

"Woah, woah. Slow down just a little. We still don't have everything." He tried to keep her from running away with something that might not be true. "Think about his family. They probably don't need to know about this if it's false, and it is totally possible that he was just exercising some fantasy online without ever having the intent of executing on that, or maybe we have things wrong here. Think about all the guys that probably watch you who make strange requests. Do you think they ever take that back and ask their wives?"

Jen *had* been asked to do some very strange things that most would never want their wife or family to know about.

He patted the bed and pillows. It had been some time since Drew had guests stay over, let alone two nights in a row.

"Where is Phil sleeping? How about Ashley? Do they need this room?" Jen asked as Drew approached the door to leave.

"No, you can sleep in here. Ashley is sleeping in Lizzy's room across the hall again, and Phil is taking the couch."

"Oh, I thought, um—awkward." She walked in close to Drew with her head tilted slightly down, looking at his chest. Her finger rose to touch the bit of skin his collared polo left exposed.

"I just thought maybe you'd want company tonight." She tilted her head to one side, then back again in a quick, innocent motion.

He hesitated. As a man, he wanted to let it happen. *When will I ever have this opportunity again?* he asked himself as he looked down into her big brown eyes.

She's twenty years younger than me! Christ! His eyes darted to the ceiling quickly.

Reaching over with her hand, Jen softly rubbed the front of his pants, making sure to stroke and squeeze gently to influence a growing bulge.

Drew closed his eyes.

"Hey?" Ashley's voice came from behind him. Drew immediately backed away from Jen, his hand on the door.

"Okay, have a good night, Jen!" he said quickly, shutting the door to Jen's room before moving toward Ashley.

Drew led Ashley into Lizzy's room for the second time in two nights. "It's not the Hilton, but at least it's clean. It's a godsend Lizzy got her mom's touch in keeping things straight and not mine. Don't know what I'd do without her."

Still reeling from Jen's seduction attempt, Drew was moving stiffly about, not quite sure how to handle the tension in the room and the awkwardness he felt.

"If you need anything, as before, I'm in the last room at the end of the hallway." He was about to shut the door.

"Drew?" Ashley called his name. She walked up to the door, opening it farther so he couldn't hide behind it.

"What's going on? You seem—" Pausing, she looked him up and down. "You remind me of a teenager having his first sleepover with girls."

Drew took a deep breath. "Why do you say that?"

"Jen tried to sleep with you?" She spoke without hesitation to his question.

"Jen tried to sleep with me," he responded just as fast, shaking his head from side to side awkwardly.

"Don't freak out. You're an adult. She's an adult."

Drew was a bit taken aback by her response. *Is she trying to play matchmaker here? Does she realize how old I am?*

"I mean, to be honest, I've slept with her a few times, and it's a wonderful thing. Sometimes company and intimacy is just what the doctor ordered." She tapped him lightly on the chest again, winked, and shut the door.

Drew walked away slowly, wondering what was going on. *I thought Jen said she only tried to sleep with her?* He tried to recall what Jen had said to him back when they first met. Before he reached his bedroom, he straightened taller.

"I'm going to do it." He went into his bedroom, opened up his nightstand drawer, and slid his hands around the bottom of the drawer, toward the back.

"Aha, here you are." He pulled out a three-pack of Trojans; flipping them over, he checked the expiration.

"Whew," he whispered, placing two of the condoms in his pocket and the other back in the drawer, although on top for easy access. Walking into the master bathroom, he looked at himself in the mirror. He felt like a teenager. Giving his room one last look over, he made sure he didn't leave anything out that could raise questions if they happened to return to his room later. A dim light caught his eye, his phone had been charging all night, and it looked like he had a missed a call, or missed message.

It's late; I'll call them first thing in the morning. Drew braced himself for whatever Jen was about to throw at him.

He headed down the hall, reached Jen's room, and knocked on the door as quietly as he could. Even with the blessing of someone he knew, he felt like he was doing something wrong. Nothing happened, he knocked again but a little louder.

"Oh my God, yes, finally," he heard Jen say from behind the door. The door swung open, and Jen stood there, wearing only her bra and panties. Her bra was light blue, her panties matching, with pink hearts scattered about. Reaching out, she grabbed him, pulling him into the room quickly.

As soon as the door shut, Jen fell to her knees looking up at him while licking her lips. Reaching up with her hands, she unbuckled his pants, making her way to the button and finally the zipper. Once they were undone, she reached up to his waistband and pulled down. He was wearing light gray boxer briefs, the outline of his shaft clearly visible through the thin material.

Jen didn't waste any time—as soon as his pants hit the floor, she reached up again and dragged down his boxers. He took a deep breath, almost as if he were about to jump into a cold pool. Trying to keep out any thoughts of leaving, he looked up to the ceiling. Reaching down, he put his hands on her head as she stroked him, bunching up her hair in between his fingers.

Her motions felt wet and perfect. Every movement was delicately coordinated with the motions of her hands, somehow maintaining a constant stream of pleasure. He didn't want to let this go on too long. He wouldn't last. He pulled his shirt off, exposing his fully naked body. Jen looked up, then stepped back, pulling down her panties and unclipping her bra, letting it fall to the floor. She moved toward the bed, towing him with her, and they kissed as they fell on the bed together. Drew pushed her hands up above her, elbows out, perking up her breasts as he massaged and gently bit them. He didn't stop there; he kissed his way down her body until his mouth was able to engulf her. He tasted sweetness as he licked and sucked, one finger slightly inside stroking her while his tongue worked in fast flicking motions. She was moaning now, her head tilting back stiffly as she had knee-jerk reactions to what he was doing.

Crack, crack, crack.

Drew looked up from below Jen's waist. She too had heard it as she was now lifted into a raised position from her back with her elbows beneath her.

Crack, crack, crack.

Someone was knocking on the door. It was quiet, but getting louder on every attempt.

"Someone's knocking?" Jen said, trying to keep a whisper.

"Lizzy!" Drew said, though he meant it as a thought for himself.

Thoughts ran through his head as he pulled his boxers on frantically. "Maybe she decided to come home and was wondering why there was a strange woman in her bed, a strange man on the couch, and I'm in the guest room!" Turning, he saw that Jen had swung herself under the covers, even hiding her head. He nodded in agreement.

The knocking came to life again. He slowly opened the door, just slightly, as he had not finished getting dressed. Peering around, he was relieved to see it was not Lizzy standing there waiting for answers.

"Hey . . . I heard you two." Ashley stood at the door. Drew was just shaking his head, trying to come up with something to say. Nothing came to mind. It was blank.

"Are you going to invite me in?" She put her left hand on his chest, coyly shifting her eyes past him to Jen hiding under the covers. Drew didn't move; he was frozen.

Unable to muster out any words, Drew continued to stand there. Pushing him aside, Ashley entered the room, shutting the door behind her. She smiled at him dangerously, winking before pulling out her hair tie so her long wavy blond hair streamed freely. She shook her head slightly, helping her hair unravel and flow straight. Removing all her clothes, she jumped into the bed, immediately beginning to kiss and touch Jen. Drew stood watching, frozen.

What in the fuck is happening? he thought. *Where the hell have women like this been my whole life?*

He felt like he was in a movie. Pulling off his briefs, he crawled up through the covers from the bottom of the bed, settling into his role as the male aid. Clearly, this was about them. He felt like a prop, a toy for their use when desired. A role he was more than happy to fill and concede to. The three tossed and turned, flipped and flopped, switched and spun for almost two hours. They had tried almost every possible combination of positions before finally succumbing to exhaustion.

Walk of Shame – 2014

Drew opened his eyes, a bit dazed from the events from the night before. He had heard that funerals, and the topic of death in general, had a tendency to bring out promiscuity. Never had he ever imagined something like that. He lifted his head off the pillow slightly, a sly smile edging into his cheeks. He saw Ashley next to him in the middle, her glowing skin staring back at him. She had just the slightest natural tan. She was still naked and the covers were mostly off. He admired her back, hips, and butt.

"Wow," he said to himself.

Ashley was on her left side sleeping, with an arm around Jen in a spooning position. He could only see Jen's hips, squeezed against Ashley's from where he was. Jen was more petite than Ashley, shorter, smaller, but she had wider hips, more curves. He turned his wrist over to check the time; it read 7:10 a.m. He thought about staying in bed until the girls woke up. *Nah.* He gently lifted off the thin sheet he had covering his legs.

Quietly collecting his clothing, he put his boxer briefs back on and headed into the hallway, closing the door behind him without a sound. He made it into his room, tossed his clothes on the bed, and jumped into the shower.

"That was amazing," he said out loud to himself, looking in the mirror, his hair still wet from the shower. Collecting some fresh clothes from his walk-in closet, Drew placed them on the bed still folded. Then picking up his pants from the previous night, he felt the pockets for his wallet and to make sure nothing would make it into the wash.

"*Shit!*" His eyes widened as he stared off into the room, his mind going back to the previous night.

Are you stupid? He pulled out of his pocket two condoms, unopened, unused. *What is wrong with you? You had two perfectly good condoms.* Thoughts of disease spun through his head.

Oh no. The thought of getting one or both impregnated smacked him in the gut. He paced the room, scratching his head above the brow, a rare nervous habit.

"Shit, shit, shit. How do I ask them?" He put on his clothes quickly, returning to the mirror in his bathroom.

Fortifying himself with a deep breath, Drew walked out of his bathroom and instinctively grabbed his phone, like he would every morning before starting the day. Leaving his room, he made it down the hall; then he made the turn into the guest room where Ashley and Jen were already up, smiling and beginning to get their clothes back on.

"Oh my. I did not expect that was going to happen when I woke up yesterday," Ashley said with an ecstatic tone.

"Seriously, though, that was amazing. Can we do that again soon? Drew, you fucking stud." Jen pointed at him, playfully biting her bottom lip as she spoke.

"Hey, what's wrong?" Ashley asked, glancing at Jen before looking back to him. "Drew, did we do something wrong?"

With horror filling his entire being, Drew could feel the blood leave his face. He looked up slowly, tears filling his eyes.

"I—Lizzy, she sent me a text," he stuttered. Getting up, Ashley approached him, gently taking the phone out of his seemingly frozen hands.

"Oh my God." She covered her mouth with cupped hands. "Is that real?" she asked.

Drew shook his head, his eyes not focusing on anything, just darting around the room, trying to comprehend the message.

"What—what's going on with Lizzy?" Jen had yet to get her pants on. "What the fuck? Talk to me!"

Looking at her with wide eyes, Ashley shook her head. After finally getting her pants on, Jen made her way quickly to Drew's side and also read the message.

"What! This can't be real. Fuck that. Do you recognize the number?" Drew couldn't hear anyone. He was trapped in his own head, replaying the previous night—Tommy asking for help to find Lizzy, pleading with him that something was wrong.

Why? Fuck! Why didn't you just listen? With that thought pounding in his head, turning, he walked out of the room without saying a word.

"Goddammit!" he yelled, his voice deep and throbbing with pain and anxiety, every muscle in his body tensing as he screamed. Tommy being there last night worried about Lizzy only gave credence and truth to this text message.

"Stay calm. Stay calm." He tried to keep himself from exploding and thinking the worse. "It could still be a hoax. It doesn't mean anything."

He picked up the cordless phone from his bedroom and dialed Lizzy's number—straight to voicemail. He hung up and redialed with the same result. He gave it another dial, for a third time, this time leaving a message. "Lizzy. Call me A.S.A.P. I am not joking around." He hung up the phone.

Throwing the phone against the wall, he screamed, "FUUUCK!" Rage, anger, and shame filled him as he watched the phone fall apart. Quickly heading downstairs, he picked up another cordless phone, staring at it. Who could he call? 911 wouldn't be able to do anything right away. They might send someone over to look at the text. But from there they would probably try to reassure him it was just a prank. They might get a warrant to request a location on the cell phone used. But that could take hours if not days. He could call one of his friends at the precinct. Maybe they would be able to get something moving faster.

"What's up?" He heard a voice speak to him from the other side of the kitchen. "Is this some sort of walk of shame? Yeah, I friggin' heard you last night. Me, and probably the neighbor. You guys were sooo friggin' loud." Phil stood drinking a cup of coffee that he had helped himself to. Drew looked up at him from the phone.

Setting his coffee down, Phil immediately said, "What's going on?"

Drew handed him the phone. "I'm trying to figure out—ahem." His voice was sticky; he needed to clear it. "I'm trying to figure out what to do." He paused. "I can't think straight."

Looking down at the phone, Phil said, "Shit, man." After a pause, he looked up. "You think this is legit?"

Drew shook his head, leaning against the counter. "It's Lizzy. I can feel it. Do you remember the kid that was at the door with you yesterday?"

"Yeah, Tommy boy. Nice guy, seemed a bit anxious."

"He told me last night that something was wrong with Lizzy. Fuck—why didn't I listen?" Drew slammed his fists down on the counter so hard the dishes in the cupboards below rattled.

"Take it easy, big guy. We can work through this."

"If I had listened—" Drew paused, shaking his head. A tear ran away from his right eye. "If I had listened to him, maybe Lizzy would be safe, and he wouldn't be dead."

"Hey, relax. We don't know for sure that he's dead. Sure, the text says it. But, you know, text messages come across wrong all the time. I think it's best we assume everyone is alive and okay with our next goal being locating them, finding them, and proving that this is just some fake text from a friggin' low-life psycho." Phil put the phone down on the counter. "Did you call this in yet?"

"No, that's what I was trying to figure out when I came downstairs."

Bobbing his head up and down, Phil listened. "I got a source that works at a cell company. Works in tech. He has access to location data. If, and it's a big if, but if it was bounced off of his company's towers, we might be able to get the location on this phone."

Drew looked up, desperation and hope in his eyes.

"If we go this route—" He paused. "It's not by the books." He dragged out his words for effect before continuing. "Right? I mean the correct thing is we call it in. They process a warrant. We call the local authorities where this text came from and hope from there we're not too late." He let Drew contemplate what he was telling him.

"How fast do you think your guy can get us a location?" Drew asked impatiently.

Phil's eyebrows went up as he thought. "Ahh, maybe a half-hour if we can reach him, and if he's in a place where he can get on his work computer." The answer was easy for Drew, whatever would get him to his daughter the quickest.

"Yeah, let's do it. Why not just call in both? That way we get the process started with the authorities. In case your guy doesn't come through?"

"Let's fucking do it!" Phil pointed hard at him, then slowly deflated a bit. "Although, if we bring in the rest of the PD, it might raise some red tape for us. In case we need to act fast to get your daughter."

Drew looked at him, not sure he knew what he was talking about.

"If you and I can get the location of your daughter quickly, we can go together. I *will* help you on this." He paused. "We can move fast. On the other hand, if we get a location and you bring in the PD, they will want to come over here and talk, review the texts, and try to locate Tommy first, and all this other stuff. Lots of friggin' stuff." Phil waved his hands in the air as he spoke. Drew started to get his point. The two of them had a chance to act fast, now; otherwise, they might get caught up in the process.

"Hey, you're her father. It's your call. If it was my kid, I would want to have control and be able to move as fast as possible." Drew nodded his head up and down. It made total sense in his semi-delirious state.

"Okay, but if your guy doesn't come through—" Drew bit his lip, almost swearing again from the thought. "Fifteen minutes. If your guy doesn't give us something in fifteen, we're already too far behind this. The text came in last night!"

Reaching out, Phil put a hand on his shoulder, looking Drew in the eyes. Drew was mixing his sentences, a clear sign of a heightened emotional state.

"My guy will come through. But you have to promise me that if we're asked about it, we say, 'Location came in from an anonymous tip.' You got that?" Drew nodded to the terms. Pulling out his phone, Phil quickly started typing into a messenger application.

"What was the number there? Where the text came from?" Phil asked as he typed out a message.

"Ah, let me see." Spinning his phone around, Drew gave him the number.

"Okay." Sending the message, Phil looked up at the clock on the stove, 7:45 a.m. glaring back at him.

"If he doesn't respond to us in fifteen minutes, we call 911." Drew paced the kitchen, his finger hovering over the send button on his cell. His gut told him to call it in and get the PD started on it. But his anxiety shouted back, focusing on the consequences.

Phil's phone buzzed immediately. Drew looked up at Phil, eager for a hopeful message.

"He says he can do it. New Hampshire. We should get in the car and head to New Hampshire."

Drew looked at him, puzzled. "He already knows?"

"Hey, I don't know how this shh-ite works. All he says is New Hampshire and that he can get more details soon." Phil tucked his phone into his pocket.

"Let's go then." Drew didn't hesitate. He grabbed his keys, ran upstairs, and opened up his closet safe. His hand hovered over a 9mm, then shifted to his 40-caliber Ruger. He ran back down the stairs, ignoring the looks from Ashley and Jen peering in from the hallway.

"You guys are going somewhere?" Ashley and Jen were huddled together, listening in on them discussing what to do.

"Yes, looks like Lizzy is in New Hampshire."

Ashley looked nervous. "Are you sure? Should we call the police?"

Drew shook his head. "We don't need them slowing us down just yet. You two can stay here. We'll text you as soon as we know more." Drew waved at Phil as he headed to the door.

"Let's go."

"Wait, Drew, I'll drive. There's no way you are driving." Drew tossed his car keys into a catchall on the counter and turned for the door.

Ashley and Jen watched them pull out of the driveway. When the men were gone, the two looked first at each other, then at the car keys Drew had left on the counter.

Concern flitted across Ashley's face, and she looked to Jen. "How do you feel about taking our own trip to New Hampshire?"

The Clean Up – 2014

Lizzy woke up to the spray of cold water hitting her bare skin. She was naked, stretched out in a large porcelain tub. Her breasts pointed up to the ceiling of a dimly lit bathroom. She was slow to wake, and her skin was covered in goose bumps from the cold water. She tried covering her breasts, but the man reached down into the tub and slapped her hand away, letting her know that he was in charge. He looked down at her crotch and focused the spray from the handheld sprayer at it, cleaning the bits of brown that were caked to her skin and delicately trimmed hair.

Tossing her a small face cloth, he said, "Scrub with this." Lizzy picked up the cloth from her stomach. When she squeezed it, soap bubbles came swelling out of it.

She groaned from her aching body as she repositioned in the tub. The back of her head was throbbing violently with pain, shooting in all directions. She felt nauseous and dizzy.

"I think you gave me a concussion." She looked up at the man with brown hair, bright blue eyes, strong lines, and wide shoulders.

"You're handsome." She was still terrified inside, but fear wasn't going to work on this man. *Maybe if I just overwhelm him with kindness?* she thought. "I mean . . . ." She looked down, letting her submissive, flirting eyes do the talking.

The man turned the water off, then grabbed her hard by the upper arm.

"Ow! You're hurting me." He dragged her out of the tub. She tried to use her feet to stabilize herself, but they slipped out from underneath her on the wet porcelain, her naked body flailing about and crashing sideways and awkwardly back down. He dragged her out of the bathroom and into a connected bedroom.

She looked around, taking in what she could. If she was able to get away, she wanted to be able to give as much information as possible to her father.

So he can put this guy away, she thought. It was a large bedroom with plush blue carpeting, light gray walls, and a large oversized king bed with a light blue comforter that was nautical style, little ship anchors scattered throughout. *It must be the master bedroom of the house.* Dragging her to the bed, with a flip of his wrist, the man spun her onto it. She landed on her chest with her legs hanging off the side of the bed, her butt exposed in the air.

"Ahh, come on. Is that necessary? Just tell me what you want, and I'll do it." She rubbed her arm where he had been grabbing it.

Her skin was red and quickly bruising from the force in which he handled her. He turned away from her without saying anything, disappearing into a walk-in closet on the other side of the room. Lizzy looked over to the door that led out of the room, briefly contemplating making a run for it.

I wouldn't get far like this. A moment later, he emerged with an elegant, slim red dress dangling from a clothes hanger that was mostly see-through.

"Ah, ha, no." Lizzy chuckled as soon as she saw it.

He tossed the dress at her. "Put it on," he said firmly.

Lizzy shook her head, not wanting to comply.

"Put it on or I'll cut your throat open right now and find someone else."

Looking into his eyes, without hesitation she stood up, slipping the dress on over her body and sliding it down snug with a shake of her hips. She glanced over to a mirror on a bureau to see what he had gotten her into.

"I look great in this." She spoke out loud, still making a play to appeal to his human nature with positive, flirty, friendly communication.

"That'll do. Take it off." He barked the order as he handed her the hanger.

"Well, do you have anything else I can wear? Or am I going to be naked for the rest of the night?" The man looked at her, a quick smile curled on the edge of his right lip. It was gone as soon as it was there, but she saw it.

"You'll be naked until I say so. You'll be wearing this dress off the jet." The moment she had the dress off, he ordered her to follow him out of the room and led her down a set of stairs. After passing through a hallway, she found herself standing in a large kitchen.

Continuing on her quest to kill him with kindness, she said, "You have a very nice house, sir." She stood near the entrance of the kitchen, covering her crotch with one hand and her breasts with the other. The man grabbed a bottle of water from the fridge, opened it, and drank half on the spot before turning and offering her the rest. Lizzy stopped her body's instinctive reaction before it manifested itself. Her hand was about to rise up and slap the bottle, but instead, she slowly reached out, keeping eye contact with the man, and grabbed the bottle gently, purposefully brushing his hand with hers. She drank the rest of the bottle without losing eye contact. She was playing a game now, a game of survival; her goal was to appeal to all of his human senses in an effort to drive out a human response, not the actions of the monster that she had seen so far.

"You will be getting on a jet in eighteen hours headed for Singapore." He paused, watching her reaction to the news. Dropping her hands to her side, she showed her body with shaky confidence.

"And what happens when I am in Singapore?" She was surprised at how smooth she was able to keep her voice, despite the terror and turmoil spinning inside of her.

He stared at her. "You're going to be sold—or, rather delivered. Technically, you were sold seventy-two hours ago." Lizzy caught her eyelids flickering from the stress of hearing her fate but stopped them in their tracks. She didn't want him to see any fear. He lived off of it, she could tell, and she wanted no part of granting him any of that satisfaction.

"Am I being sold into a sex trade?" she asked calmly, again keeping her voice smooth and level. Turning around, he grabbed another bottle of water from the fridge, tilting it in her direction as an offering. She turned it down.

"It's probably best that you do not know any more details." He turned back toward the fridge, away from her, to put the water back. In that brief moment, she felt a tear leave her eye and run down her cheek. Scooping it up quickly, she rubbed it out of sight.

"Why me?"

Without looking at her, he responded. "It has nothing to do with *you*. It's not personal. You fit the required description, plain and simple. I had led that fool Ben straight to you; he was so predictable. Feel lucky you didn't end up like your friend outside in his own trunk."

"Tommy, is he alive?" She already knew the answer.

"Please, he was dead the moment he decided to play hero, although I will give it to him. How did he find us?" The man trailed off, pondering his own question. He walked over to the sink, reaching underneath and pulling out a one-gallon bottle filled with a clear fluid. He poured it over both of his hands one by one as he leaned over the sink. The fluid gave off a very chemical smell, like a high-test cleaning solution. The man winced as he let the fluid drip from his hands. His fingers and skin turned red from the contact; Lizzy could see little bubbles sizzling from his skin.

In a friendly, concerned tone, she asked, "What is that?"

He looked over, showing his teeth, obviously in a bit of pain. "This is a custom solution I created that breaks down skin cells at a high rate." He looked down at his hands, shaking excess off into the sink. "Stings like a bitch. But when applied often, my prints are non-existent. I only use latex gloves when things get bloody." Turning on the water, he rinsed off the chemicals. "I, truly, don't ever like doing what you saw back there. It's, well, not my style." He looked over at her, but Lizzy was careful not to show anything but indifference to his monstrous attitude.

"Let's go." He motioned for her to follow him, heading back toward the hallway she had just passed through and into the basement.

"Use the bathroom. You might not get another chance for a few hours." He pointed to a door, a small half-bathroom with no windows was behind it. Stepping in, she turned and looked at her naked self in the mirror. It was shocking. She looked skinny and pale with bruises all over that had not been there before.

"That red dress did me some favors," she said sarcastically, recalling how good she looked in it.

"You have five minutes," he yelled to her through the closed door. She didn't need to pee but forced out what she could, taking his word that she may not have the availability for some time.

It didn't feel like it, but the five minutes was up, and the man was racking his knuckles on the door.

"Let's go." He led her back down into the basement, then approached the box. Lizzy frowned as soon as she saw it.

"Oh, come on, really?" He ignored her question, kicking open the lid with his foot while he had a hand on her shoulder.

"I hosed it down for you. Let's try to keep it clean this time. I promise I won't be so gentle if we have to do another bath." Lizzy crawled back in as ordered, without a fuss. The metal stung with coldness against her naked skin. She lay down on her back, tucking her elbows in and crossing her arms and hands over her breasts. She kept eye contact with him for as long as she could while the lid came down. She could here the cranks of the locking mechanism bolting in place.

At least I'm not in a bag, she thought, trying to be positive and take stock in small victories.

Dunbarton – 2014

"How far out are we?" Drew asked with a shaky voice. He had seemed to calm down on the ride, especially when they got the information containing the location on where Lizzy's text message came from. But his anxiety seemed to return as they got closer. In truth, he was undergoing a rollercoaster of emotions, ups and downs.

"It's not far. We're in the friggin' boonies now. Just down this next road, and we're there. We're very friggin' close. Are you going to be able to keep yourself together? I don't want to be accidentally shot."

Drew looked at him with disbelief in his eyes. "I'll be fine. I can handle it, and my finger will be off the trigger. How do you want to do this?"

"I think we should park on this dirt road coming up, the one we saw on the map, then hike through the small bit of trees to the house nearest the phone's last pinged location my tech buddy found. Once we're there, we split up. You go around front, and I'll take the back. Again, don't friggin' shoot me, or I will be pissed!" Phil made a hard turn left onto a dirt road that was filled with potholes and ruts.

"Should we call in the local PD? Try to get them on scene to help out?" Drew knew the answer, the right answer, but his anxiety and nerves continued to have him rely on Phil's decision making to be sure.

"Not yet. Let's have a look for ourselves. We still don't know if this is just some prank. If, at any time, it seems like something we can't handle, let's plan to just turn around and meet back at the car and call in the cavalry. Sound good?" Drew nodded, his clouded mind focused on Lizzy and what she might be into. Phil brought the car to a stop, pulling off the dirt road just slightly onto a grassy shoulder.

"All right, I'm pretty sure we're close." Pulling out his phone, he put the coordinates into Google Maps.

"Good thing I downloaded the maps before we left the coffee shop. Shh-itey friggin' service out here."

Drew and Phil had sat in a coffee shop for about twenty minutes waiting for more information from Phil's contact at the cell phone company. As soon as they got the location back, they looked it up on Google Maps to scope out what they might be running into, as well as setting up GPS.

"Looks like we're about a half mile from where we wanted to be. You want to walk it?" He looked over at Drew. Drew wasn't listening. He was staring out of the passenger window into the distance.

"Yep, I'll pull up a little further," Phil said without any response from Drew. He slid the car back into drive and drove another half mile, checking his location on his phone until he was where he wanted to be, finally pulling off the road and again and coming to a stop on a grassy patch.

"This will work out." Shutting off the car, he stepped out. "Not so bad out here. I wasn't looking forward to walking through the woods in the freezing cold."

Drew stepped out of the car with a look of pure focus. He had no interest in the banter that Phil was spouting, except for the soothing effect it had on his mind. He felt like he was a teenager about to do something he knew was wrong, but playful conversation helped sweep those feelings away.

"It's about six hundred feet through these woods to the house, right?" Drew pointed as he spoke, his arm out pointing directly into the trees, ninety degrees from the road.

Phil looked back down at his phone. "Yep. That looks about right. If you want to check out the spot where the phone last pinged from, that would be about two hundred feet from here in that direction." Phil pointed about forty-five degrees to the left from where Drew had been pointing. "Let's make our way to that spot first. These cell phone guys always tell me it's good within about twenty feet. It's probably best we check out where we know she was last, right?"

"Yeah, definitely." Drew nodded in robot-like agreement. The ground was soft and the air moist. A light snow flurry had passed through the previous night and the warm air that came up from the south this morning had already melted all the dusting, thawed the top layer of soil, and left a hanging fog in its place.

"Ah, shh-ite, a car." Phil was pointing down the road from where they came. A car was moving slowly toward them.

"This isn't going to look great. A couple of dudes hanging out on the side of the road pointing around. Should we get back in the car?" Drew said, reaching for the door handle and waiting for Phil to

244

respond.

"Nah, if they see us scrambling around, it's probably going to look weirder. Let's just hang around this tire and pretend it's flat."

"Good idea." Letting go of the handle, Drew bent down on one knee, pretending as though he was inspecting the right front passenger side tire. Phil hung over him and pulled up his arm, at the ready, to wave off any offer of help. Rolling up slowly, the car came to a stop next to Phil's car.

"God, what in all friggin' hell are you two doing here?" Phil spoke out over the sound of the car's engine idling.

"We followed you, idiot," a sharp female voice responded. Drew knew that voice.

"Jen?" He stood up, and there was Jen, hanging out of the passenger window. "I thought I told you two to stay back at my place." At that moment he realized they were in his car.

"That's my car." He pointed in disbelief, thinking back and regretting the careless toss of his keys into the catchall.

"We needed a ride, duh," Jen responded.

"I'm going to pull over," Motioning, Ashley spoke over the sound of the engine. Driving forward, she parked the car in front of Phil's car.

"You two followed us? All the way from Chelmsford?" Phil was bewildered. Ashley stepped out of the car with a smile.

"Nope. We followed you from the center of Dunbarton. Lost you about a half mile before this turnoff because we got stuck behind a damn tractor." Jen stepped out of the car.

"Yeah, who the fuck rides a goddamn tractor on the road?" Phil said. They'd passed the same tractor on the way there.

"We sped a bit trying to catch up, then realized there was no way we lost you. We figured we missed you turn off." Putting her hands, Ashley twirled her finger around in the air, indicating they needed to make a U-turn.

"We turned the car around and took a guess at which turnoff to try. Guess who got it right?"

"Okay, Ash, we all know how smart you are. You don't need to flash it to the boys constantly."

"If you didn't follow us from the house, how did you know to head up here to begin with?" Drew asked slowly, trying to put it together.

"Oh, remember last night I was telling you about IP address tracing and how I found a connection between our boy Gabe and some creep on Reddit?"

Tilting his head, Drew looked up, his mouth open, trying to recall the evening prior to the "sex-scapade."

"We were going to start in the center of town and try to Wi-Fi map the area. With only nine hundred homes—"

Jen cut Ashley off. "We figured it would be quicker than a fucking warrant."

"Wait a minute. You're here because you traced a friggin' IP address of one of your users that was creeping out on Jen's website?" Phil's eyes widened. "Fuck!" he yelled, swearing into the air. "You two should have just stayed where you were," Phil said before waving and walking away from the conversation.

"This has to be connected, right? I mean we're chasing the killer. You're chasing your daughter that's in mortal danger. And we both land in the same place? Separately?" Jen spoke, asking questions without waiting for answers, letting her logic lead her to her next statement.

"Well, boys, what do you want to do? What is the plan?" Ashley spoke calmly, ready to go.

"No, no, no, no—you two are staying here. We don't need two anchors with us. Tell them, Drew."

"Fuck you! We are not anchors. We were about to find ourselves here on our own. We are the real detectives." Jen obviously didn't understand the risks of being involved in something like this.

"Look, if this really is a kidnapping that happened here, how do you think this guy is going to handle strangers snooping around?" Phil made a gun with his hand, put it to his head, and pretended to blow his own brains out. "It's probably going to be friggin' dangerous." He finished by falling against a tree.

"There is no way you are leaving us behind at this point."

Phil grabbed his hair, almost yanking it out. "How are you two even alive? You are so friggin' stubborn, stupid, ahh! I would have guessed that evolution would have done away with you by now."

Ashley frowned at his comment before looking over to Jen. "I agree with him, Jen. Let's not get involved. Let's stay here and call the police. We can wait here for them while you guys go ahead."

Nodding up, Phil down. "Just hold off on calling the cops until you hear from us."

Ashley gave him a defiant look and said flatly, "No way! That makes no sense. Like you said, if there is any chance this is a kidnapping, and this guy, or maybe even guys, are dangerous, why wouldn't you want some backup?"

Phil looked at Drew, seemingly struggling to generate a logical response. "His daughter's life could be on the line here. Do you want some New Hampshire cow cop coming in here, putting her life at risk?" Phil let that set in, glancing at Drew, but no support came.

"Fine, you're right. You win again, Ashley." Pulling out his phone, Phil walked away from the car slightly toward the tree line.

When he came back, he said, "We have local sheriff Bill McAdoo on route, should be here in ten minutes. He'll bring a couple deputies with him. You two," Phil glared at Jen and Ashley, "will wait for them in the car while we investigate." Turning to Drew, Phil said, "Are you ready to do this?"

Drew took a deep breath before responding, feeling the air inflate and release from his lungs.

"Yes. Let's do this." He didn't know what he might find ahead, or what fate might have already befallen his daughter.

* * *

"Well, nice work," Jen said to Ashley as Drew and Phil disappeared into the woods. "Phil is such a fucking idiot."

Ashley didn't respond. Instead, an uncomfortable look stretched across her face. Her eyes tilted with confusion. Her lips curled with betrayal. Pulling out her phone, she saw that she had zero, not one bar of service.

"What cell phone provider do you think Phil has?" she asked Jen.

"Cell phone service? I don't know, why?"

Ashley put her phone back in the pocket. "Let me see your phone. Who do you use?"

Pulling her phone out, Jen handed it to Ashley. "I have Verizon, like everyone else, duh."

Ashley looked at Jen's phone. Jen had no service either.

"What company do you think Phil has to make such a clear call? You and I have no service. We couldn't even send a text message from here. We would need to get to some higher ground or something to get a call out." She looked at Jen, her eyes squinting with concern.

Phil's entire attitude, presence, and urgency to handle things his way started to turn in her gut like a bad roll of sushi. Ashley's energy drained, replaced with worry and a sickening feeling.

"Why would he not want cops here? Why go through that charade?" Jen asked Ashley, whose eyes were glossy as she was lost in thought. Her mind was trying to generate as many possible scenarios as it could, prioritizing those scenarios by highest probability.

"Oh, not him too," she whispered tensely

Jen hardly made it out. "What did you say? Not who what?"

Ashley shook her head, looking down. "Nothing good. I said, nothing good." Pausing, then looking up and into Jen's eyes, she said, "I think Drew is in trouble."

Team Three – 2014

Jen's voice escalated as she spoke. "What do you mean in trouble? What kind of trouble besides investigating the home of a fucking kidnapper! Be Tee Dubs." She used a common texting acronym meaning, by the way.

"I don't understand why everyone else is ignoring that we—" She pointed to Ashley and back to herself while she dragged on the last word. "We ended up here searching for a serial killer! And not just like some petty serial killer, this fucker is like Bundy level."

Ashley nodded. "Yes, I think he's in even more trouble than that. I don't have time to explain. You stay here with the car. I'm going to go ahead and see if I can stop them, or maybe find a signal and get a call out." Ashley stood up with renewed energy. "If I get a signal, I'll have the police meet you here and you can direct them." Ashley half-yelled as she trotted off into the woods.

"What the fuck is going on right now?" Jen said to herself, her arms flashing up in a defeated motion.

"Okay, surrrrre. I'll just wait here while everyone else is off somewhere crazy." Jen looked around, feeling alone and scared for the first time in a while. There were no cameras on her, no one to send her a chat message, no cell service, no Wi-Fi. In both directions, there was nothing to be seen except tightly packed pine trees hugging a rough dirt road. She walked around the car to the driver side. "I'll just sit in here and be ready to go if the team needs to move."

Not a moment after sitting in the car and shutting the door, she saw a car approaching form the same direction they had come from.

"Shit, he wasn't lying." She figured it was too soon for Ashley to have gotten a call out, and the car looked like a police car. Jen waved her hand in the air excitedly, getting out of the car quickly. It was a white Ford, with a thin light strip perched on the top, otherwise unmarked. The car pulled up right behind Phil's car, which blocked Jen from having full sight of it.

A man stepped out, wearing a long black coat.

"Hi, oh, fucking God, thank you. You made it quick." Jen yelled, waving to him, obviously pleased that he was there. Another man, similarly dressed stepped out of the passenger side of the car.

"Hi, ma'am," the man who got out first said. "You must be Jen?"

"Yes, yes, I am. You are in the right place. Phil called you? They wanted me to point you in the right direction." Running a hand through her hair, she looked toward the woods.

"There is a house directly through these woods, and we believe Lizzy is being held there against her will. See, we got a message that she had been kidnapped and her boyfriend was killed. Well, this was after we started working on a serial killer case. But, coincidentally, we think the two cases are related." She was rambling, her nerves causing her to talk fast.

"So, this IP address thing, Ashley said it was a bug on her end, whatever that means." The men looked at each other before trying to slow her down.

"Okay, relax, relax. There will be plenty of time to tell us what's going on." He motioned with his hands for her to pull back a bit and slow down. The man from the passenger side approached her. Beneath his coat, he wore gray business casual jeans and a white and blue patterned button-down shirt that was hanging loosely and untucked at his hip. When his coat danced from walking, she spotted a holstered black pistol hanging on his hip.

"Are you, like, a detective or something?" she asked, feeling something was out of place with their odd clothing. They looked at each other before the one closest answered.

"Yeah, something like that. We don't have time to get into it now. Where is everyone else?"

Jen pointed into the woods at his question. "Well, that fucking bitch left me alone and went running off into the woods to catch up with the others. She had the crazy idea that Phil lied and you two wouldn't be here." They remained quiet, peering into the woods, contemplating what she had said.

"Huh. Where did Ashley go then?" The one closest to her continued to do the talking. He had brown hair, brown eyes, and the slightest beard that gave him a dark complexion.

"Fuck, man, she went running in the woods, like I said. She was going to try to catch up to Drew and Phil, or find a place with better reception so she could get a call out." She was getting frustrated and felt awkward, a sensation that reminded her of the conversations she always had with Phil.

"Are you two friends with Phil?" she asked the man who had taken a few steps closer to her, from the passenger side door. He was now within arm's reach, looking into the woods where she had pointed.

"No? You guys don't want to talk about it? Are you going to go after Ashley and help or what?" The man closest to her looked her in the eyes.

"Yeah, why don't you and I head over that way? He'll stay here and wait for more backup." He flipped his head toward his partner, who nodded in agreement.

"Okay, sure. I think I can take you there. Something about a house that's about six hundred feet or so, straight through these woods." She began to walk, slowly progressing through the brush and pine trees, with the man following closely behind her.

"What else can you tell me about what's going on here?" the man asked as they moved forward.

"Well, like I was saying, not only has Drew's daughter been abducted, but we think that the guy who did it is a fucking serial killer—like thirty people at least, who knows? It's sad and super fucked up."

The man listened to her intently. "A serial killer, you say? How so?"

"From what we discovered, he likes to drown men."

The man waited a moment before asking another question. "Do you guys think he kills for pleasure or for something else? Like a job?"

Jen stopped and popped her head back. "A job? That's a weird question. Who kills people for a job?" Turning, she looked into his face. His flat, emotionless eyes made her more uncomfortable.

"I guess that is a weird question. Sorry about that. Just trying to be thorough."

Jen shook her head. "You fucking cops. You, Phil, that other guy back there. Weird. Seriously. Weird." They didn't have to walk long before the house came into view between the foliage.

"I don't see anyone." Jen winced her eyes and propped herself against a tree, attempting to keep out of view. The man behind her hovered over her shoulder.

Bleep. Sce-ew. Beep. "Team three, this is team one, report back. Over."

Jen turned her head. "Is that a radio? A walkie-talkie?" She heard the faintest beeps, whistles, and a voice coming from the man's jacket.

"Oh yes." He opened the collar of his coat and exposed a white wire that curled and hung out of his clothing with an embedded microphone and earpiece.

"We all wear these wires that connect us to a larger radio network. So we can communicate."

Jen couldn't help to feel like she was in a movie. "Why? I mean, you're cops in New Hampshire?" She was almost yelling at him. The notion of them communicating over advanced radio networks was ridiculous.

The man looked up with frustration. "It's only the four of you, right? Who else knows about what you are doing here?"

Peering for signs of anyone, Jen turned away from him. "Uh-huh. Just the four of us. Breaking this serial killer shit open."

"And you are pursuing a serial killer? That's it? What about an organization?"

Again, Jen yanked her head at the question. "An organization? What are you talking about? No, no organization, just a fucking sick dude."

In the blink of an eye, something flashed around her. She felt cold metal followed by a sharp sting wrap around her neck. Pain and pressure jammed up into her jaw. A sensation of warm liquid began to run down her neck and under her sweater.

She tried to scream, but nothing came out. She tried to pull on the tiny metal wire that had been wrapped around her, cutting into her, but it was so tight, she had no chance of getting her fingers underneath it. She put her feet up on the tree next to her, and with all her might tried to push herself away from the man. The attempt was futile. He just leaned back, expecting the move, and when she lunged from the tree, he spun her around and held her a foot off the ground by the wire, deepening its hold into her throat. The more she struggled, the less energy she had for the next burst of action. Her hands lightly slapped and pulled on his fingers from behind her head. She lifted her arms out in front of her, trying to use gravity to help put a little more strength into a swing. She hit his upper thighs with the motion, not quite where she was hoping to hit. The punches did nothing. The pain and pressure that had engulfed her neck and jaw moved. It was now in her lungs, and her chest was pounding, pinching. The muscles all in her torso were spasming uncontrollably. Her body knew it was in trouble and was sending signals to her chest and abdomen to work harder at getting oxygen. Her feet and legs kicked, pretending to tiptoe as she fought to find the ground. Her skin turned a cherry red color, which began to turn to a shade of blue. Her mind went completely blank. She tried to close her eyes to pray, but she couldn't do that either, they were bulging and stuck open. Everything around her began to fade and turn white at the edges of her vision until there was nothing left but darkness.

* * *

He could feel her muscle spasms slowing down until eventually, they stopped completely, like waiting for a bag of popcorn to stop popping in the microwave. He gave it another minute after the last muscle jerk before he dropped her to the ground, where her body crumpled lifeless into a sloppy pile, arms awkwardly raised behind her head, limbs unnaturally bent. He put the earpiece back in his ear, pulled part of the wire closer to his mouth, and spoke.

"Base Team, this is team three, agent one. Target four is off the board, unavoidable. Over." The man kneeled down over Jen's motionless body. Eyes still bulging, she looked off into the sky with a strange focus. He pulled her shirt down slightly to put two fingers on her neck.

"Base team, this is team three, agent one. We have four active targets left on site including the girl. I repeat, four active targets left on site. One confirmed down. I will leave the body for agent two to recover. Over." Standing back up, he looked at the home, a steady focus lining his features.

"Team three, this is base. Goddamn you! Fuck." There was a pause. "Fuck. Over!"

The voice squawked at him with emotions clearly rising. He shrugged them off quickly, ignoring them. This man was a professional. He accepted missions with a primary objective, and everything else was collateral. He proceeded on his missions in any way he saw fit to accomplish his primary objective. His work rarely involved someone outside of the organization. He was always called in as support to the cleanup team and only called in when the main target was someone with the set of skills and experience that Jack had been trained for.

"Base team. This is team three, agent one. Unavoidable. We expect three remaining targets in the house. Over."

His radio cracked and beeped for a moment.

"Team three, agent one, this is base team. Copy. Proceed into the home. Target one is your primary. Team two is on site currently working with the other targets, two and three. We are directing him to vacate. We have lost cameras and have no visual in the home. You are to proceed. Over."

"Base team, this is team three, agent one. Wilco." He spoke at almost a whisper, his voice steady, confirming that he'd comply with the order. He looked back down at Jen's body, grabbed her hand, and leaned her against a tree. He reached into his pant pockets, pulled out a small circular device, clicked a button on the device, then finally clipped it to her shirt.

"There you go. That'll make finding you easier."

A Bloody Screw – 2014

By the time Drew reached the house, the fog had switched over to a damp mist. A light rain was beginning to fall, keeping the day gray and dreary. He and Phil were worried that they might be spotted approaching the home, so they split off in different directions along the tree lines and made quick short dashes to ditches, bushes, hills, and rocks. Drew was breathing heavily, his chest against the vinyl siding of the home. He leaned gently to his right, peeking into the first-floor window, watching for any movement. When he didn't see anything, he moved to the next window, again peeking in and waiting a moment for any movement before repeating the same process on two more windows he had access to.

"Damn, I wish I had a signal." Pulling his phone out, he quickly slipped it back into his pocket after seeing no bars. He moved quickly to the front door, pulled out his gun, and slid the safety to the off position.

"Hang in there, Lizzy. I'm coming," he said to himself, taking another big breath before reaching for the door handle. His hand turned the knob. It was unlocked, but the door creaked a bit as he nudged it forward.

Gun raised in front of him, he slowly stepped into the home. Shutting the door, he put his free hand back under his gun hand for support. As promised, his finger hung just forward of the trigger but close enough that he could quickly fire if needed. He took slow, quiet steps into the home and toward the staircase on his right, heading up a level. The plan was that he would move upstairs at first opportunity to clear the top floor. Phil would start in the basement via a bulkhead or door and work his way up. Then, hopefully, they would meet on the first floor to clear it together.

Drew half-expected the home to be vacant by now, but he kept his guard up nonetheless. Aiming his gun up, he stepped slowly up the stairs, avoiding creaking from his weight on the wood.

"Easy, easy," he said to himself. "Keep the finger off the trigger."

He caught his finger slipping down from its prone position into a firing position, a natural reaction in a tense situation.

"A misplaced finger causes the death of innocent people all the time," he reminded himself of that fact. "Accidental shootings leading to death happen all the time. Take it easy, bud. Easy, Drew."

Making it to the top step, he had a decision to make. "Right or left?" Again, he whispered. Talking aloud helped his mind handle the tension he was feeling. He peered in both directions.

Before making a choice, he tried to listen for anything, any sound that might alert him to a presence.

When he didn't hear anything, he made the decision to start on the right side. Turning into the hallway from the stairs, he was faced with three doors: one on his right and two on his left.

"Closest first."

He moved forward. The first door that he reached was on his left. The door was open. He positioned himself at the doorframe with the gun pointing down and away. With a quick motion, he tipped his head in and saw an empty bathroom, a red patterned rug covering the floor in front of a vanity sink and a large tub and shower on the right with a glass slider, open. The tub was empty. He flashed his head in again, this time hanging it a bit longer, having a better look. His hair on his neck was standing up as all his senses were at peak performance. He was sure he would have sensed a fly coming up the stairs if one dared. He stepped into the bathroom.

The bathroom looked as though it was never used. Plastic was still covering the window pane, waiting to be peeled after shipping and installation. The cabinets were empty, and the shower had no soap, shampoo, or loofah.

He exited the bathroom in the same way he entered, carefully peeking around each corner before exposing his body.

The next door in the hallway was on his right, but the door was closed. The last door at the end, on the left, was propped open.

"Let's do the open door first," the voice continued to talk in his head, almost as if his mind had split into two from the stress of the situation. He passed the closed room on his right quietly, reaching the doorframe of the last open door and leaning in, again carefully peeking into the room. It was a bedroom with a beige plush carpet and neutral paint. There was a bed, a queen by the looks, that appeared to have been slept in at some point. He moved in slowly, and the wall hooked right on him. He peeked around. *Nothing.* Lowering his gun, he looked into an open closet.

Men's clothes. Our perp? he wondered. Pulling out a shirt that was on a hanger, he placed it against his torso.

Shit. A little bigger than me. Gently, he placed the hanger back into the closet. Making his way into the hallway, he approached the closed door that he had passed, prepping his gun in one hand pointing forward at his hip. Opening a closed door in a breach, alone, was a very bad idea. He needed to take extra precautions. "Fast? Or slow and quiet?" He stood, contemplating another possibly life and death decision.

"Fuck. How about fast and quiet?" Reaching over, he put his hand on the doorknob, which was on the left side of the door, the side he was standing at. Then quietly spinning the knob, he pushed it slowly forward away from the jam.

"One, two, three." He swung the door open quickly, ready to shoot if need be.

The door opened without much sound, just the rub against the carpet as it slid. It was a smaller bedroom, completely empty, no bed, no clothes, no furniture, nothing. He exited, once again being careful to check the hallway before jumping out.

"Half the floor down. Half to go." He walked forward slowly, his eyes focused on the other side of the floor, where just a single closed door awaited.

His mind jumped. Someone was on his left side.

Drew swung his gun toward the strange large blob of a man outside of his eye's focus, but he was too slow. The man, just as surprised to see someone standing in his hallway with a gun, was able to get his hand out quicker and smacked down on Drew's arms like an ax. The gun immediately hit the floor. The man followed the chop with a quick jab that caught Drew in the gut, forcing all the air out of his lungs.

Quickly recovering, Drew widened his stance for balance. He saw a tall man, equally as tall as himself, but younger, more muscular, with brown hair and a familiar face.

I fucking know this guy. From where? Drew thought. Drew swung with his right fist, trying to catch him in the jaw, but the man saw the punch coming and easily dodged under it. Drew pressed. The man was still on a step down from him, giving Drew a slight advantage. Kicking out his right leg quickly, he struck the man squarely in the chest, hoping to push him down the stairs. The man swallowed the slow front kick easily, falling back a step while holding onto Drew's leg to prevent him from falling backward completely.

Hopping on one foot, Drew grabbed the railing to prevent himself from falling. The man lunged with a powerful right hook that struck Drew on the side of the head. Balls of light began to flare up and dance in his vision, streaming around in a magnificent pattern. He kicked the gun, accidentally, which slid under the banister and to the first floor below with a thud. The stars kept streaming in front of him and around the corners of his vision. The streaking lights brought him back to a special Fourth of July fireworks show that he once saw from the Boston Harbor with streaming lights everywhere, reflecting off the water.

Stumbling back from the strike, Drew bumped into the wall. It had been a long time since he had been in a fight, although this was unlike any brawl he'd been in before. He shook his head, trying to expel the nausea and disorientation caused by the blow. Refocusing, he saw the man closing in on him, a flash of steel glinting in his right hand.

Drew stepped back and to the right toward the last closed room in the hallway, just missing the tip of the knife from the man's thrust. Retreating to a room he hadn't cleared yet didn't sit well with him, but his position afforded no other option.

The man swung the knife again, thrusting with his right hand toward Drew's abdomen while attempting to swing Drew's hands away with his left hand. Drew recognized the move as either a vertical thrust or forward thrust. Stepping back quickly, he opened his hands, letting the man's block attempt miss.

The knife came within an inch of his stomach. Drew watched as the man's hand rotated from palm down to palm up.

A forward thrust indeed, he thought, recognizing the technique's second step.

Drew saw the blade miss and turn; the man continued the motion into the third step of the attack, a mistake. The latter part of the technique particularly opened up an attacker to a counter attack. Sure enough, the man rotated his body to place extra weight into the follow through of the final step, and in a quick instant, he lunged through an imaginary torso. Had the knife entered Drew, this would have likely split open his abdomen, surely his intestines would have been spilling blood and matter onto the floor, a fatal strike. Drew stepped in closer now, just at the end of the push motion after the miss. Using the man's momentum against him, he grabbed his arm with his one hand and pushing the man's head forward with the other.

There was a loud thud as the man's face went splintering through the nearby drywall. Pulling the man's face back out, he slammed it back down in a slightly different direction and heard a crunch sound. The man's face stopped immediately, smashing into a stud. Drew knew all homes in New England were built with studs sixteen inches apart or less.

"Fucking asshole," Drew said, spit mixed with blood flying from his mouth, caused by the intensity of the fight.

"Where is my daughter?" he yelled insanely, a man possessed by anger. He pulled the man's head back once again, revealing a nose that was smashed, crooked, and flattened down—a bloody mess. Again Drew slammed the man's face back into the same stud, this time splitting open his forehead, blood immediately streaming out over the man's face. He heard a moan from the bloodied man as he tried to gain his footing. Pulling out a set of handcuffs, Drew slowly pulled the man toward the railing of the stairs. Halfway there, he stopped, turned, and put his boot into the man's face, teeth crunching and popping out onto the hardwood floor as blood pooled.

"Fuck you," the man spit out, mostly inaudible, looking up at Drew. What used to be his right eye was now a hole of dangling tissue and blood with a cut opening up the outside of the eye exposing bone.

"What the fuck?" Drew exclaimed. Looking back over his shoulder, he saw a bloody screw sticking out of the stud. The half-inch drywall had crumbled away from the force of the blows, exposing a half-inch drywall screw. On the last strike, he had inadvertently smashed the screw into and through the man's eye.

"Damn, I am sorry about that." Drew felt he needed to apologize. "It wasn't intentional. Fuck, man!" He strung the man's arms up around the railing bolted to the wall, handcuffing him. Stepping back, he ran his hands through his hair, looking at the devastation from the fight.

"Fuck." He tilted his head around to loosen up his neck and shoulders.

"Fuck, fuck, fuck. That was intense." He shook his hand and arms as he paced. Walking over to the knife, he picked it up, slipping it into his belt on his back before heading toward the stairs, suddenly feeling lightheaded and weak. The blow to his head had caused a concussion, and the exertion of the fight was enhancing the symptoms. His surroundings began to spin, and a throbbing headache invaded his forehead and around the ears. Raising his hands to his temples, Drew closed his eyes to try to temper the disorienting symptoms.

Two rounds were suddenly fired from his 40 caliber. Drew's ears rang violently, his painful headache multiplied by the loud noise. Sunlight finally broke through ominous clouds and pierced a nearby window, painfully striking his eyes. Seeing was suddenly a difficult task. Looking down the stairs with squinted, blurry eyes, he saw Ashley holding the gun, a small fog billowing up from the gunpowder.

Ashley's Place – 2014

Ashley moved through the woods quickly toward the house. In no time, she had made her way to the home. Unzipping her jacket's inner pocket, she pulled out her cell phone. When she touched it on, she saw that she had a single bar of service. Frantically dialing 911, she held the phone to her ear, but, no call went through. Shaking the phone with frustration, she paused, then checked to see if there were any Wi-Fi signals. *Eureka.* The home had internet.

She looked at the modern colonial home perched down the hill from her position. Just then, she saw movement toward the front of the house.

Drew! What are you doing? she thought anxiously, watching him skirt from bush to bush in the plain sight of day.

"Christ, you're going to attract more attention!" she cursed through gritted teeth.

"Phil, where the hell are you? What are you up to?" She looked around to see if he was following, or ahead of Drew, but there was no sign of him. Quickly tucking her phone back into her pocket, she looked around for a better way into the home.

"If I can sneak into the house, maybe I can get onto the network and make a call." She looked around in both directions, taking in her surroundings. Her eyes traced the tree line toward the back side of the house. It was a much shorter distance compared to the way Drew had gone in.

"I get into the basement, find the router, and try to get onto the network." She had a solid plan. Most routers came with a default randomized Wi-Fi password printed onto the unit. If she found the unit, chances were the password was never changed. In the event that it was changed, with physical access to the unit, she could hard reset it back to the default and be onto the network in just a couple of minutes.

"Good luck," she said to Drew, giving him one last look as she watched him momentarily stop to catch his breath behind a decorative boulder. With that, she turned and quickly made her way in the opposite direction.

Within a couple of minutes, she was panting, breathing hard, kneeling at the edge of the tree line. She was now looking at the back of the home, contemplating how fast it would take her to cover the fifteen feet to the door.

Looking up at the windows, she watched each one for a moment, also giving herself a chance to rest, then positioned herself into a runner's stance. She peered ahead into the French doors of the basement.

Seeing nothing, she bolted from her position, covering the distance in about a second and a half. Reaching the door, she immediately leaned against the house, sucking in deeper breaths and sitting on her heels as she recovered.

Her hand went to the door handle; gently she pushed it open, slipping into the basement. Immediately she was struck with the strong smell of bad body odor, urine, and something else foul she couldn't place. Pinching her nose, she silently stepped, quickly, across the basement, her head on a swivel looking intently for a small black device.

"What the hell is going on here?"

She stepped into a bathroom with a strange device that sat in the middle of the room over a shower pan and a weird tank to its left. Her skin crawled as she gave it a once over.

"Glad it's not in there."

Stopping at a rough door opening to the right of the stairs, she leaned into the room, an unfinished area of the basement that held the furnace, electrical panel, some small tools, and other utilities.

"Yes!" she silently touted as she fist bumped. She ran to the communications panel hanging on the wall next to the electrical panel. It held a router, modem, and some coaxial-cable TV splitters, all sitting on shelves on the wall. She grabbed the small box with three antennas sticking out of it, flipping it over to expose the default network credentials.

"Shit." She bit her lip, thinking. The network name, or SSID, that came with the unit was different than that which showed up on her phone, meaning that someone changed it from the default settings, likely changing the default password.

"Let's give it a go anyway."

She tilted her head to read the password as she punched it into her phone and watched her phone intently. *Authenticating . . . Authenticating . . .* Then the error she had expected flashed at her. *Connection failed. Check your password.*

"Damn." Her next move was to reset the unit back to its default settings. While that would guarantee her access to the network and internet, it would drop anyone else, or any wireless devices from the network. She figured that if anyone was in the house and actively using the internet, it would only be a few minutes before someone came downstairs to have a look.

"Hell with it." Pressing, she held down the little red reset button for ten seconds and waited, letting the router cycle power and come back online, watching the green lights blink then finally turn solid when ready. Immediately her phone connected, and she dialed 911.

"911 operator. What is your emergency?" the phone barked in perfectly clear tones.

"Yes, please, we need help." Her voice was strong, clear, and stern. "I—I," stuttering, she looked around the room she was in. Followeing Drew and Phil to this house, she realized she had no idea where she was.

"I—I don't know where I am. Somewhere in Dunbarton, New Hampshire."

"Ma'am, can you tell me your emergency?" the operator pushed for more information.

"We tracked down a kidnapper to New Hampshire. There has been a murder. You have to come quick."

"Ma'am, who was murdered?" The operator was calm and collected, professionally trained to pull valuable information from the most hysterical persons.

"Tommy, Tommy. Ahh! Shit, I don't know his last name. Hello? Can you hear me?" Ashley said, her voice turning desperate as she recalled Lizzy's text message.

"Yes, ma'am. I hear you loud and clear."

"You have to hurry!"

Ashley was facing the electrical panel when she felt as though someone was watching her, someone was behind her. Her heart jumping out of her chest, she spun around, pulling the phone in toward her core, a naturally defensive move.

"Ahh, oh my God. Phil!" she practically screamed. "You gave me a fucking heart attack."

Putting his finger to his mouth, Phil pointed up toward the ceiling.

"We don't know who is listening," he whispered as he got close to her, reaching out his hand and taking her phone from her in a clean motion, looking at it before shutting it off.

"What are you doing? That was 911!" Ashley said in an aggregated whisper.

"I told you I already called. They're on the way."

Ashley snapped her hands at her phone trying to get it back, but he was too quick and pulled it away from her before she could grab it.

"Phil. Give me my phone." He extended it toward her, appearing defeated. At the moment that she almost had it in her hands, he dropped it onto the concrete floor, then stomped on it with his heel, over and over until it was clear that it was unusable.

When he stopped, he looked up at her. "You see. My name isn't actually Phil." His voice was calm and no longer whispering, no longer concerned about others in the home. He seemed like a totally different person.

"You were supposed to stay by the car, Ashley. Now, you've made a big fucking mess of things." His demeanor changed; he was more frightening and intimidating. Ashley began to take a step back from him.

"What's going on here? You never called the police, did you?"

He took a step toward her for every step she took back. After only a few steps, her back bumped against the wall.

"You're one of them, aren't you?"

Her question stirred a look of puzzlement on his face. "One of who? What do you know?" He asked sharply.

Ashley held her tongue. "Go fuck yourself." He moved closer, then suddenly he was right on top of her, his left elbow forcefully across her throat, pinning her to the wall. With his other hand, he grabbed one of her arms, leaning into her left side to avoid her other hand as it clawed at him.

"You know." He leaned in close to her ear, his nose brushing against her throat. He breathed in deeply. "I could always have use for you. All these years I've watched you, all those long baths you enjoyed to take with your purple dragon."

Her eyes filled with rage at his words and his smirk smile. He was referencing some of the most private moments of her life, with her best vibrator.

"Fuck." She struggled to get the words out through the chokehold.

Reaching her free hand out wildly, she had managed to just grab the router that was now hanging loosely on the wall, tethered by network wires.

"You!"

With one hard swing, she drove a pointed side of the router into Phil's temple. Blood dripped as he stumbled away from her.

"Goddamn. You fucking bitch," he yelled angrily. He was reaching up, touching his head with his left hand, inspecting the blood. Ashley didn't hesitate. While his back was turned, she grabbed a small flathead hammer resting nearby. By the time he turned to advance on her, it was too late. The hammer struck him on the cheek with incredible force. Ashley heard crunching sounds on the impact. He fell to his knees like a sack of potatoes. Shocked he was still conscious; reaching back with more force, she struck him once again on the left side of his head. He dropped onto the floor, unconscious, with blood squirting in pulses from just above his ear.

She dropped the hammer instinctively as if she had just done something very wrong. It hit the floor with a clang. Tucking her hair back behind her ears, she leaned over, inspecting Phil for movement, poking him with the toe of her shoes. When she was satisfied that he was out, she rushed to her phone and picked it up, trying to see if it had any life left on it.

"Ahh. Fuck." She bent down next to Phil and gently reached into his pocket, afraid hard movements might wake him up. The second pocket she tried had his phone.

"Okay, come on." Turning it on, she realized it was not going to be of any help. It had a passcode on it.

"Damn." Throwing the phone onto the floor, she paused to think.

A loud, low rumbling thud reverberated from the upstairs area, quickly followed by another.

"Drew!" She picked the hammer back up and quickly, quietly made her way upstairs. As she turned the corner of the top step, peering left, she saw a gun on the hardwood floor—Drew's gun.

She could hear the movement and moaning coming from up one more level. She made a quick bolt for the gun, looking at the safety to make sure it was off. Peering up the stairs, she saw Drew with his hands on his head, and Jack handcuffed to the stair railing.

* * *

With the good eye he had left, Jack peered down at her, a glint of sadness, and a tear bubbled at the bottom of his good eye. He closed it, forcing the tear out and waiting, knowing what would happen next. He knew exactly what she would do in this situation. He knew his wife better than most, maybe better than she knew herself.

Two shots struck him in the chest. Bobby Jack Tinder kept his single eye closed as immense pressure and pain filled his chest. He thought back to all the people he'd killed, how they must have felt in this same, final moment. A sense of euphoria washed over him.

"I learned my lesson," he muttered out with his last breath.

Report – 2014

"Hmmm, ahem!" An older man stood up from his luxurious leather office chair. He continued to snort and snarl as he read a report that had been placed on his desk that morning for him to review.

"There could have been no other outcome, you say?" Slapping the report down hard on his desk, he looked across at Elle. She wore a tight black skirt that just made it to her knees and a loose-fitting white blouse underneath a thin beige sweater that sat on her pleasantly. Her eyes were confident as she met his stare through her purple, thin-framed rectangular glasses.

"As I said in my report, sir, he continued to violate our policies after repeated warnings." She crossed her legs as she spoke, looking up at him. "He put our organization at risk. You can corroborate with James. I had him come in and review an interaction I had with him before moving up our action plan."

The man stared at her a moment. "Damn!"

Picking up his coffee mug from the desk, he chucked it as hard as his old arm would let him. It smashed into the window overlooking Boston, the mug splitting into pieces, coffee splattering across the window, leaving a small spider crack in the glass.

"Do you know what this might cost us? That girl was already sold for fuck's sake. She was the first piece in putting us into a position to close this deal!" He looked at her hard. The veins above his right eye bulged with anger. She could see them pulse with each beat of his heart.

"Sir, I already took the liberty to process a refund as a result of losing the girl, and I have organized another girl to be delivered tomorrow at no cost." She paused, letting him take in the details; she could tell he hadn't yet finished reading her report.

"Early indications are that our deal with the Frenchman is still on track despite the setback." He loosened up when he heard this, walked to his chair, and pulled it in closer to the desk before sitting in it. After a moment, he picked the report back up.

"I see Rick was recovered." He flipped the pages of the report nonchalantly.

"Yes, sir. Rick took a hammer to his cheek and is in the operating room for repairs as we speak. He has yet to regain consciousness since we pulled him out."

Dipping the report from his eyes, he looked up at her.

"Sir?" She spoke smoothly, sensing doubt emanating from him. He lowered the report more until she could see his puckering, judging lips.

"Do you think that's wise?" He paused just a moment. "Rick made a mistake—exposing himself, his DNA is clearly all over the damn floor of that house. I'm sure they are already working up sketches of his appearance. He failed, failed at his cleanup duties, failed to isolate this. If he is identified and found . . . ."

Elle nodded, but she didn't think Rick was a liability. "He did well embedding with Jack's wife and neighbor. All indications prove that while they were onto Jack's personal killings, they had no idea about us, intel we would not have, had he not been able to get involved."

The old man stared at her for a minute, not saying a word, almost giving her the opportunity to adjust her strategy.

"Yes, sir. I'll have it scheduled during his surgery. Anesthesia can be a dangerous, unfortunate thing." Opening her phone, she sent off a quick text.

"Good. I always knew you were a natural at this." He smiled with a sense of pride, then cleared his throat again. "I agree with your conclusion on the girl, her father, and Ashley Tinder. At this time, it's best we steer clear from them. Let's put a checkup on the calendar though, say six months? And reassess if we need to terminate them."

Again looking down at her phone, Elle added a note to herself for six months from now. "Yes, sir."

He dropped the report back onto the table. "This was sloppy, Elle."

She looked up at him, fear creeping into the back of her mind. People died for less around here.

"Sloppy," he said it again more forcefully.

"Sir, we moved as soon as we learned that a message got out. We had to act quickly to contain it. Rick was to lead Drew to New Hampshire without the police getting notified. We had a cleanup team ready to take the girls from Chelmsford." He put his hand up to silence her.

Ignoring his hand, she said, "We almost had it contained."

"The girls ignored Rick—and that monster we sent in to assist! We had to re-task him to recover Rick as soon as we got video back and then we had to pull him out as soon as we picked up local PD converging on the home." She was spinning, reaching panic.

He raised his hand higher before speaking. "Yes. And that's primarily the reason I want Rick gone. He couldn't get two girls to stay put. But—" He took in a deep breath, considering his next words. "But you led this team. You were both Jack's *and* Rick's handler. That's now two of your operatives that have been unable to deliver, Elle." He leaned back in his chair, his eyes on her.

"Dad, I take full responsibility. You're right. I was unable to handle Jack. And, well, Rick, I take responsibility for it." She stood up, straight and confident, accepting of any penalties.

"Elle, this must be the last time." He spoke slowly and fatherly, concern in his voice. "There can be no next time . . . something like this happens again—" He flicked his eyebrows. "Well, you know what will have to happen."

She nodded. "I understand."

Standing up, he walked around the desk. Raising his hands, he placed them on her shoulders. "You are meant to replace me someday. You know that, right?"

Nodding, she looked down from his eyes in submission. "Yes, Dad." She spoke soft and beaten, shame in her tone.

"Now, now, Elle-y honey. You need to be sterner with your operatives. Listen to me. Listen to your gut. I want you to review everyone you have in the field and terminate anyone that you think might cause problems." He pushed up her chin to force eye contact. "Anyone that your gut says might be an issue, I want them gone. Because I don't want to see anything happen to you."

She nodded. "I will review them when I get back to my office, sir."

Smiling, he said, "Good," before nodding at the door.

With that Elle turned and walked out of her father's office, shutting the door behind her.

* * *

"Yes, sir?" A soft female voice spoke through the phone. He spun in his chair, holding his cell phone to his ear, facing the coffee-stained window. He watched the coffee beads slowly rolling down, hitting the carpet.

"I will need someone in here to clean up a mess. And a fresh cup of coffee. Oh, I'll need a new mug."

"Yes, sir, right away. Anything else?" The corner of his mouth twitched as he thought. He didn't want to do it—it was his own daughter—but his gut was telling him something different, and he was pissed at her for it.

"I want you to activate a clean team." His voice never quivered, wavered, or shook as he gave the order.

"Elle has made the last mistake. Make it look like a robbery gone wrong."

"Sir? Elle? Do you mean your daughter, sir?"

He sat up straight. "Yes, who the fuck do you think I am talking about?"

The woman on the other line stuttered her response. "Ah—yes, sir. A—uh. Are you sure? A robbery, sir?"

"Goddammit! Do I need to spell everything out? Give that failure what she deserves! Do you understand?"

There was a pause on the line before the woman said, "Of course, sir. Anything else?"

He didn't respond, hanging up the phone and placing it back down on his desk.

"A failure whore like her mother," he whispered as he looked down at the busy street below.

Three Months Later – 2014

"Ashley! Oh my God! You look stunning."

Lizzy smiled wide at Ashley, who spun around for Lizzy, the chic blue dress she wore flowing around her thighs.

"Wow. Really, wow."

Smiling, Ashley flipped her hand. "I feel weird wearing such a nice dress. I can't believe I bought this."

The dress was navy blue with a see-through pattern that extended down to just below the breast line where it stitched-inward and had a wide solid belt covering most of her torso before tapering back out around her hips. It accented her feminine curves beautifully.

"It's not weird. You seriously look amaz-in'. That dress is perfect for you," Lizzy chimed to ease her awkward look.

"Do you think your dad will like it? I should have bought a different dress." Her nerves spoke cautiously.

"Oh my God, stop it! My dad is going to go crazy! You look so great!"

Shuffling out of the kitchen, Ashley entered into Drew's living room so that she could twist and inspect herself in the mirror.

"I hope so," she said aloud. "You know, Lizzy. There's something I've been meaning to say." Lizzy was leaning into the living room, smiling as she watched Ashley move nervously.

"Yeah, what's that?"

"I—I am really sorry about what happened to you."

"Don't even say it, Ash. No one blames you."

"I know, but—" Ashley knew it wasn't her fault but couldn't stop herself from feeling responsible, that she should have caught on sooner.

"It's just, you and Drew letting me live here with you these past few months—I mean, I don't know what I would have done."

Moving to the couch, Lizzy patted the seat, signaling for Ashley to join her.

"I am so happy that you're here with us. I've never seen my dad so happy, like ever." She gave Ashley a serious look. "Like, never ever."

Ashley nodded with a smile hearing that.

"You two make one of the sweetest couples."

Ashley looked down, her hands fidgeting in her lap. "I don't know what I'm doing here. I love your dad, but I just shot my husband. And that's really fucked up."

Lizzy bit her lip, her eyes tightening.

"What I do know is that I don't want to leave." She smiled at Lizzy as water began to swell in her eyes.

"Aww." Lizzy put her arms around her, and they hugged tightly, like best friends might.

"What's going on in here? You two aren't getting sentimental on me, are you?" Coming downstairs silently, Drew walked into the living room, while the two were embracing. He was wearing a gray suit with a light blue button down, no tie. His dark hair was streaked back. His eyes glowed within his clean-shaven face.

"Are you ready?" Drew said.

Ashley stood up, revealing her dress. "You look fantastic, Drew! How are you so handsome?"

Drew didn't respond, instead eyeing her up and down, his mouth slightly open.

"You look stunning."

Closing in on him, she kissed him on the lips. Excitement from the way he looked at her overwhelmed her senses.

"Lizzy, hun." Drew gave her a kiss on the forehead. "Have a good day and night. Don't wait up for us." Drew turned to Ashley. "Let's get this over with and then celebrate."

Ashley grabbed a heavy, formal jacket and swung it over her shoulders. She felt a little awkward wearing it. She didn't have anything nice to wear out for their evening so she was borrowing one of Nelly's old jackets she found in a closet. Drew's hand snapped her away from stewing on the thought too long.

He tugged her out of the house and into the car. Within thirty minutes, they were standing outside of Drew's attorney's office, a large stone building with giant round pillars holding up an overhang to the entrance. Peters, Quill, & Rogers LLP. Today would mark, what they hoped, would be the last day in the drama that had become known as the Back Bay Murders by the local media. Drew and Ashley were having a final meeting with the Suffolk County District Attorney's office, the FBI's Boston branch, and the Boston police commissioner.

They stood at the entrance to the attorney's office, in awe of the upscale architecture of the building they were about to walk into.

Drew looked over at her, obviously seeing her fidgeting with her dress, and said, "Hey. Remember, this isn't an interrogation. You've been cleared from any wrongdoing."

"I know." She looked down at his feet nervously. "It's just—did I do the right thing?"

"You thought he had a gun! From where you were at the bottom of the stairs, you couldn't see he was handcuffed. It looked to you like he was pointing something at me."

She didn't look up, ashamed that she had sold that lie to Drew like everyone else. The truth being that when Bobby had disappeared, it had been a result of a fight between the two. Ashley had followed him one night into Boston, suspicious he had been seeing another woman on his work trips. Instead, she had witnessed him stalking someone unexpected, a young man named Jacob. At the time, she had had no idea about the murders. She confronted him on the issue when he had come home, a screaming fight had ensued, resulting with his hands wrapped around her neck, almost choking her to death before he had finally let go and took off, not being seen again until Dunbarton.

Shortly after Jack had disappeared, she had been watching the news one evening and a familiar face had splashed the screen, the young man Jack had been watching. His body had been found in the river, thus igniting her investigation into the drowning deaths in the Boston, New Hampshire, and Rhode Island areas. She had wondered if she should have gone to the police earlier. Denial, she realized, was a powerful thing. She didn't want to believe the man she had married was capable of such things. To protect him, to protect her own reputation, she had sought out the facts on her own.

She hadn't wanted to believe it was him, and she hadn't, up until she had seen him handcuffed to that railing, missing an eye.

"I'm really thankful that you're here with me, through everything. I mean, Lizzy, for Christ's sakes." Drew put his finger up to her lips to silence her.

"You had nothing to do with any of that. Okay?" She nodded again, looking at his feet.

"Let's go in there, listen to what they have to say. It's just a meeting to review our testimonies and their findings. We sign some paperwork; then we can move on with our lives and put this behind us."

Taking a deep breath, Ashley raised her head to match Drew's stare. "I love you," she said honestly. "I love your optimism, your strength, your heart, passion for good. I just—" She smiled. "I just fucking love you, probably more than I have ever loved anyone. I hate Bobby for—" She frowned and shook her head. "I hate him for being something else, using me, lying to me. The only positive I can take from what's happened is that I met you."

She felt his warm breath as he leaned in close to her and whispered in her ear, "I love you. Let's get in there and get this over with." He tugged at her arm, and they walked into the building.

They sat in a large meeting room on the fourth floor of the building. Michael Peters, Drew and Ashley's attorney, sat next to them on the window side of the room while the FBI special agent in charge, the district attorney, and the commissioner sat across from them. The district attorney, Miranda Ruiz-Garza did most of the talking. She was an older woman with short brown hair and black glasses. Her skin was tanned, and her personality was kind, yet, to the point.

"Hi. Thanks for meeting with us." Miranda had a slight Hispanic accent that had fallen away with her years of speaking English. "Let's get right to it, shall we." Smiling, she spoke fast, not giving anyone time to return pleasantries. Peters had worked with Miranda before and let Ashley know she was in fair, albeit very efficient, hands.

"We have worked on a finalized statement of events for the both of you." She pulled out a few thick manila folders, opening them up to reveal stacks of papers, stapled separately. Peters pulled out identical documents that he had printed earlier in the morning, handing one to Ashley and one to Drew.

"These documents," Peters began, "represent your final testimony detailing the events starting from when, you, Drew, were hired by the Ryans, and Ashley, when you began your investigation with suspicions that your husband was a victim of murder when he disappeared after a work trip to Boston," a lie she had told and decided to see through.

She stared at the papers in front of her as though they might bite her.

"By signing, you are stating that the events here, recalled to the best of your ability, are truthful and complete." He flipped to the last page and pointed to the signature line for both of them. Drew leaned in and signed it quickly. Ashley hovered her hand and pen over the line.

Sensing her hesitation, Miranda said, "Is something wrong?"

"Oh, I just—what about Jen and Phil? It feels weird, incomplete to me that he is still out there and Jen is missing."

The man who stood next to her, the FBI special agent in charge spoke up. "Yes. I agree. We are still actively investigating and searching for their whereabouts. At this time, we don't believe you are in any danger."

Nodding, Ashley looked back down at her papers.

"Do we even call him Phil?" Drew asked.

"We don't know who he is yet." The FBI agent took a deep breath. "The real Detective Phil Trenhon's body was found in his apartment, garroted. His time of death occurred prior to your first encounter with the imposter. We spoke to the officers that visited Ashley's residence. They had never worked with Phil before and had also been duped." He was obviously distraught at the topic.

Putting the pen down, Ashley started rubbing her stomach. She suddenly found herself in a flashback to when Bobby had his hand around her neck the night he left. As he choked her, he leaned in and whispered in her ear. She was hardly able to make it out.

"You don't understand. The organization. I have to do it. They won't let us be. It's my job." His words were mumbled and barely cohesive, but she understood enough to know that there were more like him. Just then she felt something, pulling her out from the flashback she had yet to tell anyone about.

Ashley looked down at her stomach. Her hand rubbing over a spot on the mid-section of her heavy, dark blue coat, lined with thick fake animal fur. Inside the material, at the edge of the coat opening, on the inside of the flap, was a small, thin square box hidden in the dress. She looked up at Drew puzzled. She felt the other side of the coat, which lacked such a feature.

"Ashley, we need you to sign this." Peters reached over with another pen. "Here, try mine."

Ashley looked down at the paper, picked up her pen quickly, and signed. "I'm sorry, everyone. This has been very difficult for me." Standing up, she looked at Drew. "Can we go?"

Drew looked at everyone else in the room.

"Yes," Peters answered. They stood up and began to leave when Ashley was stopped by Miranda.

"Ashley." Miranda reached her hand out for a handshake. "No one blames you. What you did, that was very courageous. Everyone thinks you two are heroes. You stopped the Back Bay Murders from continuing. Your direct work has helped us link forty-two deaths to him." She stopped and peered at the police commissioner sitting at the table, a newly appointed commissioner, as the previous one resigned after the links were made between Bobby's victims.

"And I think we all owe you. You have forced changes throughout our ranks that have been sorely needed." Ashley nodded and shook hands with Miranda before leaving the room.

"Drew! Ashley!" Peters yelled as they exited the conference room. He hurried up to them and said, "They are going to do everything they can to find Jen, okay?"

Somehow, Ashley felt that wouldn't help. Her heart told her Jen was lost to them.

"Thanks, Mike. You were great on this case. I'll give you a call in a couple weeks to check in." Drew spoke quickly as Ashley had already turned from them and was making her way toward the steps to leave the building.

"Ashley, why are we moving so fast?" Drew asked incredulously as she pulled him down the street at almost a jogger's pace.

"You have a utility knife in the car, right?"

Drew looked at her, confused.

"Ah, yeah, what for?"

She looked over at him, her eyes wide, the same look she had when she was excited about solving a problem or finding a way to hack into Gabe's account, a look of triumph and pride.

Drew had told her one evening about Nell-a-bell and how his last moments with her were confusing and a challenge for him to accept. He had told her one night, after a bottle of wine, how when Nell left she had told him to "find the box."

Ashley looked ahead, her hand back pulling Drew along at an uncomfortable pace. Looking up, she could see the first level of the parking garage was in sight with Drew's car patiently waiting.

"I think I might have found it!" she said again with excitement. One hand on her stomach, her fingers twisted and spun around the little box that was stitched into the coat.

"Found what?" Drew had no idea what was happening.

"Just wait," she said as they got to the car. Unlocking the car with keyless entry, she jumped into the passenger seat. Quickly, she opened up the glove box and pulled out a folded utility knife. Flipping it open, she pinched out the small sharp knife.

"What are you doing?" Drew reached out to stop her as she began to carefully pick at the stitches.

"Wait, just wait. Trust me." She pushed his hands away. After a couple of nips, she had worked a hole into the inner seam of the coat big enough for her finger. Reaching in, she hooked her finger around the object, pulling it all the way out.

A matchbox.

"I found the box!"

ABOUT THE AUTHOR

Andrew Bonar is an author, engineer, and entrepreneur telling raw, gripping and compelling stories. A longtime New Hampshire USA resident, often featuring New England locale in his works. Andrew graduated from the University of Massachusetts, Amherst with a B.S. in Electrical Engineering and works as a Software Engineer when not writing fiction novels.

Andrew comes from a long line of published authors, a natural story teller, who carefully crafts intricate plots, and expertly captures character nuances. Andrew is married with three young children, Jem, Madison, and Cooper.

Learn more about Andrew at andrewbonar.com